**Novels by Michael J. Deeb**

Duty and Honor 2007

Duty Accomplished 2008

Honor Restored 2009

The Lincoln Assassination 2011

# THE LINCOLN ASSASSINATION

## WHO HELPED JOHN WILKES BOOTH MURDER LINCOLN?

*Dear Melinda*

*Regards*

*Michael J Deeb*

# MICHAEL J. DEEB
### AUTHOR OF *THE DRIEBORG CHRONICLES*

iUniverse, Inc.
Bloomington

The Lincoln Assassination
Who Helped John Wilkes Booth Murder Lincoln?

iUniverse books may be ordered through booksellers or by contacting:

iUniverse
1663 Liberty Drive
Bloomington, IN 47403
www.iuniverse.com
1-800-Authors (1-800-288-4677)

ISBN: 978-1-4502-9618-2 (pbk)
ISBN: 978-1-4502-9619-9 (ebk)

Printed in the United States of America

iUniverse rev. date: 03/15/2011

The Lincoln Assassination is for my daughters:
Susan, Ann and Mary Jacqueline.

# O Captain! My Captain!

"O Captain! My Captain! Our fearful trip is done,
The ship has weather'd every rack, the prize we sought is won,
The port is near, the bells I hear, the people all exulting,
While follow eyes the steady keel, the vessel grim and daring;

But O Heart! Heart! Heart!
  O the bleeding drops of red,
    Where on the deck my Captain lies
      Fallen cold and dead.

Walt Whitman (1819 – 1892)

Michael J. Deeb was born and raised in Grand Rapids, Michigan. His undergraduate and graduate education centered on American studies. His doctorate was in management.

He was an educator for nineteen years, most of which saw him teaching American history and doing historical research. As a businessman, he owned an accounting and investment advisory practice for twenty five years.

His personal life found him as a pre-teen spending time regularly at the public library, reading non-fiction works of history. This passion has continued to this day. Teaching at the college, university and high school levels only increased his interest in such reading and research.

Since 2005, he and his wife have lived in Sun City Center, FL. In the fall of 2007, he finished his first historical novel, Duty and Honor. It was followed in succeeding years by Duty Accomplished and Honor Restored.

# Grand Rapids, Michigan

It was not yet dawn and the new fallen snow glistened in the bright light of a March full moon.

A few days earlier, there had been a thaw. Warm temperatures and a light rain had melted much of winter's accumulated snow. High banks of snow on either side of the city streets virtually disappeared.

Could this have been the first sign of spring? Or, was it was just one of those swings of temperature typical in Michigan that filled winter weary people with hope of an end to the cold, ice, snow and dark skies?

Sure enough, a day later the temperature dropped below freezing and snow began to fall once again.

"Michael, are you awake?"

Mary Jacqueline and Michael Drieborg had been married for just four months. He had met this beautiful dark haired widow while in Charleston, South Carolina. The Joint Congressional Committee on Reconstruction had sent him there in the spring of 1866. She and her four-year old son Charles were living in the home of her father-in-law, Col. Pope.

"Yes, sweetheart, I am."

*I thank you Lord for bringing Mary Jacqueline into my life.* Michael thought. *After Julia and our son Robert died, I thought I would never allow myself to fall in love again.*

He turned on his side and moved toward his wife.

"Yes sweetheart. I'm awake." Michael slid his right arm under her head and pulled her toward him. She put her hand on his leg.

"Wow! Your hand is like ice!"

"I'm cold all over, Michael. I can't wait for this winter cold to end. Hold me close darling."

"You're not alone with that wish, dear. Right now every farmer is praying for spring. Every one of them is just as sick of winter weather as you. Believe me, they're anxious to get into their fields and plant this year's crop."

"But do they feel chilled all the time like I do?" Mary Jacqueline complained. "The only time I feel warm is when I'm in your arms."

"That's nice to hear, sweetheart." Michael pulled her closer. "But you've experienced Northern winters before, haven't you?" Michael teased her. "In Pennsylvania where you were raised, you had plenty of snow and ice."

She snuggled closer to her husband.

"That was a long time ago, Michael. I left my home and all that ice and snow in the summer of 1861. So, this is my first winter north of South Carolina in almost six years. I guess my blood thinned during that time. Right now, I'm sick and tired of winter."

Michael moved his free hand under her wool nightgown. "I know how to warm you up." He began to move his warm hand over her skin.

"Don't you dare let cold air into this bed, Michael Drieborg," she warned.

"As I recall it, not long ago you told my mother you couldn't understand why I would choose to be out in our shed milking a cow when I could be in our nice warm bed, with you. Are you now telling me you don't want me to keep you warm?" He continued to caress her under the blankets.

"I want you to keep doing those devilish things with your hand, Michael. I just don't want you to let the cold air in while you're doing it."

"So you want me to stop?"

"Don't you dare, mister!" She began to do some touching of her own, to him.

*Thank you Lord for bringing this good man into my life,* she prayed.

"Momma," Her five-year old son, Charles was standing at the side of the bed.

She twisted away from Michael to face her son. "What is it, son?"

"I feel hot and like I'm going to throw up, Momma."

Mary Jacqueline threw her covers back and swung out of bed. In her robe and slippers she led Charles to his bedroom.

"Oh! Damn!" Michael mumbled into the pillow. He waited under the covers in hope that his wife would return. After a while, he gave up. He peeked into Charles's bedroom and saw that Mary Jacqueline was under the covers holding her son.

I hope the little guy isn't sick again. The boy had never seen ice and snow before moving to Michigan. This has been a rough winter for him.

Mike retrieved his robe and slippers and headed downstairs to start a fire and get some coffee going.

He had been sworn in as Federal Marshal for Western Michigan last December of 1866. Then, he and his new wife purchased a home on the corner of Prospect and State Streets. This was an upscale neighborhood within walking distance of downtown Grand Rapids. The home was a two story wooden structure with a veranda on all four sides. Mike's own daughter, Eleanor and his wife's son, Charles, each had a room on the second floor. He and Mary Jacqueline did, too.

Mike thought of his parents who lived in the nearby village of Lowell.

*By this time of the morning, Momma will have the fire going and bread baking. Poppa will be in the barn feeding the stock and milking the cows. He will join her before too long for a good farmer's breakfast of meat, eggs, and potatoes with plenty of hot coffee. Not too long ago, I was a farmer doing those chores each morning, too.*

*That was before my wife Julia and our son Robert were murdered. After I avenged them I fled my farm to work as a marshal in Washington DC. So much had happened since. Seems strange how things turn out.*

Now he was sitting in his Grand Rapids home sipping coffee at the kitchen table while reading yesterday's local daily newspaper, the Eagle. He didn't hear his wife enter the warm room.

Mary Jacqueline slipped her arms around him from behind. "I looked for you in our bed, Michael. I had hoped you would be waiting for me."

"How is Charles?" Mike asked, putting down his paper.

"He was a little feverish," she responded. "But I think he'll be fine. Sorry we were interrupted."

"Nothing you could do about that, sweetheart," Mike assured her. "One of the sacrifices of parenthood I guess."

Mary Jacqueline moved around the chair and sat on her husband's lap.

"Don't think you're off the hook, Marshal," she chided giving him a squeeze. "Believe me; I'll not forget where you left off this morning. As soon as the children are in bed tonight, you're all mine."

Mike chuckled. "Demands; you're all the time making demands. Anyone tell you that you're a hard woman?"

"Such a hard life you have Marshal Drieborg," she said as she kissed him. "I suppose you don't want me to kiss you, either."

Mike pulled her closer and answered that question with another kiss.

She leaned back after a time. "I see you've already made coffee. Any left for me?

"Does that mean no more kissing?"

"We'll see after I get some of that good smelling coffee."

"More demands; all the time demands."

"A girl has to look after herself, don't you know."

Truth be known, Mary Jacqueline was willing but not yet very comfortable around a kitchen. An only daughter who had been raised in a Doctor's home, she had never been expected to perform household or kitchen duties. As a teenager she married into a landed South Carolina family. There, she wasn't even allowed to wait on herself, much less cook for others.

So Mike wasn't surprised that the Negro woman, Helen had come north with them to cook for Mike's household and continue to be a nanny for young Charles, too.

Helen was a slender five-foot two-inch tall, light-skinned Negro lady; she had been a slave in the Pope household. It was thought that she was in her late twenties, although nobody actually knew for sure. As a slave it wasn't necessary to have birth records about such things. Nor was it common to know if a slave had any family. So, it was assumed Helen had none.

Besides cooking for the Drieborgs, she looked after Charles and Eleanor, too. She took them to school and walked them home in the afternoon. Then she would insist that they do their homework, pick up their rooms and hang up their clothing before going out to play.

When they would complain, she often said, "What you think; dat I be your slave?" Then she would smile at her own humor and all three of them would laugh.

"You don't have to remind me, Helen." Charles would protest. "I know you're not a slave anymore."

"Seems ta me you need remindin, chile. Cause sometimes it pears you done forgot."

Actually, the three of them got along very well. In fact, after school Eleanor and Charles even tutored Helen by helping her with reading and arithmetic. She was determined to become educated and the two children were determined that she would succeed.

Her own room adjoined the kitchen. This morning, she walked in on Michael and Mary Jacqueline. "Good morning ma'am, Marshal," she greeted. "If'n y'all don mind, I best be getting da bread goin. Can I get' y'all anything, before I start on dat?"

Mary Jacqueline answered first. "No thank you, Helen. The marshal has already made coffee and warmed up some rolls from last night. That will do me nicely, too thank you."

"What about you, Marshal?" Helen asked. "Fer a big man like you; rolls ain't nuff. You sure I can't get you somethin; eggs maybe? It be no trouble a' tall, sir."

"Come to think of it," Mike decided, "that would be a good idea. While you're getting your bread dough around, I'll get dressed. Give me ten minutes, Helen. Then I'll have those eggs; scrambled and some ham, if you don't mind."

As Mike left the kitchen, Mary Jacqueline turned to Helen. "While he's getting dressed, I'll just watch you make your bread dough. I might surprise you one of these mornings and wake you up to the smell of baking bread."

"Dat would be a pleasure, ma'am." Helen smiled in response. "It surely would. Let me show you where I keep all da fixins. Den we'll mix up some dough before da Marshal gets back down here lookin fer his eggs and ham."

The two ladies were busy mixing the ingredients when Mike returned to the kitchen.

"If you two are in the middle of something," he told them. "I can skip the breakfast."

"You jus sit yourself down, Marshal," Helen told him sternly. "Miss Mary Jacqueline can do jus fine by herself with our bread dough. Take me but a minute to rustle up dose eggs n' ham I promised. Not right for a grown man to go off on a cold morning like dis without a good breakfast. I don want nobody saying you leave Helen's kitchen with a empty stomach. You want grits, Marshal?"

"You bet, Helen," Mike assured her. "Amos served them with most every meal. I got to liking them."

Helen turned from the stove toward him. "Dat, 'you bet' business," She asked with a sly grin. "Dat Yankee talks fer, yes?"

Mary Jacqueline answered. "Yes, it is, Helen. He means, 'Yes, thank you. I would like some grits with my breakfast, please'."

Helen turned back to the stove and began to scramble eggs in her bowl. She continued to talk to no one in particular.

"Bad enough a body gotta get used to all dis freezin weather. But yer Yankee talk got ta' be da worst. Why can't a Northern man jus say what he means?"

Properly chastised, Mike sat quietly. Finally he spoke up. "Helen, how was it you were allowed to cook in the Pope house? I thought they had a cook."

"Dey did, Marshal," Helen, answered. "An she didn't want anyone foolin around in her kitchen, neither. Dat cook and me had hard words more dan oncet about me in her kitchen, fer sure. But I be in charge of feedin Master Charles. Oncet she unnerstand dat, we get along. Why you ask? You aren't fixin ta bring somebody else ta cook in my kitchen is you?"

"Absolutely not, Helen." Mary Jacqueline interrupted. "The marshal was only making conversation. This is your kitchen and you are the cook in the Drieborg house."

"Dat 'making conversation', anoder Yankee ting? I swear. Such talk be da death of dis poor colored girl."

Mike didn't say another word. He just ate the food set before him and left the kitchen without another word.

At the front door, Mary Jacqueline gave him a hug.

"See you for lunch, dear?"

"Not today, sweetheart. I have business downtown. Besides, I think I need to give Helen time to cool down. She wouldn't poison me would she?"

Mary Jacqueline gave Mike a quick kiss. "She might if I ever stop loving you. So just you be careful and not neglect me."

Mike laughed and grabbed his wife. "So, you're the dangerous one?"

"You got that right, mister big shot US Marshal. And, don't you forget it. We'll just see how you perform tonight."

"There you go again, threats and demands! You can be a tough one, lady," Mike squeezed her in a big bear hug. "I hope I'm up to the challenge."

"I do, too." One last kiss and Mike was out the door.

\*　　\*　　\*

Later, both Helen and Mary Jacqueline were upstairs getting the children ready for school. Charles was reluctant.

"Why do I have to go to school this morning, Momma?" Charles complained. "You know I don't feel well."

"I'll keep you home when you have a temperature or are truly sick, Charles. Otherwise, you'll go to school whatever the weather."

To his mother's back as she left the room, Charles continued, "But Momma, it looks terrible outside. I could get sicker."

His five-year old sister Eleanor whispered, "It won't do any good Charles. Momma has made up her mind. You're going to school. Both of us are."

"It's not fair, Eleanor." Charles insisted. "You're used to this kind of weather. I'm not."

Helen was still in the room helping the children dress.

"Won't do no good to complain, Master Charles. Eleanor be right. You're goin ta dat St. Andrews school dis mornin, an' I'm walkin y'all der. So, gets a move on you two. You know how dose nuns at da school gets angry if'n we're late. Sides, your breakfast is gettin cold."

Between spoons of hot oatmeal, Eleanor asked, "Are you staying for a reading lesson today, Helen?"

"Yes I am chile," she responded. "Sister Aquinas be in charge of da school. She tol me dat I be welcome to learn reading and doing numbers any day I get da time. Jus so happens, today, I gots da time."

"You know, Helen," Eleanor continued. "I think the other kids are jealous that we three do homework together."

"An I preciate your help chile; believe you me I do," Helen confided. "But dat don't change things. We gots ta get goin. I don want ta be late. Com'on now you two, gets yer coats on. We can talk while we walk."

"But its cold out there, Helen." Charles complained.

"Dat's right chile," Helen agreed. "So's you better bundle up real good, you hear?"

# The Marshal's Office

Mike walked into his office and the middle of a conversation.

"Good morning, gentlemen." Mike greeted.

"Morning, Marshal," Craig Haynes replied.

Stan Killeen was asking, "Is Ohio weather as cantankerous as this Michigan stuff, Craig?"

Stan was a Michigan farm boy, like Mike. He was a good deal shorter at five-foot-five. He had a sharp tongue and could spin tales at the drop of a hat. While still a teenager, he had fled the nagging of his four sisters and the dawn-till- dusk work on his father's farm. He went to cut tall trees in the dense forests of northern Michigan. Later, he joined Mike when he volunteered for the Sixth Michigan Cavalry in 1862.

"Depends just where you're standing when you answer that question, Stan," Craig responded. "Up around Cleveland, the moisture from Lake Erie keeps that city well covered with snow and ice clear into April. In the southern part of the state, why the farmers down that way are already harvesting the first cutting of hay and complaining about the heat."

Craig was Mike's Chief Deputy. He was a slender six feet of muscle, with brown hair and a trim mustache. He had a way of looking at you that made you wonder if you had done something wrong. Haynes had been sheriff in the city of Cleveland, Ohio before joining Mike's team of marshals last year. He stayed when Mike was appointed US Marshal in Grand Rapids, Michigan.

Another deputy, Bill Anderson, chuckled at that. "I believe Craig has taken a leaf from your book of whoppers, Stan, and told us a tall one."

Bill was in his forties, the oldest of Mike's wartime buddies. He was almost as old as Mike's father. Before the war, he and his wife had owned a general store in the nearby farm community of Wyoming. Walking barefoot while hanging clothes in the backyard, she stepped on a nail and died from a tetanus infection. Soon thereafter, Bill sold the place and joined the newly formed Sixth Michigan Cavalry Regiment back in 1862. That's where he met and served with Mike and Stan.

Pretending to be irritated, Stan asked. "What falsehood have I ever told you?"

"You still spouting all that stuff about Paul Bunyan; a man ten feet tall who carried an axe with a blade four feet across? That sure was stretching the truth, seems to me."

"That ain't a falsehood, Bill. That's gospel."

"How about you insisting he had a dog as big as most mules? You telling us you didn't exaggerate that one, just a mite?"

"If you seen the footprints in the snow, like I did, you wouldn't be doubt 'in my word none."

Mike just listened. He leaned his chair back against the wall and had lit his pipe.

*These guys are something. Craig hasn't been with me that long, but Stan and Bill have since September of '62. We met in training camp when the 6th Regiment was being formed. We survived the war together and even fought Indians in the Dakota Territory. I've listened to this banter all that time. I love it.*

*I only wish Riley, Stewart, White and Austry were here, too. Each of them had other obligations. So, they turned down my invitation to join me here as deputies. My First Sergeant, Riley stayed in the cavalry out in the Dakota Territory; a Platoon Sergeant, Dave Stewart is raising his family and farming up near Newaygo; my Executive Officer, Phineas White is running a bank in Lapeer; and Henry Austry, another of my platoon leaders, is working the family farm in Illinois for his ill father. There isn't anything I wouldn't do for these men. I love them like brothers.*

Mike leaned forward and his chair legs hit the floor with a bang.

"All right; let's us move on." He announced. "Did anything happen of note during the night?"

"The log is clean of any reports, Mike." Bill reported.

"Is there anything new in that business with Amos?"

Stan answered that one. "We've been over this when we first heard about it. Things are still the same. Seems that one of the cooks at the Cosmopolitan Restaurant felt a wartime buddy of his should have the cook's job Amos was given.

"The guy complained to George that it wasn't right that a nigger should have the job over a buddy who was a white war veteran. George told him he could work someplace else or stay and accept his employer's decision.

"The guy shut up, but it appears that back in the kitchen he harasses Amos. He'll dump salt into a pot of soup Amos has cookin or spill stuff, even trip Amos when he's carrying something. Thinks it's real funny."

"Has Amos been physically attacked?"

"Not that we know."

"You're in charge of this one, Stan. But today you and I are going to talk with George at his restaurant. Maybe he can solve the problem quietly. If the cook turns out to be a slow learner, you're going to have a conversation with him in the back room here.

"The guy probably doesn't know it, but there's a federal civil rights law on the books. That law makes it one of our jobs as federal marshals to protect freedmen from guys like him. I'm not sure just how far we can go under this new statute, but Amos won't be mistreated whatever this new law says."

"Damn right, Mike." Stan agreed.

"Are there any other issues?"

Mike and his men worked for the Federal Judge and the U.S. Prosecuting Attorney for the Western District of Michigan. They were immediately responsible for the men and a few women being held pending trial, others who were awaiting sentencing and some who were waiting to be transported to a federal prison somewhere.

Craig Haynes was the Chief Deputy. Mike had assigned him to travel with the Federal Judge to courtrooms as far away as Marquette, the largest city in the Upper Peninsula of Michigan. Bill Anderson supervised the Grand Rapids area jail and all the prisoners being held there. Stan headed up the field staff and worked with Mike on issues like the Amos affair.

Bill and Craig brought Mike up to date on the prison population and the Federal Court schedule. Aside from some overcrowding in the prison, things seemed to be under control.

# Washington D.C.

Congressman William Kellogg arrived at his office at his usual time, 7:30 A.M sharp. A widower, he was an energetic man in his early fifties, well dressed and contrary to the custom, a man who did not have any facial hair.

His staff had been there since 7 A.M. Most congressional staffers were not even in their offices until 8:30 or 9 A.M, but Kellogg wanted to get a running start on each day. And he expected, in fact he required, the members of his staff to reflect that attitude.

His new chief Aide was Peter Oppewall.

"Morning Congressman. I have some hot coffee in the conference room."

"Good, Pete. I intend to have some. I could use some warming up. It's damp and chilly outside this morning. As soon as I get rid of this overcoat and grab some papers I'll join you there."

"Yes sir."

Oppewall was a Grand Rapids native. Almost six-foot four inches tall he frequently had to stoop to enter a room. Rather gaunt as well, his boss thought he looked a lot like Abraham Lincoln.

Finally seated with cups full of steaming hot coffee, the two men began to review the day's schedule.

"At nine a businessman from Grand Rapids, Mr. C. C. Comstock, has an appointment to see you in this office. He has his family with him. I've arranged for you to take them to lunch at the Willard Hotel, too. Afterward a staff member will take them on a tour of the city."

"Why are we doing all of this for Comstock, Pete? What makes this man and his family so special?"

"They are special, sir because he gave a good deal of money for your last election campaign. I expect he'll be willing to do that again."

"How much did he contribute?"

"He happens to be your largest contributor. He gave $2,000, sir."

"My! That is a lot. Do you know if he expects any special favors from me in return?"

"His company makes desks, tables and chairs. I think he would like you to help him obtain a government order for office furniture. Toward that end, I've already arranged an appointment for him with the appropriate people. He'll meet with them in this very room at 11 A.M. this morning. I'll handle that meeting before you take him and Mrs. Comstock to lunch."

"How many men does he employ back home, Pete?"

"He has almost 100 people working at his Grand Rapids factory. What is interesting about it is that he has a policy of hiring relatives of employees. So, most of his workers are related. And, he employs women, too. I'm told that the ladies do any sewing or artwork that might be needed. Unlike the ornate furniture his competitors manufacture, he produces a line of inexpensive furniture particularly designed for offices."

"I sense that you are recommending that we make every effort to help him get an order."

"No question in my mind, sir," Pete responded. "I recommend we do everything we can for him. And, by cultivating his friendship, I believe he can bring in money from other Grand Rapids manufacturers, too.

Pete continued, "I'd also like your permission to contact a gentleman new to the household market, Mr. Melville Bissel. He has a new carpet sweeper that could become widely used. Along with him, I've made a list of other businessmen I believe we should cultivate, too sir."

"Thank you Pete. Just glancing at your list, I see that I know some of these men already. I hadn't realized how rapidly the list of factory owners has grown in the Grand Rapids area lately. Do we really have six beer breweries in town now?"

"Yes sir."

"I've read some articles in the Eagle newspaper about them. Temperance groups are on the warpath about what they call the 'silver foam'. I don't know if I want to get too close to this brewery group."

"If you don't, sir, your next Democrat opponent will. Besides, what is so wrong with a workingman having a glass of beer now and then?"

"Absolutely nothing is wrong with that, Pete. I just don't want to be known as their political patron. Arrange for me to meet with Henry Fox of the Fox Beer Company the next time we're in Grand Rapids. We'll see what develops. You can invite the Fox fellow to the next shindig, but hold off on inviting the rest."

"Yes sir. But if it is all right with you, I'll draw up lists of guests I suggest for this spring's Easter gatherings in Grand Rapids. How about I ask Mr. and Mrs. Comstock to chair one of the gatherings?"

"If he gets a government contract, suggest it to them. Otherwise you and I need to talk about it, first."

"Yes sir."

"Do you have anything else, Pete?"

"Yes sir. Before we talk about it though, I suggest you read this article from the Chicago Tribune. It is an interview with Mrs. Lincoln. In the article she is quoted as accusing President Johnson of being part of the Booth conspiracy to kill her husband. You should read the article before your Judiciary Committee meeting this afternoon, sir."

"Thanks Pete," Kellogg said. "I will. Mrs. Lincoln was probably egged on or tricked by the reporter into saying something outrageous about the death of her husband. Maybe in her loneliness and anger, she was just lashing out. I can't believe she actually believes the president was involved.

"Besides, Stanton and his military court failed to prove that the assassination was anything but a Booth led conspiracy and did not involve anyone in the government. I didn't realize that the old rumor about President Johnson still floated about."

"Despite that, sir," Pete continued. "My sources tell me that some of your more radical colleagues intend to demand an investigation of her charges. It appears that they see this as another opportunity to embarrass President Johnson."

"I've always hated to see power abused in that way, Pete," Kellogg reminded him. "We Republicans have the majority in Congress now. To use that majority in our fight against the president's Reconstruction policies is one thing, but to weaken him personally in that effort is another, especially when we already know he had nothing to do with the assassination plot."

"Your feelings aside, sir," Pete assured Kellogg, "I'm told that a proposal to pursue an investigation will be made by a member of your committee this very afternoon."

"I may not be able to stop it entirely, but I'll see if I can't control it some."

"Good luck, sir."

# THE JAKE DRIEBORG FARM IN LOWELL, MICHIGAN

It was Saturday afternoon. In the barn, Mike was in the stall across from his father. Each man was milking a cow. Mike and his family were visiting for the weekend.

"The Congressman sent me a telegram," Mike said. "He'll be in town before Congress reconvenes in May. He wants me to meet with him at his local office."

"You have any idea what he wants?"

"I have a feeling he's going to ask me to do some work for him in Washington."

"What does your wife think of dat?"

"She's fine with it, as long as I take her with me."

"And, da children?"

"I'm not quite sure. Most people who can leave Washington in the summer to avoid the typhus and other sicknesses that seems to infect people that time of year there. I'd not want the children with us during that time of year. Actually, I would like to leave them with you and Momma. I believe the kids would love it. What do you think of that idea, Papa?"

"That's fine with me, Michael. I think Charles would like it, for sure. By the time you returned he should be a seasoned farm boy. Momma would love to have Eleanor spend time with us and work with her in da kitchen and garden dis spring, too."

"Let us wash up and go in for supper, Michael. You know how Momma gets if her men are late getting to da table."

"Some things never change do they, Papa?"

"I'm surprised you haven't found dat out already, son."

"Just don't bring it up in front of Mary Jacqueline, please." Mike chuckled.

*       *       *

At the dinner table, the family discussed the possibilities.

"If Washington is so dangerous during the hot months, Michael," his mother, Rose began, "why would you ever consider having Mary Jacqueline there?"

"Don't talk to me about that, Momma," Mike defended himself. "She's the one who is insisting."

"Mary Jacqueline?" asked Rose.

"I don't intend to sit quietly alone at home while my husband runs all over the country doing favors for the Congressman. We promised each other before we married that we would have supper as a family every night. Am I the only one who remembers that promise, Michael?"

"No, sweetheart," Mike protested. "I remember it and I have kept that promise."

"Yes you have," his wife agreed. "For all of four months you've kept it. And now, at the first hint of an invitation, it appears you are itching to go off on a new adventure, without me and the children."

Jake interrupted calmly. "Children, Momma," he broke in. "Let me make a suggestion." Everyone was quiet.

"Michael, if you're asked to go to Washington for dis work, I think da both of you should go der. Leave da children with us. When da hot weather comes dis summer, Momma and me will bring da children to Philadelphia. Mary Jacqueline, you and Michael can ride da train from Washington and meet us der."

"I think Papa has a good idea," Rose added. "What do you think, Mary Jacqueline?"

"I've known for some time that Grampa Jacob was a smart man. Now, I know he is a wise one, too. I would like to discuss it with Michael, of course. But with my baby due in August, going to Philadelphia in June or early July would get me out of the worst of the season in Washington and the entire family together for the birth of our child."

"What do you think, children?" Mary Jacqueline asked.

"Would you teach me to milk a cow, Grampa Jake?" Charles asked excitedly.

"Yes, Charles. Dat could be one of your afternoon chores."

"And sleep in the loft like Mike did?"

"Ya, you could sleep in da loft, Charles."

"Would you like to stay here and help gramma in this house, Eleanor?" asked her mother.

"Yes, Momma," the child responded, somewhat quietly. "Remember, I grew up here for a long time. I love it now, too; especially when Charles and I stay overnight here. But this is for a long time, Momma. What of our schoolwork? Will we be with you when you have your baby, for sure?"

"Those are good questions, Eleanor." Mary Jacqueline agreed. "Let's talk all those things over with gramma Rose in the morning. We don't have to decide anything tonight. Would that be all right with you?"

"Yes, Momma," Eleanor responded. "That would be fine with me."

"Oh, come on, Eleanor," Charles prodded. "Don't be a spoilsport. This will be great fun."

"Hold on now, Charles," his mother cautioned. "Eleanor has a right to voice her opinion. We'll all just take our time here and talk it out before we finally decide. Everyone will have a voice in the decision; not just you Charles."

"Oh, all right, Momma," he grumbled.

"Michael," Mary Jacqueline continued, "I have one request to make of you before any decision is made."

"What would that be sweetheart?"

"I'd like the congressman to join us for supper one evening. Then he can explain to me, too, why only Michael Drieborg can ensure the success of his project. You wouldn't mind that, would you, dear?"

Jake choked on his coffee and Rose smiled broadly.

*She's got me, again. What a woman!*

∗    ∗    ∗

Later, the house was quiet. Rose and Jake were in their room preparing for bed.

"Listen to that rain beat on the roof, Papa," she told him.

"If da temperature drops much lower, Momma, we'll have a coat of ice covering everything in da morning." Jake observed. "No church for us if dat happens."

"What do you think of the children staying here, Papa?"

"I like da idea, Momma," he responded. "It is too quiet around here for me, anyway. I like having da children around, noise and all. It will be fun for me to teach Charles all da farm things his fader and his uncle Little Jake learned from me years ago, too."

"Truth be told, Papa, the house does seem empty. Little Eleanor was an infant when we brought her here. So, she's like a daughter to me. I miss having her around the house."

"I do too, Momma," Jake continued. "Not long ago we had four children under our roof. Michael left for da Army in '62; den Susan got married; Ann was next; and den Little Jake ran off to da Army out West in '66. It was like, one day our house was all noise and talking and da next it was quiet as a church. It is hard for me sometimes, Momma."

"It is for me as well, Papa. The weekends are better, though. That's when Ann and her husband bring their children here after church on Sunday. Susan is so tied up with her restaurant she seldom gets out here with her children. So, I go there just to be with them. It is some better with Michael and his children living in Grand Rapids."

They both got into bed. "Remember what the Hechts did, Papa?"

"You mean, when dey went to Germany and came back with two babies?"

"We could liven things up here too if we did the same in Holland."

"Turn out da light, Momma."

"I'm cold, Papa. Move over here and get me warm."

"Dat's a good idea."

"Jacob."

"Yes Momma?"

"We could get a baby the old-fashioned way, you know."

"Dat's a better idea, even."

They shuffled around under the covers and pushed aside their woolen bed clothing.

"Oh! Jacob. And I thought maybe you had lost interest."

"Not hardly, Rose."

Then, all you could hear was the rain falling on the roof.

# Grand Rapids

Mike and Stan walked into the Cosmopolitan Restaurant and Bakery for lunch.

The owner, and Mike's brother-in-law, George Neal greeted them. "Hi, Mike."

"Damn! Don't I get a greeting, George?" Stan Killeen asked irritably.

George was another of those who had joined the Union cavalry with Mike and Stan back in '62. They trained and fought together throughout the war. George had been discharged a year early when he came down with a severe case of dysentery. He was sent back home to Grand Rapids.

George had no family, so the Drieborgs took him in while he recovered. That's when he and Mike's sister Susan fell in love, married and bought the Grand Rapids bakery where George had apprenticed before the war. It was a successful enterprise, now.

"Keep your shirt on, Killeen. My Lord you are touchy. Give a guy a chance."

"I'm just keepin' ya honest, George."

"Crying out loud, has all this Deputy Marshal business gone to your head?"

"Why don't you get one of yer employees to bring some coffee to our table, George? I'll worry about my head."

Settled at their table, the two men looked over the menu. George sat with them.

"I don't know why you even look at my menu, Stan," George chuckled. "We all know you want some of Amos's gumbo."

"There ya go, worrying about another part of my anatomy, George," Stan snapped. "By God, that sure is comforting. Just knowing how much you care."

Mike spoke up. "Speaking of Amos, how is he doing, George?"

Amidst the confusion in the South Carolina countryside of the spring of 1865, Amos left the plantation where he had been a slave since birth. Wandering aimlessly, he had been captured by some bushwhackers and was cooking for them. Mike came upon their camp, hung the thieves and took Amos along as a cook for his troop. Amos stayed with them throughout Sherman's drive through the Carolinas. When the war ended, he stayed in South Carolina.

A pretty good-sized fella, Amos was almost as tall as Mike. Slender, he had a ready smile and a mild disposition. Mike had returned to South Carolina as a U.S. Marshal on an assignment for the Congressional Committee on Reconstruction. He and his team stumbled upon Amos cooking in a Charleston eatery.

After an altercation with a local redneck, the local sheriff suggested.

"You best get your nigger out of here, Marshal Drieborg. The guy your deputy killed surely had it comin' but it will go hard with Amos if you leave him here."

So, Amos joined Mike and his deputies as a cook and member of his team. When the assignment ended, Amos went back to Washington with Mike and was subsequently sent to Grand Rapids and a cook's job in George's restaurant.

"He is a jewel, Mike," George told him. "I've told you guys a million times how much I appreciate you sending him north to work for me. He's a hard worker, here early and leaves late. The customers love his soups, especially his gumbo. I'd put him in charge of my kitchen here in a minute, if'n he wasn't a colored."

"Shouldn't be that way, George," Stan cut in. "Guy does the job, shouldn't make a damn bit of difference what he looks like, seems ta me."

"Com'on, Stan. You ran a grain elevator up north of here. You had guys working for you. Would they have been willing to take orders from a colored?"

"No! But it still ain't fair."

"Maybe not," George continued. "I pay Amos a fair wage and let him manage the soup an' such. The other guys get along with him just fine the way it is. I'm not about to ruin that and my business ta boot, just because something I can't control ain't fair; neither would you Killeen. Besides, then Amos and me could both be out on the street lookin for work."

"No one is accusing you of anything, George," Mike interrupted. "Stan just was pulling your chain. You should realize that by now."

"Ya, I know it, Mike." George admitted. "He could always get a rise out of me, though."

Mike continued. "After lunch we want to talk to one of your guys, Bob I think his name is. We hear he's been harassing Amos. Just so happens, there's a new federal civil rights law that outlines the rights of the new freedmen. The way I see it, George, this employee of yours is breaking the spirit of that law."

"Look, Mike," George countered. "There's a lot of kidding around in my kitchen between the men. My Lord, the guys in our old squad got into it with one another all the time; you just heard how Stan and me were funnin' with each other a minute ago. What'd you say; Stan was pulling my chain? How is what my guys do, so different?"

"Because Amos is a colored," Mike said with some heat. "Because your guy, Bob's kidding around will probably lead to Amos getting a beating after work for taking a job a white man wanted.

"Stan and I saw that kind of thing when we were down south, George. I want this stopped right now before that happens. If this gets out of hand, and your people have to take sides between Amos and Bob, the white cook, do you think it would hurt your business?"

"I'd have to believe it would, Mike," George agreed. "What do you want me to do?"

"Get Bob out here right now. We'll take him over to the jail for a little conversation."

"Can you wait until the lunch rush is over? I can have him in my office at two this afternoon. Ok?"

*        *        *

Bob Thomas entered the office of his employer at 2 PM sharp.

"You wanted to see me, boss?"

"This is Deputy Marshal Killeen, Bob. He wants to have a visit with you."

"Ya; I've seen him in the restaurant before. But I ain't done nothin wrong boss. What does he want to talk with me about, anyway?"

"The deputy will tell you, Bob."

Killeen took charge at this point. You and me are going to take a little walk over to the jail, Bob. I got a special room just for conversations. Since ya haven't done anything wrong, you wouldn't mind havin a friendly talk with me over there, would ya?"

"But I got work ta do, boss."

"That's all right, Bob. I won't dock your pay. You just go along and cooperate with the deputy. You can finish up here when the two of you are done with your talk."

# The Drieborg Home

"Good evening, Congressman," Mary Jacqueline greeted. "Michael will take your coat and hat."

"What a nice home you have Mrs. Drieborg. Did you know that mine is just up Prospect Street, a couple of blocks?"

"Yes, Michael told me," she answered. "We like it. It's close to the children's school and not far from Michael's office, either. Supper will be ready soon. Please, join us in the living room."

"How has the winter treated you?"

"I was raised in Pennsylvania, Congressman," she began. "My father, Dr. Miles Murphy, was a professor at the university medical school; still is, actually. In any case, the weather there is not much different than here."

"But you spent some years in the South, did you not?"

"Yes. And, I'm afraid I've struggled this winter getting used to the cold and snow, once again. With spring, I'll be fine, I'm sure."

"Michael tells me you are expecting."

"Yes, that's true. I believe the Doctor predicts that August will see the birth of our first child together."

"That's right. You each brought a child to the marriage."

"My son Charles and Michael's daughter Eleanor are almost the same age. They get along beautifully."

"I was only blessed with one child, Mrs. Drieborg. Her mother died when she was very young, too."

"Mrs. Drieborg is so formal for friends, Congressman. Please call me Mary Jacqueline."

"Thank you. But only if you call me William."

"I met you daughter Patricia, William. She and her husband, George Krupp, attended the reception you held for Michael last Christmas."

Throughout this back and forth, Mike sat quietly, just listening, letting them get better acquainted.

The Drieborg's cook, Helen came into the room and announced, "Dinner is served, everyone."

"Allow me, Mary Jacqueline," Congressman Kellogg said, and offered his arm.

She took it, and allowed him to escort her to the dinning room. Mike followed along, still very quiet.

He sat at the head of the table, and began passing the serving dishes.

"Let us thank the Lord for this food, shall we?" Mary Jacqueline suggested.

"Of course," Kellogg agreed.

"Bless us oh Lord, for these thy gifts, for what we are about to receive from thy bounty, through Christ our Lord. Amen."

Mike spoke for the first time, "Thank you, dear."

"This is an excellent stew, Mary Jacqueline." Kellogg decided. "The biscuits are especially tasty. Give my compliments to your cook." He nodded to Helen who was standing by the kitchen doorway.

"Weren't me who done it." Helen told them. "No sir. Mrs. Drieborg done it, bread, rolls an all. I only helped a little bit."

Mike looked as surprised as Kellogg.

"I agree with the congressman, sweetheart. It is all very good."

"Thank you, Michael. Thank you, William. I hope you like my dessert as well."

A bit later Kellogg asked, "Where are the children, Mike? I haven't seen your daughter Eleanor since she was an infant. Remember when I had them all at my home in Washington back in '64?"

"Yes, I do. She's not tiny anymore."

"I had looked forward to meeting your son, too, Mary Jacqueline. Charles is his name, isn't it?" Kellogg continued.

"Yes it is." Mary Jacqueline answered, "They'll both join us for dessert, William. They ate with Helen earlier."

"Before they join us, could I ask you about this new assignment you are suggesting my husband take on?"

"Of course you can."

"Michael has told me that your Judiciary Committee wishes to reopen the investigation of the Lincoln assassination. Is that correct?"

"Yes, it is."

"Why is Michael so necessary?" she began. "With all the government employees at your beck and call in Washington, why bring him into what appears to be just another round of political infighting?"

"There are two reasons I have pushed for Mike to head up such an investigation." Kellogg responded. "First of all, Michael can be trusted. And, while my colleagues know I am his mentor, they also know he will conduct an honest investigation.

"Much is at stake for the nation right now, Mary Jacqueline. Allow me to explain."

"Please do, William. Michael has told to me of your conversation with him. But I would like to hear what you have to say, too."

Kellogg began. "It is critical that a thorough investigation is conducted and an honest report is issued."

29

"There is no doubt that Booth alone shot President Lincoln. And, we believe his immediate accomplices were caught and punished.

"Including a woman, Mrs. Surratt?"

"Well, many of us believe her hanging was a grave mistake." Kellogg admitted. "But it was done, can't do anything about that now."

"The question remains, though," he continued, "did Booth receive support from others who have not yet been identified? Rumors around Washington insist that such aid was given Booth before he fired the fatal bullet, and especially afterward to facilitate his escape."

"There are already many in Congress and people in the North who want the South punished severely for starting the past war. Imagine the uproar if it were discovered that Confederate leaders had a hand in killing President Lincoln.

"Even before Lincoln's reelection in November of '64, Radicals in Congress were on a collision course with him over his Reconstruction policy. Many of them tried to get the Republican Party to select General Fremont as their candidate for president instead of Lincoln. So, another theory has men from this group encouraging an attack on him, or taking an active part in it.

"And another theory suggests that President Johnson was somehow involved. In an interview recently, Mrs. Lincoln claimed that he had a hand in the killing of her husband. Did he? Some in the North believe her accusation. Remember, he is actually a Democrat who was put on the ticket in 1864 by Lincoln to help hold the Border States in the Union. So, he was never popular among Republicans. Now, the Republican Radicals in Congress would love to see him brought under suspicion and his Reconstruction policies discredited.

"I mentioned a second reason I want Michael to come to Washington and assist in the investigation of all these theories, Mary Jacqueline. Employees of the Congress and the Justice Department are appointees whose investigation and report could be easily influenced and thus suspect from the outset, thereby worthless."

"But William," she interrupted. "Michael is an appointee and employee of that same Justice Department, too, is he not?"

"Yes, that's true." Kellogg agreed. "And, that brings me back to my first point. Mike has a reputation in Washington for honesty. He will be trusted to render an honest report."

"But really, Congressman," Mary Jacqueline continued. "Surely no one actually thinks members of Lincoln's own administration or members of Congress conspired to have him killed."

"I hate to even entertain that thought, my dear," Kellogg responded softly,

"Unfortunately, there are powerful people who do believe it. Some would love to see that very possibility confirmed. So this investigation must be thorough and honest. Given the impact, Mary Jacqueline, the very fate of our nation might well depend upon it."

Kellogg went on arguing his case with Mike's wife.

"I know Mike is considered Kellogg's man; my man. But he is also seen as a man who would come to this assignment with clean hands. I must confess, such a person would be virtually impossible to find in Washington today."

"That was a very thorough explanation, William. Thank you. Now, I would like to ask you a practical question."

"Please do."

"I pay the bills for this household. So, I am aware of our financial situation. Do you expect that Michael's current salary will have to cover travel and Washington expenses, too?"

"No," Kellogg quickly assured her. "Michael and his team will receive their salaries plus expenses."

"That's good to hear," Mary Jacqueline said. "You should also know, though, that his family will not stay in Grand Rapids while he's in Washington. We haven't decided about the children, but I certainly will be with him there. And, I do not intend for us to stay in some boardinghouse."

"Mike already told me that."

Mary Jacqueline relaxed some, paused, and quietly said. "Thank you, Michael."

"I told you sweetheart, I had not forgotten my promise to you."

"I'll thank you later, Michael, in private." Mary Jacqueline smiled.

\*     \*     \*

Just then, Helen brought the children into the room.

"Sorry ta interrupt," she said, "but des children have school in da mornin. So, dey has ta get ta bed."

"Children," Mary Jacqueline began, "our guest tonight is Congressman Kellogg."

"Hello children," he greeted.

Barely seated, Charles asked, "What's a congressman?"

"I work in Washington D. C. and help make laws for our country. Are you Charles Pope from South Carolina?" Kellogg asked.

"I'm Charles Pope Drieborg from Michigan, now," he exclaimed calmly.

"Well said, son. Would you mind living in Washington, when your father works there for a while?"

Eleanor piped up, "We might stay with our grandparents."

"Is Washington full of Yankees?" Charles asked.

Kellogg chuckled. "I'm afraid it is, son. Aren't you a Yankee now, too?"

"I'm not sure. Some of the kids at school call me Reb," Charles continued. "They say I talk different, too. But I think they talk funny."

Eleanor added. "There's a boy in our class who likes to push and shove other kids. When we're on the playground, he calls himself Yank and Charles, Johnny Reb. If Sister Aquinas would let him, I think he would like to start a fight. But most of the kids treat my brother fine."

"Is this Sister Aquinas in charge at your school?" Kellogg asked.

Helen answered this time. "I help her some to keep order on da playground. But dat lady is definitely in charge. An, is she quick! My goodness; I 'spec she has eyes in da back a' her head, even."

Mary Jacqueline interrupted. "Let's have our dessert, everyone. It's getting late for you children."

"Aww, Momma," the children responded, almost in unison. "It's still early."

# The Federal Marshal's Office in Grand Rapids

"Go right on in, Bob," Stan Killeen directed. George's cook went into the marshal's office.

Deputy Marshal Bill Anderson was at the front desk.

"Who are you dragging in here, Killeen?"

"This guy works for George in his kitchen, Marshal Anderson," Stan explained. "He's the one who seems ta have a problem working with our old friend, Amos."

"I don't know what the hell you're talkin about, deputy," Bob objected.

"Oh, so you're that guy," Anderson remarked. "I've been wanting to you. Right this way mister. I got just the room for us to visit in."

Killeen pushed the man toward a doorway. Once through, the man came to a stop.

"Hey, this is a jail. Why am I here" I ain't done nothin wrong."

"We'll just see about that, my friend," Stan said pushing the man into an empty cell.

Bill Anderson closed the metal door behind them. Only three chairs were in the five by five foot room. Light came from a small barred window a good seven feet from the floor. The heavy door had a window, too. But it was only big enough for a guard to survey the inside of the bare room. And, there was a slot at the bottom of the door through which a food tray could be slid into the cell.

"Sit down, Bob," Killeen directed. "Let's have a talk about your military record."

"What about it?"

"I hear tell you're a veteran, Bob."

"I'm damn proud of it, too. So, what's it to you?"

"Deputy Anderson and me are vets, too, Bill," Stan continued. "What unit were you in?"

"I was in the 4th Michigan Infantry. I joined early in the war."

"Serve to the end, did ya?" Anderson asked.

"Naw, I didn't make it. I got a medical discharge."

Stan opened a folder and began reading. "It appears that you couldn't keep yer hands of'n the property of the other soldiers in your unit, Bob. In fact, this here record says the guys in your unit turned you in to the Provost Marshal."

"That's all lies." Bob protested. "Where'd you get that pile of crap?"

"I got it from this official record of the court where your case was heard. It seems as though you were convicted of stealing, dishonorably discharged, and sent to the military prison in Detroit for a term of two years."

"I can see why you'd be awful sick over that," Anderson chuckled.

"What's this got to do with my being a cook, an all? I'm just trying to make a living. No crime in that. After all, the past is the past. I served my time."

"Yes you did, Bobby," Anderson told him. "While all the other vets in town here were dodging bullets, living out of doors in all kinds of weather and eating crap, you were safe and warm in a military prison eating three squares a day."

Stan asked, "Do the vets down at the GAR meeting hall know about your real military record, Bobby?"

"Nobody's damned business."

"That's fine with us, Bob. None a' this information need get outside a' this room, Bob."

"Then, why am I here?"

"Listen real careful, Bob," Anderson leaned close.

"It's come to our attention that you've been harassing one of your fellow cooks over at George's place. Something about how a buddy of yours wanted the job but George gave it to this colored guy."

"So you're going ta' put me in jail fer, what; having a little fun by teasing a nigger, some? Fact is he did take a job away from a white guy, a veteran, too."

"Ya best listen ta' us on this, Bobby." Stan cautioned. "Amos served with us in the war. And, when we were in Carolina last year on a mission for the folks in Congress, he was with us then, too. We got real fond a' him."

Anderson finished by saying, "So, if we hear of any more harassment of our friend Amos; any at all. If he even slips on the ice, or burns his little finger in the kitchen, we're going to hold you responsible, Bob. Then, this little room here will become your home, real fast."

"That ain't fair." Bob protested.

"He's not listening, Deputy Stan," Anderson decided. "He's just not getting our message."

"Afraid yer right, Deputy Anderson," Stan agreed. "Tell you what, Bob. We're going to leave you here for a while. I'll tell George you got tied up. When you think you understand our message, we'll let you get back to work.

"Don't take too long though, Bob," Anderson continued. "We might just have' ta' tell everyone about how you got thrown out of the army an' all. Yer beer drinkin buddies who served honorably in the army probably don't know how you stole from the other soldiers in your unit."

"I can't believe this. You're gonna put me in jail? Fer what?" Bob shouted standing up. "Funnin with a nigger? I ain't even broke no laws, or nothin'."

The two deputies stood and left the room.

"Oops!" Stan said coming back into the cell. "I forgot the chairs."

"Hey!" Bob shouted, "What'll I use?"

"Let's see if this will do."

It was his turn to move his hips.

"Oh, yes Michael! You are able."

Later, they lay side-by-side in one another's arms, and slept.

# Trip to Philadelphia

It was still dark outside the Drieborg home. But everyone was up, dressed and in the kitchen.

"I don't know why we have to go to Philadelphia, Momma," Charles complained. "Grampa Jake told me he needs me here to help him do chores on the farm."

"You'll get your chance, Charles," his mother assured him. "But Grampa Miles and Gramma Judy want to visit with you, too. You'll be back in Lowell sooner than you think."

"But there's nothing to do at their house, Momma," Charles continued.

Eleanor interrupted. "It's been decided, Charles. We're going to visit Grampa Miles and Gamma Judy first. Then we'll go to Lowell. You might just as well stop complaining. If you keep talking like this their feelings will be hurt. You want them to think you don't want to see them?"

"I guess not, Eleanor."

"We'll have fun. You'll see."

"You children finish your oatmeal, now, you hear?" Helen ordered. "We don't have all day a' fore we leave for da train station. You pack da school books, Eleanor?"

"Yes, Helen, I did. And the chalk and writing slate, too."

"And I packed our reading stuff, too," added Charles.

"What you bring, Charles?" Helen asked.

"I brought our school readers, Helen. Eleanor and I each picked out one book for the train trip. Gramma Judy will take us to the library in Philadelphia for more."

"What did you bring to read, Helen?" Eleanor asked.

"I'm still readin' "Uncle Tom's Cabin" ya know."

"I thought you've read that before," Charles observed.

"No, I haven't finished it. Der is some hard words in dat book, Charles. So I use da dictionary ta help me figure dem out. Takin' me a long time dat way. Dat's all right though. I'm learning lots' a new words dat way."

"Sides, I likes dat story. When we gets to your grandma's, maybe I'll find a new one when we go to da library."

*    *    *

The sun was barely up when the train left Grand Rapids headed southeast toward Michigan's capital city of Lansing. The Drieborg family would change trains there and board one headed for Detroit.

"This is my third time riding on a train, Eleanor," Charles calculated. "How many times have you been on a train?"

"Let's see," she began. "I was a baby when my aunt Julia carried me to Michigan from Maryland where I was born. That's one time. The next time was when Grampa and Gramma Drieborg took me to meet you in Philadelphia, last fall. That's when your Momma married my father. So, this is my third train ride, too."

"I've an idea, Eleanor," Charles began. "Let's see who can count the most barns or cows or something as the train moves between Grand Rapids and Detroit."

"All right Charles. But there are probably too many animals to count. So, let's do barns that are painted red."

"Why are most barns painted red, do you think?" Charles asked.

"That's a good question, Charles. I never thought about it. But I'll bet Grampa Jake would know. Let's write him a letter and ask. He would like a letter from us, and his barn is red. So, he should be able to tell us why he painted it that color."

So, the children began looking out the windows for barns painted red. Helen sat up front, too, reading. Mike and Mary Jacqueline sat close together in the back of the car and watched. They took advantage of the opportunity to talk, too.

"Well, dear. We're on our way," Mike observed. "Do you regret that I accepted this assignment?"

"Absolutely not, Michael," she quickly responded. "I told you before we married that you could pursue whatever career you wished as long as we did it together. Do you remember our conversation on that subject?"

"Yes, I do, sweetheart," Mike told her. "And, I hope you know that I never want to be apart from you. Thank you for your willingness to be with me."

"And you should know by now, Michael Drieborg, that I'll not let you get far from my side, if I can help it."

"Good thought. I want you close, always."

"We'll be in Detroit by noon," Mike explained. "After we change trains there for Cleveland, we can have lunch in the dining car."

"Did you forget our talk yesterday, Michael? I told you I wouldn't trust any train food. Who knows where it came from or where it's been sitting around?"

"I guess I did forget, sweetheart." Michael admitted. "So, what's your solution?"

"I brought sandwiches and hard-boiled eggs from home. It should be all right to buy train coffee for you, Helen and me. But I'll have the children drink the water I brought. I even have a slice of pie for each of us in my picnic basket."

"Sounds like a feast."

"Not quite. But I don't want anyone getting sick on train food."

"Neither do I dear," Mike said. "Thank you for taking care of me and the children."

Smiling and giving his arm a squeeze, Mary Jacqueline replied, "Somebody has to look after my mister big shot, Marshal Drieborg."

"Is that right?" Mike taunted. "Just wait until we get to Washington and I walk on water. Then you'll be sorry you made fun of this big shot marshal."

"I love you dearly, Michael," Mary Jacqueline assured him. "But sometimes you are so full of it."

"It's part of my charm, dear."

Mary Jacqueline just snuggled closer to her husband.

# Washington D.C.

"What in the devil are you up to now, Kellogg?"

Congressman Webster from Tennessee was speaking.

He and Kellogg were meeting with Congressman Clark from Ohio and Judiciary Committee Chairman George S. Boutwell from Massachusetts in the Congressional Office Building. Several aides were present as well.

These men were all members of the House Judiciary Committee. Webster was the only elected Democrat present.

"Whatever are you talking about, Harry?" Kellogg responded.

"Don't pull that innocent crap with me." Webster snapped. "I saw the request for funds your people sent to the Justice Department. You want money to pay your darling, Marshal Drieborg and his buddies to stir up more trouble. What's it all about?"

"Can't hide a thing from you Harry," Congressman Davis admitted. "You're the ranking minority member of the Judiciary Committee, so I might as well let you know."

"Mighty nice of you fellas," Webster replied. The congressman from Tennessee was very portly; fat actually. He was serving on a committee dominated by Republicans. He had been considered a Peace Democrat during the Civil War. As such he was suspected of sympathizing with the Confederate cause.

"Since you guys took over Congress last fall, I don't know what the hell is going on most of the time. I only find out after you've made a decision."

"I don't see what you have to complain about, Harry," Owen Lovejoy from Illinois interjected. "The president is a Democrat and from Tennessee, to boot."

"Are you gonna tell me why you asked me here, or not?" he asked irritably.

"I'm getting to that, Harry," Boutwell promised. "You read that article in the Chicago Tribune quoting Mrs. Lincoln?"

"Ya, I read it. Everybody knows she's a bit addled."

"Maybe she is, but not everyone thinks so. In fact, there is growing pressure for us to look into her charges."

"That is so much crap, Boutwell," Webster retorted. "You're just looking for an excuse to embarrass the president."

"Not at all, Harry," Lovejoy declared. "When a charge is made it's our obligation to check out all the possibilities. Besides, I'd think the president would want to be cleared of such suspicion."

"You boys are just trying to distract the country from the real issue, reconstruction. Like Lincoln, President Johnson wants each of the states in the former Confederacy to resume its place in the Union. You Republicans want to keep your military boot on the neck of the South and use the coloreds to take over their state governments. You're into punishment, not forgiveness and reunion.

"And, I find it hard to see such an investigation helping the president." Webster went on.

"Why the devil are you asking me, anyway?" he challenged. "You have the majority in Congress. You can do whatever you damn please."

"While that's true, Harry," Boutwell admitted. "We'd rather have you on board with this investigation."

"I bet you would, now," Webster snapped. "With a Democrat or two, this investigation would not seem so much like the witch hunt it really is."

"Now, Harry," Lovejoy interjected. "You know we value your views."

"In a pig's eye you do, Lovejoy. All right, let's get down to cases. What's in it for me?"

Boutwell spoke to this issue, first. "I know there are some bridges that need rebuilding in your district, Harry. Folks back home might like some help with the cost of those projects."

"Not enough; not for the political cover you're asking me to give you."

Kellogg joined the discussion. "I'm aware that the rail lines around Chattanooga are still in disrepair since the war. That was a rail center important to Tennessee before the war, wasn't it, Harry?"

"Don't forget Nashville, Kellogg," Webster added, "the boys in blue tore that up pretty good too; it's still not up to full operation and the war's been over for almost two years."

"Harry," Boutwell concluded. "I think the committee staff has enough to start with, don't you? Let them work on this today. We can meet again tomorrow. Do we have an understanding, Harry?"

Webster put up his hand. "Wait just a minute, here," He cautioned. "I don't want to be signing off on just any investigation you birds come up with. I can go along with Kellogg's man, Drieborg heading it up. The boy's sort of violent, but he's a pretty straight arrow. I think I can trust him to do an honest job. But he's still a Yankee. I want a couple of southern boys on this team; men who actually fought for the Confederacy."

"An, I want to pick 'em."

"Not a problem, Harry," Boutwell conceded, "get their names to my office as soon as possible. My people will arrange for travel expenses and so on."

"There's another thing," Webster insisted.

"My Lord, Harry, Don't push it. We can probably find another Democrat, you know."

"No you can't, Lovejoy. I'm the only so called Peace Democrat who presently serves on the Judiciary Committee. And I was on the Joint Committee on the Conduct of the War during the late conflict. Besides that, I've been on the Reconstruction Committee since the war ended.

Them three aces will trump the cards of any other Democrat in Congress."

"All right, Harry." Kellogg asked. "What else?"

"The scope of this investigation needs to be expanded."

"What the hell!" Lovejoy exclaimed.

"Damn right!" Webster shouted. "To appear nonpartisan it must be broader. It has to look into two other conspiracy theories if it is to appear bipartisan, complete and fair."

"I can't wait to hear this." Boutwell chuckled. "What are they, Harry?"

"While everyone agrees that Booth committed the murder, there have always been questions about the possibility that he had help from inside the government. I want our investigators given full authority to look into that."

"Holy Mother of God," Lovejoy shouted, "that will create a storm of protest from our side of the aisle. Can you imagine how Seward, Stanton and the boys at the Justice Department will react?"

Webster retorted. "How do you think my side of the aisle will react to just investigating the president?"

"I can't say I give a damn what you Democrats think," Lovejoy retorted.

"If you fellas agree with Lovejoy," Harry asked. "Why are we here?"

"Cool off Lovejoy," Boutwell urged. "I agree with Harry on this one."

"An, the other one that should be given another look is that Jeff Davis and others in his government ordered Lincoln's killing."

"So," Congressman Boutwell summarized. "In addition to the Johnson accusation, you want our investigators to also look into those two possibilities."

"About time, too," Webster quickly said. "After all, the president already issued a statement claiming that some Confederate officials did support the assassination. Be good to check out the questionable testimony that supported that conclusion."

Rep, Lovejoy wasn't done. "While we're at it, Webster, why don't we have our investigators check-out the accusations of Charles Chiniquy, the defrocked Catholic priest? You know; that the Pope had a hand in Lincoln's killing?"

"Good idea," Webster laughed. "I'll get a big atta-boy on that one back home. Most people back my way don't trust Catholics anyway."

The chairman of the Judiciary Committee, Congressman Boutwell brought the meeting to a close.

"I'll see you tomorrow morning at ten, gentlemen. We'll conclude our arrangements at that time. Don't forget those two names, Harry."

# CADES COVE, TENNESSEE

As he saw Bose Faute enter his general store, Noah Burchfield shouted, "Hey, buddy," got a telegram here fer ya. It's all the way from Washington D.C., too."

"Who the devil;" Bose asked of no one in particular." a telegram for me?"

It was Saturday, and the general store was crowded with locals, women mostly, on their weekly visit. Some picked up catalogue orders, others just some staples like tobacco, coffee and sugar; most came for the local gossip. Kids were underfoot noses pressed against the glass side of the candy counter, hoping for a sample of licorice or a piece of hard candy.

"What' those Yankees want with you, Bose?" Dan Lawson, Justice of the Peace, asked.

"It sure beats tha hell out' a' me. Gimme that telegram, Noah. We'll find out right now."

People gathered around. There were few secrets in Cades Cove. Located in the Great Smoky Mountains, the Cove was connected to the valley 1,750 feet below and the town of Gatlinburg by a single road. So, the 47 families and 250 people had to be virtually self-sufficient.

The floor of the Cove was very fertile. Several thousand acres had been cleared to support several crops: wheat, corn, oats, barley and rye. Garden vegetables were grown and cattle and farm animals were raised as well.

Despite the fact that Tennessee joined the Confederacy, the men of Cades Cove fought for both sides. The anger of that split and the wounds created were still felt, but most folks got along. Pretty well, anyway; Union families traded at a different general store though.

"Can't believe it," Bose exclaimed. "Webster, our Congressman, wants me to join him in Washington. Says he needs me right away to help him out. He wants to make me a US Marshal to help investigate the killing of Lincoln."

"Don't that just beat all?" Dr. Calvin Post exclaimed. "Why'd he pick you, Bose?"

"Remember when he was up here last fall, Doc? He was lookin fer our votes a course," Bose reminded the group. "I put him up at my place and showed him around the Cove some. We hit it off real well. He sure had a taste fer my moonshine, too.

"He says he needs a good Southern boy from his district who's a Confederate veteran. Wants to make sure those Yankees don't end up blaming us Southerns for the killing."

"What' a' ya gonna do, Bose?" John Myers, another man listening to all this, asked.

"My seed's in," he mused out loud. "All I got 'ta do is watch em sprout' 'n grow. He says this business won't take more n couple' a months. Heck, that would get me back here in plenty' a time fer the harvest; maybe even the first cutting. Pick' in up some Union greenbacks wouldn't hurt neither."

"Noah," Bose decided, "warm up that telegraph key a' yours caus' I'm goin ta' Washington DC."

# PHILADELPHIA

"It doesn't seem near as cold here as it is back in Grand Rapids." Charles told his father.

The Drieborg family had arrived in Philadelphia and was waiting for their luggage to be unloaded. Mary Jacqueline's father, Dr. Miles Murphy had agreed to pick them up.

"Daddy is so prompt," Mary Jacqueline observed. "I would guess the train was a bit early or he would probably be waiting impatiently for us."

"Isn't that him getting out of that carriage at the other end of the station?"

"I think you're right, Michael. Children, that's your grandfather up ahead. Run to greet him."

"I'll race you, Eleanor," Charles challenged. He got the jump on her and reached his grandfather first.

"Grandfather!" Charles shouted.

"Oomph!" Dr. Murphy exclaimed when Charles crashed into him.

"Easy there, my boy."

Eleanor approached her stepmother's father in a much more reserved manner.

"Grandfather Murphy," she said quietly. "Remember me? I'm Eleanor."

"Of course I do, child," he told her equally reservedly. "It's nice to see you again." He patted her head softly.

By this time, Mary Jacqueline had reached the three and opened her arms to embrace her father.

"Father," she said. "It's so good to see you."

"Good to see you, too, Daughter." He allowed her to hug him for a brief moment, and stepped back.

"Didn't your husband, the marshal, come with you?"

"Michael is my husband's name, Father," she reminded him. "He's looking after our luggage."

"Of course it is dear. My carriage will take you and the children to the house. Your mother is anxious for your arrival. I'll go with your husband in the wagon with the luggage."

# Macon, Georgia

Sunday mass at St. Andrew Catholic Church was just letting out. Fr. Urbanski was standing in the entryway greeting members of his congregation as they left the church.

"And, how is the Stanitzek family this beautiful day?" he asked.

"Just fine, Father," Frank Stanitzek answered as he shook the priest's hand. "Are we going to see you this afternoon for dinner, Father?"

"I wouldn't miss tasting your homemade sausage, Frank. Or, your dear wife's peach pie."

"It's a bit early in the season for peaches, Father," Peg Stanitzek told him. "You may have to settle for pecan pie, instead."

"Such a problem the saints in heaven should have, Peg. Are you still expecting me at four o'clock, Francis?"

A line was forming behind them, so they knew they needed to move along. "That will be fine, Father."

As they rode toward their farm outside of the town, Peg asked. "Frank, are you going to tell Father Urbanski about the job offer to work in the Yankee capital, Washington DC?"

"Do you think I should, Margaret?"

"Yes I do, Frank."

"You might be right. He knows how much I hate them Yanks for what they did to our people here. He might help me decide whether or not to help out on this investigation thing."

"Do what you think is best, Frank," his wife counseled him. "Please remember, though, that one of our own Georgians, our boy's regimental commander, Col. Toombs, asked you to go to Washington and do this thing; no Yankee asked."

"I know, Margaret," he admitted. "I'm just having a hard time separating the two. Besides, I'm busy with our meat business."

"Francis Stanitzek," his wife snapped. "You have two perfectly capable sons who can butcher animals and cut meat as well as you. And, they've been running the farm, butchering and delivering meat and sausage to our Macon customers since before the war. Besides, I'm here to run the business side, am I not?"

"You've got me there, Margaret," he agreed. "You already run the business, truth be told. And, yes, the boys are very capable. Our meat customers in the city sure like them, too."

"And thank the good Lord for that, Frank." his wife said. "Both boys came home from the war a good deal thinner, but without a scratch. Now they're both married and their wives are expecting. I thank God every day, Frank."

"So do I Margaret."

After supper, the Stanitzek family and their guest, Father Urbanski sat around the table with their coffee and pie.

Never shy, Father Urbanski asked the question that was on the mind of everyone present.

"Are you goin to Washington, Francis?"

"I don't want to go, Father," he answered. "I really don't."

With the question finally out in the open, Frank's son joined in.

"Dad," Fritz began. "Are you worried that Francis, John and me can't handle the business?"

"I'm not worried at all, son," Frank assured him. "You three and your Momma practically run it without me now. When I come to this country from Poland, I was only a boy. I only had my health and my faith. The Good Lord saw to it that I learn the butcher trade and find your Momma."

"We've all heard you tell that story, Papa. We're proud of our heritage, too. But tell us; what bothers you about going to Washington?" Frank's youngest son, John asked.

"I just don't know if I can be around all those damn Yankees and control my anger, John! There it is everyone. I hate those savages. Most of the burning, stealing and killing they did against the citizens of Georgia were not necessary; it is too much to forgive in my book. Am I wrong to feel this hate, Father?"

"Francis," Father Urbanski began. "I can understand your feelings. Most Georgians feel the same way, me included. But as difficult as it is, it is time we move on.

"Remember, the Lord forgave his executioners even when He was dying on the cross. Can we do less? Accepting this invitation from Col. Toombs might be a good way for you to forgive, too. I think you should accept. Show them Yankees that we Georgians are men of character and not still wallowing in self-pity and hatred."

"What about you, Margaret?" Frank asked. "Do you agree with the father?"

"Yes, I do, Francis," she told him. "I will miss you, of course. But my dear man, I see this hatred eating you up. And, it's become like a barrier between you and me in the process.

"Confront it, Francis!" she urged. "We'll all be better off if you can get it out of your system."

"My goodness, Margaret," Frank exclaimed. "I never thought it was something that stood between you and me."

"It has Francis, believe me," his wife assured him.

Son John recalled being home during the war. "When the Yankees went through Georgia, I watched your anger grow, Papa. I hated them for what they did, too. But I think that hate is keeping you from enjoying life now because you haven't gotten over the hate you still feel."

Fritz reminded his father. "The war and the destruction it brought to Georgia has effected everyone, Papa.

"We're all angry about what happened," he continued. "But I agree with Momma about you. You can't talk of anything else. I swear, you'd probably shoot a man dead on your front porch if'n you thought he was a Yankee. In the war Frankie and I shot our share; believe me. But it's over, Papa. We have to spend our energy recovering, not hating."

Frankie chimed in. "I agree with Fritz, Papa. But I have another reason, too. My wife and I will have our first child soon. I don't want to raise our children hating people, not even Yankees. So, I don't want them to see you going into one of your rages about the Yankees. Right now, that's what they would hear, all the time. I don't want them seeing their grandfather as a hater. Or, grow up thinking that hating others is acceptable.

"Who knows," he continued. "Maybe we wouldn't have had the war in the first place if leaders from the two sides didn't hate so much. So, Papa, if it would help you come to grips with your feelings, I think you should go to Washington."

"Phew!" Surprised at the outburst, Frank sat back in his chair.

Father Urbanski broke the heavy silence.

"Francis," he began quietly, "everyone at this table loves you. We all want to see the sweet hardworking man we knew before the war return to us. Help us out here, Francis. Go to Washington. Maybe then you can make your peace with those Yankees and set aside your anger in the process."

A somber look came over Frank's face. Family members had seen that dark look before, and expected the worst.

"That will do it, everyone. I think I've heard just about enough of your opinions on this subject." He paused and everyone at the table held their breath.

"Fader Urbanski, will you lead us in a prayer - for my safe return?"

# KELLOGG'S WASHINGTON HOME

Mike and his wife just arrived at Congressman Kellogg's Washington home.

Adam, the longtime Kellogg butler greeted them at the front door.

"My goodness, it gladdens these old eyes to see you again, Marshal Drieborg," he said. "Please step inside."

"It's good to see you too, Adam," Mike told him. "I don't think you've met my wife Mary Jacqueline."

"Where are my manners? Welcome to our home, Mrs. Drieborg. Here, give me your wrap. Please, take your wife into the drawing room, Marshal. Let me call Mable. She'll skin me alive if I don't tell her you're here, right now."

Mike led his wife into the familiar drawing room. "Adam was the first person to greet me here back in the winter of 1863, Mary Jacqueline. He and his wife, Mable had been with this household since just before Congressman Kellogg's wife died twenty or so years ago."

The door opened and in walked Mable. "Saints be praised. Who brought this beautiful lady into my house?" Mable walked across the room and took Mary Jacqueline hands in hers.

"This lady loves you very much, Marshal. You're expecting his child, aren't you, dear?"

"How can you tell? And, yes I am."

"It's in your eyes, child." Mable told her. "It's in your eyes."

"You know how lucky you are to have this lady as your wife, Marshal?"

"Yes I do, Mable."

"You can be sure we'll look after her here."

"I have no doubt of that, Mable."

"My husband, Adam, will show you to your room upstairs. You have some time to rest before supper. I'll be sure to call you."

*    *    *

At the supper table that evening, the Congressman and the Drieborgs talked of Mike's assignment.

"So, William," Mary Jacqueline began. "Just what will this job demand of my husband?"

"Mostly office work around Washington, I expect."

"He and his team will examine boxes of testimony and probably interview a pretty good number of government officials, too. People at all levels of government will be required to speak with him. Mike and his men will have access to any documents they believe necessary.

"The power we've given Mike's team to investigate the assassination of Lincoln is rather unprecedented. I don't actually know just how far Mike and his team will take it. But I do hope they will leave no stone unturned in searching of the truth."

"Have my men arrived yet, Congressman?" Mike asked.

"Yes they have, Mike. I've put them up at the same boardinghouse your men used the last time.

"Peter Oppewall has taken over George's old position as my administrative assistant. I've had him schedule a meeting for you with your team tomorrow morning in my offices."

"Seems strange not working with George Krupp."

"Oh! Haven't I haven't told you, Mike? The Judicial Committee has retained George as legal counsel. He'll be at the meeting tomorrow to begin working as a member of your team."

58

"Is this another one of your surprises, sir?" Mike chuckled. "There seems to be no end to them, from you."

Kellogg ended their conversation. "I'm just trying to keep you on your toes, Michael."

"I've a request of you, too, Mary Jacqueline."

"Yes?"

"Dinner parties are an important part of doing business around this town. As you know, Mike, I have used such occasions to push for things I support. In the past, you have been an important part of those efforts."

"Yes I have." Mike interjected. "Before you continue, Congressman, I want to warn my wife of something. Once my charge is announced, and we agree to attend dinner parties, we'll probably be swamped with invitations. It will not be possible to deny some and accept others without causing problems. So, we may have to be out several evenings every week while we're here. These could be exhausting for you, sweetheart."

"Michael," Mary Jacqueline responded in that soft tone she often used with her husband. "I assume you'll be working a full day, every day. If you must attend an evening affair, your day will be very long, too. I expect to accompany you and be your pleasant companion.

"Actually, I look forward to getting out of the house with you Michael. It should be fun. Don't worry about our baby. I'll just stay home if I'm too tired."

"You promise?" Mike prodded.

"Yes dear. I promise."

"But that is not quite all I'm asking of you, Mary Jacqueline."

"Well, William," she shot back. "You look so serious. How difficult can your request be, for heaven's sake?" Mary Jacqueline continued.

"You know my cooking skills are limited," Mary Jacqueline continued kidding him. "Besides, Mable wouldn't welcome another cook in her kitchen, even if I was a competent cook. I can do laundry, I suppose. Cleaning the house might be a chore as my baby grows."

"It's nothing like that, my dear." Kellogg chuckled at her little joke. "I would like you to act as my hostess when I hold dinner parties in this house."

"I would have thought your daughter Patricia would fill that role."

"She did at one time. But now that she is married to a Washington attorney, she keeps busy doing that very thing for him."

"I wouldn't want to overstep or intrude on her territory, as it were. But if you wish I'll be happy to assist you in any way I can, William."

"Excellent. Pete will contact you tomorrow. We need to get our invitations out quickly if we are to get the most important guests lined up."

"I'm going to turn in, you two." Kellogg announced. "I'm an early riser, and tomorrow will be a very busy day. If you need anything just ring for Adam."

"Goodnight, William," Mary Jacqueline wished him.

*     *     *

As they prepared for bed, Mike and his wife talked some about the tasks ahead of them.

"Are you comfortable, Michael with my helping you and acting as a social hostess for William?"

"Yes I am sweetheart. I love the idea that you'll go with me to the evening affairs. Kellogg and I did the rounds the last time I was in town. It can be a real chore; especially because every mother in attendance tried to pawn their daughter off on me."

"You were single at the time?"

"Yes, I was. The talk then, was that I was expected to marry Patricia. That didn't stop the mothers from trying to fix me up with their daughter just the same."

"Is that the only purpose I serve, to protect you from predatory Washington mothers?"

"Oh! Not at all, sweetheart!" Mike moved to hold his wife in his arms.

"That was a long time ago. Now, I look forward to showing off my beautiful and intelligent wife."

"That's better, mister." She snuggled closer to her husband.

"By the way Michael, I have a surprise for us from the children. They wrote a letter to us. I promised not to open it until we had arrived in Washington."

*     *     *

*Dear Momma and Papa*

*We miss you already.*

*Grampa Murphy is not around much and doesn't talk to us when he is. But he likes to hear us read from our books before we go to bed. Gramma Judy told us Grampa has not had children around since Momma was young and is just getting used to us. She hugs us and reads to us all the time. She and Helen get along very well.*

*Grampa is making us go to school while we are here. Eleanor thinks that is great. I (Charles) do not. When will you come to visit?*

*Please write us a letter, too.*

Love
Eleanor and Charles

# Kellogg's Washington Office

Mike and Congressman Kellogg arrived at 7:30 AM.

"Mike," the congressman began. "This is Peter Oppewall. He'll go over today's schedule."

"Heard a lot about you, Mike," Pete extended his hand to Mike. "I look forward to working with you."

"It's mutual, Pete," Mike assured him. "This investigating business is new ground for me. I'll really need your help."

"Whatever you need, just ask." Pete responded. "I've got coffee and fried cakes in the conference room. Care for either?"

"You bet. I'll have some of both. The congressman ushered me out the door this morning before I was hardly dressed. I had forgotten how early he begins his day."

Pete chuckled. "Around here, it seems we're always running just to keep up with him."

"When will the men of my team arrive?"

"They'll join us at nine."

*     *     *

Earlier that morning, three members of Mike's team joined Craig Haynes for coffee in their boardinghouse.

"Good morning, gentlemen."

Amid mumbled responses, all the men took their seats. Henry Austry was the first to speak.

"So, we get our instructions this morning, eh?"

"That's what I'm told, Henry," Craig responded. "We'll meet with Marshal Drieborg at nine and the members of the congressional subcommittee charged with this investigation at ten. Beyond that, I have no information."

# LOWELL, MICHIGAN

Rose and Jake Drieborg were supper guests at the Hecht home.

"Jake," Ruben Hecht began. "Have you read da' newspaper article about Michael?"

"No, I haven't, Ruben. I didn't have time for much of anything yesterday when I was in town. Do you have a copy of the paper?"

"Ya, I do Jake. You can read it for yourself."

"Read it aloud, Papa," Rose asked. Jake picked up the copy of the Grand Rapids Eagle.

*Local Man Heads Washington Investigation of Lincoln Assassination*

*The chairman of the Congressional Judiciary Committee, Rep. George F. Boutwell [*] of Massachusetts, announced the formation of a team to investigate the assassination of the late president, Abraham Lincoln.*

*Marshal Michael J. Drieborg of Grand Rapids is to head this investigation. A US Cavalry officer during the late conflict, he was awarded the Congressional Medal of Honor. The Judiciary Committee drew the men of his team from both the North and the South in an attempt to pursue an unbiased investigation and report. It is made up of:*

*Craig Haynes: Former Sheriff of Cleveland, Ohio and lately Drieborg's Chief Deputy Marshal in Grand Rapids, MI.*

*Henry Austry: An Illinois farmer and resident: formerly a US cavalry officer in the late conflict.*

*Frank Stanitzek: A businessman and resident of Macon, Georgia: formerly a CSA elected official in that community.*

*Bose D. Faute: A farmer and resident of Cades Cove, Tennessee: formerly a CSA cavalry officer in the late conflict.*

*George Krupp: Attorney and resident of Washington DC: Formerly Chief Aide to Congressman William Kellogg ® MI.*

*Robert Stephan: Attorney and resident of Columbia, SC: formerly a CSA Judge Advocate Division officer during the late conflict.*

*Drieborg and his team are charged with the responsibility of looking into several conspiracy theories of the assassination.*

*1. That President Johnson was involved in, or had prior knowledge of, the assassination of Abraham Lincoln.*

*2. That high ranking officials of the late Confederate government in Richmond were complicit in the assassination of Abraham Lincoln.*

*3. That there were members of the federal government, who were involved, or had foreknowledge of, the assassination of Abraham Lincoln.*

*4. The Judiciary Committee may direct these investigators to look into* other *matters dealing with the assassination as circumstances dictate.*
*.*

*This investigation faces many obstacles. Will the Johnson administration cooperate? Will Drieborg's team be given access to all pertinent government documents? Will we ever know if any of the Radicals who tried to deny the late president the Republican nomination in 1864, were involved in the assassination? How will Drieborg and his team handle the intense pressure to ignore the possible involvement of such men? How will he handle the pressure to identify CSA officials as co-conspirators in the assassination?*

*There are more questions than answers at this point. We at the Grand Rapids Eagle wish Marshal Drieborg and his team our best wishes and lend this paper's support to their efforts.*

*The Judiciary Committee is to be applauded for including former CSA men on Drieborg's team of investigators. Time will tell if this effort is another whitewash or a serious effort to reveal the truth.*

*To our readers, we pledge that we will keep them as fully informed as we can of this investigation's work and final report.*

\*      \*      \*

"My goodness, Papa," Rose exclaimed. "I didn't realize that Michael's new job was so important. Did you?"

"He told me about it some, Rose," Jake replied. "But I am surprised, too."

"I thought dat actor, Booth killed President Lincoln," Ruben stated. "What is dere to investigate dat could be so important?"

"He did Papa," Emma joined in. "But some people think he would not have been able to do it without help. Mrs. Lincoln thinks President Johnson had something to do with it. Others think the rebels in Richmond helped Booth."

Jake interrupted. "Michael told me dat some of the Republicans in Congress who disagree with Johnson and his Reconstruction policies want to weaken and maybe destroy his authority with dis investigation."

"Well, anyway," Emma concluded. "You should be proud that they trusted this important thing to Michael."

"We are, Emma," Rose told her. "Thank you for saying so." Emma had lost both of her adult daughters. And, Rose knew that Michael was closely associated with the pain her friend still suffered from those losses. Rose felt tears forming, just thinking about it:

Michael was wounded at Gettysburg in July of 1863. When he arrived at a Washington hospital he was suffering from infection, dehydration and a high fever. In fact, Congressman Kellogg had found him unconscious, in the hallway of an office building. He contacted the Hechts and they took Michael to their Maryland farm where Emma Hecht began treating him. Her daughter Eleanor helped with his care. She and Michael fell in love and married before he returned to duty. A year later, while Michael was in Andersonville Prison, Eleanor died giving birth to their daughter.

To escape the war and marauders, the Hecht family moved to Michigan in 1865. There, Emma's other daughter Julia and Michael fell in love. They married in 1865, after he returned to Lowell from his military assignment in the Dakota Territory. On a Saturday the following March, when shopping in that village, Julia was killed by assassins hired by an enemy of the Drieborg family. I loved those dear girls, too, Rose thought.

# KELLOGG'S WASHINGTON OFFICE

Kellogg began the meeting and introducing himself.

"This office will be your primary workplace during your investigation. Marshal Michael Drieborg here will be in charge. My assistant, Pete Oppewall is here to facilitate your work. I will assist you with any problem you might encounter on the Republican side of the aisle. Congressman Webster of Tennessee will assist on the Democratic Party's side of the aisle. He will be with us later, I assume.

"Each of you has in front of you a folder. It contains your charge from the House Judiciary Committee. If you will open it, I will walk you through it and answer any questions you may have.

"Pete," Kellogg told him, "will you check with Webster's office? He should be with us for this."

"While we're waiting for Congressman Webster, we can get better acquainted," Kellogg announced.

"On my right is Marshal Michael Drieborg. He will be in charge of this team. He was my military aide back in 1863, until he joined his cavalry troop for the Gettysburg campaign. He was wounded there and returned to active duty in January of 1864, with General Meade's forces in Virginia. He was captured that March, spent some time in Libby Prison and eventually ended up at Andersonville Prison. During a transfer of prisoners to Savannah, he escaped to Union lines.

"Later, he was a major when he joined Sherman in Savannah to work with the Union prisoners-of-war recently liberated there. Once that task was finished he took over a troop and marched north with Sherman.

"When the conflict ended, he and the 6th Regiment were sent to the Dakota Territory until they were mustered out in the fall of 1865. In 1866, I asked him to rejoin me in Washington and lead a team to gather information in South Carolina for the Joint Committee on Reconstruction. When that task was completed, he took over the position of marshal for the western district of Michigan.

"Did I leave out anything, Marshal?"

"No sir," Mike responded. "I think you covered things completely."

"I'll leave it up to you to introduce the members of your team."

Mike turned to Henry Austry who had been a platoon leader in his wartime troop.

"Good to see you Henry," Mike began. "I hope you father is doing better."

"Yes, thank you, Mike. He is up and about some now, or I'd still be back working on his Illinois farm. He was a big Lincoln supporter. So, he was thrilled that I was asked to work on this investigation. Besides, my brother is older now. He can do a lot of the farm work that my father can't."

Mike asked his chief deputy, Craig Haynes, a question.

"Is the boardinghouse going to work out for the team, Craig?"

"I think so, Mike. The location is good. It's just a thirty-minute walk for us to these offices. Mrs. Mitchell keeps it nice and clean and manages a good kitchen, too. Anyway, I haven't heard anyone complain."

"Mr. Stanitzek," Mike began. "Welcome to the team. When we're working together or in private, I suggest we be on a first name basis. When we are on committee business, I will use your title of 'deputy'. Please follow that rule with your colleagues and me. Will that be ok with you?"

"That will be fine, Mike."

"Mr. Faute," Mike continued. "Welcome to you as well. I see from your file that you are from a rather isolated Tennessee mountain community. I hope Washington City is not too confusing or crowded for you."

"It's like night versus the day, Marshal. I mean Mike," he responded. "But I'll get used to it."

Then, Mike told every one of his wartime ties with Henry Austry. "Henry was a platoon leader with my cavalry outfit. We served in Sherman's march through the Carolinas and in the Dakota Territory right after the conflict ended. He was also a deputy in my team that traveled to South Carolina in '66. So, he and I are well acquainted. I value his participation greatly."

"Thanks Mike."

"Craig joined me for the Carolina investigation, too. He was my chief deputy. Prior to that had been the sheriff in Cleveland for several years. He's an investigator. I suggest we look to him to lead us in that pursuit. I trust his instincts on such things, as well. Currently, he is my chief deputy marshal in Grand Rapids, Michigan."

"George Krupp and Robert Stephan will help us review testimony, assist us to prepare for interviews and generally give us legal advice. During the war, George was the chief aide to Congressman Kellogg. He is now an attorney here in Washington City. Mr. Stephan was a member of the Confederate Judge Advocate's Division during the conflict and is currently an attorney in Columbia, South Carolina.

"We'll get to know one another better as we work together. I expect we'll have lunch together most days, too. Peter will meet with each of you to work out your pay and expense reimbursement paperwork. Any other problems please come to me. If I can't take care of it, I'll enlist the help of either Congressman Kellogg or Congressman Webster. Do any of you have a question?"

In the immediate silence, the door flew open and Congressman Webster filled the doorway.

"Gentlemen!" he bellowed. "I'm so happy that you did not start without me, Kellogg. I wouldn't want any members of this team to receive erroneous information." He chuckled.

Kellogg did not chuckle or even crack a smile.

"You're late, Webster. We start work in my office during daylight hours. In thirty minutes we're due to appear before the Judiciary Committee and we haven't even explained the committee's charge to this team. We need to get moving."

"Very well," Webster admitted, "it's your office Kellogg, so get going already."

"Please open your folder, gentlemen." Kellogg then reviewed the team's charge from the Judiciary Committee.

The congressman could have been reading virtually word for word from the Grand Rapids Eagle article on this subject that I read the other day.

"Did I cover everything to your satisfaction, Congressman?" Kellogg asked Webster.

"You did, thank you very much. But let me add a word for the benefit of Mr. Faute of Cad's Cove Tennessee, Mr. Stanitzek of Macon, Georgia and Mr. Stephan of Columbia, South Carolina. President Johnson has already announced the complicity of Confederate government officials in the assassination of President Lincoln. Some of us believe the testimony that led to this declaration is questionable. Take a close look at it, gentlemen. We want the truth.

"Others suspect Union officials of complicity. Look carefully at the evidence behind that possibility as well. Remember, we want the truth."

Kellogg ended the meeting. "I couldn't have put it better myself, Congressman. Now, we must get to our next meeting. When the Judiciary committee has finished with your team, Marshal Drieborg, Congressman Webster and I will take you all to lunch at the Willard."

"Can't happen too soon for me," Webster announced. "I need a drink. You bring any of that good Tennessee moonshine with you, Faute?"

"I wouldn't leave home without it, Congressman."

# PHILADELPHIA

The Murphy family was sitting at the dining room table having their evening meal.

"Grampa, can I ask you a question?" Charles wondered aloud.

"Of course you can, my boy. What is it?"

"Why can't Helen go to school with us?"

"I'm not sure what you're talking about, Charles."

Dr. Murphy's wife interrupted. "It would appear, Miles, that the school principal insists that Helen leave the building after she escorts the children to school. In Grand Rapids, she was allowed to stay and learn right along with the children."

"Is it a matter of paying tuition for her, Ruth?"

"It doesn't appear so dear. I already offered to pay whatever fee might be required. The head of the school, a Sister Margaret, feels that it is not proper for a person of color to be in her building with white children."

"Is our church pastor, Father MacMahon aware of this woman's decision?"

"Not to my knowledge. I felt it was your place to discuss this matter with him, not mine."

"She was allowed to attend school with you children back in Grand Rapids?

"Yes Grampa. Sister Aquinas at St. Andrew's School said she was always welcome to stay and study with us and the other children," Eleanor informed him.

Her calling him Grampa was new. He noticed.

"And, you want her to attend school with you here, too?"

"Oh, yes, Grampa." Charles repeated. "Back home, we all helped one another with homework every day."

He thought a moment. "Before we go any further with this, I'd like to talk with Helen."

The children jumped off their seats and ran out of the dining room. A moment later they returned, each child pulling Helen by a hand, into the room.

"Here she is, Grampa."

"Helen," Dr. Murphy began after she had taken a seat. "I understand that you want to attend school with the children. Is that your wish?"

"Yes' sur," she began. "This chil's ben kept ignorant long 'nuff. I want ta read, rite and do numbers as good as ana' body; so' I can make my way in dis word."

"Do you wish me to see what I can do to enroll you in the children's school?"

"Yes' sur, I do."

After pausing some, making everybody nervous, he said, "I'll see what I can do."

The children jumped up and ran over to him. "Thank you, thank you, thank you, Gramps" they chorused. Much to his surprise, they hugged him in the bargain.

"My goodness, Miles," his wife chuckled. She had to hide her wide smile with her hand.

"I can't remember seeing you blush so, Miles."

*          *          *

The following morning, Dr. Murphy attended eight o'clock mass at St. Patrick's Church.

After the service he asked one of the altar boys to get Fr. MacMahon for him.

"Dr. Murphy," greeted the priest. "To what do I owe the happy surprise of this visit?"

"I have a delicate matter to discuss with you, Father. Can we go somewhere private?"

"Of course, Doctor. Just follow me if you would."

Once at the parish rectory, the priest asked, "What is it, Doctor?"

"I'm afraid it will be necessary for my family to move our support to another church, Father."

The priest sat forward in surprise. "My heavens, man! Why ever would you do that?"

"You're aware that my grandchildren are now attending school here at St. Patrick's."

"Yes I am, Doctor. And, most pleased we are that you chose our school for them."

"I thought so, too. That is, until your principal denied our request that the children's nanny be allowed to sit in on lessons with the children."

"You mean be a student, too?"

"Yes. That's it exactly. Back in their Michigan home parish, the Dominican Sisters there welcomed the young lady. Here, your Sisters of Charity believe it is not appropriate for a woman of color to be educated in their school."

"Oh! She's a Negro. Even so, Doctor," the priest added, "I am sure there is some mistake. The church here in Philadelphia fully supports the education of colored people."

"Then, you will see to it that my children's nanny be allowed to attend school with them?"

"There are schools for coloreds, you know."

"So, you're refusing my request?"

"The good sisters who teach in our school might withdraw their services if I overrule our Principal, Sister Margaret, on this matter. Surely you can understand my position, Doctor?"

"I see, Father." Standing, Dr. Murphy informed the priest. "It would appear that I must remind you that in this country, we Irish have been called, 'The Niggers of the North'. After all the prejudice we Irish have experienced here, I would have thought our church would not tolerate such bigotry toward others; certainly not in its own schools. Possibly, you priests and the good sisters have been insulated from the bigotry we Irish in the real world have endured.

"But I have not. Nor have most adult Irish members of this parish, I expect. Do you have any idea how difficult it was for me to even be accepted into medical school; or later, allowed to teach at the University of Pennsylvania Medical School? I expect not; or you would be appalled at the bigotry you are supporting here. Frankly, Father, your ignorance disgusts me.

"I will withdraw my two grandchildren from your school, immediately. I won't allow them to be infected with such attitudes. And, Mrs. Murphy and I will withdraw our financial support from your church as well."

Father MacMahon interrupted. "Oh, please Doctor; all this fuss over an ignorant Negro woman? Aren't you being a bit extreme?"

"But that's not all, Father. I also intend to go further. I will contact your superior, the Archbishop and the Philadelphia press," Dr. Murphy continued. "I intend that the people of this entire city know that a young woman came to you for help in furthering her education and you turned her away, just because she is a woman of color.

"It appears to me that it will be instructive for you and the good Sister Margaret to read your Bible. Luke's gospel and Christ's parable of the 'Good Samaritan' comes to my mind. Good day, Father."

# THE WILLARD HOTEL – WASHINGTON D.C.

The entire team sat around the table at the Willard. Congressman Kellogg and Webster were present as well. They had hardly gotten seated when a waiter came to the table.

"Can I get you gents something to drink before I take your lunch order?"

Kellogg ordered first. "I'll have a bottle of Fox DeLux beer, I think."

Mike was next. "That's brewed back home in Grand Rapids, isn't it, sir?"

"Yes it is, Michael. In fact, the Fox family volunteered to support my reelection campaign next fall. So, I thought I'd best try their product."

"I'll take one of those, too," Mike told the waiter.

"What other beers do you have?" Frank Stanitzek asked.

"One of our biggest sellers is a German beer from Pennsylvania called Yuengling. I think it's pretty tasty."

Craig Haynes cut in. "I know that beer. Bring me a bottle of Yuengling."

"Don't you have a beer made in the South?" Frank wondered.

"We just started carrying one brewed in Missouri. It's called Anheuser Busch."

"Give me one of those," Frank decided.

Henry gave the waiter his order, too. "I'll have a bottle of that Busch beer, too."

The waiter turned to Congressman Webster. "And you, sir?"

"Beer is for sissies. Faute, let's you and me have a man's drink; some of that Tennessee moonshine."

"I'm with you Congressman," Faute commented as he got out a flask and poured some of the amber liquid into a glass. "We call this golden liquid, 'Happy Sally'."

Webster took a sip. "I don't care what you call it, Faute. This is good stuff. I hope you brought plenty."

Mike interrupted. "Take it easy with that stuff, will ya Bose? We have a full afternoon of work today."

"Not a problem, Marshal Mike," Faute responded with good humor. "I'll be as alert as a young man on his wedding night."

While waiting for their orders, the two congressmen regaled the men with stories of the Willard Hotel.

Kellogg shared some history.

"About twenty years ago," he began. "The Willard brothers opened this hotel. They have enlarged the original building several times. So, now they have several floors each with running water, bathtubs and toilet facilities. Those swinging doors our waiter just ran through lead to the kitchens, which are ninety-four feet long and said to serve over 2,500 meals each day. One of the reporters who has a room here, said he overheard a traveling salesman complain of the Willard:

"Beelzebub surely lives here, and the Willard is his temple."

Congressman Webster interrupted. "There are probably more decisions reached in this room than in Congress or the president's office combined," he suggested. "At those tables, right now, men are trying to obtain government contracts. Some are probably offering bribes to ensure or sweeten the deal."

"Is that the way you Yankees run your government?" Frank asked, sort of shocked at that revelation.

Webster laughed aloud. "Truth be told, Frank, the Confederate government in Richmond was most likely no different. Every capital in the world has its Willard, my good man. No government could function without a place like this; wouldn't you say, Kellogg?"

"On that we can agree, Webster."

Kellogg continued. "It was rumored, too, that in this very room spies for your Confederate government hung about. Don't look surprised, Mr. Faute. It wouldn't have been the first time in history that liquor loosened some lips. I'm sure that information learned in this room was passed to you Confederates.

"Probably happened right at the bar over there," he revealed. "Men bought drinks for Union officers, generals even, in hopes of gaining such information."

"If that's the way you Yankees run your government, how in the very devil did you blue bellies win the war?" Faute asked.

After the laughing died down, Kellogg offered an explanation.

"Mr. Faute," he said. "Believe me when I tell you, it is a mystery to me how we ever managed to beat you fellas."

No sooner had the men finished their lunch when Mike hustled them back to work.

\*     \*     \*

"Empty your sock now gentlemen, and get your coffee," Mike directed. "It will be a good couple of hours before we take a break."

Frank asked Henry, "What is this 'empty your sock' business?"

"I think he is telling us to use the men's lavatory down that hallway."

Once everyone was settled, Mike began.

"You each have a folder in front of you. The contents are the same in each folder. On the first page you will see your name assigned to a team. George Krupp will head up one, Bob Stephan the other. Craig will head up our office and coordinate the activities of both. He will also be in charge of our field investigation efforts."

Bose Faute spoke first. "So, I'm to work with our Yankee lawyer, George Krupp and Henry here is assigned to our South Carolina lawyer, Bob Stephan."

"You got it, Bose."

"What's first, Mike?" Henry asked.

"That's on the second page, Henry. As you can see, you and Stephan will meet with the lawyers for Mrs. Surratt in this room at three.

"George, you and Bose will meet with the lawyers for Payne, Atzerodt and Herold in room 312 at three, just down the hall.

"While you're doing that, Craig and I will talk with the lawyer for Spangler and Dr. Mudd."

"We want to know what they think of the judgment the military court handed down. Did that tribunal make every effort to seek information from the accused? Or, did they rush them to the gallows to keep them quiet? Do the attorneys believe their clients could have implicated men in either the Union or Confederate governments? If so, is there documentation to support such accusations?

"We'll be better prepared for this interview after we review some of the court documents that are in our packets. We'll meet here afterwards to discuss what we've learned."

# Kellogg's Washington Home

Mary Jacqueline and Patricia had invited Robert Stephan's wife to lunch at the Kellogg home.

Adam showed her into the house. "Welcome to Washington City, Mrs. Stephan." Mary Jacqueline said. "I'm so pleased you could join Patricia and me today."

"Thank you for inviting me, ladies. Please call me Mary Alice. You have truly rescued me from another horrid day of staring at the walls of our boardinghouse."

"Well, we'll take care of that, won't we, Patricia?"

Patricia Kellogg Krupp had risen to greet their guest. "Yes, let me welcome you to my father's home."

"Did you have any problem with your trip here from Columbia?"

"Oh my, yes! We did. With all the spring rain we're having south of here, the roads were a mess. Several times, we had to get out of the carriage with our entire luggage just so the horses could pull it out of the mud. I'm afraid my shoes and clothing took a terrible beating."

"We're not strangers to mud around this city, either, Mary Alice." Patricia informed her.

"Thankfully, there are several shops here where your shoes and clothing can be restored. I'll take you to the one I use, if you like."

"That would be so kind."

"I'm told you are from Columbia, South Carolina," Patricia continued.

"Yes, I am; what's left of it. After our mayor surrendered the city to Sherman, he still allowed his army to burn most of the city to the ground."

Patricia couldn't resist, "That's what's liable to happen, sweetie, when you start a war."

Mable came into the sitting room. "Ladies, lunch is ready."

"Thank you, Mable." Mary Jacqueline said. *Whew! Yes, thank you very much, Mable. Leave it to Patricia to start a fight with our guest.*

After a light lunch, the three women were chatting over a cup of coffee.

Patricia surprised the others when she lit one of the new smoking devices called a cigarette, and inhaled the smoke.

"Nothing like a good smoke with my coffee," she commented to the stunned women.

"Mable, could I have a plate for my cigarette ashes?"

"Oh, my goodness," Mary Alice softly exclaimed.

Patricia smiled mischievously, "Never seen a woman smoke?"

"Well," Mary Alice responded. "Not exactly; I hear tell that among our hill folk, women smoke tobacco and drink moonshine right along with their men. I've just never seen women do it in polite company, that's all."

"Bother you, Mary Alice?" Patricia teased.

"Not really, Patricia," she responded. "I'd been warned to expect all sorts of weird things in the North. This is just one of those oddities, I expect."

"Well put," Mary Jacqueline interrupted, chuckling. "You'll also find that Patricia is very outspoken on political matters as well."

Mary Alice was quick to respond. "In my opinion you couldn't do much worse than our menfolk, Patricia. Are you a suffragette, too?"

"As a matter of fact, I am," Patricia, admitted. "We women can do more than just have babies and cook."

Mary Jacqueline interrupted. "Speaking of babies, I'm due to deliver one late this summer."

"Congratulations! Is this your first?" Mary Alice asked.

"No. I have a five-year-old son. He was born in Charleston after his father died early in the war."

"I thought you were from Michigan or somewhere up north."

"I am now," Mary Jacqueline told her. "I met Michael in Charleston last year. The Congressional Committee on Reconstruction had sent him there on a fact-finding mission.

"He stopped some colored soldiers from harassing me and my son on our way to church one Sunday morning. As a result of that chance meeting, my father-in-law, Colonel Pope, helped Michael with his mission. We became acquainted and fell in love."

"Oh, my goodness," Mary Alice exclaimed. "Out of the ashes of war, comes something beautiful."

"Please, Mary Alice," Patricia piped in, "Keep talking like that and I'll gag."

Perplexed, Mary Alice said, "Well, it is beautiful, Patricia."

"Please excuse Patricia," Mary Jacqueline began. "She has a bit of a problem with me, I expect. It seems that not long ago, she and my husband were close – rumor has it they were even lovers. I'm also told that she had three opportunities to marry Michael, and let each of them slip away."

"Oh, my goodness," Mary Alice exclaimed.

"However you put it, Mary Jacqueline, I'm just happy that you're satisfied with my leftovers." Patricia snapped.

"That would be fine if I could trust you in the same room with my husband. But since I can't, in the future, Patricia, you will not be welcome in this house without your husband."

Red-faced, Patricia virtually shouted, "Look here, you prissy rebel bitch; I don't need your approval to come into to my own father's house."

"You shouldn't be concerned about my approval, Patricia," Mary Jacqueline said calmly. "You'll never receive it."

Mabel had stepped into the room with a pitcher of water in her hand.

"Water anyone?"

"Yes, thank you, Mable." Mary Jacqueline turned in her chair and as she rose to her feet she took the pitcher from Mable.

"Patricia," she continued. "Listen carefully. I'll not say it again. As long as Michael and I are staying in this house, you are not welcome here without your husband."

Still seated, Patricia glared across the table.

Mary Jacqueline stepped around the table and calmly emptied the pitcher of water over the Pat's head.

"Cool off, my dear."

"Oh, my goodness," Mary Alice exclaimed.

"I'm so sorry, Mable," Mary Jacqueline said. "I've splashed water all over your clean table cloth."

"Should I get a towel for Miss Patricia?" Mable asked.

"No, Mable, she's leaving." With that Mary Jacqueline grabbed Patricia's hand and dragged her out of the dining room and toward the front door.

"Adam!" Mary Jacqueline shouted. "Open the front door. Mrs. Krupp is leaving."

Adam barely got the door open before Patricia was pushed outside; the door slammed behind her.

Back in the dining room, Mary Jacqueline apologized.

"I'm so sorry for the mess I made, Mable. Here, I'll help you clean up."

"Don't you worry none, Miss Mary. I knowd that chile since she was borned, an' that's the furst time someone took a strap to her. I can't wait for the Congressman ta find out."

"Oh, my goodness," Mary Alice said. "I don't know what to make of you Yankee women."

All three women laughed heartily.

"Bob," Mike asked Robert Stephan. "You go first. Find out anything of interest?"

"Once you get by their anger at the tribunal, these attorneys don't have much to offer, Mike. I was stunned to learn that of the fifteen objections made by the lawyers for the defense, the presiding judge overruled all but two. On the other hand, of all the objections raised by the prosecution, not one was declared out of order. Anyway, these attorneys just gave up trying. I find that unbelievable, even in a Yankee military court."

After the laughter subsided, Stephan continued. "More specifically, they couldn't reveal anything we have not read in the documents you provided, Mike. These lawyers believed their clients acted at the direction of John Wilkes Booth. If the plot went beyond Booth, these lawyers did not believe their clients knew of it."

"Thanks, Bob."

"What did you find out George?"

George Krupp had little to add. "The attorneys we interviewed had been allowed so little time with their clients, they did not know much besides their client's immediate role. I don't think these lawyers will be of much help to us, Mike."

"Thanks, George."

"All right, gentlemen," Mike concluded. "Thank you for your efforts today. Tomorrow will be busy, too. We'll be talking first with the Special Judge Advocate, John A. Bingham who acted as prosecutor in the assassination trial."

"Just so I'll be prepared," Henry asked. "Who will be assigned to interview this man?"

"Good question, Henry," Mike said. "This fellow not only played a critical role in the trial and the sentencing of the conspirators, he also insisted that

Jefferson Davis and other Confederate officials were behind the entire plot. So, I think we should all participate in this interview."

Bose Faute spoke up.

"Good idea, Yank. I wouldn't want ta' be left out of this little chat. From what I read, if this buzzard Bingham is dealin' the cards, you better cut the deck first."

Krupp offered an observation, too. "Mike, I thought his case against Davis was blown out of the water last year by Congressman Rogers."

"According to what Congressman Kellogg told me, George, you're right. And, it seems that view is generally accepted. Just the same, our group has been told to look into the charges made against Davis and other Confederate officials as part of our overall investigation. So, we will.

"The man most familiar with the perjured testimony against the Confederate leaders is Congressman Rogers (D) from New Jersey. He has agreed to join us tomorrow, too. I expect him to give us very revealing information since he's the one who in open hearings, pretty much destroyed Bingham's witnesses against Jefferson Davis."

"I'm looking forward to watching this Rogers in action, tomorrow," Stephan said. "His cross examination of Bingham's witnesses is among the documents you gave us, Mike. I'll go over them tonight. Tomorrow, Bingham won't have a biased court to support him like he did during the conspirator's trial. So, it should be fun to be part of it."

\*     \*     \*

That evening, Michael, Mary Jacqueline and Congressman Kellogg were sitting in the dining room beginning their supper.

"Adam," the congressman asked his long-time servant. "Weren't George and Patricia supposed to join us this evening?"

"Yes, sir," Adam answered. "But Mr. George sent a message to please excuse them because your daughter Miss Patricia was feeling poorly, sir."

"I'm sorry to hear that," Mary Jacqueline said. "I was looking forward to a nice chat with Patricia; unless of course, she chose to join you men for brandy and cigars after dinner."

The congressman looked up, surprised at the comment.

Michael almost choked on his food.

Mable hid a smile behind a hand and walked out of the room.

# Washington Interview

"Gentlemen," Mike began. "Allow me to introduce Special Judge Advocate John Bingham, currently congressman from Ohio. Thank you for taking the time to visit with us today, Congressman."

"I am always ready to assist my colleagues on the Judiciary Committee, Marshal Drieborg. It is an additional pleasure to see Craig Haynes as a member of your team. I remember him well as the very highly regarded sheriff in Cleveland, Ohio."

Mike concurred. "Deputy Haynes was with me in South Carolina last year, Congressman. I also feel fortunate having him as my chief deputy in Grand Rapids, Michigan. Before we begin our work though, sir, allow me to introduce the other members of my team.

"Deputy Bose Faute is from Cades Cove Tennessee. He served in the Confederate cavalry during tha late conflict. In civilian life he is a farmer and businessman.

"Deputy Henry Austry is from Virden, Illinois. In the late war he served in my troop as a platoon leader. He currently works as a farmer.

"Deputy Stanitzek was an elected official in Macon, Georgia prior to and during the war. Currently, he is a businessman there.

"Mr. Robert Stephan is an attorney from Columbia, South Carolina. In the recent conflict he served on the Judge Advocate's staff for the Confederate Army.

"Mr. George Krupp is an attorney in Washington D.C. and formerly Congressman Kellogg's chief of staff here.

"Chief Deputy Haynes, you already know.

"Of course, you know Congressman Rogers. He has graciously agreed to assist us in this phase of our investigation. So, I will give the gavel to him at this point."

"Excuse me, Marshal." Bingham interrupted. "I don't understand what the congressman from New Jersey is doing here."

"I'm sorry I didn't make that clear to you, Congressman Bingham," Mike told him. "We have been charged with the responsibility of looking into the charges you made that the president of the Confederate States of American conspired with Booth, and possibly others, to assassinate President Lincoln. The Judiciary Committee wants to very publicly put such accusations to rest if they are not true; or take the proper legal steps if they are.

"Toward that end, the members of my group are simply taking advantage of the fact that the two men most familiar with your charges and the witnesses who supported them, are in town and available to us; that would be you, and your colleague, Congressman Rogers.

"Possibly, Congressman Bingham," Mike concluded, "you would like to make a statement before we proceed."

"Damn right, I do." Bingham exclaimed.

"First, the legal standing of this so-called investigating body of yours, Drieborg, is virtually non-existent.

"Second, I want you to understand that I am here as a courtesy to my colleagues on the House Judiciary Committee. I am not here because of any legal obligation.

"Third, it is highly irregular for you to record what is said here, today.

"As to the involvement of leaders of the late Confederate States of America; I think it very clear that President Davis and others in that government supported efforts to kidnap President Lincoln. When that failed they conspired to kill him and other members of his administration.

"The actual perpetrators of that crime have been tried and punished. Now, just because it no longer seems good politics to legally pursue the Confederate leaders it does not diminish their involvement in the planning for and the actual assassination of Lincoln."

After a brief silence, Mike asked. "Are you finished, Congressman?"

"For now I am, yes."

"Very well; I'm not going to argue legal points with such an eminent jurist as you, Congressman. So, whether or not this investigating committee has legal standing or not is of no concern to me. I'll leave that to the legal experts. But I will say this: "You are here because you have been legally subpoenaed by the Judiciary Committee of the Congress of the United States.

"As a courtesy to you, the chairman of that committee has told us to hold this legal hearing behind closed doors. So, I assure you sir, that if you do not cooperate, I will arrest you and put you in the same jail cell in which you imprisoned Mrs. Surratt. As a legally sworn United States Marshal, I will do that in a heartbeat.

"And, sir," Mike continued loudly, warming to the subject, "transcripts of these hearing will be kept and provided the Judiciary Committee.

"Finally sir", Mike continued, "if at any time you refuse to cooperate, this hearing will be held in a place open to the press and the public. And then, Marshal Stanitzek from Macon, Georgia and Marshal Faute from Cades Cove, Tennessee will bring you from your jail cell to that public place, chains and all."

"Do you wish our clerk to read back anything I have said, sir?

Bingham sat and said nothing.

"You will answer, Congressman or I will hold you in contempt and order your immediate arrest," Mike informed him calmly.

"You wouldn't dare!" Bingham replied.

"Craig," Mike ordered. "You and Marshal Faute chain the congressman's wrists behind him, place a hood over his head and take him to a jail cell at the Old Capitol Prison. Once there, do not remove the wrist manacles or the hood. Do not allow him to talk with anyone. Guard his cell and do not allow him out for any reason. You will be relieved in two hours."

As he was led away, Bingham shouted, "You don't know who you're dealing with, Drieborg. You'll pay for this!"

Everyone in the room could hear him despite the hood.

He may be right. Mike thought. But if I don't call him on his challenge, right now, this investigation will be dead in the water before it's hardly begun. Might as well find out right away if our subpoena power is worth anything and if the Judiciary Committee will back me up, or if our work is just more Washington window dressing.

"We'll take a recess. In fifteen minutes we will return, this time with Congressman Rogers."

*    *    *

Mike went into Congressman Kellogg's private office.

"Could I see you a moment, Congressman?"

"Sure. Close the door if you wish."

Mike did. Then he explained the situation.

"Whew!" Kellogg exclaimed. "You don't horse around, do you Mike?"

"Either our subpoena power is worth something and we get cooperation or we don't, sir." Mike explained. "If this investigation is all a charade, tell me now and I'll approach it as such. If you want us to honestly search for the truth, Bingham's challenge has to be answered."

Kellogg couldn't help but chuckle. "Holy smoke, don't you think using a hood over his head was a bit much?"

"Maybe, sir," Mike responded seriously. "I might admit to being angry at the time; Bingham's arrogance pissed me off. But he will know now to take me seriously. I intend to bring him back after lunch. We'll see, then."

"As to the question you asked me," Kellogg told Mike, "most of us on the committee take this investigation seriously. That is not to say there will be no obstacles or resistance from those who fear an investigation they do not control. Keep the pressure on; don't back down, Mike. I'll see if I can't get your move on Bingham covered until after lunch."

"Fine, sir," Mike told him. "But I intend to keep the pressure on Bingham; even if it means he spends a night shackled and hooded in jail. Because if word gets out in Washington that this investigation is without authority, we will not be able to do the job requested of us.

"What do you say, sir?"

"Do it, Mike," Kellogg assured him. "That's exactly why I chose you to take on this job."

# COMMITTEE HEARING RESUMED

"This hearing is hereby resumed," Mike declared. "Congressman Rogers, do you have a statement to make before we begin?"

"I must admit to being a bit hesitant, Marshal," Rogers began. "The last congressman to give opening remarks to this committee was dragged off to a jail cell."

After the men present stopped chuckling, Rogers continued.

"Believe you me; I'll measure my words very carefully.

"Allow me to begin by thanking the Judiciary Committee for its determination to get the truth on the public record. Beside the proven fact that John Wilkes Booth killed President Lincoln, several conspiracy theories which suggest that others were involved, have gained the attention of the public.

"During the trial of Booth's colleagues, then Special Judge Advocate Bingham spent over a quarter of the court's time arguing that the Confederate President, Jefferson Davis, and others in the his government were co-conspirators in the Lincoln assassination. He argued this so forcefully that President Andrew Johnson signed a proclamation to that effect.

"Because there was a good deal of controversy over this issue, Judge Advocate Holt called for a public examination of the witnesses Bingham used to support the charges against the Confederate leaders. Have you gentlemen had an opportunity to read the court record of my examination of those witnesses?"

Robert Stephan spoke first. "I think we all have, Congressman. I must say I admire your method of questioning."

"Thank you, Marshal Stephan. Coming from a trial attorney like you, that comment is especially appreciated.

"Since you all have read the hearing record, I'll just point out what I believe is important and summarize the rest.

"First and most important is the testimony of Charles Dunham, alias Sanford Conover. I was able to establish that the Secretary of War paid him for his testimony. In addition, Conover admitted that he tutored two key witnesses; a Mr. Snevel and a Mr. Campbell, to say they both heard Judah Benjamin, the Confederate Secretary of State, and President Davis approve a plan to kill Lincoln.

"Conover admitted coaching the men on this testimony at Washington's National Hotel. In fact, Judge Advocate Holt's own office paid the witnesses for their perjured testimony.

"Despite this admission of perjury, the House Judiciary Committee indicted Jefferson Davis and other Confederate officers for their supposed role in the conspiracy to kill Abraham Lincoln; and the committee asked President Johnson to initiate a war crimes trial of the men.

"But Conover, their chief witness, fled to Canada. To the credit of the administration, he was pursued, captured, tried and sentenced to ten years in Albany Prison for his perjury. During his trial, Conover blurted out the entire scheme that Stanton's Bureau of Military Justice had devised.

"So, I think it safe to say that the entire case against the Confederate leaders was compromised."

Immediately, Stephan had a question;

"Does this mean that there was no involvement of high Confederate officials in a conspiracy to kill Abraham Lincoln?"

"No, Marshal Stephan, it doesn't mean that at all," Rogers replied. "It just means that this particular attempt to implicate them failed for lack of credible evidence."

Frank Stanitzek asked a question. "If you were to speculate, Congressman, do you think there was confederate government involvement?"

"If you're asking for my personal opinion, Marshal," Rogers said, "this is the answer I would give:

"After the Dahlgren raid of 1864 was foiled, the Confederates found papers on the person of Colonel Dahlgren that authorized him to kill

President Davis if he had the opportunity.

"Following the discovery of these documents, I believe the possibility of assassinating Lincoln was discussed by highly placed members of the Confederate government. Beyond that, I can only wonder."

Mike interjected, "We are scheduled to interview Mr. Davis soon, Congressman. We'll ask him about that very topic."

"One more question, Congressman," Frank continued. "It appears that you had little trouble easily proving that the Judge Advocate's case was based upon perjured evidence. How do you explain that?"

"You mean aside from my thorough investigative work and brilliant examination of the witnesses?"

The men in the room laughed heartedly. Even the always serious Frank laughed.

"He's got you there, Frank," George Krupp chuckled.

"I believe that Secretary Stanton at the War Department, Judge Holt and Special Prosecutor Bingham, all believed in Confederate government involvement.

"They believed it so strongly that they took shortcuts to develop their case. When support for their belief was not easily available, they made up evidence. They never thought anyone would challenge what they believed to be self-evident. Their attitude was, take whatever means to justify an end.

"That's only my opinion, of course," Rogers concluded. "I can't prove any of that."

"Thank you Congressman," Mike said. "We're going to break. The soup and sandwich lunch I ordered has arrived. No beer this time gentlemen, coffee only. Frank, you and I will go and help escort Bingham back here for the afternoon session. Hopefully, he'll be more cooperative."

Mike turned to Rogers. "Congressman, I hope you're willing to stay for the afternoon session. Of course, you're welcome to join us for lunch, as well."

"If I declined your invitation, Marshal, I'm afraid I'd quickly find myself in jail with Congressman Bingham. So, I accept your kind invitation to stay and have lunch."

Mike made no reply.

Frank Stanitzek probably spoke for him and said, "I think that's a wise choice, Congressman."

# KELLOGG RESIDENCE

Peter Oppewall was working at a desk in the parlor with Mary Jacqueline.

"That should just about wrap up the guest list," Peter said.

"I hope so, Peter," she replied. "And, now we're going to tackle the seating arrangement?"

"Yes," Peter confirmed. "And, that could be even more important to the success of the evening than who attends."

"I had no idea planning a Washington dinner party could be so time consuming, and challenging. I suspect this will take us awhile. We can work through lunch if you can take the time, Peter."

"That's kind of you, Mrs. Drieborg. But you don't have to bother," Peter assured her. "I can pick something up on my way back to the office; or go without, for that matter."

"Maybe you can, Peter. But I can't. I'm eating for two, you know. So, if you'll excuse me for a moment, I'll ask Mable to set another place at the table. And please, Peter. Call me Mary Jacqueline."

The two continued planning the dinner party right through lunch.

"Mary Jacqueline," Peter asked. "Why do you want to sit directly across from the Secretary of War Stanton during the dinner?"

"Can we have a secret about this, Peter?"

"Of course, if you wish."

"I want to be able to look the man in the eye when I tell him what it was like for civilians like me to live in Charleston during the very unnecessary nightly Union bombardments; and how much it was resented."

"Your secret is safe with me," Pete assured her. "But I want to warn you; that man has a reputation for having a nasty tongue and a vindictive streak ta' boot. Possibly the presence of Mrs. Seward will temper his reaction to your words."

"We'll see, won't we Peter?"

"I wouldn't miss this dinner party for anything, Mary Jacqueline."

# KELLOGG'S WASHINGTON OFFICE

The lunch dishes had been cleared and the men returned to their seats.

"We officially resume this hearing," Mike announced. "Frank, would you tell Craig to bring the prisoner in?"

With Marshal Haynes on one side and Marshal Faute on the other, the hooded Congressman Bingham was led into the hearing room and rather forcefully put into a chair.

"You can remove the hood, Marshal."

Immediately Bingham spoke. "Can I speak without the risk of being thrown into a broom closet again?"

"After you're sworn in, Congressman," Mike told him. "If you refuse, it will be a real jail cell next time."

"Very well, Marshal."

When that part of the oath requiring him to recognize the legitimacy of Drieborg's investigation was reached, Bingham paused.

*Ok, my man. What will it be?* Mike wondered to himself.

The clerk said that portion of the oath once again. This time, Bingham repeated it.

*Thank goodness! Easier is better any day,* Mike thought.

"Now, do you have a statement, Congressman?"

"I don't think so," Bingham said in exasperation. "Will you get these manacles off my wrists?"

Haynes got a nod from Mike and removed the metal bindings holding his arms behind him.

"In your absence, Congressman Bingham, your colleague Congressman Rogers reviewed some of the recorded testimony and cross-examination of the witnesses you presented during the late assassination trial. We were especially interested in those witnesses who claimed the involvement of Confederate officials in the Lincoln assassination.

"Mr. Rogers focused on the testimony of Mr. Conover, Mr. Snevel and Mr. Campbell. It appears that the record shows these men were paid to give perjured testimony. I am sure you're familiar with their testimony. Would you like to comment on this?"

"My respected colleague, Congressman Rogers is an outstanding trial attorney," Bingham began. "He did a masterful job confusing these witnesses. As a result, they would have said most anything to get away from his questioning.

"I might point out, Marshal Drieborg, that after Mr. Rogers was finished cross-examining these men, the Judicial Committee you serve still voted to indict Davis and his cronies as co-conspirators. As we speak, the Committee is pressing the president to try these men as coconspirators in the killing of Abraham Lincoln."

George Krupp interrupted. "May I ask a question of Congressman Bingham?"

"Have you concluded Congressman?"

"I've quite finished, Marshal; for now."

"Congressman," Krupp began. "I've had an opportunity to review the written record of the testimony and the examination of your witnesses by Congressman Rogers. Is the committee's transcript accurate, sir?

"The Judiciary Committee has excellent court clerks, Mr. Krupp. So, I would say they accurately transcribed the testimony given."

Krupp continued. "Then, sir, relying on this record I must come to several conclusions.

"First: that every one of these men confessed to giving perjured testimony at the assassination trial. Second: that every one of them admitted to having been coached by Conover and lawyers from your office in pre-trial sessions at the National Hotel. Third: that every one of them admitted to being paid for their testimony."

"Do you disagree with these conclusions, sir?"

"Your first question focused on the accuracy of the clerk's work, Mr. Krupp. I think I answered that. To the third question only, I must tell you that I have no knowledge of paying any witness."

"What is your answer to my second question, sir?"

"We did no coaching of testimony," Bingham insisted. "My office staff interviewed these men as potential witnesses. We helped them organize their testimony; we did not coach them to lie as you concluded."

"So, if you did not coach them," Krupp continued, "did your witnesses lie when they admitted giving the false testimony or did they lie when they told the court of the coaching?"

"They lied both times," Bingham snapped.

At this point, Krupp turned to Mike Drieborg. "Correct me if I am wrong, Marshal Drieborg. But I believe we are holding this hearing to examine the veracity of the charges that highly placed Confederate officials supported the conspiracy to kill President Lincoln."

"That's correct, Marshal Krupp." Mike responded.

"Then, it would appear that we must report to the Judiciary Committee that there is no credible testimony tying Jefferson Davis or other Confederate officials to the Booth plot to kill Abraham Lincoln."

"Comment, Congressman Bingham?" Mike asked.

"I still believe that Jefferson Davis and his cronies were co-conspirators in the assassination of Abraham Lincoln."

"Are there any other questions of Congressman Bingham?'

"I have one, Drieborg," Bose Faute said. "Based on perjured testimony, the president of the United States was convinced to sign a proclamation stating that Jefferson Davis and other Confederate officials were, what' cha call' em, co-conspirators; and he did. Since everyone now knows about the lies that led to Johnson's decision, when the hell is he going to revoke his declaration?"

"That's not our job right now, Bose," Mike told him.

"If our job is to set the record straight, Yank," Faute continued heatedly, "we damn well ought ta' say something about that in our report. People back my way knew that proclamation was a pile of Yankee shit, to begin with. Now that it's been proven we were right all along, it's important ta' us that the Yankee president fess up to it."

"You ungrateful traitor," Congressman Bingham virtually shouted. "You caused the deaths of several hundred thousand loyal citizens of the United States. Now, you have the nerve to demand an apology from the president of the United States? Such gall; you should be shot."

"I almost was, mister," Bose answered good-naturedly. "Twern't no fault' a yours I wasn't. But answer me this, mister big shot. If we Southerns were such a terrible burr under yer saddle, why did ya kill all those thousands of us who just wanted to leave in peace?"

Bingham threw back his head and rolled his eyes. "I can't believe I'm arguing with an ignorant hillbilly." he mumbled.

Faute wasn't done, either. "An' another thing, you pile of crap. I may be a dumb hillbilly, but I've read the last speech Lincoln gave in 1865. You might give it a read, too. Cause' his idea of bringing the South back into the Union was probably this country's best bet; still is.

"Given the chance, we Confederates would have placed a guard around Lincoln ta protect him from tha likes a' you damn Radicals. You wanted vengeance, but he was havin' none a' that. I'm especially lookin forward to checking out the possibility that you Black Republicans had a hand in killin him, not us Southerns."

"Do I have to sit here and listen to this drivel, Marshal?"

"Yes, you do, Congressman, "Mike assured him. "And, if I may be allowed, let me remind you, sir; you are still under oath. If we find that you have lied about anything to which you testified here, you would be held in contempt and jailed immediately, hood and all.

"Are there any more questions or statements?" Mike asked.

"Hearing none," Mike concluded. "Thank you for your time Congressman Rogers and Congressman Bingham. A copy of the comments and testimony you made here today will be sent to your office as soon as they are made."

Once Mike was alone with his marshals, he warned them.

"Thanks for your participation today," he began. "I don't think we've heard the last of Bingham. He is a member of the majority party in Congress. And, after his role as chief prosecutor in the assassination trial, he has a good deal of power in this town."

Bose commented. "That peacock wouldn't last a week back in the Tennessee hill country I come from."

Craig Haynes broke in. "Maybe not, Bose," he said. "But none of us will go anywhere alone while we're in this town. So, you all listen and listen real well. Always go in pairs, gentlemen. And, you must always be armed. I provided each of you with a shoulder holster and a revolver after you arrived. I don't want to catch you without it. No discussion, no excuses."

"Another thing," Mike added. "No visiting the ladies of the evening or the bars. We have a reputation to protect. Besides, those places are just full of trouble. Are there any questions?"

# EVENING AT THE WASHINGTON BOARDINGHOUSE

The men were relaxing after their evening meal.

"That was a very good meal, don't you think?" Henry Austry said.

"I was so hungry after only soup this noon; I swear that my stomach thought my throat had been cut. I sure liked those taters we got tonight. What did you call' em, Henry?" Bose asked.

"We call'em scalloped potatoes, Bose. Back home my mom would fix' em that way whenever we had ham. You never had' em before?"

"Can't say as I have, Henry. You'd think I'd remember with all the taters we eat in the Cove. But you can believe I'll get my woman to cook' em that'a way when I get home."

"What's it like up in them mountains, Bose?" Frank Stanitzek asked.

"A little piece of heaven, Frank," Bose told him. "It is so quiet up there a man has to start a fight or kick the dog just ta' keep from fallin asleep.

"I don't know how you fellas get any sleep in this town. I sure ain't used to all the city noise, ya have here. Back at the Cove only thing makin' a sound after dark is tha frogs an' suchlike."

Austry agreed. "It's like that on the farm back in Illinois, too. At night, it's as quiet as a church after services."

"What about Cleveland, Craig?" Austry asked. "Is it as noisy as Washington?"

"Pretty much the same" He figured. "Town's grew a lot during the war. It had already been a major Great Lake port and rail center. The war traffic just accelerated the growth. It's still not as big as Washington though; at least not yet."

"My folks have 200 hundred acres cleared back in Illinois. How big is your place in Tennessee, Bose?"

"It's about that big, Henry. Might surprise you fellers that there are several thousand cleared acres up in them mountains. People started comin around the 1820s; pushed the Indians right out. Afore the war, we grew to around 100 families as I recall. Got to be more than the area could support, so people moved on; about half that, now.

"With a limestone base and plenty of water, the soil is real fertile. Wheat, rye, corn and all kinds of vegetables grow real well. In fact a' fore the war we lugged a lot' a that stuff as far as Knoxville; traded' em for coffee, tobacco, cloth an tools. Since the war ended, we sort' a pulled in our horns some. Market's collapsed in East Tennessee. So, we're gettin along with less' a' that big city stuff.

"Mostly, we use barter in the Cove, anyways. Not much need for cash there. But the Yankee dollars I earn here will come in handy at the general store I own a piece of. I'll stock the store better with goods and farm tools from Knoxville, I expect."

"Sounds like a pretty simple life, Bose," Craig decided. "How do you handle lawbreakers?"

"Pretty much like the folks handled bushwhackers 'n marauders during the war, Craig. When most' a' the men were gone fightin, the folks' at home hung some, banished others, whatever seemed ta' fit; still do. Our Justice of the Peace has always been a person who didn't tolerate thieving an such, or hesitate to use tha hang in' tree.

"My daddy was a real rough old coon during his day as a circuit judge. Yankees killed him in '65 for being a secesh. After he died, my family lost over 14,000 acres, his mill and the forge he owned, too. I was lucky to hold on ta my few hundred acres."

Frank changed the subject. "I got a telegram just before supper. My wife said she would be arriving here tomorrow or the next day. You fellas know anything about that?"

"Now how would I know anything about your wife, Frank?" Bose kidded. "Maybe she heard about those bawdy houses Mike told us about. Worried about you, is she?"

"She says she was invited by Mike's wife to join us here while we're doing this investigating. You sure you don't have a telegram too, Bose?"

"Well, ya, I got one today, too."

"Why'd you keep it a secret, Bose?" Henry asked.

"No secret, Yank. I hadn't got around to telling ya, that's all."

"Does that mean you and me can get female companionship too, Craig?" Henry asked.

"That seems only fair to me, Henry," Haynes answered.

"Now isn't that a fine kettle' a fish, Frank," Bose complained. "These birds get a sweet young thing to escort around, an' what'd we get? We get our old mostly used up wives. Don't that just beat all?"

With a big grin on his face, Henry asked Craig, "You're the chief deputy. Are you gonna ask Mike about it?"

"Not me, Henry. Are you?"

"You must be joking, Craig."

Frank told the men. "I can't recall but a few nights spent away from my wife, Peg, in all the years we been married. I must confess it was a new feeling for the first few nights, here. But the blossom is off that tree for me. I flat out miss her. Like me, she's old, fer sure. But not used up. Fact is; I think she's still a knee-weakner."

Bose had the last word. "Truth be told, you guys. I was just funnin. My old lady is a good ol' gal. I'll be happy to have her here by my side."

\*　　　\*　　　\*

Across town, William Kellogg, Mike and Mary Jacqueline were also eating supper.

"You created quite a stir today, Mike," he began. "I can't remember a time when my colleagues on the Judiciary Committee were so perplexed. Some were outraged. Others virtually cheered.

"I thought Webster would have a heart attack. He laughed so hard he had tears streamed down his face. Our committee chairman, Congressman Boutwell, just sat and stared into space for a time. Finally, he said, "That's what we asked of Drieborg; be tough but fair. So, gentlemen, it's too late to back down, now. The horse is out of the barn for sure."

Kellogg wasn't finished. "Here Mary Jacqueline, read the afternoon edition of the Daily Evening Star."

## Congressman Jailed

*This morning, Congressman John A. Bingham \* Ohio, defied a congressional committee. In response to committee questions, he said,*

*"The Judiciary Committee has no legal standing to require me, a member of the Congress, to testify under oath, to anything. Most galling was that among my interrogators were three former Confederate traitors."*

*The result of the Congressman's refusal was to be put in irons and jailed. Later today, the Rep. Bingham thought better of his earlier decision, and agreed to testify. He was then released.*

*Judiciary Committee chairman, Congressman. John A. Bingham \* OH had this to say in response on the matter:*

*"My committee is determined to investigate the various rumors suggesting the possibility that government personnel conspired with John Wilkes Booth to kill the late President Lincoln. In that pursuit, we will not tolerate refusal to cooperate from anyone. Therefore we fully support the actions taken by Chief Marshal Drieborg this morning."*

*Marshal Drieborg was not available for comment.*

Finished reading, Mary Jacqueline asked, "Michael, did you really do this?"

Mike explained what had happened.

"Oh my Lord!" she exclaimed. "You actually put manacles on his wrists, a hood over his head, and threw him into a jail cell?"

"Actually we locked him in a broom closet down the hall from the congressman's office."

"We'll hear about that in the Congress for a while, I'm guessing," Kellogg chuckled.

Mike teased his wife. "See what happens to people who cross me?"

"Guess I'd better watch myself, huh!" Mary Jacqueline replied in jest.

With a mischievous smile on his face, Mike told her. "You think I'm kidding?"

# Grand Rapids, Michigan

"Hi, fellas," George greeted his old buddies from the war.

"Got a seat for us for a couple of hungry marshals today?" Bill Anderson asked.

"There's always one for you guys; even if you are the law," George assured them. "I got a table for two over in the far corner."

After a waiter took their order, George came over and pulled up a chair.

"We had a bit of a problem last night." He told them.

"Is that right?" Stan Killeen responded. "Happen in the restaurant, did it?"

"I suppose you could say that. You guys know, Amos stays at my place over the old bakery. He got roughed up when he was walking there last night. It must 'a happened just before he got to the place. A couple of men dragged him into the alley behind the building and punched him around some. They told him to leave town."

"How bad is he hurt, George?" Bill asked.

"Doc said his ribs are bruised; got a cut on his head and a split lip, too. But other than that, he's fine. He'll be sore for a while, but nothing broken, it seems."

"Your cook, what's his name, Bob? He involved, you think?"

"Don't really know, Stan," George told him. "He's at work right now in the kitchen. I suppose you'll want to see him."

"Not until I've eaten, though" Bill told him. "My stomach believes I've forgotten it."

The two federal marshals walked into the kitchen of the Cosmopolitan Bakery and Restaurant. They already knew who they were looking for, so they went directly to him.

"Put your hands on yer head while we search ya, Bob," Stan ordered. Once satisfied that he was not armed, Stan pulled his arms down behind him and cuffed his wrists together.

"What tha hell you guys doin?" he complained. "I ain't done nothin wrong."

As they led him out the back door of the building, Bill explained.

"We warned you, Bob," Bill told him. "Anything happen to Amos, we were going to hold you responsible. Well, somethin did, so that's why we're taking you to jail."

"That ain't legal, is it?"

"Not your concern right now, Bob." Stan told him. "Your only worry right now is what going to happen after we put you in that dark cell. You remember that small, dark room, don't you, Bob?"

"But I ain't done nothin wrong ta be in jail."

"We'll talk about that after you get a chance ta' think about it for a while in your cell, Bob."

Bill slammed the metal door shut behind his prisoner and turned to walk away.

"What about these cuffs? Aren't you going to take' em off?"

"We'll talk about that later, too."

"But they's hurtin my wrists!"

"Supposed to, Bob."

# National Hotel – Washington D.C.

"Right this way, ladies." The headwaiter led them toward a large round table. "I'll be right back to take your orders."

"Thank you for arranging this lunch, Patricia," Mary Jacqueline told her. "Did you choose this place for any special reason?"

Pat had reserved a table for five: Peg Stanitzek, Ethie Faute, Mary Alice Stephan, herself and Mary Jacqueline. Peg and Ethie had just joined their husbands at the boardinghouse the previous evening. So, this was the first opportunity for all the wives of Mike's team members to get together.

"The Willard is the largest in town, and the well-known to visitors. But it's the meeting place for all the politicians, lobbyists, and favor seekers with their bribes. Crooks frequent the place, too; truth be' known. Besides it's the most crowded place in the city this time of day. And, it's so full of cigar smoke, you can hardly see across the room."

"So, I thought we would enjoy ourselves somewhere else. I chose the National because it is the more prestigious hotel. Most of the important congressional leaders and their families stay here. And, its dining room is the much nicer."

"Well, I must say, this room is very elegant." Mary Jacqueline agreed.

Their waiter had returned with a glass of water for each lady at the table.

"Can I get anyone a drink before you order?"

Patricia spoke first. "I'll have a beer. What brands do you serve?"

*Here we go again. Pat's out to make her statement – whatever it is today,* Mary Jacqueline decided.

"I'll have tea, please," Mary Alice told the waiter.

Peg told him, "Tea for me, too."

"It'll be coffee for me, young fella." Ethie directed.

"Can you recommend anything on the menu, Patricia?" Mary Alice asked.

"Most everything is very good. I favor the Caesar salad with flame-cooked chicken. It is excellent," she replied. "So is their egg salad sandwich."

After they gave the waiter their orders, Mary Jacqueline asked Ethie,

"Just where is Cades Cove, Tennessee?"

"We're northwest of here several days riding in good weather; at the eastern end of Tennessee in the Great Smoky Mountains, almost 2,000 feet up."

"I still can't picture it, Ethie," Mary Alice protested. "Is it anywhere near Knoxville?"

"It is, sort of. We're southeast a' that town about a day's ride in good weather, an' 1,500 feet up tha mountain. Once or twice a year, a' fore the war, we took wheat an' such there to trade for tabacca, coffee and the like. Not much call right now given the bad times in East Tennessee.

"So, now if we trade at all, we pretty much take our goods down tha mountain to Gatlinburg a small town bit north a' us.

Ethie continued, "The Cove's not even on any map I ever seen, neither. We're down to about forty or so families right now, so we only got some 250 people livin' in the Cove."

"Sounds awfully isolated, Ethie," Peg chimed in.

"That it is, Peg. We don't get passers-by in our neck a' the woods. People don't often just show up at the Cove. You must really want to go there. We got one road and it's a steep climb, all the way. Sometimes it's flooded, sometimes it's covered with ice, sometimes it's so muddy ya need spikes on yer shoes just ta' keep yer footing. It is never easy traveling.

"But I wouldn't trade it fer all the Knoxville's or Washington's in the world. No sir. The Cove is sometimes rough on a body, but it's a little piece of heaven ta' me."

"Give me Washington any day," Patricia told those at the table.

"I must admit, Pattie," Ethie added. "I ain't never been waited on afore like I am here. I sort' a like that part."

"When I heard that you were coming, Peg, I looked for Macon on our map," Mary Alice told everyone. 'It didn't look to me that it was very far south of Atlanta."

"That's right," Peg answered. "It's not. Our farm is just outside of Macon actually; but most of our meat business customers live in that city. My husband, Francis, and now our two sons, manage the farm and the sale of meat. We raise our own feed for a good-sized herd of cattle and several hundred pigs. The boys do all the butchering and sausage making. I do the record keeping and of course take care of the house and a big garden. It's a family operation. Everyone keeps busy. Now, Francis and I are waiting to become grandparents.

"By the way," Peg asked no one in particular. "Before I forget to ask you Mary Jacqueline; just where is the Catholic Church around here?"

"I'll show you. Peg," Mary Jacqueline offered. "The Stephans went with Michael and me last Sunday. You're welcome to join us this coming weekend."

"I never met a Catholic a'fore. None' a them live in the Cove," Ethie said. "I'm a Baptist, don't ya know. You ladies don't seem to fit the image I had a' Catholics. I thought they all had horns, spoke some popish language and carried a pitchfork around to herd folks into Hades."

The ladies laughed heartily at Ethie's description; at least the Catholics laughed. Pat drank her second beer. The food was served, too.

"This salad is very good, Patricia," Mary Alice decided. "Do you have any other good eating places on your list?"

"As a matter of fact, I do," Patricia, answered. "The place I have in mind is so unique I won't try to describe it to you. You'll have to see it for yourself."

"Oh, come on, Patricia," Mary Alice complained. "Don't keep us in suspense."

"You'll just have to trust me when I tell you that the food is the best of its kind in Washington. I guarantee that it will be an experience you'll never forget."

"It sounds exciting," Peg said. "I can't wait to go there."

*Here she goes again. Should I warn the others?* Mary Jacqueline wondered. *No, let Pat have her fun. This adventure might just be a good one,* she decided.

After the plates were cleared, the ladies were served coffee and a light dessert. Patricia chose brandy and a cigarette.

Only Ethie Faute said anything. "What you're havin looks good, Patti. My dessert is mighty tasty but next time, I might let you order fer me."

# President Johnson's Office

Mike began.

"Mr. President, please allow me to thank you for seeing us on such short notice."

"That is quite all right, Marshal Drieborg," President Johnson replied. "Given the circumstances, I fully understand and support the need to proceed with this investigation as quickly as possible.

"Some unscrupulous people are using the deranged comments that Mrs. Lincoln made to suggest that I had something to do with the assassination of her husband, President Lincoln. I more than anyone want to put that thought to rest."

Johnson continued. "In fact, I'm trying to implement Mr. Lincoln's Reconstruction plan to bring all the states together with the greatest possible speed and heal the deep wounds of the recent conflict. But some powerful men argue that instead, we should punish those who led the Southern states out of the Union and to war.

"They are using Mrs. Lincoln's accusation to discredit me personally, and with it my administration's Reconstruction policies. So, I more than anyone want to put that charge to rest. Therefore, you can be assured of my full cooperation."

"Thank you, Mr. President," Mike said.

"If I may, Marshal Drieborg," Johnson asked. "Can I ask one of your marshals a direct question?"

"Of course you can, sir."

"Marshal Faute," Johnson began. "It has been a long time since I visited Cades Cove. Did the people there suffer much during the war?"

"I was away serving in a Confederate cavalry unit during that time, sir. But I'm told that toward tha end, our women and the men too old to be in the big fight had to deal with some deserters and bushwhackers.

"Much to our shame, most' a' them thieves were Southerns. But all n' all, the folks managed pretty well. We are isolated some there, you might remember."

"I do remember that. Tell me, Marshal Faute. Why did you volunteer to participate in this investigation?"

"The money was good, sir."

After the laughter subsided, Bose continued. "Actually sir, Congressman Webster asked me ta volunteer. He said he needed ta' find a good Southern boy or two ta' help sort out tha truth of this tragedy."

"You think Lincoln's assassination was a tragedy?"

"Fer us in tha South, it sure enough was. Anyone with a brain could see he was goin ta let us up easy. With all tha harsh comments you made in '64, everybody thought you'd go along with tha Black Republican's plan to punish tha old Confederacy."

"I can see why you might think that Marshal," Johnson agreed. "But the presidency changes a man. I had a choice to make; either pursue a policy of retribution or one that would help the people of the South recover from the devastation they suffered.

"As president, I saw that my job was to help all Americans set aside hate and anger so we could be one united county again. So, I chose recovery over retribution; Lincoln's way."

Mike Drieborg asked. "Can we assume then, Mr. President, that you will direct all the members of your administration to assist us in this investigation?"

"I will, absolutely, Marshal Drieborg. Let me take care of that right now."

President Johnson picked up a bell from his desk and rang it. Shortly a door opened and a man stepped into the room.

"How can I help you, Mr. President?" he asked.

"This is my personal secretary, gentlemen: William Browning. William, I want you to write a memo to each of my cabinet members. Direct them to give Marshal Drieborg and his committee their fullest cooperation. Write that up for my signature immediately."

"Yes sir."

"I understand that you have been in this office before, Marshal Drieborg."

"Yes sir," Mike replied. "I had the privilege of meeting with President Lincoln twice during the war in this very office. Congressman Kellogg was with me on both occasions. A third time, I was in another room of this building to receive the Congressional Medal of Honor from him personally. My entire family was present on that occasion. I'll never forget it."

"I imagine not."

"Before we leave, sir, can I ask you a direct question?"

"Yes, you can; certainly."

"You said that Mrs. Lincoln's comment about your involvement was deranged. Excuse me, sir, but was she correct in her accusation?"

Johnson noticeably colored some and shifted in his chair. "I know you had to ask, Marshal," he responded quickly. "No, her accusation has no foundation."

"Thank you, sir," Mike responded. "I have one thing more, sir. Can you explain why Mr. Booth would leave his calling card at your hotel?"

"Of course, I do not know what was in Mr. Booth's mind. He and I had met after one of his Nashville performances before I became Mr. Lincoln's running mate in '64. In fact, I think we had a drink together at my hotel's bar. A Confederate friend of his was in one of our prisons and he asked me to obtain the release of the man.

"In those days such requests were made of government officials all the time. So, there was nothing unusual about such a petition. Even Mr. Lincoln was known to have granted the release of Confederates held in one of our prisoner of war camps at the urging of a friend or other influential person.

"Booth and I never met after that."

At this point, the president's secretary entered.

"Copies of the memo you requested, sir."

"Thank you, William. Let me sign them right now. And, please give one of the originals to Marshal Drieborg."

"Yes sir."

"Do you or members of your team have any more questions, Marshal?"

"I do, Mr. President," one of the men said.

"Would you be Marshal Stephan from Columbia, South Carolina?"

"Yes sir, I am."

"What would you like to ask, Marshal?"

"On May 2, 1865 you signed a proclamation naming former President Davis and other members of the Confederate government, co-conspirators with Booth in the assassination of Abraham Lincoln."

"Yes, I did."

"Was that proclamation based largely upon the testimony given at the trial of the conspirators and presented to you by Mr. Holt?"

"Yes it was," Mr. Johnson answered. "I questioned Mr. Holt vigorously about the veracity of the witnesses. He assured me, and the members of my cabinet, that the testimony could be relied upon."

"I see," Stephan commented. "Let me tell you, sir. The members of this committee have read the testimony Mr. Holt presented to you back then. We have also read the more recent court testimony given by the same men when they were being questioned by Representative Rogers. During his cross-examination, they admitted to having perjured themselves when giving their earlier testimony. In fact, sir, as Congressman Rogers of New Jersey told us, not only did Mr. Holt know their testimony was a bunch of lies, he saw to it that they were paid by your War Department to give that perjured testimony.

"This is now a matter of record; it is a fact, sir."

"I can see you learned your interrogation skills well in the Confederate Judge Advocate Department, Marshal. What is your question?"

"It seems that neither you nor your cabinet members knew Mr. Holt suborned perjury or that he lied to you in the bargain. But sir; are you now aware that no credible evidence has been produced which links President Davis or his staff with the killing of Abraham Lincoln?"

"Yes, Marshal Stephan, I am aware of that."

"Sir, it has been over two years since your proclamation of May 2, 1865 was issued; and several months since the testimony it was based upon was shown to be all lies. So, sir, when are you going to revoke that proclamation?"

"I assure you, Marshal, such a step is under consideration."

"One more thing, Mr. President," Stephan continued. "The Judiciary Committee has asked you to bring Mr. Davis to trial as a coconspirator in the assassination of Mr. Lincoln. Do you intend to grant their request and bring him to trial?"

"Mr. Davis will not be brought to trial on that charge, Mr. Stephan; for the reasons you so clearly pointed out."

"Marshal Drieborg, I must move on with my schedule. I thank you all for joining me today. If I can be of help as your investigation develops, please do not hesitate to call upon me again."

"Thank you, Mr. President."

# PHILADELPHIA

"Children," Mrs. Murphy called, "a letter just came for you."

Eleanor and Charles came bounding down the stairs into the living room.

"Is it from Momma and Mike?" Charles asked excitedly.

"Calm down, Charles," she said, "and I'll share it with you."

"Oh, all right." He grumbled.

"There is a letter for me and Grampa Murphy and one for you children," she told them. "You'll take turns reading. Eleanor, you read the first paragraph."

*  *  *

*My Dear Children*

Your father and I are finally settled in Washington City. We are staying at Congressman Kellogg's home while Papa works. It is a very nice home, but I wish we were all back at our house in Michigan. We miss you both terribly. I am helping the Congressman plan a dinner party he will hold in his home soon. I have met the wives of the other men who work with your father. They are all very nice.

One of the ladies is from a mountain town in Tennessee; another from Georgia; another from South Carolina and still another lives right here in Washington.

I hope you two are minding Helen and Gramma Murphy and doing your homework. School will be over soon, as summer is almost upon us. Just imagine, I will be with you shortly, too. And then, we can greet my new baby, together.

We both loved your last letter. Please write another. Remember to say your evening prayers. Give everyone a hug for us.

Love you, Momma

# WILLARD HOTEL - WASHINGTON

Mike and his men were having lunch at the Willard.

"Mike," Craig Haynes began. "Are you satisfied with what Johnson told us about his relationship with Booth?"

"I don't know whether or not I should be," Mike replied. "You have one of your 'feelings' about it?"

"Yes, I do," Craig told everyone. "My information is that he and Booth sort of partied together. Word around town is that when Johnson was the military governor of Tennessee, the two escorted ladies around town on a number of occasions, even here in Washington, too. I think we should look into it."

Frank Stanitzek interrupted. "What is this 'feeling' business you two are talking about?"

Mike responded. "On a number of occasions Craig has mentioned this 'feeling' he gets about a person. You know, like he thinks the person is lying or is just not telling us everything. I've learned to trust it. In the past I've told him to pursue the issue and see where it takes us."

"So, he thinks there is more to know about a Johnson/Booth link?"

"Don't know, Frank. Craig will look into it, though."

"This intrigues me, Mike," Frank told him. "Mind if I tag along with him on this?"

Craig cautioned him. "You're welcome to join me, Frank. But I'm going to check out a few things tonight at one or two of the brothels. I'm not so sure Peg would like you visiting there, especially since she just arrived in town.

"So, I'll take Henry with me tonight. Come with me tomorrow when I'll check out a place or two during the day. Will that work for you?"

"Sure, Craig," Frank agreed. "You're right about tonight with the wife. I best spend it with her. I'll go with you tomorrow, instead."

George Krupp asked, "When do we interview Mr. Davis, Mike?"

"We've got him scheduled for day after tomorrow. It will be an overnight trip. So, tell the wives that there will be no exceptions; everyone goes."

Faute spoke up. "You couldn't keep me away from that interview with a team of horses, Mike," Bose assured him. "Never met President Davis; but I sure won't pass up the opportunity, even if he is only a citizen like me, again."

"Craig," Mike continued. "Check to see that everyone is armed."

"Yes sir."

Stephan asked, "Do you really think we need to go around armed, all the time?"

Krupp spoke up. "Let me tell you a story, Robert. A year or so ago, Mike was working here with the congressman on Reconstruction issues. I noticed he was wearing a revolver, even when we met in Kellogg's office. In fact, I kidded him about it."

"But you learned your lesson about laughing last, didn't you, George?"

"I must admit it, Mike. I did."

"What the hell happened?" Faute asked.

"Mike and I had our supper in this very room one evening," George began. "Afterwards, we decided to walk off our meal. We took something of a shortcut back to our lodgings. It took us down through Hooker's Way where all the brothels and a bunch of abandoned buildings were located; still are. After a while we began to walk down this dark and rather deserted street. We were talking and not paying too much attention to our surroundings.

"Two guys suddenly jumped us," George continued. "One of them knocked me to the ground and was hitting me with a piece of wood, or something. I didn't know what Mike was doing."

Mike explained. "I sort of saw a guy running at me. So I was more prepared than George. I just took his charge and threw him on the ground. I didn't know if he was armed, so I pulled my revolver and shot him in the chest before he could get up. Then I pulled the other attacker off George."

"Good thing, too," George told everyone. "Next thing I see is Mike holding his gun barrel against this guy's head.

"I heard him tell the guy to look at his dead companion. Mike wanted to know who sent these guys to attack us."

"I just told him I'd kill him if he refused," Mike added.

"When this guy stays quiet, Mike gave me his revolver and pulled a big ass knife from his boot. He held it up close to this guy's face. Then Mike grabbed the man's right hand and says, I'm going to cut off your little finger."

"I told Mike that I thought there were just muggers looking for some quick cash."

"Not likely," Mike said. "Didn't you hear this one use my name? They were paid to attack me, George. You just happened to be along."

"Once more, Mike asked for the name of who paid the attacker. The guy still didn't say a word."

"Naw; He didn't, did he?" Frank asked.

"Damn right, he did; quick as a flash."

"Did Mike ask, again?"

"He didn't have to. The guy couldn't talk fast enough. Mike was calm as could be, holding that big knife by the next finger. I believe he would have continued chopping fingers off until this guy answered his questions. I didn't know whether to laugh or cry. Could've pissed my pants; honest to God!"

"That was it?"

"Not quite. After we got the guy to the police, we went to the nearest bar and had few drinks. Next day, I bought a revolver."

"Well, I swear. Right here in Washington," Bose marveled.

"Damn right!" George exclaimed. "It's dangerous hanging around with Mike."

# Interview with Jefferson Davis at Fortress Monroe

Mike's team arrived at the prison early. After everyone checked his weapon, he and Craig Haynes were ushered into the office of the commandant.

Colonel Andrews looked up from behind his desk, but did not stand to greet the visitors. "Be seated," he told them coolly.

Mike recognized the arrogance and refused to sit. "We have little time for pleasantries, Colonel," he said. "As you can see from these documents, we are authorized to interrogate your prisoner, Jefferson Davis, today."

Andrews did not accept the documents Mike held out to him. He did not even look at them.

"I'm in charge of Fortress Monroe, Drieborg! No politician's lap dog is going to order me around. I decide what happens here. I have orders from Judge Holt to give you one hour with my prisoner. So, I don't give a rat's ass for your documents. You'll get one hour with Davis, not one minute more. If we are clear on that, Marshal, I'll take to see him."

This guy is a real horse's ass. No sense arguing. I'll take the hour and when I get back to Washington, I'll look into it, if it turns out we need more time with Mr. Davis,

"Fine, Colonel," Mike agreed. "Let's get on with it."

The Colonel led Mike and his men to an isolated part of the prison. He showed them into a room about ten feet by ten feet, not much larger than a common cell. There was only one chair and no table. The metal door was closed with a loud bang and locked behind them.

Jefferson Davis was chained to the only chair. He could not stand, but he extended his hand to Mike in greeting just the same.

Mike was first to shake his hand. "President Davis, I presume."

"Are you Marshal Drieborg?" Davis asked.

"Yes, I am Mr. Davis," Mike confirmed.

"Please excuse the accommodations, young man," Davis said. "My hosts here have not been willing to extend even the barest of courtesies to my visitors."

"We found that out on the way in, sir," Mike told him. "I doubt Col. Andrews was appointed warden because of his people skills."

Davis chuckled. "He would not be my choice as a salesperson in a retail establishment, I assure you."

"We have been allowed only one hour, sir. So, I suggest that we proceed. First, allow me to introduce my colleagues."

Once the introductions were complete, Davis said. "I am glad to see that at least three of your men served the Confederacy; Tennessee, Georgia and South Carolina. Seems like a good representation to me. Welcome to all of you. I'm sorry there are no chairs for you."

"Do you wish to make a short statement, sir?"

"Well put, Marshal." Davis chuckled. "I see you are aware of my verbosity. Very well, I know we are short on time."

"First, let me state without qualifications, I did not approve any plan to assassinate President Lincoln. And, to my knowledge, no member of my cabinet did, either.

"Second, I was appalled that any sane person would think Lincoln's death would help our cause. On the contrary, killing him was a tragedy for the South. Once our struggle for independence was denied by force of arms, he wanted to bring each of the states that formed the Confederacy back into the Union quickly with the fewest hurdles.

"I suspect and fear that Lincoln's successor will not be strong enough in his struggle with the Republican Radicals. They want to punish not heal. No, gentlemen; Lincoln's death was a tragic loss for the people of the South."

"Do you men have any questions of me, at this time?"

"Yes, sir," Frank Stanitzek said. "In March of 1864, I think the Union army conducted a cavalry raid aimed at Richmond. Do you recall that incident, sir?"

"Yes, I do. I recall it very well, Marshal."

"One of the Union officers carried instructions to capture or kill you. He was killed and the documents discovered. Were you aware of those documents?"

"Yes, Marshal Stanitzek, I was," Davis admitted. "It surprised us that such a thing had even been discussed by our enemies, much less ordered. It caused quite a stir in Richmond, let me tell you. As a result, some of my advisors wanted to retaliate and send men to kill Lincoln. That approach was voted down; I wouldn't tolerate that action.

"Instead, it was decided to kidnap him. As you know, prisoner exchanges had stopped. So, we hoped to obtain the release of thousands of our soldiers held by the Union in exchange for President Lincoln. That plan failed, however."

"Could anyone on your staff have ordered an assassination without your knowledge?" Robert Stephan asked.

"Toward the end of our struggle for independence, Marshal Stephan, there was much confusion. I'm ashamed to admit it, but the control we had over the men and women working in our clandestine service was definitely diminished. So yes, it is possible that such an order was given.

"But allow me to suggest something else, gentlemen." Davis continued. "Is it not also possible that members of one of your radical Northern groups were involved? Could such people have represented themselves as Confederate agents to Southern sympathizers like Booth, and given instructions to kill the President of the United States? They could have said the instructions were coming from me."

Craig Haynes broke in at this point. "Yes sir. In fact, we are looking into the possible involvement of those Northerners who opposed President Lincoln's renomination in1864, and his Reconstruction program."

"I'm happy to hear that, Marshal," Davis said. "I regret that so many of our government's documents were destroyed. The minutes of my cabinet discussions would have shed some light on this subject."

A loud bang was heard on the metal door of the room. When it was opened, Col. Andrews stepped into the room. "Your time is up Marshal Drieborg. I must return my prisoner to his cell."

\*        \*        \*

Mike's team was seated around a table at a local rooming house. The meal that came with the room was about to be served.

"It's a shame we only had an hour with the man," George Krupp told his colleagues. "He must have a great deal of information stored in that head of his. I've got a long list of questions I was hoping to ask, too."

"We'll go over them and anyone else's, George." Mike told him. "If we decide we need more time with Mr. Davis, we'll get it. But there was no sense trying to get around this Colonel Jacobs, today. His orders will have to come from Washington."

"So we'll go back to Washington in the morning, Mike?" Bose asked.

"Might as well, Bose; we've done all we can here. Tonight, we'll talk over our interview with Davis, and decide if we need more time with him."

"I've got another idea I think you should consider, Mike," Craig proposed.

"Spit it out, Craig." Mike urged.

"You know how hard it is to work in the congressman's office, everyone running in and out with stuff. The noise alone drives me to distraction," he began. "I suggest we stay right here tomorrow. After morning chow, we settle down and lay out the rest of the investigation.

"Now that we've seen Johnson and Davis, I think we should identify what information we still need, who we should see next and why. Up to now, we've not done that, Mike; we really should."

"Makes sense to me, Craig," Mike told him. "Anyone have a comment on Craig's suggestion?

"I hated to leave the girls alone back in Washington." Bob Stephan told everyone." But as long as we're here I think we should devote tomorrow to coming up with a plan for the rest of our investigation. I'm for staying and getting it done."

"If there's nothing else on that, it's decided. We stay here tomorrow, and work."

"I wouldn't worry much about the ladies," George Krupp said, "My wife made some plans for all the wives to go out for dinner tonight. She's taking them to Harvey's Oyster House, as a matter of fact."

"Well, I'll be," Henry exclaimed. "Remember when you took us there, Mike?"

"Yup," he responded. "That was quite an evening. Killeen wouldn't even try an oyster; said they were slimy looking. He went back and ate leftover stew at the boardinghouse. I bet those biscuits he ate there were hard as bricks."

"Not to hear him tell it, though," Craig remembered. "He swore the entire next day that his stew' n biscuits had been sooo delicious."

"Would you go again, Craig?" Mike asked.

"Sure would, Mike," he said. "I'd had oysters back in Cleveland, on special occasions. But none of them were as tasty as at Harvey's Oyster House."

"This Killeen sounds like a good ol' sensible farm boy ta me," Bose told everyone.

"My wife's not used to that kind of food," Frank added. "I just hope she don't get sick or something."

"I don't think she will, Frank," Mike told him. "All of Washington's rich and powerful go there. No one has complained yet."

"Ever had oysters, Frank?" Bob Stephan asked.

"I'm a butcher by trade, Bob; a meat' n potato guy," he replied. "I don't think I ever saw one' a' them things, even."

"You'd love it, Frank," Krupp spoke up. "Mike, we ought to take everyone over to the Oyster Bar before we're finished with this investigation."

"Gotta warn ya, boys," Faute warned. "I'm with Frank on this one."

"Think of it as an adventure, Bose," Mike urged, half laughing.

"If we go there, think I'd just watch."

The food arrived; steak not oysters.

*      *      *

The next morning after breakfast, the men stayed right in the dining room of the boardinghouse. Their host even agreed to supply them with hot coffee throughout the day.

Once the dishes were cleared, the coffee cups and pipes were filled. The men were ready to begin their day's work.

Bob Stephan spoke first.

"To begin with, I believe it is apparent that there is no foundation to support the charges against President Davis; that he was part of a conspiracy to kill President Lincoln. Any comment on that?"

"Just a pack a' lies to find a scapegoat, seems ta me," Faute concluded.

Stephan continued. "If that is the finding we include in our final report, I suggest we spend no more time discussing or investigating those charges. Any comment?"

Mike had one. "Bob," he began. "I can support what you initially said and what you concluded, too. But I want to remind all here; if we find evidence to the contrary, we'll have to take another look at Mr. Davis.

"This will apply to all individuals and groups we look at. President Johnson is a case in point. We're probably going to have to interview him again before this is over. Does everyone understand what I'm saying here?"

Stephan was the first to agree, "Not a problem with me, Mike."

"Frank and Bose?" he asked. "You have any problem with what I just said?"

"As long as it applies to everyone we're investigating," Frank answered, "I got no problem with it."

Mike turned to Krupp, "George, what do you think of taking a look at Parker, the President's guard on April 14th?

"There is almost nothing in the records we were given about this guy. In fact, it appears that no one seriously questioned him after the assassination. Parker does his job and President Lincoln does not get shot; it's that simple.

"But of all the arrests made that night and later, no one lays a hand on him. In fact, he has continued to be a White House guard, to this day. It's unbelievable. Has someone been protecting him? If that's the case; why? This situation screams for us to investigate."

"Henry," Mike directed. "You keep minutes here, please. Write down the suggestion George just made. Anyone else have anything?"

Stephan spoke up, "Remember what Mr. Davis told us, yesterday? He wondered if some of the men who tried to dump Lincoln as the Republican Party candidate in the election of 1864, might have been part of a conspiracy. What about that?"

"Bob, he was talking about the Radical Republicans," Mike told everyone. "There was and is a bunch in Congress and within Lincoln's administration too, who opposed his postwar policy. Let me take just a minute to go over it for you.

"As early as 1863, President Lincoln held out an olive branch to the South. He proposed what was called, The Ten Per Cent Plan. Under its provisions, when ten per cent of those who voted in the presidential election of 1860, swore allegiance to the Union, that state would be readmitted to the Union with all the rights of the other states.

"The people of Louisiana qualified, held elections and petitioned to be readmitted. But the Radicals in Congress refused to admit their elected representatives. In response to Lincoln's plan, the Radicals passed a bill that required fifty percent of the voters to take the oath before a secesh state would qualify for readmittance.

"As the war was winding down, it became obvious that Lincoln would seek to bring all the Confederate states back into the Union as quickly as possible with the fewest requirements.

"That was a real problem for the Republicans in Congress and the Senate. It was especially galling because it seemed likely that the people of the former Confederate states would elect to office the very men who had led their states out of the Union. So, the same people who had cost the people of the North so many lives and so much money would just waltz back into Congress and the Senate as though nothing had happened. Then, those men could combine with the Peace Democrats of the North and possibly control Congress.

"This very possible situation was considered intolerable to the Republicans and many others in the North. You see, if it was allowed to happen, the losers of the war could dominate and control the peace.

"A Congress controlled by Peace Democrats and the new delegations from the former Confederacy could shape the peace to their liking. That majority could possibly decide to honor Confederate war bonds, repudiate the North's war debt, disband the Union army, or even restore slavery in some form. Oh! All sorts of things might be possible in such a situation.

"This scenario did not seem as likely with Andrew Johnson as president. When he was the wartime governor of Tennessee and later as vice president, he appeared to be a real fire-eater when it came to secession and those who led it. He called them traitors who should all be hung. He advocated confiscation of their lands, too. As president, the Radicals thought he would never let the former Confederates up easy. Before the assassination, he had agreed with them and so they thought he was their man.

"But between the assassination in April 1865 and the new session of Congress in December of the same year, President Johnson did a complete about face and embraced Lincoln's approach.

"By December of 1865, all the former states of the Confederacy except Texas were ready to send representatives and senators to Washington. It seemed that the worst nightmare of the Radicals was about to become true.

"So, they refused to seat these newly elected representatives. And, they began to fight Johnson's Reconstruction plans and implement their own.

"Now that we all know this, we can return to the spring of 1864. The war was not going all that well and the people of the North were weary of the war. The Republicans had already lost heavily in the midterm elections of 1862 over the war issue. And with casualties mounting it was considered very doubtful that Lincoln could even win the general election in the fall of 1864.

"So a group of Republican leaders supported by Northern money began a movement within the party to dump Lincoln and select General Fremont as the party nominee. This man had been the first nominee of the party back in 1856; and he was known to favor a harsh peace.

"The movement failed; Lincoln was renominated. There were several Union military victories and Lincoln was subsequently re-elected president."

George Krupp entered the conversation at this point.

"That brings us back to the conspiracy to kill President Lincoln," George continued.

"In 1865, military victory was assured. As soon as it was over, Lincoln still wanted to quickly restore the states of the Confederacy to their former rights in the Union. This meant he wanted to restore the Union as it was before secession with the exception of slavery.

"Also remember, before the assassination, Vice-President Andrew Johnson agreed with the Radical Republican's approach to Reconstruction. Therefore they considered him a perfect fit for their post-war approach and weak enough of a personality for them to control.

"So, the question for us is; did any of the Radicals have anything to do with Booth and the assassination?"

Frank Stanitzek was the first to comment. "It seems strange to me that Lincoln would allow the Democrats to take over his government. You think those Radicals in his party wanted to get rid of him so bad they would kill him?"

Stephan answered. "That's exactly what we are expected to determine, Frank."

"I can't believe they would go that far," Henry commented. "No way! One thing's for sure; I want to get to the bottom of this as much as you rebs wanted to clear your President Davis."

Mike directed the next question to Craig Haynes.

"What steps do you suggest we take, Craig?"

"Like any other investigation, Mike," Craig began. "We talk to the men most likely to have been involved and see where it takes us. The documents we've plowed through have given us no clue to a conspiracy involving federal officials in Washington. So, we talk to people. We may get something useful from such conversation, especially if they are under oath.

"Also, Booth was reportedly engaged to Lucy Lambert Hale, the daughter of former Senator John Hale of New Hampshire. She wasn't even questioned after the assassination or Booth's death. I was told that this was out of respect to her father. But we should talk with her anyway because she might have heard things from Booth that could be important to our investigation."

"We should also interrogate all known associates of Booth; actors and workers at the playhouses in Washington and other cities. He may have talked with them. They may have seen him with people we should question."

"Weren't those types questioned back in April of 1865?" Henry asked.

"I doubt that they were, Henry," Craig countered. "Cause' there's not much of what they had to say in all those boxes of information and testimony we were given. Virtually nothing is there.

"Remember, gentlemen, the investigators back then were looking to convict Booth's assumed accomplices, assure the public that Booth did the killing, and that he was assisted by only the people who were put on trial after his death. Additionally, it was decided to link Booth and those accomplices to officials in the Confederate government."

Bose Faute broke his silence. "So, Chief Deputy Marshal Haynes," Bose began. "You're saying that tha War Department people had Booth shot, tha people accused of assisting him hung; and Jefferson Davis proclaimed by tha president of the United States as a co-conspirator; period and end of story. Have I heard that right?"

"So it would seem to me, Bose," Craig responded. "At least it currently stacks up that way."

Henry wasn't convinced. "Just because you repeated to us what actually happened, doesn't mean that you can say, therefore, Union government officials were involved."

"You're right, Henry." Craig agreed. "I'm only trying to justify the need for us to take a look at the possibility some of them were involved. It has never been seriously investigated, you know."

Mike spoke up at this point. "I just want to remind you fellas," he warned. "We go down this path and we run up against the most powerful man in Washington; Edwin Stanton, the Secretary of War."

Henry said, "I thought the president of the United States was the most powerful man in the city, Mike."

"Maybe he is, Henry," Krupp interrupted. "Then again, maybe he's not."

Stephan had an opinion on this as well.

"We've been directed to take this investigation to wherever it leads. We've already imprisoned one powerful congressman; interrogated the president of the United States; and visited a former president in his prison cell.

"My Lord, George," Stephan asked. "Just how much more backbone must we have to take on this Edwin Stanton?"

Bose had a question. "I was told there was another theory floated about tha assassination."

"Oh. Sure. And what would that one be, Bose?" Henry asked.

"That the Catholic Church played a part in Booth's conspiracy ta' kill Lincoln; that one, Henry."

Frank Stanitzek jumped up from his chair. "That's as bad a lie as to say that President Davis had something to do with the killing."

"Well let me tell ya, my Catholic friend," Bose continued. "A former priest from Illinois claims your church leaders didn't like Lincoln much; and helped Booth ta' kill him."

"That's such nonsense!" Stephan insisted.

"Come on, you two," Bose continued. "Just cause' you're Catholic don't mean this guy's a liar. We should talk ta' him, too."

"There's a lot of anti-Catholic Baptists in Georgia," Frank snapped. "Are you one from Tennessee, Bose?"

"All right you guys; all right!" Mike chuckled. "Calm down. Whew! This is the first heat I've seen since we began to work together; probably not the last either.

"But Bose is right. Just like the other possibilities, this one should be part of our investigation as well. Remember, it got a lot of press in the North after the former priest went public with it."

"My Lord, Mike," Stephan countered. "The only guy throwing mud at the Catholic Church is this defrocked priest. His superiors threw him out after he slandered his bishop. What does that have to say about his veracity?"

"I don't know what that word 'veracity' means, Bob," Bose countered. "But if'n we're going to look inta every nook' n cranny during this investigation, I believe we've got' ta put this one ta rest, too. "

"I'm a Catholic like you Bob," Mike revealed. "But I have to agree with Bose. Let's give this the same examination as the other possibilities. There's a lot of anti-Catholic sentiment in the country; North and South. It was seriously fueled by this guy's accusations. Be good to see if it has any foundation, seems to me."

\*　　　\*　　　\*

"I agree with you, Mike," Craig said. "Right now, though, I think it's time to set some priorities. We need you to decide where we go from here. Where do we start?"

"First," Mike began, "I want Bose and Henry to find Parker and bring him in for questioning. Craig, bring in his boss, Richards of the National Police Force," Mike began. "We'll interview him in our offices."

"All right, I'll do that as soon as we return to the city,' Craig promised.

"What else?"

"Bob, Frank and George, you interview that defrocked priest Charles Chiniquy. He's the one who insists that the Catholic Church was involved. Make sure he produces all the documentation he has for the charges he made.

"George, you and Frank take a look at Booth's appearance schedule for at least six months prior to the assassination. Talk to all the theater people who worked with him. Start here in Washington; other cities if necessary. Include the maids, bartenders and other workers wherever he roomed during those engagements. Start with the National Hotel, where he stayed here in Washington.

"That will be all for now," Mike concluded. "We've got another session with President Johnson already arranged. We'll work out a schedule for the congressional Radicals and Secretary Stanton, next."

"What about Dr. Mudd?" Bob Stephan asked.

"We've sent a subpoena to Stanton's office requesting the transfer of Mudd to Washington from Fort Jefferson. You inquire about that one Bob. I expect each of you to get on your assignment first thing tomorrow," Mike told them.

"Back in Washington this evening, I suggest all of us relax. I know my wife will welcome me home for an evening. I suspect yours will too. So, hang around the boardinghouse with them tonight. I'll expect to see you at the office tomorrow morning, bright eyed and bushy-tailed."

"What's this bright eyed and tail business, Henry?" Frank asked.

"It's some Michigan term; means rested and wide awake, I think."

# Girls Night Out

It was already dark, and the five women were crowded into a horse-drawn carriage headed into Washington's downtown. The window shades were down on the carriage, so no one could see the city as the vehicle sped along the almost abandoned streets.

"Isn't this fun, everyone," Mary Alice said. "I love surprises."

Ethie Faute added, "This stomach a' mine will be surprised, too if' n it doesn't get something soon."

"Don't worry, Faute," Patricia assured her. "Your stomach will get a treat this night that it will long remember."

"I had the flu once last winter, Pattie," Ethie snapped back. "Just because I remember it don't mean my stomach liked it."

Ethie sure handles Patricia well. I love it! Mary Jacqueline thought. It saves me the trouble.

The carriage came to a stop at the corner of Pennsylvania Avenue and 11th Street.

"Everybody out, ladies," Patricia told them. "My surprise is just down 11th street a few doors."

They soon found themselves standing outside of a building looking at a sign: **Harvey's Oyster Saloon.** The place appeared to be full of well-dressed people.

"Oh, my goodness," Mary Alice said.

"What in the devil are oysters?" Ethie Faute asked.

"You'll find out soon enough," Patricia said. "The carriage won't be back for an hour, at least. So you're stuck, ladies. Wouldn't of thought you'd be afraid of anything, Faute."

"I'm not, Pattie," Ethie responded. "But I don't want 'ta make my stomach mad at me fer gettin it into trouble."

"You won't, I assure you, Faute." With that Patricia led the ladies into the oyster bar. The main room was crowded with women as well as men.

"Hi ladies," a man shouted over the noise. "Come right over this way, please."

With her companions trailing along, Patricia followed the waiter to a far corner in the smoky room. There were no chairs; instead they stood around a table that was waist high. Patricia told them the history of the place.

"During the war years, the Harvey brothers started this business in the most rundown part of town. Despite that, it became so popular that even President Lincoln and his wife ate here regularly. It only cost 25 cents for a gallon bucket of oysters. The brothers moved into this building last year."

She stopped as a waiter came by, "Bring us each a mug of beer and a gallon of oysters. Don't forget the hot bread and butter."

"I'll be right back with the beer and bread, ladies," the man told them. "It will be a few for the steamed oysters."

In no time at all, each woman had a mug of beer and some hot bread on the table in front of her.

"Just tear off a piece of bread and dip it into the hot butter in front of you," Pat instructed.

"Oh my goodness," Mary Alice exclaimed. "This is so good, I can't believe it."

"It is tasty," Peg agreed. "It is so far, anyway."

It wasn't long before two men came with a heated plate for each diner. More hot butter, pepper and saltshakers were placed on the table, too. Another man arrived with a bucket filled with steamed oysters, one for each of the ladies.

"Watch me, ladies," The waiter directed. "This is how you eat these succulent morsels." He picked up an oyster in his left hand and with a small fork in his right hand pried it open. Then he used the fork to pull out the sort of slimy looking meat inside; the oyster. He dipped it into the warm butter, sprinkled some salt on it, put it into his mouth and swallowed.

"Remember, you don't chew the oyster; you just swallow it."

Pat said, "Watch me." She demonstrated, too.

"Pattie," Ethie warned. "I'm goin ta jump inta this full bore. If' n my stomach rebels, though, these oysters will end up on yer shoes."

"Come' on, Faute," Patricia teased. "You can do it."

Everyone watched as Ethie used her fork to spear an oyster out of its shell, dip it into butter, sprinkle on some salt and swallow it. She followed each swallow with a piece of buttered bread and some beer. Before she paused to take a breath it seemed she had a dozen shells at her feet. She paused with a big smile.

"Not bad, Pattie," she decided. "Not too filling, though."

Peg was next. "It's not bad, actually," she decided after she had consumed a few.

Mary Alice Stephan had already thrown a dozen or more empty shells on the floor.

"You seem to be familiar with oysters, Mary Alice," Peg observed.

"Living in South Carolina, it would be hard to avoid this tasty treat," she told everyone.

"Down home, we eat' em raw. This is the first time I've had' em steamed; they're still tasty. They'd be even better if we had some hot sauce to go with."

Patricia turned to Mary Jacqueline. "What about you, Drieborg? Are oysters and beer too much for ya? Are you going home hungry?"

"Not on your life, Patricia," she responded. "Remember, I lived in Charleston during the war years. Oysters were sometimes all we had to eat. Like Mary

Alice, I just never had them steamed. Don't you worry, I'll eat my share tonight."

It didn't take long for a good-sized pile of shells to accumulate at the feet of each lady. At Ethie Faute's call, a waiter brought another beer and more bread. The gals made short work of that, too.

"I wonder what the men are doing tonight." Peg Stanitzek wondered.

"Can't say I give a hoot," Ethie laughed. "I speck they'll look after' em selves without any help from us."

Patricia was finishing her third mug of beer and was smoking one of her cigarettes. "You got that right, Faute. Besides, they're probably having a good ol time."

"Give me one' a those smokes, Pattie," Faute demanded. "You look like yer havin too much fun 'ta be doin it alone."

"Anybody else want to try it?" Patricia asked.

"Oh, my goodness," Mary Alice exclaimed. She couldn't help but chuckle at the sight.

# The Second Meeting With President Johnson

Mike and his men were seated in the president's office.

"Your request for this meeting suggested that you had some new information to give me, Marshal. What is it?"

"You might be aware, sir," Mike began, "that there are various rumors being spread by men seeking to discredit you."

"I think a former president said that such things came with the territory, Marshal," Johnson replied. "Which rumor is it this time?"

"Chief Deputy Haynes was responsible for obtaining this information. So I'll let him tell you, sir."

"Mr. President," Haynes began. "When were here last, you told us that you had met Booth only once. And, on that occasion he sought the freedom of a Confederate soldier held in one of the federal prisons."

"That is correct."

"Senator Howard of Michigan has been telling anyone who will listen another story, sir," Haynes began. "He charges that while you were Military Governor of Tennessee, you and Booth kept mistresses in Nashville and were seen on occasion together escorting them around that city. So he insists, sir that you had a close relationship with Booth."

"Is the Senator accusing me of conspiring to kill President Lincoln or is he suggesting I have engaged in immoral conduct, Marshal?"

"The context in which he is speaking, sir," Haynes explained, "is that, since Booth's actions made you president, your pre assassination relationship with him was close enough to warrant an investigation. I don't think he cares whether or not you kept a mistress."

"I believe the senator from Michigan is so upset with this administration's Reconstruction policy that he will make up anything to discredit me," the president observed. "He is also one of those laying the groundwork to impeach me."

"So, sir," Haynes continued. "The senator is mistaken?"

"I did not keep company with Mr. Booth in Nashville, Marshal."

# CONVERSATION WITH LUCY HALE

"Tell me why you and I are doing this again, Pattie." Ethie Faute asked.

"Aside from the boys being too busy, my husband George gave me the impression that none of them felt comfortable interrogating a Lucy Lambert Hale about her affair with the scumbag John Wilkes Booth."

The two ladies were riding in a carriage to the National Hotel. Their appointment was for ten that morning.

"And, I'm along because?"

"Because I've taken a liking to ya Ethie; that's why," Patricia answered. "They boys are doing all their interviews with at least one Yank and one Reb. George told me to pick one' a you. Drieborg and I don't like one another; I'd plain suffocate with either of the other two ladies from the South. So, you're the Reb on this assignment. Do you really care why you were picked?"

"Not' a tall, Pattie; not even a little bit," Ethie said. "I was just curious. Actually, I'm glad ta be along cause I'm dying of boredom back at the boardinghouse. Sides, I like yer idea of fun.

"I hear that this fella Booth had bedmates in every town he visited. The gal we're goin ta talk with; she must be dumb as a stump thinkin Booth wanted to marry her."

"My husband agrees with you on that score, Ethie," Patricia confided. "In fact it appears to run in the family. Her father lost his appointment as Senator from New Hampshire because he was sort of an embarrassment around Washington. And just before the assassination, Lincoln named him ambassador to some far away land of no importance, as a favor to the politicians from New Hampshire; just to get rid of him."

"So, we're supposed to find out if Booth shared anything with little Lucy."

"That's the plan, Ethie," Patricia told her. "Pillow talk is notorious in this town. Several military men of some importance ruined their careers during the war because they shared secrets with their bed companions who turned out to be Confederate agents."

"I'm shocked, truly shocked, Pattie," Ethie feigned. "You mean women of the South used their bodies to spy for the Southern cause?"

"That's a fact. The hoot is that the men actually believed these women bedded them because they liked them."

\*     \*     \*

After their arrival at the hotel, the two ladies sat in the ornate lobby in front of the check-in counter.

"She's supposed to check at the front desk," Patricia told Ethie. "They'll direct her to us."

"Pattie; see that fella standin over there?" Ethie pointed. "What's he lookin at us that way for?"

"Oh! I forgot. That's Henry Austry. He's one of the marshals working on this thing. After we go into the room where we're conducting our discussion, he'll knock on the door and then administer an oath of some sort to our friend Lucy. Because of that oath, we can tell her she'll be arrested if she doesn't answer our questions honestly."

"You mean ta say we could have her arrested fer not answering, or fer lying?" Ethie asked.

"That's the idea we want planted in her empty head."

"Well, I'll be. That would be something fer these tired rebel eyes to see. A Yankee arrested fer lying."

"Look, Ethie," Patricia whispered. "See that sort of frumpy girl at the front desk? Think that's our Lucy?"

"We're gonna find out pretty quick," Ethie responded. "She's headed our way."

"Is one of you ladies, Mrs. Patricia Krupp?"

Patricia stood. "That would be me," she greeted, hand extended. "And you must be Lucy Hale."

"Lucy Lambert Hale, if you wouldn't mind."

"Of course," Patricia responded coldly. "This is my partner, Ethie Faute. So that we can talk in private, I've reserved a sitting room for us. Right this way."

Once in the room, Lucy said, "I do hope you've also made arrangements for lunch. I've got to have my lunch."

"Don't you worry yer pretty little head, sugar," Ethie assured her. "We'll have a waiter take orders in a wink. While we're waitin though, have a glass of wine. You like wine, don't you, dear?"

"Oh my, yes."

Their glasses were no sooner filled than there was a knock on the door.

"You seem to have an accent, Ethie," Lucy surmised. "Just where are you from, anyway?"

"I'm from Tennessee, dearie; the mountains of Tennessee."

"Weren't you' all rebels up that way?"

"Still are, sugar, truth be told."

Patricia opened the door to Henry Austry.

"Oh, do come in, Marshal," Patricia greeted. "We were just about to begin our visit."

"Lucy dear, this is Marshal Austry. He is here to swear you in, before we begin."

"Swear me in?" She looked puzzled. "I never heard of such a thing. Whatever does that mean?"

"Well dear," Patricia explained. "If you were in a public courtroom, you would swear to tell the truth and answer all questions asked of you. I expect that many of the questions would be about your love affair with Mr. Booth.

Would you want to talk about that in a public courtroom full of newspaper reporters?

"Oh! Good gracious, no!" Lucy exclaimed.

"So, to protect you from the embarrassment of the press reporting everything you said, you're being allowed to give your testimony here in this private room. Isn't that better than in public?"

"Oh my, yes," Lucy agreed.

Then, Lucy swore to tell the truth and signed a paper stating that she had been so sworn.

"Remember, ladies," Henry assured them. "I'll be right outside the door if you need me."

Seated once again, Lucy asked. "Is he really a marshal and everything?"

"He's a marshal and everything, Lucy," Patricia assured her.

"He's cute," Lucy gushed. "Can I talk with him later?"

"Sure, Lucy," Patricia promised. "You can after we're done. How is your wine, dear?"

"It's just fine. Can I have a bit more?"

Patricia poured, and Ethie asked the first question. "Were you actually engaged to marry that good lookin Booth?"

Lucy tittered, "It was a secret," she said. "Johnny said we would announce it after some big project of his was finished."

"What was that project, Lucy?" Patricia asked.

"He never told me what it was," Lucy revealed. "But he said he had a lot of important people helping him."

"Who would those people have been dear?" Ethie urged.

'I can never remember names very well," Lucy revealed.

"Does the name of Andrew Johnson ring a bell?"

"Of course it does, silly. He's the president; everyone knows that. Actually, Johnny hated him. You see, during the war, Johnny happened to meet Johnson in Nashville. He asked him to use his influence and get one of Johnny's rebel friends released from a Yankee prison. Johnson refused; rather rudely, as I remember the story."

"I'm told your fiancé was such a sweet man," Patricia cooed.

"Oh, yes he was," Lucy agreed. "He knew how to make a girl feel loved."

"I know my husband loves me because he tells me everything," Ethie revealed. "I spose your Johnny did, too."

"We had no secrets from one another," Lucy said. "That's why I was so shocked to learn that his life was in danger here in Washington."

"He talked to you before he fled the city?"

"Oh, no," Lucy protested. "He wrote me a note."

"You must treasure that piece of paper and keep it close to your heart," Patricia prompted.

"Oh, yes," Lucy put her hand over her bodice and took a deep breath. A moment later she released a button, reached in and brought out an envelope.

"Oftentimes, when you share a treasure like that with others, the pain is more bearable. Read it to us, Lucy," Patricia urged.

\*        \*        \*

*My Love*

*I must flee the city and your loving arms, but only for a short time. The tyrant Lincoln is dead. Now, I fear that the powerful men who supported me will try to silence me, too. When all is known, I will return to my Lucy, a hero.*

*Your Johnny*

\*        \*        \*

"Oh, the poor man," Ethie gushed. "Who would such men be, Lucy?"

"Once, Johnny told me he had friends on the Washington police force. Another time, we were just resting in bed, you know how you do, afterwards," Lucy tittered. "He told me something I didn't understand."

"What would that be, dear?" Patricia prompted softly.

"You see, in his heart of hearts Johnny was a Rebel; a Confederate supporter. Despite that, he believed that important men in the Union War Department were helping him on some big project. That seemed strange to me, him being a rebel and all. But my mind was on something else at the time," Lucy tittered, again. "I didn't remember that he mentioned that, until just now."

"Have some more wine, dear," Ethie urged.

"Excuse me ladies," Lucy said. "I need to use the pot." She was directed to the adjoining bedroom to relieve herself. "When is lunch?" she asked.

"We'll see to it, sweetie." Ethie assured her.

After several minutes, "What is keeping that girl?" Patricia wondered aloud. "I had best check on her."

From the other room, Ethie heard Patricia calling.

"Isn't that the berries? The little twit has fallen asleep on the pot."

"Too much wine, I expect," Ethie surmised. "Let's lay her on the bed and order lunch. I'm hungry."

*       *    .    *

Sometime later, Lucy burst into the sitting room.

Henry Austry stood, "Miss Hale."

"Where are the ladies who were talking to me?"

"You were resting so soundly," Henry told her. "They didn't have the heart to awaken you. They had to leave."

"Are they done asking me questions?" she asked, "I haven't even had lunch."

"If you wish, miss. We can order something downstairs in the restaurant. Then I'll take you home after we eat."

"Give me a moment, Marshal," she cooed. "I want to fix my hair and freshen my makeup first. I'll be right out."

When the couple walked into the dining room, the headwaiter addressed them.

"How may I help you, sir?"

"A table for lunch, please." Henry told him.

"Normally you would need a reservation, sir," he told them. "But we certainly can accommodate Senator Hale's daughter. It's a pleasure to see you again, Miss Hale. It has been too long."

Lucy beamed.

"This way, please."

The two were looking at the menu when a man in the uniform of an officer of cavalry suddenly appeared at the table.

"Henry, my boy," General Sherman said, extending his hand. "I didn't know you were in town."

Henry stood and shook the general's hand.

"Good afternoon, sir," Henry responded. "May I introduce Miss Lucy Hale?"

"Lucy Lambert Hale, if you please," she corrected.

"Of course," the general responded taking the offered hand of the girl. "You're Senator Hale's daughter; a pleasure, Miss Hale."

"May I borrow this gallant young man for a moment, miss?"

"Of course you may, General."

Sherman took Henry into the hotel lobby.

"Actually I did know you were in town, my boy; working on that investigation of President Lincoln's death. There are no secrets around this town, you know. A word to the wise, though; if your young lady knows that you are a relative of mine, all of Washington will know it shortly. I suggest you tell her you were on my staff during the war.

"Your group is creating quite a stir with this investigation, my boy," Sherman told him. "Be especially wary of Secretary of War Stanton. He is my enemy; and will be yours, too when he discovers we are related. Call on me at my office when you get a moment, I want to talk with you privately."

"Off you go," he concluded. "Have a good time with Miss Hale. I'll write your mother that I saw you and that you are well."

"Thank you, sir."

As soon as he returned, Lucy began to question him.

"I'm very impressed," she began. "May I call you Henry?"

"Of course you can, Miss Hale."

"Please," she said covering his hand with hers, "Call me Lucy."

"How do you know such an important man as General Sherman?"

"I served on his staff during the war," Henry told her. "Of course, I was only one of many."

"You must have been pretty important for him to remember you all this time and to take the trouble to leave his table just to say hello."

"It is nice that he remembered me," Henry admitted. "But he is known to write letters to men who were privates, even. So, I'm not all that surprised, really."

"You are most likely being modest, Henry," she insisted. "Truth be told, I'm probably having lunch with a war hero or something." She squeezed his hand.

"Let's order lunch, Lucy."

"I already did, silly," she told him. "I was too hungry to wait for you to get back from your important general."

After eating, Henry led Lucy out of the restaurant.

"I'll get a coach and escort you home, Lucy."

"Oh my, Henry," she announced. "I forgot my purse in the bedroom. Please, I must have it."

"Fine," Henry assured her. "Would you like me to fetch it for you?"

Lucy clutched his arm, "Oh no, Henry. I don't want to be left alone in all the hustle and bustle of this lobby; please take me with you."

Back in the suite, Lucy went into the bedroom.
Henry waited in the sitting room. After a few minutes, Henry called out. "Have you found your purse, Lucy?"

"Can you help me in here, Henry?"

He pushed open the half-closed door and saw Lucy lying across the bed, naked.

"Would you like to join me, Marshal Austry?"

# Grand Rapids, Michigan

In the Cosmopolitan Restaurant and Bakery, George Neal was meeting with his silent partner, Mrs. Paula Bacon.

Mrs. Bacon asked, "Could this problem with Amos seriously affect our business, George?"

"It isn't at the moment, but it could become an issue," George told her. "The marshal's office is not going to allow Amos to be openly abused. But some of the veterans could organize a boycott of the restaurant. That's not against any law I know about.

"The issue isn't that Amos has a job; it is that he was given a job a white veteran wanted. As you know, Mrs. Bacon," George said, "aside from household servants there are a few people of color working in Grand Rapids. This hasn't caused much trouble because their jobs are very menial and not highly sought after.

"Besides, only a couple of men have made an issue of Amos taking a cook's position a white veteran thought he should have. I might have handled his hiring better, but it's too late to turn the clock back."

Mrs. Bacon interrupted. "I have an idea, George," she offered. "Let's set up a kitchen in the old bakery. Amos can cook his soups there and sell them to our restaurant. We could have a different soup or two each day on the menu saying something like, 'soups of the day', or 'soups by Amos'."

"That's a great idea," George agreed. "That could work."

"Amos lives in your old apartment upstairs as it is," Mrs. Bacon continued, "it would be convenient for him to prepare his soups there and it would solve our problem, too, since he would no longer be an employee of the restaurant."

"Before we go any further, though, let's ask Susan's opinion."

Mrs. Bacon agreed. "Good thought, George. After all, she manages the finances of our enterprise, here. Maybe she could see a problem or two we've overlooked."

"She's at the bank right now," George told Mrs. Bacon. "I'll get her to join us as soon as she returns. In the meantime, let's get a table out front and have some of Amos's famous soup."

*     *     *

In the federal jail, a few blocks away, Stan Killeen and Bill Anderson were discussing the 'Amos' problem, too; only from a different angle.

"You think our cook prisoner is ready to talk?" Bill asked Stan. "Or, should we keep him in isolation without food for another day?"

"I don't think that would work, Bill," Stan told him. "In another day he'll stink so bad the other prisoners will start to complain. Remember, yesterday, we didn't leave him anything in his cell; not even a pot to piss in. So, he probably already stinks to high heaven. Think I'll stay outside his cell when we talk with 'em."

"Where'd that saying come from, anyway?" Stan asked. "You know, 'so poor he didn't have a pot to piss in'?"

"City folks, I guess," Bill responded. "You know, folks too poor to own a pot just for relieving themselves."

Standing outside the cell, Stan commented, "Whew, I can smell him though this steel door!"

Bill pounded on the cell's door. "Hey Bob," he shouted. "You awake in there?"

"Awake? Do you expect me to sleep in my own shit, fer God's sake?" he shouted back. "Get me outa here. I smell so damn bad I can't stand being close to misself."

"Gotta have some information from ya first, Bob."

"Well ask, damn-it all! I ain't even done nothin ta be put in here. What do ya want ta' know, fer God's sake?"

"Who beat up on Amos, Bob?"

"I can't tell you that. You want me ta' get killed, fer God's sake?"

"God isn't goin ta help ya in that cell, Bob," Stan retorted with a chuckle. "Answer our questions an' you get ta' clean up and you're outa here. Who beat up Amos?"

There was no response for a few minutes. "If'n I tell ya, you'll protect me from them guys?"

"You tell us the truth, Bob," Bill promised. "These guys won't be able to touch you. I'll have them in jail. Besides, whose goin to let' em know it was you told us? Not me."

"All right, But I'm outa here, right?"

"Sure thing, Bob," Stan promised. "Bill here, will write down the information; names and where they hang out."

Bob rattled off several names. After being pressed, he even revealed where the men lived, places they worked, and the bars they frequented.

"You done real good, Bob," Stan told him. "We're going to check this out. We'll get back you."

"Hey!" Bob shouted. "You promised I'd get outa here."

Bill answered. "Stan promised you, Bob. I didn't; and I'm in charge of this jail, he isn't. It'd be against jail policy to let you go. You might get out of here though, after we check out the information you gave us."

"Damn-it all, you lied 'ta me!"

"I never lie, Bob. But Stan does."

\*        \*        \*

Back at the Cosmopolitan Restaurant, Susan Neal had joined her husband and Mrs. Bacon for some crackers and hot soup.

"I don't see any problem in buying soup from Amos," Susan informed the others. "It would be no different than with other things we buy. Except this time, the product would be soup already cooked and ready to heat for serving."

"Will you help Amos organize this thing, Susan?"

"What do you mean, George?"

"You know, come up with a price for his product, billing issues, packaging his soup, getting a bank account; that sort of thing."

"I suppose I could," Susan told them. "I can do it, but I'm concerned about the time it will take."

"Look you two," Mrs. Bacon said. "I'm nervous about you spreading yourselves too thin, too. Why not let me work with Amos. In fact, I'll be his partner, sort of like I am with you."

Mrs. Bacon continued. "Susan, you've got your hands full with the children and the restaurant bookkeeping. George, you've done a tremendous job marketing and managing the restaurant. Let's keep things the way they are. I'll need advice from you, of course, but let me take on the responsibility of working with Amos."

"Sounds good to me," George decided. "Are we ready to ask him if he likes our plan?" George asked.

The two ladies looked at one another and nodded. "I think we are, George," Susan said. "Why don't you ask Amos to join us?"

# KELLOGG'S WASHINGTON OFFICE

"Where do we stand with our interviews?" Mike asked Craig, his chief deputy.

"We have another one scheduled with President Johnson. We're finished with Jefferson Davis, and with Congressmen, Bingham and Rogers. We have yet to interview Baker, Secretary of War Stanton, Dr. Mudd, the various members of Congress who cheered Lincoln's killing, and the defrocked priest who claims the Catholic Church was in on the assassination.

"This afternoon we have Col. Lafayette Baker, Chief of the National Detective Force and John Parker, the officer who was Lincoln's security man the night of the assassination. And of course, we have to review the information gathered during the questioning of Lucy Hale, yesterday."

Mike asked. "Anyone have a comment on the list Craig just read? Are there any additions or deletions?"

"I have a suggestion." George Krupp offered.

"Yes, what is it, George?"

"I think we should contact Judah Benjamin. He was the right hand man to Jefferson Davis. He was a prominent lawyer before the war and Confederate Secretary of State during the conflict.

"I'll just bet he kept pretty good notes on his discussions with Davis; especially about something as important as the possibility of assassinating Lincoln. Rumor has it that he fled to England. He might just be willing to answer a few questions for us."

"Want to go to England, George?" Bob Stephan asked with a chuckle.

"I wouldn't mind someday, Bob," he responded. "But I can't make any money sitting on a boat traveling there and back. Besides, right now I've got too many other irons in the fire, including this investigation, to spend that kind of time on what could be a wild goose chase. Just the same, I think we ought to ask him a few questions."

"Ya know, George," Frank Stanitzek broke into the conversation. "I just have a feeling that President Davis might write a letter urging Benjamin to answer those questions."

It was Henry Austry's turn to get into the discussion. "Who'd believe whatever Benjamin would say?"

"Good point, George," Mike said.

It was Bob Stephan's turn to get into the conversation. "Benjamin has a brilliant legal mind. He'll see the problem you raised, George. If he chooses to respond at all, his answers will be so compelling as to earn the belief of even the harshest critic. I also think we should ask President Davis to join us in our search for answers from Benjamin, like Frank suggested."

"In an investigation," Haynes added. "You can never gather too much information. I believe we should ask the man."

"Does anyone have anything else, gentlemen?" Mike asked. "Hearing none, I suggest that George and Bob bring us a list of questions and a cover letter for Mr. Benjamin, as well as a letter to Mr. Davis. Would day after tomorrow be all right with you two? Put it on our agenda for Wednesday, Craig."

"We have a treat today, gentlemen," Mike announced. "The wives of two members of this group are going to visit with us. As you know I asked Mrs. Patricia Krupp and Ethie Haute to question a young lady, Miss Lucy Hale. She is reliably reported to have been Booth's mistress and fiancée. She was never questioned after the assassination and Booth's death out of respect for her father, the former United States Senator from New Hampshire. Our team of female investigators held their meeting with Miss Hale in a private room at the National Hotel.

"The ladies are in the outer office waiting to join us. George, would you ask your wife and Mrs. Faute to come in, please?"

After the ladies were seated, Mike introduced them to his team.

"Would you tell us of your meeting with Miss Hale, ladies?"

Pat began. "When the good Lord was passing out brains, I'm afraid Miss Hale was at the back of the line. She is pleasant enough, but very unaware."

Ethie Faute joined in. "Patty's right. And the girl has either blocked out what Booth did and what happened to him or all those events just passed her by somehow."

"Did Booth share anything of interest with her?" Mike asked.

"Once again, she played the innocent," Patricia Krupp reported. "She claims she is terrible with names; besides she claimed that when they talked she was still in the throes of passion or something."

Ethie pick it up, "But she did tell us her Johnny was always running off to meet with an important government person. Just the same, as Patty said, Lucy couldn't remember if Booth mentioned any names."

"There was one thing, though," Pat continued. "He sent her a note as he fled from Washington."

"Does she still have it?" Mike asked.

"Yes, she did" Faute offered. "In fact, she carried it close to her heart."

With that, Pat produced the handwritten note Lucy had given her and handed it to Mike.

Mike read it and passed it around the table.

"Well ladies," Mike asked. "Do you feel there is anything more to be gained from visiting with her again?"

Pat Krupp responded first. "It's hard to say, Michael," she began. "She seemed willing enough to answer our questions. But it's hard to understand how her mind works. The little twit could remember something useful, out of the blue."

"She'll want that note back, I'm thinkin," Ethie Faute asserted. "She treasured it; carried it under her clothing, close to her heart. She'll remember when she takes off her clothes, next time. Getting it back might just help her shake loose a name or two out of that foggy brain' a hers."

"We'll hold on to it for now," Mike said.

"I'll get it to a handwriting expert," Craig Haynes said. "We need to know that it's actually in Booth's own hand. We have the journal that was found on his body. So we have a recent sample. Our expert should be able to validate the note Lucy gave you."

"She already knows you ladies have her note," Henry Austry told the group.

After a brief silence, Haynes asked. "How do you know that, Henry?"

"Miss Hale fell asleep in the bedroom right during her interview. The ladies asked me to wait for her to wake up. I was in the sitting room when she did. She insisted on having lunch, so I took her downstairs to the dining room. She told me that she had given the note to you ladies and that you had not returned it."

Haynes continued. "Do you agree with Mrs. Krupp and Mrs. Faute about Miss Hale?"

"Do you mean that she would not be the brightest student in most any classroom, Craig?"

"Yes."

"I'm inclined to agree with them," Henry concluded. "She is pleasant enough, but not much for carrying on a challenging conversation."

"What did Booth see in her, Henry?" Bob Stephan asked. "From what I hear, he could have had most any woman he wanted."

Henry responded, "I think she gave him the adoration his ego demanded. I also suspect Booth thought marriage to the daughter of a former US senator could be useful."

"Remember," Henry continued, "Booth was said to be losing his stage voice at the time of his death. And, he was broke. Becoming a member of the Hale family might have seemed to him a good move."

"You're probably correct, Henry," Craig agreed. "Do you think there's anything more Lucy Hale could give us?"

"I'm with the ladies on that one, too, Craig. It's hard to predict just what she could come up with. But I may find out because she asked to see me again."

Ethie Faute was the first to react. "Well, ain't you the foxy one, Henry. Remember, Pattie, Lucy was taken with Henry; said he was cute."

"And you found out all that over lunch?" Pat Krupp kidded.

"Not entirely," Henry admitted. "We spent the afternoon together."

"Back in the hotel room; upstairs?" Pat continued to prod.

"Well, yes."

Bose Faute slapped the table. "That' a way Henry; all in the line' a duty, too. You Yanks ought a give the lad a medal."

When the laughter died down, Mike concluded the meeting.

Stifling his laughter, he said. "I think we had better end our meeting for now. When Henry has something to tell us that is important to this investigation, I'm sure he'll let us know."

Addressing Pat Krupp and Ethie Faute, "Thank you for your assistance on this matter, ladies. We are grateful for your help."

"Not as much as Henry is, I expect," Bose Faute shouted. The room erupted again in laughter. Much to Henry's embarrassment, no one laughed louder than the two ladies.

# THE NATIONAL POLICE HEADQUARTERS

Mike and his men entered the offices of the Washington Metropolitan Police and strode to the reception desk atop a raised platform. Looking down on them was a man dressed in a dark blue uniform buttoned to the neck.

"I'm Sgt. Cattleman, gentlemen. Can I help you?"

"Yes you can, Sergeant," Mike replied presenting his credentials to the sergeant. "I'm Marshal Drieborg; these men are all Deputy US Marshals. We have an appointment with Superintendent Richards."

"If you'll give me a moment, Marshal, I'll see if he's ready to see you."

The sergeant returned, followed by a tall, distinguished looking gentleman.

Extending his right hand, he greeted Mike. "Good afternoon, Marshal Drieborg. I'm Superintendent Richards, gentlemen. Welcome to the offices of the Metropolitan Police. If you'll follow me, we can have our talk in the conference room just down this hall."

Once they were seated, Mike began the conversation.

"Thank you for seeing us on such short notice, Mr. Richards. Hopefully, we will not take up too much of your time today. As you know, the House Judiciary Committee asked us to look into various conspiracy theories surrounding the Lincoln murder.

"Because men of your force were responsible for the protection of the president, you have to be part of our investigation."

"Marshal," Richards bridled, his face reddening some. "Are you suggesting that I was part of the plot to kill the president?

"No sir, we don't have any evidence to suggest that; at least not yet. But the glaring security lapse left the president unprotected and made it possible for Booth to kill Lincoln. That fact requires us to look at responsible personnel who were under your command at that time."

"You mean Officer Parker?"

"Yes I do; and his superiors, too."

Richards retorted sharply, "The military court's investigators didn't think it necessary to question me at the time. They didn't even question Parker. Why now? Why almost two years later?"

At this point, Craig Haynes commented. "Mr. Richards," he began. "As the former chief of police in Cleveland, Ohio I cannot imagine why you and Parker were not questioned in the aftermath of the assassination. You are being questioned now because such an obvious omission has given support to rumors of a government cover-up in which you and your security personnel might have participated."

"Hells bells, Mr. Richards," Frank Stanitzek continued. "Some a' your Yankee newspapers I'm reading say that you fellas might even have been involved in the killing."

Richards snapped. "President Johnson says you rebels were behind it. Did that make it true?"

"That's why we're here today, sir," Mike concluded. "Before we begin, though, Marshal Krupp will swear you in."

Once that was completed, Bob Stephan began the interrogation.

"Is Officer Parker still assigned to your team, protecting the president?"

"Yes."

"Isn't tha current president just a' mite nervous about that?" Bose asked with a mischievous grin on his face, "I sure enough would be."

With a straight face, Richards answered, "Our office has heard no complaints, Marshal."

Stephan continued the questioning, "In the aftermath of the assassination, was he disciplined for leaving his post at Ford's Theatre, thus allowing Booth unobstructed access to the president's box?"

"No."

"Why wasn't he?"

"Apparently, the review board did not feel it necessary."

"Parker was under your command at the time, Mr. Richards," Stephan pressed on and asked. "Since it was well known that Parker deserted his post that night, tell us why you did not discipline him? You were his immediate superior, after all."

"It was too long ago," Richards claimed. "I don't remember."

"It seems that there was a formal hearing held on May 15th of 1865. Is that not true?"

"If you say so, Marshal."

"I don't say so, Mr. Richards. Your own departmental records say so."

"Why did it take you a month after the assassination to bring Parker before a review board?"

"I expect we were too busy to do so any sooner."

"You weren't too busy to arrest and interrogate the owners of Ford Theatre and all their employees. Why did it take you so long to look at the possible involvement of Parker in the assassination conspiracy?"

"As I said, Marshal," Richards responded. "We were probably too busy."

"We haven't been able to find minutes of the hearing you held on May 15th, Mr. Richards. Why is that?"

"I don't know. Maybe our review board didn't take written minutes of the Parker hearing."

Stephan continued his questions. "Parker was brought before your review board on several occasions prior to this for various breaches of discipline like: falling asleep on the job, abusing prostitutes, conduct unbecoming and the like. We know this because we have read pages and pages of minutes kept by the board of their hearings for those minor breaches of proper police conduct.

"But you mean to testify here today that his dereliction of duty, the result of which allowed John Wilkes Booth to kill the president of the United States did not meet the test for keeping minutes?"

"It must not have. It wasn't my responsibility, anyway. You'll have to ask whichever officer chaired the board at that time."

"Who would that have been, Mr. Richards?"

"I don't recall. You must remember that it was a very chaotic time for us. Any one of several officers might have taken that responsibility. All I know is that I didn't."

"Has there been any pressure to retain Officer Parker on the team protecting the president?"

"No pressure whatsoever."

"So, despite his failure to protect President Lincoln you kept him on that team."

"Yes."

"Why?" Stephan asked.

"That decision was made some time ago. I don't recall the reason."

"Where is Officer Parker today?"

"Today is his day off."

"This is a subpoena for his appearance. You are being served because you are his superior. You will be held responsible for his compliance."

George Krupp picked up the questioning.

"Superintendent Richards," Krupp began. "Who appointed you to the position you now hold?"

"The late President Lincoln did."

"Did President Lincoln know you well?"

"No."

"Who recommended you for the post?"

"I don't know."

"Our records show that Secretary of War Stanton recommended you."

"Nice to know who my friends are."

"You were a schoolteacher before your appointment. How did that qualify you for this position?"

"You'll have to ask him."

"We will, sir. We will."

Mike interrupted the questioning. "Thank you for your time, Mr. Richards. We expect to see Officer Parker at our offices on the date specified.

"I expect we will be calling on you again, too; very soon. Please remember, sir, unless your memory improves by that time, you just might be facing a contempt charge, loss of your present position and end up spending time in your own jail."

Outside, the men talked as they walked away from the building.

"That man was lying," Frank told the others. "He knows more than he let on."

\*     \*     \*

In another part of Washington, Henry Austry and Bose Faute were watching Parker's home on L Street. They intended to arrest him when he showed up. Waiting hours on end is boring duty, and they were whiling away the time by talking of farming.

"So, you don't worry so much what the market is like for the grain you grow?" Henry asked.

"Not really, Henry," Bose told him. "We grow mostly for ourselves. We save some for bartering in the valley; sometimes even fer Knoxville. But it don't bother us much if there ain't a market fer our stuff. "

"What about stuff you don't grow, though? What do ya do for coffee, sugar and material for clothing?"

"We get sweetener from our hives an' some wool from our sheep fer cloth; but getting coffee and such can be a problem, fer sure.

"But we barter a good deal; did, even before the war. So we get by without Yankee greenbacks.

"Up in Illinois, is what you farmers get for your grain controlled by a big market somewhears?"

"Pretty much, Bose," Henry admitted. "I don't fully understand it. But I think it works like this; we pay the local grain elevator people to store our grains until we see on the telegraph a price per bushel that we like. Then, we sell it and get the railroad to ship it to cities like Chicago or St. Lewis. The buyer then telegraphs the payment to our local bank and we get paid. Then, we pay the railroad and elevator their fees."

"You trust all those folks ta pay ya proper?"

"Sometimes I wonder about that, Bose." Henry admitted. "The cash we end up with seems awfully small. And, with what we have left, we have to pay our mortgage, the bill at the general store and also set some money aside for spring planting. It seems like there's never enough.

"After the war, the government stopped buying much in the way of grain, wool and such. So, prices really went down for our crops. A lot of farmers couldn't even pay their mortgage and lost their farms. We barely survived.

"There's a new method my father is trying this growing season. The big grain company in Chicago offered him a contract for his grain. It isn't even harvest time; but he already knows what he will be getting for his crop and how many bushels he'll have to deliver to get that payment. A' course, if his harvest is short and he can't come up with the number of bushels he promised, he'll have to buy bushels of grain on the open market. It's pretty tricky – but all of farming is that way."

"Seems too complicated ta me, Henry," Bose concluded. "I like my simple mountain life."

"Bose," Henry pointed. "That fella comin down the street is wearing the uniform of a Washington policeman. I think that's a nightstick he's carrying, too. He's walking toward the Parker house. Should we take him now?"

"Let's see if'n he goes into the house, Henry."

"There he goes. He walked in as though he owned the place. Let's go."

Bose knocked on the door to the Parker home. Someone opened the door an inch or two.

"You again?" the lady said. "What da you want, now?"

"Mrs. Parker?" Henry said. "We need to speak to your husband."

"He ain't here," she insisted. "Go away."

Bose pushed against the door. "Either he comes out here, ma' am or we come in an arrest him in front of your children," Bose threatened. "It's your choice, lady."

She stepped aside and let Bose push the door open. "The good for nothing went into the back ta sleep."

Weapons drawn, Henry and Bose moved quickly to the room at the rear of the small house. Parker was just lying down. They jumped him.

"What the hell are you doing?" Parker shouted.

"Check him for weapons, Henry." Aside from the nightstick lying on the dresser, they found none.

"Officer Parker," Henry told him, "you're under arrest for failing to obey a federal subpoena. Put on your shoes and grab your coat. You're coming with us now."

As they handcuffed him, Parker shouted, "Ya can't do this to me." Bose shoved him toward the front of the house.

On the street, Parker continued to shout. "I'm a police officer. Colonel Baker will have your ass fer this."

"He'll have ta' find ya first, fella," Bose told him. "Henry, did you bring along that hood?"

"Time to use it, ya think?"

"Most anything ta keep this scumbag quiet," Bose declared. "He's hurtin my ears with all a' his holler' in."

Even after the hood was in place, Parker continued his shouting. Bose poked him in the ribs with the nightstick they had taken from his house. "If ya don't shut up," Bose threatened, "I'll use yer nightstick on yer ribs, hard next time."

The shouting stopped. "There, that's better."

They hustled Parker around the corner from his house and into a carriage and were soon headed out of the city. Craig Haynes had rented a farmhouse outside of Washington. He planned to use it as a place where reluctant witnesses could be held and interrogated without fear of interruption. Parker was considered a reluctant witness.

# WASHINGTON DINNER PARTY

Congressman Kellogg, Michael and his wife, Mary Jacqueline, were in a carriage on their way to a dinner party.

"Are you sure you're not too tired for an evening out, sweetheart?" Michael asked.

"I'm fine, Michael!" Mary Jacqueline responded. "I've really excited about this evening. Just imagine, Michael. We'll be at the Executive Mansion, the home of the president. I wouldn't miss this event for anything."

Kellogg joined the conversation. "Most of the important people in Washington will be there, my dear. It is a good opportunity for Michael to meet some key players in this town, and for them to meet his beautiful wife."

"His very pregnant wife, you mean. Thank you just the same, William. A woman always enjoys a compliment especially when she is big as a house and feels so ugly."

"As I'm a newcomer to the Washington party scene, do either of you veterans have any advice or instructions for me?"

Kellogg was the first to respond.

"Just be your charming self, my dear."

"Michael?"

"I agree with the congressman, sweetheart."

*      *      *

The three were soon at the home of their host and in the receiving line.

"Good evening, Kellogg," President Johnson greeted with a handshake. "Welcome to my home.

"It is my pleasure, Mr. President," Kellogg responded. "I would like to present Marshal Michael Drieborg and his wife, Mary Jacqueline."

"Welcome to my home, Mrs. Drieborg. If I recall correctly, Kellogg, I'm to be interrogated by this young man very soon. Am I in danger of going to jail, Marshal Drieborg?"

"Hardly, sir," Mike responded with a handshake. "I most appreciate the time you have set aside on your schedule to help us with our investigation of the assassination of your predecessor."

"Well said, Marshal. I look forward to our meeting."

As the three moved away, Kellogg looked around the ballroom and saw congressional colleagues and members of the administration standing in small groups sipping their drinks and talking.

He took Mary Jacqueline by the arm and led her toward one such group.

"Good evening, Kellogg."

"Good evening, Secretary Stanton. Allow me to introduce Marshal and Mrs. Michael Drieborg."

"Nice to meet you," he responded. "This is my wife Ellen."

Mrs. Stanton looked at Kellogg. "William Kellogg, when will you learn not to forget that even we wives have first names? Who is this beautiful lady you introduced as Mrs. Drieborg?"

"I'm sorry, Mrs. Stanton. This is Mary Jacqueline Drieborg."

Ellen took Mary Jacqueline by the arm and led her away a step or two from the three men. "Kellogg has been single way too long. He needs a good woman to sharpen up his manners. You're new in town, I take it, and expecting a child, too. Am I right?"

"As a matter of fact, Ellen, it is yes; on both counts."

"If you need maternity clothing I know just the place; beautiful stuff and not too expensive. I had two children during the war in this town. In fact, you and I are about the same size. Maybe you could use some of my things. I'm through having children."

"That's most kind of you, Ellen. But let me catch my breath here."

"Don't let my going on make you dizzy, dear," Ellen cautioned her. "You'll get used to the fast pace of my conversation. If I've got something to say, you'll hear it straight out."

She led Mary Jacqueline toward a table with full wine glasses. "Let's get a glass of wine. If we wait on those men of ours, we'll never have one before dinner is served. Do I detect a Southern accent in your speech, dear?"

"How could you," Mary Jacqueline chided laughing. "I've hardly gotten a word out since we met."

Ellen Stanton threw her head back and laughed loudly. "You got me there, dear. You got me there. I think you and I will get along just fine."

# KELLOGG'S WASHINGTON OFFICE

"Morning, Mike," Pete Oppewall greeted. "Coffee and rolls are ready in the conference room."

"Thanks Pete," Mike responded. "I sure could use a mug of coffee. Don't know about those rolls, though. My wife warned me that my waistline is catching up with hers. She's pregnant, you know."

"The boss wants to see you before your men arrive."

Mike got his coffee and went to Congressman Kellogg's office.

After he knocked on the closed door, he heard the congressman call out.

"Come in." Mike stepped into the office.

"Morning, Mike," he greeted. "Sorry I missed you at breakfast. But I had a bunch of things to get out of the way before my official day begins, so I ate early."

"You wanted to see me, sir?"

"Yes, Mike," he responded. "Close the door, will you? Have a chair. I have three items to share with you. Have a seat.

"First, you received a note from one of your team advising you that the pigeon was at the farm. Pete didn't mean to read the note, but it wasn't sealed or addressed. What the hell is this farm? And who is the pigeon?"

"Sir, trust me. You don't need or want to know the answer to either question. What you do need, sir, is the ability to truthfully deny any knowledge should you be asked."

"You know I trust you, Michael," Kellogg assured Drieborg. "Just keep in mind that there are people in this town who would like nothing better than to discredit you and thus discredit the entire investigation you are conducting."

173

"Thank you for the trust, sir," Mike responded. "We are at a point where some leads are critical. I assure you that my team will be selective in our use of the 'farm'."

"The second item, sir?" Mike wanted to move the discussion forward and get away from the subject of the farm.

"Just a thank you for your charming wife, Mary Jacqueline," Kellogg began. "She is doing a top rate job planning the dinner party. Peter tells me that she is a fantastic person with whom to work."

"Thank you, sir. I'll pass that along."

"The third item deals with your brother, Jacob."

Mike couldn't hide his surprise. "Holy smoke, sir; I never expected to hear about him from you. Nothing bad, I hope."

"It's quite the opposite, actually. His troop commander, Capt. Quinn and your old friend, Sgt. Riley have both written me about your brother and your former brother-in-law Kenny Hecht. They recommend both boys for appointments to the West Point Military Academy."

"Wow!" Mike responded excitedly. "That is great news. Anything special bring this on?"

"I would say so. It appears that a sudden blizzard caught each of the squads the boys were leading miles away from their fort. Your brother led his squad back to the fort after hours of struggle through snow and high winds. All his men survived safe and sound.

"But Hecht's squad got lost on the plain. Quinn and Riley say Hecht's men would not have survived if not for his leadership. They tell all about it in their letters. They sent along letters from some of the troopers, too."

"Can I hold on to these letters overnight, sir?" Mike asked. "I'm up to my ears in meetings today. Besides, I'd like to share them with Mary Jacqueline. She's never met either of the boys, you know."

"Certainly, Michael," Kellogg told him. "I will need them if I decide to recommend the boys for the academy. Do you think they'd make good officers?"

"I've not seen the boys since they ran off and joined the cavalry; and I don't know this Captain Quinn enough to have an opinion about his judgment. But I do know Sgt. Riley. He wouldn't give a recommendation like this without good reason. I'd trust his judgment any day. If he thinks the boys are good officer material, I'd bet they are. How the boys will handle the studies at West Point is another question."

Kellogg concluded the discussion. "I know you've got a full day, Mike. I'd like more of your thoughts on this before I make a decision. So, let's review our conversation about this tomorrow over breakfast. If I'm going to recommend the boys, I have to do it soon if they are to make it in time for the fall term."

"Shall we talk tomorrow at breakfast, Congressman?

"We'll talk then Michael."

# THE FARM

"When am I gonna get somethin ta' eat?" Parker complained. "I'm starvin here."

"You couldn't eat tied to that chair anyways," Bose teased him. "Overweight like ya are; do ya good to lose a few pounds."

"You two are in big trouble," Parker warned. "Kidnapping a Washington police officer an all?"

Henry chuckled. "From where I sit, mister; you're the one in trouble. And we haven't got to the part of you letting Booth kill President Lincoln."

"He done that on his own; everyone knows that."

"But if you hadn't left your post that night, Booth couldn't have done it, now could he?"

"If I'd a stayed, he'd a killed me, too."

"Promised ta do that, did he?" Bose prodded.

"He was crazy! He could' a, easy as not."

Henry picked up on that, "So, you left your post to avoid being shot?"

"Wouldn't you? The guy was crazy, remember!"

"Henry," Bose said. "It sounds ta me like this fella knew Booth was comin."

"It appears so, Bose."

"Wait just a minute. I didn't say no such thing. You're putting words in my mouth; trying to trick me. I'm not goin ta say anything more."

"Oh, darn!" Henry said. "And just when we're having such a good talk."

"I know, Henry," Bose said. "I have just the thing to help Parker here remember more about that evening. Do you recall how you Yankees helped folks in Tennessee remember where they hid their valuables; the old rope trick?"

"I heard of it being used in Carolina, too, Bose, if my memory serves. I was told it worked every time."

Bose picked up a coiled rope with a noose at one end. He threw the other end over a ceiling beam and put the noose around Parker's neck.

"What are ya doing?" Parker shouted.

Bose pulled the rope taut until the noose was tight under Parker's chin.

"Here's how this works, Mr. Policeman," Henry explained. "We pull you off the ground and count to five. Then, we let you down and ask you a question. If you still refuse to answer, we start again and pull you off the ground. This time we count to seven."

"You could kill me doing that." Parker protested.

"It's your choice, Parker," Bose reminded him. "Are you going to talk with us, or keep silent? Silent, eh? All right, take a deep breath, cause here we go, chair 'an all."

"Three, Four, Five," Henry counted. Bose let him down. "How did you know when to leave the door to the Lincoln box unguarded?"

"You gonna stop hangin' me if I tell ya?"

"We'll stop if you answer all our questions. Won't we Henry?"

"Whatever ya' say, Bose."

"Booth found me in a brothel one night, drinkin an' such. He said he'd give me fifty dollars in gold to leave my post during some play that was gonna be performed on April 14th. I was to leave before a certain line was spoken in the play. He threatened to have me killed if I told anyone 'bout our conversation. Then, he laughed and said he might have me killed anyways."

"How did he know the president would be attending that evening?

"I didn't ask him an' he didn't say."

"How did he know you would be the man guarding the president's box that night?"

"He said that important people would arrange for me to be on duty instead of one of the other three men in the president's guard detail."

"What important people?"

"Booth never mentioned any names," Parker insisted. "He only said 'important people'."

"So, he paid you fifty gold dollars?"

"He gave me twenty five the last time we met. I was supposed to get the rest on April 15th. But he stiffed me; never got a cent more."

"How did a sleazebag like you ever get assigned to guard the president?" Henry wondered.

"Turns out Mrs. Lincoln is a relative; a cousin or somethin, on my mother's side," Parker revealed.

"An aunt of mine asked her to help me. I was already a policeman on the Washington Police force, so the job was easy to arrange. Anyways, Mrs. Lincoln was the one who asked that I be assigned to guard the president. She even got me an exemption from the draft late in the war."

Henry interrupted Parker, "I read that after Lincoln's death, she made a fuss over you leaving your post. She demanded that you be punished. How come there is no record of your review board hearing or any punishment?"

When Parker hesitated, Bose pulled on the rope to tighten the noose. "Well?" he said.

"I expected to be fired, maybe even thrown in jail," Parker admitted.

"But I wasn't. They didn't even punish me a' tall. Instead, I was returned to duty as though nothing had happened. Later, my boss, Superintendent Richards told me that some people of influence in Washington put pressure on the Police Review Board to dismiss all charges. He reminded me how lucky I was that important people were pleased that Lincoln was out of the way. That's all I know about that."

"What' ya think, Henry? Bose said. "Should we give this pile of shit a rest?"

"He can rest while I write up everything he told us. Then, he'll have to sign the statement before I'd agree to give him any rest."

"Gimme some food," Parker complained. "I'm starving here."

"We'll give ya some water," Bose told him. "You haven't earned food, yet."

"Besides, we'll probably have some more questions fer ya, don't ya know."

After Bose gave him some water, he put the hood back over Parker's head.

"Hey!" Parker shouted. "What ya' doin?"

"I'll be' a doin more with yer nightstick, ya little shit, if'n ya don't shut yer yap."

Parker quieted down.

# THE RADICALS

Several men sat around a table in a private room at the Willard Hotel.

Secretary of War Stanton spoke first.

"Colonel Baker has something to tell us."

"After Drieborg and his deputies questioned me yesterday, Parker went missing. His wife told my deputies that two men burst into her home and took him away in cuffs. By her description, I concluded that they're members of Drieborg's team."

"I don't understand why this is a problem for us." Judge Holt said. "What can Parker tell them that should concern anyone in this room? He doesn't know anything, does he?"

Baker responded. "I don't think so, Judge. But he might know just enough to lend authority to the rumor that administration officials helped Booth."

"Are you willing to take that chance, gentlemen?" Stanton asked.

Congressman Bingham spoke up. "This whole damned investigation has gotten out of hand. We have to stop it, right now! I'd especially like to square things with that damned Drieborg."

"Come on, Bingham," Congressman Butler chuckled. "You're just angry because he called your bluff and you shit your pants in that broom closet he locked you in. Get over it, man. There's a lot more at stake here than your hurt pride."

"Butler's right," Congressman Julian stated. "Just remember gentlemen, without Parker, they have nothing. So, I suggest we concentrate on eliminating that threat.

"Colonel Baker, I propose you make sure Parker disappears again. And, I suggest you put his family on a ship bound for the West coast. Give his wife a nice stipend and a new name, too. Anyone disagree with that?" No one in the room objected.

"Why me?" Baker asked. "Parker's not even one of my men. Why not ask Richards to handle that?"

"Think about it for a moment, Colonel. Richards doesn't know anything more than the Parker whitewash. We don't want him more deeply involved, do we?"

"I suppose not. Do you want me to do anything about Drieborg and his deputies?" Baker asked.

"You take care of Parker, Colonel," Butler spoke firmly. "You leave Drieborg to us."

"By the way," Baker asked, "when am I going to get my share of the reward money for capturing Booth?"

Stanton spoke up, "As soon as things cool down. Now, leave us. We have other issues to discuss."

After Baker left, Congressman Julian told the group.

"As soon as possible, we have to do something about Baker. He's weak and knows too much."

"Just keep calm, Julian," Butler urged. "We'll take care of that matter soon enough."

"Henry," Mike began. "Thanks for bringing these statements Parker signed in last night. It will help us when we question Superintendent Richards this afternoon.

"Will Bose be all right at the Farm, alone?"

"I believe he'll be fine, Mike," Henry responded. "We figured you could use these documents today. And, I was less likely to get lost getting back to town. Besides, he didn't mind staying alone. I think Bose could happily carry on a conversation with a stump, if he was of a mind."

"Good man, Bose," Mike added.

Bob Stephan spoke up. "I've been thinking about this comment Parker made about his conversation with Richards. Parker insists that Richards told him that important people in the government pressured him to drop all charges against Parker. That means that Richards knows who those important people are. Now, I think we have Superintendent Richards by the balls."

"Not so fast, my friend," Krupp jumped into the conversation.

"Remember it was Officer Parker who made the statement; not the most reliable witness, I'd judge. In addition, the statement was given under rather questionable circumstances. It wouldn't be hard to make a case that he would have said anything to avoid another round with that rope around his neck."

"Should we give Superintendent Richards a dose of the 'Farm'?" Henry asked.

Krupp virtually shouted. "Not on your life! My God, Henry! He's the chief of Washington's Metropolitan Police. He's not a Parker who nobody gives a damn about."

Mike got into the discussion at this point.

"What do you think about this idea, George? Knowing that the statement we have from Parker was coerced, we arrange for Parker to go on trial for being part of the conspiracy to kill the president of the United States. After all, he did admit to taking money in exchange for abandoning his post."

George held his ground. "Admitted under duress, remember. Mighty flimsy grounds, Mike."

"Not really," Mike insisted. "I remember reading Rep. Bingham's argument made at the trial of Booth's crew of conspirators. He argued that people like Mrs. Surratt were equally guilty of killing the president because she had knowledge of the planned act.

"With Parker, we have a fellow who admits having taken a bribe to leave his post and expose the president to danger. So, according to Rep. Bingham, I see Parker as part of a larger conspiracy even though he didn't know that killing Lincoln was the objective of the plan. Like Mrs. Surratt, I believe Parker could hang."

"Henry, do you think Parker might be willing to testify in court about Richards and possibly others?"

"I think he's basically a coward, Mike," Henry said. "But if we can protect him from being killed now, and the hangman's noose, later, it's my guess that he'd say most anything."

"Put that way, Mike," Krupp agreed, "we might just be able to use his statement as a threat. When confronted, Richards might worry about the hangman's noose and implicate others to save his neck."

Stephan added. "I think we should give it a try this afternoon with Richards. After all, right now we don't have any other leverage with that man. Who's going to handle the interrogation, Mike?"

'I think I will, Bob," Mike decided. "You lawyers can sit on either side of me and pass me notes. Give me a kick under the table if either of you wants to step into the questioning or thinks I'm going down the wrong path."

Krupp added a suggestion.

"In case Richards asks about when we found Parker and how we came to have these signed statements from him, we might have a problem if

Henry is present. But if Henry's gone, we can claim ignorance."

"Good suggestion, George," Bob Stephan agreed. "So, Henry shouldn't be present when we confront Baker with Parker's statements."

"Henry," Mike decided, "Before we meet with Richards, leave for the Farm. You might just as well pick up some supplies on the way, too. Stay there with Bose and Parker. Frank and Craig will relieve you later today."

*    *    *

At one o'clock sharp, Mike greeted Colonel Baker in the outer office.

"Good afternoon, Colonel," Mike greeted him with a handshake. "Please join us in the conference room, if you would."

"Your subpoena doesn't seem to give me much choice, Marshal," Baker responded. "Will this take long?"

Mike shut the door behind him. "That depends on you."

"We'll begin the questioning with Deputy Stephan."

"Do you report directly to Secretary of War Stanton?"

"Yes."

"The secretary has said that the daybook Booth kept was given him with seventeen pages missing," Stephan began. "Under oath, you said that the daybook was completely intact when you turned it over to your boss.

"Did you make that statement?"

"Yes."

"But the secretary has said he received the day book with seventeen pages already torn out. So, Colonel, are you lying, or is Secretary Stanton?"

"I do not lie, Deputy."

"After killing Lincoln, Booth wrote in this in his day book,"

184

*"I have almost a mind to return to Washington to clear my name, which I think I can do."*

"What do you think he meant?"

"I have no way of knowing what was in his mind," Baker said. "My Lord, man, he had been observed entering the president's box just before the shot, and he jumped to the stage from that box immediately after Lincoln was shot. And, there were three other people in the box who identified him. There was no doubt that he was the one who shot the president. If Booth thought otherwise, he was delusional."

"Because he was killed, we will never know, will we?" Stephan observed. "His killing was convenient, wasn't it, Colonel."

"What are you implying?" Baker shot back irritably.

"Secretary Stanton made you responsible for the manhunt to capture Booth and his conspirators," Stephan reminded him. "Was killing Booth part of those instructions?"

"It was not; absolutely not!" Baker exclaimed. "My men were told to find him, not kill him."

"What did you do with Booth's body?"

"I was ordered to bury it in the prison compound along with the other conspirators."

"There has been some suggestion that Booth is actually still alive," Stephan said. "Any chance the wrong man was put in that grave?"

"Such nonsense," Baker retorted. "I assure you, Booth was killed in Virginia and buried right here in Washington."

"Let me get a clear picture of this," Stephan continued. "In dead of night a man was shot in the back while standing in a dimly lit barn. Your people identified the body of this man as that of John Wilkes Booth, primarily because Booth's daybook was found on the body. Do I have this correct so far, Colonel?"

"Yes."

"Later, when some of your men were mistakenly shown a photograph of his brother Edwin, they thought the photograph was one of John Wilkes Booth. Is that correct?"

"Yes."

"So your people might have killed and buried the wrong person. Is that possible, Colonel?"

"Possible, but it's not likely."

"Convenient, though," Stephan challenged.

Baker jumped to his feet. "I resent that suggestion; especially coming from a person so recently a traitor to the United States."

"Throughout the history of the world, Colonel," Stephan quietly lectured Baker. "Losers of a civil war are always traitors and winners are always patriots."

Mike interrupted the exchange. "I think we'll resume this interview at another time, Colonel. Thank you for your time."

# OUTSIDE OF WASHINGTON D.C.

Henry had left the Kellogg office and was driving a carriage toward the Farm. He was a mile or so outside the city when several masked riders emerged from a forested area and blocked the road.

He pulled back on the reins. "Whoa!" he shouted to his horse.

"I wouldn't reach for a weapon, Deputy," he was told by one of the riders. "We just want to visit with you some."

Two men rode alongside and another two led the carriage horse off the road.

When they finally stopped, Henry confronted them.

"It would appear that you know I'm a federal marshal," he said. "So far, your action is not a serious crime; carry it any further and it will be."

"Don't worry about us, Deputy," one of the men told Henry. "You should worry about what you must do to survive our little meeting here."

"All right," Henry responded calmly. "What must I do?"

"Tell us where you're keeping Parker."

"If you're referring to John Parker, who is a member of the Washington National Police Force, he is in the custody of US federal marshals."

"His wife told us about your abduction of her husband. Tell us where you're keeping him and you can go on your way."

Still appearing calm, Henry told his captors, "You can present a subpoena for him at the offices of the House Judiciary Committee. I'm sure they will obey the law concerning such things."

"I see we're going to have to do this the hard way, deputy," The man drew his revolver. "Step down from the carriage, please."

Instead, Henry threw himself backward into the second seat of the carriage. The first shot went over his head. Before another, Henry had a shotgun in his hands and fired once, then again. He could hear the screams of horses.

His carriage horse reared and pulled away from the men holding its bridle. Off it ran, pulling the carriage toward the main road. Still crouched in the back seat, Henry grabbed the reins and urged his horse on. He heard the report of gunshots behind him. Unhurt, the horse foamed at the mouth while it raced in panic toward the city.

Henry expected riders to catch up with the carriage. So he reloaded his shotgun. This time he would be ready for them. Fast approaching the first buildings of the city, he would be safe in a few hundred more yards.

Suddenly, he felt a blow on his right shoulder, then heard the report of a shot. He lost his hold on the reins and fought to remain conscious as the horse increased its pace. Despite being dizzy, and feeling the rush of pain, he still regained control and was able to direct the horse through the streets toward Kellogg's Congressional Office Building.

As soon as the horse stopped in the street in front of the building, Henry pushed himself out of the carriage. He didn't have the strength to walk, though. Instead, he collapsed on the sidewalk and called out to passersby.

"Help me! Help, please," he called weakly.

# KELLOGG'S WASHINGTON OFFICE

Later that afternoon, Superintendent Richards joined Mike's team in the Kellogg conference room.

"Before we continue, Mr. Richards," Mike began, "do you wish Mr. Byron, our recording secretary, to read any portion of your earlier testimony?"

"That will not be necessary, Marshal," Richards responded. "Can we proceed? The sooner this charade is concluded, the sooner I can return to my duties."

"Certainly, sir," Mike calmly responded, "At our last interview, you admitted under oath that your men disciplined Officer Parker for abusing a prostitute, but chose not to punish him for allowing President Lincoln to be murdered."

"I admitted no such thing!" Richards shouted, hitting the table with his fist.

"Now, now," Mike chided. "No need to get upset. Mr. Byron, would you please read to us Superintendent Richards' earlier statements about this matter?"

The recording secretary did so.

"You're twisting my words." Richards insisted.

"Now," Mike resumed. "Let us move to your role in the review of Officer Parker's actions on the night of April 14th. You are chief of the Washington Metropolitan Police, are you not?"

"Yes. I was made the Superintendent of that force in 1864."

"You were given the responsibility for the safety of the president?"

"Yes. We had an eleven man unit assigned to that task."

"When was Officer John Parker assigned to protect the president?"
"He joined the group protecting the president in early April of 1865. He had been a member of the Washington Metropolitan Police before that assignment."

"The records show that during that service, Parker was brought up on charges several times. His offenses included sleeping on duty, beating prostitutes, drunkenness, dereliction of duty; the list goes on. Why would a man with such a poor record be assigned to such an important position?"

"Mrs. Lincoln requested he be assigned to the team that protected her husband."

"Why would she do that?"

"I have no idea. You'll have to ask her."

"On the night of April 14, 1865 he was assigned by your office the responsibility for guarding the doorway to the presidential box at the Ford Theatre. He left that post unguarded long enough for an assailant to enter that very doorway and shoot the president of the United States, Abraham Lincoln."

"Is this all true?"

"Yes, it is."

"Subsequently, the record shows that you proffered charges of neglect of duty against him on May 1, 1865. And, sir, I quote:

"In this, that said Parker was detailed to attend and protect the president, Mr. Lincoln; that while the president was at Ford's Theatre on the night of 14 of April last, said Parker allowed a man to enter the president's private box and shoot the president."

"Is this true, Superintendent Richards?"

"Yes, it is."

"The records also show that a trial was to be held on May 3$^{rd}$, 1865. Is that true as well?"

"If the records so show, I suppose it is."

"Were you present for this trial, Mr. Richards?"

"I probably wasn't. Events were occurring at a terribly fast pace back then. I was probably too busy."

"I find that strange, since you are listed as having given testimony against Parker."

"Then it would appear that I was present. I simply don't remember any of that."

"We have detailed records of Officer Parker's previous hearings. Were written records kept of this hearing?"

"We've already gone over this ground, Marshal. I told you at our last meeting that I don't remember who chaired that particular trial. My Lord, man, I was busy in the aftermath of the assassination of President Lincoln."

"I had hoped, Mr. Richards," Mike reminded him, "that by now you would have remembered who was in charge of the hearing. We have testimony that you were."

"That's not true."

"Do you have any records of the hearing?"

"No," Richards insisted. "If records were kept at the hearing, I don't have them; never did."

"I have questions for the superintendent, Mike," Frank Stanitzek said.

"Go ahead, Frank."

"All this review board business you've been telling us about has me confused. At the time of the assassination, were you Officer Parker's superior?"

"I was; still am, too."

"As such, you were actually in charge of this review board trial you keep talking about?"

"I suppose."

"It also appears you dismissed your own complaint against Parker on June 2, 1865. Then, you returned him to duty without restrictions; not even probation or enhanced supervision.

"Is that true?"

"Yes."

Frank was still not satisfied, however. "But the man was obviously guilty of the charge you yourself brought against him; of deserting his post and allowing Booth to kill the president. Why was Parker not found guilty of at least that?"

"Sometimes guilty people manage to escape justice."

Mike asked a question. "You heard no complaint when Parker was returned to the squad protecting the new president?"

"I don't know of any."

"Wasn't even President Johnson a bit nervous having Parker as a protector?"

"It wouldn't seem so," Richards said.

Robert Stephan asked Richards, "According to a statement from Officer Parker, you told him that important people did not want him punished.

"Is that true, Mr. Richards?"

"I never said that at all."

"What did you say, by way of explanation to Parker?"

"I don't recall saying anything."

"So, sir," Stephan continued. "Parker's sworn statement is a lie?"

"Look at the man's record, for God's sake," Richards retorted. "Would you trust his word?"

"Whether or not I trust this man is not why we're here, sir," Mike reminded him. "It will be interesting, though, to see whether or not a jury trusts his word."

"What in heaven's name are you talking about, Drieborg?" Richards asked. "What jury?"

"A grand jury will be impaneled to determine whether or not there are sufficient grounds to bring Parker to trial for participating in conspiring to kill Abraham Lincoln," Mike informed him.

"That could be the trial at which your role in protecting Parker will be revealed for the public; that trial, Mr. Richards."

Richards turned red, calmed himself and said, "You delude yourself, Drieborg. Parker's record alone will taint anything he has to say; any accusation he makes will be dismissed on its face."

"I think the grand jury might be more interested in your lies, Mr. Richards."

"What lies?"

"You'll find out when you are called before a grand jury." Mike assured him.

"Excuse me, Marshal," George Krupp interrupted. "May I ask the superintendent a question?"

"Of course you may, George," Mike told him.

"Mr. Richards," he began. "If Parker was so untrustworthy why was he assigned the rather important task of protecting the president of the United States?

"I already told you, Marshal. Mrs. Lincoln requested he be assigned to that task."

"There were four men on the president's guard detail, were there not?"

"Yes."

193

"Did Mrs. Lincoln ask for Parker on April 14ᵗʰ by name?"

"She might have. I don't recall. But I think that it was simply Parker's turn in the rotation of the four members of the president's guard detail. Parker relieved Officer Crook, who had the daytime duty on April 14, 1865."

"It is interesting that you remember those details, but have forgotten everything else," Stephan taunted.

Before Richards could respond, the door swung open and Peter Oppewall rushed in. He went right to Mike and gave him a message.

After reading the note, Mike stood. "Craig," he ordered abruptly, "you stay with Richards. Search him for a weapon and chain him to his chair. Do not open the door of this room except for me. You stay too, Bob. Frank, you and George come with me."

"You can't do this to me!" Richards shouted. "I'm the Superintendent of the Washington Metropolitan Police Department!"

"Not today my friend," Craig told him. "Maybe you'll not be ever again, either."

\*　　\*　　\*

In the outer room, Mike and his men joined Pete. They all hurried down the stairs to the street level. At the entrance of the building, they were just in time to see a medical team carrying Henry on a stretcher to a military ambulance.

"We'll follow them to the hospital," Mike ordered. "Frank, you drive Henry's carriage."

Inside the carriage, Krupp sat in the second seat.

"Blood all over back here, Mike," George reported. "There's a hole in the carriage's rear curtain, too. A shotgun is lying here, loaded; a basket of supplies, too."

Mike told them, "One of the medical guys who's with Henry said it looked like a shoulder wound; not fatal. But he said that there was so much blood, it was hard to tell. It could be worse. I hope Henry will be able to tell us what happened.

"We'll get him to a private facility as soon as we can, too. With the poor care and the high rate of infection around military hospitals, staying there could be more dangerous for him than the wound.

"While he's in the hospital though," Mike continued, "you two will stay with him as guards. Take the shotgun with you, George. I'll contact General Sherman. I'm sure he'll furnish round-the-clock security for his nephew."

At the hospital, Henry was taken to an operating room. His clothing was removed and the blood cleaned from his torso.

"Doctor," the orderly said. "I only see one wound, it's in the shoulder. I don't see an exit wound, so the bullet is still in him."

"Use some ether, Sergeant. We'll get that bullet out of there. Strap him on the table."

"Yes sir."

*       *       *

Surgery finished, the Doctor approached the men waiting outside of the operating room.

"What are you men to my patient?"

"I'm Marshal Drieborg," Mike began. "The wounded man is United States Deputy Marshal Henry Austry. I am his superior officer. How is he Doctor?"

"He should recover. I extracted the bullet. If I remember my combat surgery days correctly, I think it was a projectile from a Henry rifle. The wound had some cloth in it, but I think I got it all. He should be coming around shortly. I assume you'll want to move him to a private facility. I'd give it till morning. I'll check on him later today."

"Thank you, Doctor. These men are also deputies. Because Marshal Austry might still be in danger from his assailants, they will remain with him."

"In that case, I'll order Austry placed in a private room. Oh! By the way, here is the bullet I took out of him."

Mike turned to Krupp and Stanitzek. "I'm going to inform General Sherman. Stay with Henry until I return."

\*      \*      \*

Mike entered the War Office and approached the guard seated in the lobby.

"I'm United States Marshal Drieborg. Where can I find General Sherman's office?"

"If you'll give me a moment, Marshal, I'll see if the general is available. Do you have a message you'd like me to give his secretary?"

"Give him my name and tell the general that this afternoon, his nephew was shot while on duty."

Very shortly, General Sherman himself came bounding down the hallway.

"Drieborg!" he began. "What's this about Henry?"

As they retreated to his office, Sherman was full of questions.

"What can I do at this point?"

"First, General," Mike began, "we need to get him out of that hospital."

"I agree," Sherman cut in. "Too much risk of infection there."

"Next, he is still in danger, sir. I believe those who shot him were members of the Washington Police force. They botched the job and very probably will try to finish it."

"My Lord!" Sherman exclaimed. "Richards had a hand in this?"

"I have no proof, at this point, sir; if not him, possibly Baker. Henry might be able to help us on that score. That's why I think the danger to him is very serious."

"Let's get right on that, Drieborg. I'll personally take a guard detail to the hospital right now. I'm staying at the National Hotel. I suggest we get a suite of rooms for Henry there. I'll have my staff take care of that as soon as we leave here."

"Send in Captain Sowle," Sherman ordered one of his people. "Get him on the double!"

"One other thing, sir," Mike said. "Henry was on his way to a farmhouse we are using outside of the city. We have a man there in the custody of one of my marshals. Can you send a squad of men there to guard them, at least until we get a better understanding about Henry's shooting?"

"Not a problem, Drieborg. I'll have that squad report to me at the hospital. You have one of your marshals there ready to lead them to the place."

"Thank you, sir."

Captain James Sowle arrived. "You sent for me, sir?"

"Yes, I did, Sowle," Sherman told him. "I want you and two cavalry squads of fully armed troopers to meet me on the street, right now."

"Yes sir," Sowle saluted, and virtually ran out of the room.

*        *        *

General Sherman stormed into the hospital. Captain Sowle and a squad of five armed troopers had to almost run to keep up. Drieborg wasn't doing much better and was walking several feet behind, too.

The doorway of the building was deserted. "Who's in charge around here?" Sherman shouted as he entered.

As soon as a frightened orderly could find him, the Doctor in charge appeared and stood in front of the general.

"This is a hospital, sir," the man began, "We don't shout in here."

The man with the red beard moved forward until he was almost touching the man wearing the blood stained coat. "I'm General Sherman. I want to see the butcher who operated on Marshal Henry Austry, right now!"

"That's me. I mean, I'm Doctor Andrews, sir. I operated on Marshal Austry."

"Will he recover?"

"I believe so, sir."

"He had better, Doctor," Sherman demanded. "Or you will find yourself assigned to a field hospital in the Dakota Territory. Do you understand, sir?"

"Yes sir. I understand, sir."

"Now, take me to him."

He turned to Captain Sowle. "Sowle," he ordered, "assign guards to the hospital entrance and bring the others to Henry's room."

"Yes sir."

"As soon as it gets dark," Sherman continued, "we'll move Henry to the National Hotel. You will have a detail and a medical team there when he arrives, too."

"Yes sir," Sowle promised.

"Oh, yes," Sherman said as he stopped abruptly in the hallway and faced Doctor Andrews again.

"You, Doctor, will supervise the movement of Marshal Austry to his rooms at the hotel. And, Doctor, come equipped with supplies sufficient for you to stay with him until he recovers from the surgery you performed. I also suggest that you pick a medical orderly to work with you, there.

"Questions, Doctor?"

"No sir."

The Lincoln Assassination

After General Sherman left, Sowle had a few words with Mike. "Your two marshals left with a squad from my unit. They have supplies for a week. When do you need your men back in Washington?"

"They already have instructions to be back in the morning. We have an investigation to pursue. I can't afford to have three men babysitting one witness; one will stay there. That should do it."

"I understand," Sowle said. "By the way, I hear you're from Michigan. That true?"

"Matter of fact, I am; I live in Michigan's second largest city, Grand Rapids. Why do you ask?"

"Just curious, I guess. My brother Pete and I grew up in that town."

"Well, I'll be." Mike exclaimed. "How'd you end up an army regular?"

Sowle told him. "I had a pretty stern father. It didn't help that I was a bit of a rascal. Even so, I can't ever remember getting a hug from him or an atta' boy either. Nothing I did ever seemed good enough, ya know. So, when the war broke out, I lied about my age and joined the army. My brother Pete followed me a year later; neither of us has ever been back to Grand Rapids."

"Can't say I had it rough at home; quite the opposite actually. But my town's Justice of the Peace gave me a choice; join up or go to jail for assaulting the town banker's son. I was of age, so I joined."

"I suppose there's an interesting story behind you and the banker's son."

"It would take a lot of beers to tell that tale."

"Let me know when you have a free evening. I'll supply the beer, if you tell the tale."

"That sounds good. I'd like that."

# KELLOGG'S WASHINGTON HOME

Mike was a bit late arriving home. Kellogg and Mary Jacqueline were already at the table.

"Sorry for the hold-up, everyone," he said as he gave his wife a kiss on the cheek and sat down next to her.

"We're just enjoying a moment together over a glass of wine, Michael," Kellogg told him. "Allow me to pour you some. It is excellent Chianti. I opened it especially to have with this evening's spaghetti supper."

"Thank you, sir," Mike said. "The first taste of wine I ever had was at this very table a million years ago. Remember how I happened to be there, sir?"

"No, I'm afraid I don't, Michael. You have attended so many of my gatherings, I get them confused. Refresh my memory."

"I've never heard this story, Michael," Mary Jacqueline. "Tell us, will you?"

"It was in early December of '62, shortly after the Michigan 6th Cavalry arrived in Washington," Mike began. "We were camped at the north end of the city. Between picket duties, many of us walked into town to see the sights. We were all from rural Michigan and were quite taken with the capitol. Anyway, I was standing on a street corner with another member of my squad. There was a light rain falling.

"I saw this girl coming toward us from across the very muddy road. She picked her way rather slowly through the mud, concentrating more on her footing than road traffic. She carried her umbrella against the rain in such a way that she could not see to her right.

"From that direction a horse drawn wagon rounded the corner and headed right toward her. The driver seemed to have lost control of his horses. Anyway, I jumped off the boardwalk and sprinted for her. I was able to get my arms around her and push her out of the way just as the wagon rushed by.

"Turns out, the young girl was your daughter, Patricia."

"I must say, Michael," Kellogg reminded him. "I was most grateful you were there and acted as you did."

"Thank you for the walk down your memory lane, Michael," Mary Jacqueline told him. "Now, I can better understand Pat's attraction toward you; the handsome young man who saved her from serious injury. You were her knight in shining armor. But what has that to do with having wine in the Congressman's home?"

"I'm coming to that, dear," Mike told her.

"As a result, Congressman Kellogg invited my troop commander, Captain Hyser and me to a dinner party here. I had never been inside a home as elegant as this or to a dinner party of any kind. And here I was, this farm kid meeting the congressman's other guests, General Scott, who was the head of the whole Union army, and several congressmen. If that wasn't daunting enough, when I got to the table, I didn't even know what all the spoons and forks at my plate were for."

"I imagine Patricia helped you with that, though," Mary Jacqueline offered with a knowing smirk.

"I just followed her example. As each course was served, I picked up the same spoon or the same fork I saw her pick up. Wine was served, too. I had never tasted wine before. Actually I thought it tasted sort of funny. But I just followed her lead with that, also. With each of the many toasts offered, I just took a little sip."

"I remember that dinner party, now," Kellogg told them. "You really impressed the general. He wanted to snatch you up as an aide, as I recall."

"Is that how you came to be assigned here in Washington, the first time, Michael?" Mary Jacqueline asked.

Kellogg answered her question. "Actually, I tried to convince Michael to leave his squad and join my staff. He turned me down cold; said he had to stay with his men."

"Why did you leave them, Michael?' Mary Jacqueline persisted.

"Back home the Bacon family had it in for me because their son, a second lieutenant in my cavalry regiment was court-martialed and dismissed from the service after a run-in with me. I was just a corporal. But he ordered some of his men to attack George Neal and me. As a result, Bacon was court-martialed and sent to military prison. The family blamed me and took it out on my parents."

"How could the Bacons do that, Michael?"

"Mr. Bacon was the banker in Lowell," Michael explained. "If you needed to borrow money in that town, you had to go to him. Like most of the farmers, my father had a mortgage on his farm. After his son was dishonorably discharged from the army, Mr. Bacon took his anger out on my family. He demanded the full payment of my parents' mortgage. He knew they would not be able to pay it and would have to forfeit everything."

"Allow me to explain the rest, Michael," Kellogg cut in. "I was made aware of their dilemma. So, I offered to buy their mortgage if Michael would join my staff as an aide."

Mary Jacqueline finished the story. "So, Michael, that's why you changed your mind and left your squad. William got you to accept the offer you had refused earlier. And, your parents' farm was saved from foreclosure. You both got your way, seems to me."

"You make it sound so simple, dear," Michael admitted.

"Wasn't it?" she smiled and took another sip of her wine.

After dinner, the three rose from the table.

"Excuse me gentlemen," Mary Jacqueline told her dinner companions. "I'm feeling more tired than usual this evening. If you don't mind, I think I'll turn in early."

Mike gave his wife a hug and a kiss on the cheek. "I'll be up shortly, dear," he promised.

"Thank you, Michael," she told him. "Have your cigar and brandy. I'll read a bit until you come up."

In his study, Kellogg poured a snifter of brandy for himself and one for Mike.

"Pete told me what happened to Henry this afternoon. How is the young man?"

"The surgeon said that he is on the mend."

"Any idea what was behind it?"

"I believe it was Lafayette Baker's men."

"Why?"

"My guess is that when Baker realized our interest in Parker he sent men to look for him. In the process they found out we had already picked him up. I believe they wanted to silence him."

"What are you planning to do about it?"

"We've got Baker in custody as we speak; or to be more accurate, General Sherman does," Mike revealed. "As soon as Henry is capable, I believe he'll be able to identify the men who attacked him."

"I'll bet that redhead is steaming about his nephew getting shot," Kellogg guessed.

"Your bet is a safe one, sir," Mike agreed. "Sherman has the surgeon who operated on Henry in fear of his life. The general threatened to send him to Indian country if Henry didn't fully recover. Sherman has actually taken over Henry's care; put guards on him, too."

"I can understand his concern," Kellogg added. "But why did Sherman get involved with Baker?"

"After I told him of my suspicions," Mike explained, "I also shared my fear that Baker was a flight risk. We did not have a secure facility to keep him, so I was going to have to let him go.

"Sherman would not hear of that. He volunteered to keep Baker under guard until we could question him further. Baker has to suspect we have something on him. This poorly executed attack on Henry might just be the break we need to pry information out of Baker."

"This investigation has taken on an entirely new sense of urgency," Kellogg told Mike.

"The word in the hallways is hushed. As your group dismisses one theory after another, my radical colleagues are losing their cover. And, with Baker arrested and the disappearance of Parker, I'm sure they feel the increased heat."

"Are you troubled about the course we've taken, sir?"

"Not at all, my boy," Kellogg assured him. "Turn the heat up if you need to. You may get to the bottom of this mess, yet. I hope you do."

"Thanks for your support, sir," Mike said. "If you don't mind, sir, I think I'll head up to check on Mary Jacqueline."

"Not at all, Michael," Kellogg assured him. "We can talk over your brother's West Point appointment at breakfast."

"Good by me, sir. Good night."

\* \* \*

Mike turned the doorknob slowly and pushed the door open carefully. He didn't want to wake up his wife by just storming into their bedroom.

Mary Jacqueline was sitting up in bed, reading.

"I thought you'd be asleep, honey. That's why I was so careful coming into the room."

"Thank you, that was thoughtful. I was hoping you would join me soon. I have a letter for the children I want to mail tomorrow. I thought you would like to add something."

"Of course," Mike told her. "I'll do it before I leave in the morning. But how are you feeling? Is all this activity too much for you, honey?"

"Thank you for being concerned, Michael," she said, patting the bed for him to join her. "I just suddenly felt a bit more tired than usual this evening. I'll be fine. Are you coming to bed soon? I need some hugs."

"It just so happens, young lady, I have a few unused hugs right here. Besides, I'd welcome some, too. Just give me a minute to wash my face and brush my teeth. Then, I would like nothing better than to fall asleep in your arms."

"Actually, Michael, sleeping was not what I had in mind." Mary Jacqueline ran her hand up his leg.

"I like what you have in mind," Mike said in surprise. "Just give me a minute to get out of these clothes."

As he undressed, he saw his wife unbutton her night dress and pull it open. Very quickly she was lying on the bed, naked. If he hadn't been aroused before, he certainly was now.

Mike blew out the light and lay alongside Mary Jacqueline. She moved quickly into his arms.

"I thought you were too tired for talk."

"This isn't talking, is it?"

"It's definitely not, sweetheart! In fact, what you're doing with those hands of yours, will not get us to sleep any time soon, either," Mike warned his wife.

"Good! Hopefully, you're finally getting the picture. Sleep's not what I had in mind when I prepared for bed."

As Mary Jacqueline had grown larger with her unborn child, she and Mike had made adjustments to their customary lovemaking. Now, she moved over him. "Help me get your nightshirt off, Michael."

She threw it on the floor and quickly found her husband ready for her. She was ready for him, too.

After they were joined she swayed back and forth atop him, "Isn't this better than your smelly old cigars and brandy?"

Michael gripped his wife by the hips and helped her move on him.

"Oh yes, he agreed. "It is, any day of the week."

She leaned forward and brought her lips to his. He knew she was about to come when she began to gasp and whine softly. He slowed to prolong the union.

"Don't you dare slow down if you know what's good for you, Michael Drieborg!" She took control and quickened her movement. He lost his control and came with her.

Later, they rested in one another's arms. Covered with perspiration, they had thrown the sheets back. Now, Michael ran his hand over his wife's enlarged belly.

"Do you think our little one will come on time?"

"I suppose so. I was right on schedule with Charles."

"We haven't talked about a name," Mike reminded her. "Have you given it any thought?"

"I have. But I've not seen one that captured my fancy. Have you?"

"I thought you would have some in mind. But since you haven't, I do have a suggestion."

"Oh? What would that be?" Interested now, Mary Jacqueline sat up beside him.

A bit alarmed at her reaction, Michael reminded her. "This is only a suggestion, sweetheart. But if it is a boy, I'd like to name him William; if it is a girl, Maxine."

"Why do you like those names?"

"The boy's name would be for the congressman, William Kellogg. He's looked after me ever since I saved Patricia from that runaway wagon back in 1862. Every time I've had a problem he's been there to help me. It's as though he regards me as the son he never had. In some ways I think I look upon him as another father. The girl's name was his late wife's."

Mary Jacqueline stretched out, alongside her husband. "I like the names and I like why you chose them, Michael," Mary Jacqueline agreed. "Let's tell him together; sort of ask his permission."

"Good, I think he'd like that."

Finished talking, Mary Jacqueline ran her hand down Michael's chest; then lower. "Mary Jacqueline!" Mike exclaimed in mock shock. "Such shameless things you're doing with your hand; and you a dignified pregnant lady."

"I'm a dignified lady when I must be, Michael," she teased him. "But in the dark of night in bed with my husband, I am shameless. Can you live with that, my love?"

For a second time this night she slipped on top of her husband.

This time, Michael used his hands on her. "What I must do for love."

Mary Jacqueline settled on him. "You poor thing; am I too much for you, Michael?"

"We'll see about that, young lady."

\*        \*        \*

It was hardly much past six in the morning. Congressman Kellogg was enjoying his morning coffee and last night's edition of the Daily Evening Star newspaper. Mike and Mary Jacqueline walked into the dining room.

"Good morning, you two," he greeted them. "What a treat to have you join me so early, Mary Jacqueline."

Once his wife was seated, Mike took a chair for himself.

"We have a question for you," Mary Jacqueline told Kellogg. "And we wanted to ask it together."

"My goodness; what could be so important to get you up this early, young lady?"

"It's about a name for our child."

Mike spoke up. "If the child is a boy, we want your permission to name him, William; after you, sir."

No one spoke for what seemed a long time.

"William?" Mary Jacqueline said softly.

He cleared his throat and spoke with some effort. "Yes, of course. I would be honored."

"If the child is a girl, though," Mike began.

Clearing his throat again he seemed to regain his composure. "Yes, what if the child is a girl?"

"We would like to give her your late wife's name, Maxine."

"Oh my," Kellogg said; pushed his chair back and stood. "Please excuse me." He hurriedly left the room.

Mike sat quietly, not knowing quite what to do. He saw a tear on his wife's cheek and realized their request had deeply touched the congressman and her, too.

Shortly, Kellogg reentered the room and walked toward Mary Jacqueline. She rose and stepped into his open arms. Tears flowed down her cheeks.

"Thank you so much, my dear," Kellogg said, tearing up once again.

Mary Jacqueline gently pushed back from the congressman's embrace.

"It was Michael's idea, William. He was the one who thought it out and wanted our child to have your name. I am here to assure you that both of us want it to be so."

Kellogg reached out his hand to Mike. "Thank you, my boy. Thank you both."

# THE NATIONAL HOTEL

Mike entered the National Hotel on his way to Kellogg's office. He noticed that there were armed troopers at the head of the stairs in the hallway to Henry's room as well as outside the door to his suite of rooms. Inside, Mike spoke to the Doctor.

"How is Henry, Doctor?" Mike asked.

"His temperature is elevated some. We're using cold compresses to keep it down and giving him all the water he can swallow. Fever is a common reaction to injuries of this type. He should be fine, though."

"I'm happy to hear it, Doctor. I had this type of wound during the war. I also had a high fever. In my case it was caused by dehydration and infection. A rural healer opened my wound so it could drain and applied a poultice. That eventually took care of the infection.

"Afterward, my temperature went back to normal. Of course, she also forced me to drink so much water I thought I would drown. Then it was only a matter of the wound healing and regaining my strength."

"Of course, I've heard of using a poultice. It seems to be a popular rural remedy for cuts, punctures and such. If you can obtain the ingredients for me, I'll try it on Marshal Austry if his temperature does not respond to our traditional treatment."

"I know just where to find the lady who treated me, Doctor. I'll telegraph her this morning and have the ingredients for you tomorrow. Can I talk with Henry?"

"You might catch him awake, Marshal. I gave him some laudanum for the pain earlier this morning, so he might still be sleeping."

Mike entered the darkened bedroom.

*My Lord! This room would never pass muster at Emma Hecht's house. The air is stale and smells like a sick room,* Mike thought.

He went to the window and pulled back the heavy curtain. The room was filled with light. Then he opened the window as far as it would go. The room was suddenly filled with the sweet air of the outside summer morning.

"Good morning, Henry," Mike said.

Barley awake, Henry blinked at the bright light from the window behind Mike.

"That you, Mike?"

"That's right, buddy. How are you feeling?"

"I'm groggy as all get out. My mouth feels dry and I've got a hell of a headache."

"That's what happens when ya get yourself shot, my man," Mike kidded him.

"Thanks! Got any other interesting news?"

"I have a question. Who shot you?"

"I'm pretty sure it was one of Baker's men," Henry told Mike. "The four of them wore masks, but I saw a police badge on the vest of one man. Each of them had on a dark blue suit just like they all wear, too. One rider had red sideburns; and, they all rode horses with a US brand."

"That's pretty observant, Marshal Austry. I sort of suspected something like that. So I kept Baker in custody. I'll be having a serious talk with him about this, shortly."

"Don't forget, Mike," Henry rasped. "Faute is all alone at the Farm. He has a few supplies, but not many. Besides those guys are looking for Parker. It would be risky to leave Faute alone out there."

"Good thought, Henry. Craig and Frank rode out there last night with a squad of soldiers. That should secure the situation."

"Where am I, anyway? Looks like a hotel room, not a hospital."

"Uncle Billy moved you here yesterday. The Doctor who operated on you is here as well, with a squad of troopers ta boot. Place is like a fortress. Your uncle threatened the Doctor with exile to the Dakota Territory if anything bad happened to you. You die and the poor man is in deep trouble."

"I'll try not to inconvenience him."

"Good man, Henry," Mike chuckled. "I have to get my detectives to work on the case of the wounded marshal. Can I get you anything?"

"Thanks, but I'm too dopey to enjoy much of anything," Henry revealed. "I know! Get me some ice to suck on."

"Even though it's July, Henry, I'll get some ice for you. But please, while I'm gone don't get into any more trouble."

"Very funny, Mike!"

On his way out, Mike encountered Sherman's provost marshal, Captain James Sowle.

"Captain," Mike greeted. "How is everything going?"

"It's pretty hectic, actually. I've got men here and out at your farmhouse. When the general sets a course, you get with it or get off the ship."

"Sherman hasn't changed his approach to command. Lincoln assigned me to the general's staff back in Savannah," Mike informed Sowle.

"Sherman didn't like it at all. But because it came directly from the president, he tolerated the order. I stayed out of his way as much as I could because I saw what he did to officers who did not jump as fast or as high as he thought proper. I think he approved of my work since he assigned his nephew, the wounded marshal you're guarding, to my troop."

"That's the general, all right," Sowle agreed. "And, believe me, if anything happens to Austry while I'm in charge, the Doctor isn't the only one who will be sent to the Dakota Territory."

# KELLOGG DINNER PARTY

In the parlor of his home, Congressman William Kellogg stood alongside his hostess for the evening, Mary Jacqueline Drieborg. They were waiting for the first guest couple to arrive for his dinner party.

"I hope everything will go well this evening," she said, wringing her hands.

"Mary Jacqueline," the congressman whispered. "Don't worry. I've hosted dozens of these dinner parties. You've done a superb job preparing this one; believe me. Everything will be just fine."

"Thank you William," she responded. "But this is our nation's capital. And it happens to be my first such party in Washington. So while I appreciate your assurances, I'm still nervous."

"Yes, it is Washington, my dear. And I'll have you know that you're fitting in very well."

"Thank you."

All the congressman's dinner parties were formal affairs. So, he wore a tuxedo and his hostess, Mary Jacqueline Drieborg, wore a pale blue full-length dress suitable for a lady six months pregnant. Her black hair was simply pulled back and tied with a blue ribbon. She also wore her husband Michael's wedding present, a pearl necklace with matching earrings.

The Kellogg butler, Adam would be the first to greet the guests. He had been with the Kellogg family for the last twenty years. This evening, he waited for the guests in the vestibule.

Because it was early July, he would not have overcoats to check. But each male guest would most likely wear a hat. And some of the ladies would have a wrap to wear home later. He would take both before showing them into the parlor.

Robert Stephan and his wife Mary Alice had arrived early. They were already in the parlor.

Mary Jacqueline gripped Mary Alice's arm for a moment. "Thank you for coming early. I'm so nervous."

"Stop that kind of talk, you hear," her friend commanded. "Everything will be just fine. The Washington Yankees I've met can't hold a candle to the ones who occupied my town back in South Carolina. You'll manage this bunch just fine."

Adam appeared in the parlor doorway, "The honorable Edwin and Mrs. Stanton, sir," he announced.

"Speaking of butchers," Mary Jacqueline whispered to her friend. "The head Yankee has just arrived. Excuse me."

Mary Jacqueline moved to Congressman Kellogg's side.

"Mr. Secretary," he greeted extending his hand. "You met my hostess Mrs. Mary Jacqueline Drieborg, at the president's dinner some weeks ago."

"A pleasure, Mrs. Drieborg," Stanton responded with a slight bow. "Allow me to present my wife, Ellen."

"We've met Mr. Secretary," Mary Jacqueline reminded him. "She and I met at the president's dinner."

"Of course; now I remember," he responded, a bit embarrassed.

"Excuse us, gentlemen." Mary Jacqueline reached out for Ellen Stanton's hand and led her aside.

"It is such a pleasure to see you again, Mrs. Stanton. May I offer you some refreshment?"

"Please call me Ellen. And yes, I would like something; cool if at all possible."

The two ladies moved toward a table with a punch bowl. "First, I want to thank you for sending over those maternity dresses. They're just what I needed."

"You're welcome, my dear. Would you like me to have my midwife call on you?"

"Thank you, Ellen. But that won't be necessary. My father is a physician in Philadelphia. I'll be going there soon to have my child."

Mary Jacqueline led Ellen across the parlor.

"I think it's too hot this evening for wine. My friend Mary Alice is serving lemonade. Would you like a glass with ice?"

"That sounds absolutely marvelous."

"It is," Mary Alice told her. "I can't claim to have made it, but I can promise that it's delicious."

Ellen Stanton took the offered glass. "Just where did you get that sweet accent, dear?"

"In Columbia, South Carolina, ma'am."

"Oh! My heavens, Mary Jacqueline! You've got someone here from the very heart of the rebellion! We'll be murdered in our beds for sure." Ellen Stanton gasped in feigned surprise.

Their laughter was interrupted by Adam, who appeared again in the doorway.

Adam announced, "The Honorable George and Mrs. Julian."

"Welcome, George," Kellogg greeted his congressional colleague. "It is so good to see you again, Laura. It has been too long."

"Yes, it has, William," she responded. "And it's entirely your fault, too."

"Not true, Laura. In spite of my past invitations, George has kept you all to himself."

"I'm not so sure, William. My spies tell me that you have another lady who has captured your attention; her name is work."

"Ouch! I'm afraid you've got me there, Laura."

Kellogg dodged further conversation by turning to his hostess.

"Laura, allow me to introduce Mary Jacqueline Drieborg."

"I see you're expecting, Mrs. Drieborg. When are you due?" she asked.

"Late August, actually," Mary Jacqueline told her. "I will join our two children at my parents' home in Philadelphia soon. My father is a Doctor you see. So I'll deliver there."

"I certainly wish you well, Mrs. Drieborg." Congressman Julian told her.

The guests' attention was drawn to the parlor doorway once again.

Adam announced another guest, "The Honorable Andrew and Mrs. Rogers."

"You're just in time, Andrew," Kellogg told him. "I had about given up on you. My cook is demanding that we go into the dining room or she won't be responsible for a ruined supper."

"Have you met my wife, Grace, William?"

"I have not had that privilege, Andrew. Welcome, Grace. In the future, you must not allow your husband to keep you such a secret."

*　　*　　*

Everyone was in the dining room.

"Before we begin, let us bow our heads and thank the Lord for our blessings," Congressman Kellogg asked his guests. "Michael, will you lead us in a prayer?"

"Bless us Lord for these thy gifts. And, for what we are about to receive from thy bounty through Christ our Lord, we give you thanks. Amen."

"Thank you, Michael."

After the women were seated, Kellogg announced. "Before you take your seats, gentlemen, please raise your wine glasses and join me in a toast.

"To the future; and to a united and prosperous America!" he proposed.

"Hear! Hear!"

*       *       *

Between the soup and the main course of ham and sweet potatoes, Secretary of War Stanton asked Michael a question.

"Marshal Drieborg," he began. "Several years ago, I recall signing the paperwork awarding you the Congressional Medal of Honor. Are you aware that we are in the process of withdrawing many of those awards?"

"I've heard, sir. Not much is secret in Washington," Michael responded. "Back in '64 when President Lincoln told me of the award, I protested that I had not done anything to deserve it. But he insisted that he had a role for me to play. He asked me to trust him and accept his decision and the award. Of course, I did.

"Now, political necessity has changed, I suppose. If you fellows want the medal he awarded me returned, I have no objection."

Congressman Julian had a question. "I imagine you realize, Marshal Drieborg, that you've created quite a stir around Washington with this investigation of yours."

"It's odd you put it that way, Congressman. I thought my men and I were conducting this investigation at the request of the House Judiciary Committee. Wouldn't that make it their investigation? What do you say, Congressman Rogers? Am I mistaken about that?"

"No, you're not, Marshal."

Julian's face colored some. "I mean the methods you're using. Were they approved by the Judiciary Committee?"

"We use the subpoena power we were given by your congressional colleagues to do the job requested of us. It's that simple. Even congressmen and members of President Johnson's administration are subject to it. Are you suggesting, sir that some people should be protected from the subpoena power of the Congress?"

Ellen Stanton interrupted with a question. "How is the investigation going, Marshal?"

"Very well, Mrs. Stanton," Mike responded. "We have a few more interviews to complete and a few loose ends to tie up. But we're nearing the point where we can make at least a preliminary report to the Judiciary Committee, ma'am."

The dinner plates were cleared and the dessert was being served.

"Will you give us any hints about the conclusions you've reached, thus far?" Secretary Stanton asked.

"Can I address this question, Mike?" Bob Stephan asked.

"I believe we've said enough, Bob. We'll be visiting with the secretary and Congressman Julian soon enough."

Mary Jacqueline asked Mrs. Stanton a question of a different sort.

"Ellen. You told me that two of your children were born here during the war."

"That's correct, Mary Jacqueline. With Edwin so busy, I must confess I was surprised that I even became pregnant once, let alone twice.." When the polite laughter died down, Mary Jacqueline continued.

"Michael and I met last year when he was sent to Charleston by the Congressional Committee on Reconstruction. I was born and raised in Pennsylvania, you see, but went with my husband to his home in Charleston after we married. He was a Doctor and died shortly after the war began, serving the Confederacy. I stayed there with his family.

"My first child was born during the war, just like yours, Ellen. Unlike you, though, I had to nurse my son in the root cellar of my father-in-law's home during the nightly bombardments from Union guns.

"Ellen. Did you know that the nightly shelling had no military purpose? It was conducted to punish the civilians of that unprotected city?"

"No, I didn't."

"But you knew that, didn't you, Mr. Secretary?"

"War is not a pleasant business, madam. As a matter of fact, it is ugly. Actions taken in wartime often seem unjustified later in the quiet of the victory once won."

Robert Stephan joined this conversation, too.

"I wasn't in Charleston during the war, Mrs. Drieborg. I was stationed in Columbia, the capital of South Carolina. Near the end of the war, the city was undefended when General Sherman's army approached. I was a member of the delegation that met with him outside the city.

"At that meeting, the mayor of the city assured the general that Columbia was an open city and that no resistance would be offered to his army's occupation. The mayor also presented him with a petition from the city council asking him to spare Columbia.

"Just the same, Sherman allowed the shelling of our city. The resulting fires burned for three days. If that wasn't enough, his troops were allowed to run wild, rape our women and pillage our homes. Another necessity of war, I suppose, Mr. Secretary?"

"My disagreements with General Sherman are well known, Mr. Stephan. Had I been present with him before Columbia on the occasion you mentioned, I would not have allowed such conduct. But unfortunately, I was not."

Kellogg stood by his chair and made an announcement. "Excuse me, everyone; I'm sorry but I must interrupt this stimulating conversation.

"Ladies, my cook Mable tells me that she has refreshments waiting for you in the parlor. Gentlemen, if you will follow me, I have brandy and cigars waiting for you in my library."

\*       \*       \*

In their bedroom later, Michael was helping Mary Jacqueline unlace her shoes.

"Thank you for helping me, Michael. I'm so big I can't even bend over to untie my own shoes."

He was thinking of something else. "Don't you think you were a bit tough on Stanton this evening, sweetheart?"

"Sit next to me, Michael, please."

He joined her on the bed.

"Try to put yourself in my place, darling. Like thousands of other women, children and men too old or crippled to fight, I was living in Charleston during the war. During that time, we all had to endure Union shelling of the city almost every night for weeks on end.

"I sat in a root cellar for hours night after night, shaking with fear that the next shell would crash through the house above me. Charles was with me, Michael. That's where our infant son slept most every night.

"Don't you think my anger about that is justified? Do you really think that I should have been silent when offered the chance to confront the man who allowed his agents to attack a defenseless city and it civilians?"

"Sweetheart," Mike responded, "I'm sorry for even suggesting that you were harsh this evening. Forgive me?"

"It depends."

"It depends on what?"

"It depends upon what happens after you join me in this bed tonight."

Much later, Mike was trying to catch his breath.

"Well? Did I earn your forgiveness?"

"Maybe."

Mike rolled on his side, facing his wife. "What in heck does 'maybe' mean?"

Mary Jacqueline pushed him on his back and moved atop her husband.

"It means, sweetheart, that the night is still young."

# THE DAKOTA TERRITORY

Sgt. Riley was going through mail pouch and telegrams that had just arrived from Fort Leavenworth.

There was a telegram for Corporal Jacob Drieborg and another for Corporal Kenny Hecht. The return address on each envelope showed that they came from the office of Congressman William Kellogg, Washington D.C.

"Captain Quinn, sir," Riley announced to the commander of this post. "I expect we've got an answer about the appointment of the Hecht and Drieborg boys to West Point. Each'a them has a telegram here from Washington."

"Get' em in here, Sergeant," he ordered. "We'll find out soon enough."

It wasn't long before both young men were standing at attention in front of Captain Quinn's desk.

"At ease, men," he ordered. "A telegram for each of you arrived. Riley told you about the West Point recommendation I sent your congressman last spring. These telegrams should contain the answer."

Both Hecht and Drieborg stood as they each read their telegram.

"Well?" Riley asked. "Don't keep me waiting here. What's he say, lads?"

Drieborg spoke first, "I am instructed to travel by the fastest means available and report to West Point Military Academy."

"What about you, Hecht?" Quinn asked.

"My telegram says the same, sir." Kenny answered. He handed the paper to Sgt. Riley.

\*   \*   \*

TO: Cpl. Kenneth Hecht US Army
FROM Congressman William Kellogg:

*Each year I am asked to give two deserving young men an appointment to West Point Military Academy. Based upon the recommendations of Captain Quinn and Sgt. Major Riley, I have chosen you for one of those appointments.*

*Upon receipt of this communication, proceed by the fastest means possible to West Point Military Academy.*

\*   \*   \*

"Congratulations, lads," Riley exclaimed slapping each on his back. "It'll be a week or so a'fore we can get ya goin east, though. In the meantime, I expect ya to continue yas duty as squad leaders."

"Yes sir!" Both men came to attention.

"Off with yas, now," Riley ordered.

Walking back to their barracks, Kenny brought up the subject bothering them both.

"What are you gonna tell your squad?

"Shit! I have no idea what to say," Jacob responded. "They already know the captain recommended us; Riley let that cat out' a' the bag two months ago. With both of us called to the captain's office at the same time, the guys are sure to figure something's up; gotta tell'm something, I suppose."

The two were not a step inside the barracks when one of the troopers shouted.

"Gather 'round lads," Bill O'Brien yelled. "Our two big shots are back."

"Crap!" Kenny Hecht mumbled. "Watch yer tongue, Bill."

"I warned ya, boys," Ben Shaw chuckled. "Power's gone to Hecht's head already."

Drieborg went over to Shaw's bunk. "I'll be doing some banging on that head of yours, Ben, if you're not careful."

"Take it easy, you two," Hans Krause urged. "We're just kidding ya some. Come right down to it, we're proud' a ya."

The men gathered around their two squad leaders and congratulated them with hugs and backslapping.

"Easy you guys!" Hecht shouted. "You're pounding me to death here."

Ben Clark asked the first question. "When do you leave for West Point?"

Kenny Hecht answered. "All we know is that the next wagon train east is in ten days. We're to head east with it and report as soon as possible for fall classes."

"I'll bet Riley expects you to keep doing your job, just the same." Hans said.

"He knows better than to leave you guys unsupervised," Jacob Drieborg kidded. "My Lord; ten days without our supervision and this barrack would be a shambles and your horses probably gone back to being wild."

*　　*　　*

"Ya know, Riley," Capt. Quinn said. "Good men, those two. I hate to see them go. I expect the men in their squads will miss them, too."

"Yes sir. They was boys when they got here but theys goin off as men. I'm proud a' the both' a them."

"So am I, Sergeant; so am I," Quinn agreed.

# The National Hotel

It was seven in the morning. The guards General Sherman assigned hadn't been relieved yet, but Mike was already looking in on his wounded deputy.

"Morning, Henry," Mike greeted. "How was your night?"

"I've got a fever, according to the doc." Henry told him.

Mike was puzzled though. "Why are you laying on your stomach?"

"It's because of that smelly poultice the doc put on my back last night. Kellogg's people got a telegram yesterday from their Grand Rapids office listing all the ingredients. The lady who took care of you back in '63 sent it. I guess it's the same stuff she used on that saber wound of yours back then."

"Phew!" Mike exclaimed. "It smells as bad now as I remember it, too."

"Before he put it on, the doc opened my wound. I wanted to hit him; that hurt."

"Believe me, my friend," Mike assured him. "You're lucky. Even though you had bled like a stuck pig when we found you, the wound wasn't very deep. So, the doc got the bullet out without having to cut you much. Now, if a little fever is your only problem, you'll be fine. Remember, get lot of sleep and drink a lot of water."

"That's easy for you to say, Mike. You don't have to breathe this smelly stuff."

"You're right. And, I'm leaving before I have to smell any more of it."

Mike paused. "One more thing Henry; if we pick up a few of Baker's deputies, I may have to bring them up here for you to identify. Are you up to that?"

"Sure. The guy with red hair should be easy. I'm not so sure about the others."

"Identify one and we have a chance at the others, Henry. See you later."

# DOCTOR MUDD INTERVIEW

Two uniformed soldiers led a man in ankle irons into Kellogg's office. The prisoner's hands were manacled to his waist and he had a hood over his head. One of his guards handed Peter Oppewall some paperwork.

"This is Dr. Mudd?" he asked.

"That's what it says on the paper, mister," one guard said. "All I know is he's one' a' the scum what killed President Lincoln. But under his hood, it could be Santa Claus for all I know."

"Why is this man chained like this?" he asked the guards.

"He was chained and hooded this way when we picked him up at the Old Capitol Prison," one of the soldiers answered. "Col. Wood told us we were told to keep him this way until you signed for him."

"Well, you've delivered him and I've signed your paperwork. So, give me the keys to all these chains and wait out in the hall. I'll call you when we're done with your prisoner."

"Fraid not, friend," one soldier insisted. "We've been ordered to stay with him at all times."

Oppewall stepped close to the soldier who spoke, "Look, 'friend'. I've got several armed United States marshals in the next room," Pete told him. "Unless you leave now, I'll call them. They would be all too happy to kick your ass down the stairs. So, what will it be, tough guy?"

The two soldiers left.

*     *     *

Pete put a chair behind the chained man.

Pete helped him sit back onto the chair and removed the hood. "I'll be back with Marshal Drieborg in a moment, Doctor."

"Thank you."

Pete led Craig Haynes and Mike into the room.

"Welcome, Doctor. We have many questions for you."

Craig removed the ankle chains and led Mudd into the meeting room.

"Before we begin, Doctor," Mike said. "Would you like to say anything?"

"First, I would like to thank you for getting me out of that hell-hole, Fort Jefferson. I believe I was sent there to die. I almost did, you know. Despite them, I survived the yellow fever epidemic we had there. But I don't think I could have survived that cell of mine much longer."

"You said, 'them', Doctor," Haynes said. "Who is, 'them'?"

"The people at the Department of War: that crowd."

"Who would be in that crowd?"

"Stanton, Holt and Bingham were the ringleaders. The members of the military court just went along."

Stephan asked, "In your opinion, Doctor, what did these people do to earn your anger?"

"My attorney told me that Prosecutor Bingham presented a conspiracy theory to the court which made anyone who played any role whatever in Booth's plot, co-conspirators and thus equally guilty of the president's killing. The court accepted Bingham's line of reasoning as a legal principle.

"In addition, Bingham convinced the court that there was never a plot to kidnap President Lincoln; that it was always an assassination plot. Since I had treated Booth's broken leg at my home during his escape, I was considered a co-conspirator, too. Consequently, I was guilty of murder."

Bob Stephan commented, "This is a good time to remind everyone that the records clearly show that War Department people knew early in 1865 of Booth's kidnapping plot. But Chief Prosecutor Bingham kept that information from the court while maintaining there was never a plot to kidnap Lincoln."

George Krupp resumed his questions of Dr. Mudd. "But you did know John Wilkes Booth?"

"Yes, I did," Mudd, admitted. "We were both part of a Confederate spy system. I don't think he did anything of note before the assassination. But yes, I knew him."

"According to the information we have, the officer who escorted you to Fort Jefferson was Captain George Dutton," Stephan told Mudd. "Do you remember telling him that you met with Booth at Washington's National Hotel in December 1864?"

"Yes, I do."

"So, in wartime, you traveled from your farm in Maryland to meet with Booth here in Washington."

"Yes, I did. We met for the first time in December 1864. The second meeting was in March of 1865."

"Why did you meet?"

"He wanted me to help him kidnap President Lincoln. I was sympathetic to his plan and agreed to provide a place for him to bring the president and enlist the help of another physician, Dr. Queen. We were to have fresh horses and provisions ready for the next leg of their journey as they fled with their captive to Richmond.

"We had a second meeting in early March to firm up arrangements. The kidnapping was scheduled for later that month. But as you know, it never happened. Booth never mentioned the possibility of killing President Lincoln at either of our meetings. I didn't see him again until he showed up at my home after he killed the president."

George Krupp continued, "When you met Booth in December and March or at your home after the assassination, did he mention any help he expected or had received from a member of the Union government?"

"Yes, he did," Mudd, said. "When he spent the night at my farm after the assassination, he said that a man from Secretary Stanton's office assured him that Lincoln would be unprotected at the Ford Theatre. Booth also told me he was promised that he would have no trouble escaping Washington."

"Why did none of this come out at the trial?" George asked

"If you read the court documents, Mr. Krupp, you will see that I wasn't allowed to speak. My lawyer didn't even ask that I be allowed to testify, either. He told me that with Booth dead my testimony was unsupported and thus would not be taken seriously by the court."

Mike broke into the conversation at this point.

"We're going to pause for some lunch. We might have more questions for you later today, Dr. Mudd. For now, though, Marshal Haynes will escort you to another room where you'll have lunch and wait until we call you back. Thank you for your cooperation."

"You're welcome, Marshal."

After Mudd was led out of the room, Mike turned to George Krupp and Bob Stephan. "Prepare a document, gentlemen, stating that we're not finished questioning Dr. Mudd and that we intend to keep him in our custody until further notice."

Frank asked, "Where we gonna put him, Mike?"

"I think there's room at the boardinghouse, Frank. We'll keep him there for now.

"George," Mike added, "Please send a request by messenger to General Sherman to assign a guard detail to our committee. With Henry injured and Bose out at the farm, we're a bit short-handed."

Before they adjourned for lunch, Stephan made a parting comment. "I have a few observations I'd like to make while everything is fresh in my mind, Mike."

"Go right ahead, Bob."

"After the assassination, the search parties found evidence that Booth had been hidden at the Mudd home and that the Doctor had treated his broken ankle. So, Mudd was arrested in the process, as were many others. Most were released, but not Mudd.

"They kept him in jail because during his interrogation, they discovered he had been part of Booth's failed plan to kidnap Lincoln in March of 1865, not kill him. Stanton and his people had known of the plan in early March but failed to take it seriously.

"Had Stanton's people taken the March kidnapping plot seriously it was first discovered, the president would have been more closely guarded thereafter.

"In fact, Stanton's people knew that Booth was the leader of the kidnapping plot. Had they arrested him and his team members when they found out about the plot, the Booth assassination probably would have been foiled.

"Therefore after the assassination, it would have been very embarrassing for Stanton and his War Department if the public were to find out about this failure to protect President Lincoln.

"So they had to deny a kidnapping plot ever existed, keep Mudd quiet and instead include him as a co-conspirator in Lincoln's killing."

Mike closed the meeting. "Thank you, Bob. Your summation makes sense. Now, gentlemen, let's get something to eat."

"This afternoon, I'm going to escort my wife to Philadelphia. She'll deliver our child there next month. I'll be back in town on Sunday evening and will meet you in Kellogg's offices on Monday morning."

"I thought we're interviewing Charles Chiniquy this afternoon, Mike," Frank said.

"You will, Frank. Craig will be in charge of the prisoners until I return. You other three can handle the questioning of the fellow.

"George," Mike continued. "You and Bob get a subpoena ready for the arrest of any member of Baker's Secret Service who has red hair. If you find him tomorrow, Craig, hold him for questioning at the Farm.

"On Monday we'll request a search warrant for all documents held by Baker's people that have anything to do with the assassination. But I don't want to present the search warrant before then. If they know about it before the search, they will probably destroy things that might be helpful to us.

"Craig," Mike continued, "I'm thinking we can use the redheaded police officer Henry identified to crack Baker. In the meantime, you and Bose stay with Parker, Mudd and the redheaded police officer at the Farm. You can supervise Sherman's people there, too.

"Stanton and his crowd are probably on guard, now. So, be especially careful. Frank, I don't want you or Bob to leave the boardinghouse this weekend; not even for church on Sunday. Be sure not to allow your wives to go out. Remember to stay armed. You and Pat stay home, too, George.

"Keep alert, gentlemen. I think we're approaching an important point in this investigation. I believe Stanton and his radical friends are beginning to sweat, some. Let's not leave ourselves vulnerable."

"Do you have any questions?" There were none.

"Wait a minute, Mike. I got one," Frank said. "What about you in all of this? Seems ta me that you are the most important part of this investigation; it might even fall apart without you. How are you protecting yourself and your missus on that trip to Philadelphia and back?"

"Thanks for your concern, Frank. But I think Mary Jacqueline and I will be all right," Mike insisted.

Craig wasn't convinced. "Wait just a minute, big shot. I think Frank has a point. If I were Stanton or any one of those other men worried about this investigation, I'd figure that if you were eliminated the whole business goes away; or is so damaged no one will pay any attention to the final report."

"We're under siege in this town, Mike. You know that as well as anybody. And, here you go gallivanting off on a public train with your wife like a couple of honeymooners without a care in the world. Think of your wife's safety, for God's sake!"

"Come on, Craig," Mike protested. "Aren't you making more of this than is justified?"

"As I recall, one Saturday afternoon in your quiet little town of Lowell, Michigan your pregnant wife, Julia, was killed by some hired thugs. You probably thought she was safe, too. Maybe you've forgotten that!"

"Whew!" Mike exclaimed. "That was a wake-up call. I have to admit, I didn't think of the current situation that way.

"All right, you have my complete attention. What do you suggest, gentlemen?"

Craig took the lead. "Off the top of my head, Mike, I have a plan.

"First: You and your wife do not board that train this afternoon for Philly. Instead, I'll get a Pinkerton man and a female agent to go in your place. That outfit will also supply two other agents to go with them disguised as passengers. We'll see what might have happened to you and the missus had you been alone.

"Second: The two of you will go to Baltimore this evening escorted by some of Sherman's troopers and board a train later tonight. Frank and Bob haven't got an assignment this weekend. They and their wives will go with you as the only passengers on a sleeper car. With the doors to the car locked from the inside, and with your Spencer repeaters, the three of you will take turns standing guard until the train arrives in Philadelphia; that ought to get you there safely.

"Lastly: The return trip will be Saturday night, without your wife. The Pinkerton agents will return tonight as you had originally planned for yourself. Frank and Bob will escort you back to Washington early Sunday morning."

"The rest of us have our assignments. We'll be fine until you return Sunday."

"Sounds like a good plan, Craig. Does that sound good to you, Frank?"

"Makes sense to me, Mike," Frank responded. "Sides, I never have been to Philadelphia. You think I could see the room where the men signed the Declaration of Independence."

"I would guess so. How about you Bob? You mind sitting up most of the night to guard this Yankee?"

"I don't mind at all, Mike," Bob retorted. "Ya see, my friend; you may be a Yankee, but you're my Yankee. An' no one fools with you if I can help it."

"Good. Now who wants a beer before we order lunch?"

*    *    *

While they were waiting for their orders to arrive, Mike had a side conversation with Craig Haynes.

"Craig," Mike began. "I received a report from the guys back at our Grand Rapids office this morning. It appears that some local Grand Rapids toughs roughed up Amos. Stan and Bill got Neal's cook to give up the names of the attackers and they picked them up."

"Even so, I don't figure it will amount to much legally, Mike," Craig figured. "It would be Amos's word against theirs. Besides, it'd be a Negro testifying against a couple of white men. Not even a Grand Rapids judge would take his word against theirs. So, what are you planning to tell Bill and Stan to do?"

"What they're doing already. Keep the thugs locked up for a few weeks. Solitary confinement would send a good message. These men are trying to get the sympathy of the veteran organizations in town. They're claiming Amos took his cook's job away from a veteran.

"But I sent the boys their service records and they've been spreading the word about their very bad service performance and the dishonorable discharges they received during the war. That ought to isolate them some, and give Amos some cover.

"George, my sister Susan and their partner, Mrs. Bacon, are all helping, too. They're using George's old bakery building to set Amos up in his own business. He lives upstairs, anyway. Amos will cook his soups there and sell them to George's restaurant. I gather Mrs. Bacon will obtain other customers for Amos, too."

"You're telling me that the cook's job the men we have in custody wanted, has been eliminated? But George still can sell the soup Amos makes, too?"

"That's about it, Craig."

"Sounds like a win. Chalk one up for the good guys, Mike."

"I hope so. You can read the entire report later, back at the office."

\*     \*     \*

"Can I help you, sir?" The desk sergeant in General Sherman's office asked.

"Yes, you can, Sergeant. I'm Federal Marshal Craig Haynes. I have a personal message for the general from Marshal Michael Drieborg."

"If you'll wait here, sir, I'll check with the general's aide."

It was only a few minutes before the sergeant returned.

"Go right into that office, Marshal," he told Haynes.

General Sherman rose from behind his desk.

"Good afternoon, Marshal. What's this about a personal message from Drieborg?"

Haynes handed the general Mike's message.

*       *       *

General: *It is becoming clearer as we proceed that there are men in the government who wish to stop this investigation I'm heading. I strongly suspect that Secretary Stanton is among them. I also believe what happened to Henry was only the first effort to impede and eventually end this inquiry.*

*Henry was involved in questioning and guarding a key witness we have in custody outside the city. I don't believe Baker would have sent his officers to search for him or to attack any of my marshals without Stanton's knowledge.*

*We need two squads of troopers assigned to our investigation to protect our witnesses and my marshals from attack.*

*We also believe my pregnant wife may be in some danger as well. So, I intend to remove her to Philadelphia. If you could provide us with an escort to the railroad station, it would be appreciated.*

*Please accept my chief deputy, Marshal Craig Haynes as my representative and have your troopers report to him.*

"Marshal Haynes," Sherman asked. "Did you read this memo from Drieborg?"

"No sir. But I'm aware of its contents."

"How soon do you need men from my Provost Marshal?"

"I need them immediately, sir."

"Captain Sowle!" the general shouted. "This is Marshal Haynes. You are to assign a platoon of troopers to him. You will accompany the troopers and supervise their actions in accordance with the marshal's orders. Do you have any questions?"

"No sir."

# GRAND RAPIDS, MICHIGAN

Bill Anderson ran the jail for the Federal District of Western Michigan. Anyone arrested for breaking a federal law was housed there awaiting arraignment and trial before a federal judge.

The two men Stan Killeen had arrested for the beating of Amos were in cells on different floors of this jail.

Stan looked in on one of the men. "When are ya gonna let me outa here?" the man shouted at him.

"Probably when you tell us why your buddy we put in another cell beat up that black guy, Amos the cook."

"I don't know nothin bout no beating. I ain't ever seen a nigger named Amos."

"Now, there ya go, getting me angry by lying," Stan told the man. "We know what your buddy Wilson did. He's already dead meat as far as we're concerned. We're goin ta leave him in solitary and let him rot.

"If you cooperate, Williams, you'll have a chance to avoid all that. Ya see, we already know that he did the beating while you watched. If you help us here, you'll get out of here a hell of a' lot sooner. Otherwise, you might just have to grow old in that cell like your buddy."

"It's beginning ta' smell like a' outhouse in here. I had ta shit on the floor, even. When can I get cleaned up?"

"Tell me what you saw yer bud do to that Negro guy. Then we can arrange something about getting you and your cell cleaned up."

"Go ta' hell!"

"Suit yourself, friend," Stan concluded. "Enjoy the smell."

Back in the office, Bill asked Stan.

"Any luck with Williams?"

"Not yet. I'll try Wilson later this afternoon. They're both cowards at heart. I'm pretty sure they'll both crack and rat on each other before long."

"What about the veterans' organizations in town?" Bill asked. "Are they still angry with George for hiring Amos instead of one of the so called veterans we have in our jail?"

"He and I are meeting with some of their leaders this noon. Join us, Bill. It should be fun telling them about the sterling characters they've been supporting. I even have that service record for Amos that Mike had Kellogg's office request of the War Department. It sounds so good, I'm jealous, some. Why don't you join us?"

"My relief gets here at noon," Bill told him. "You go on over to the restaurant. I'll join you as soon as I can."

*     *     *

At noon, the tables at the Cosmopolitan Bakery and Restaurant located on Monroe Street in Grand Rapids were filling rapidly. The most asked for item on the menu was one of Amos's soups. The second most ordered was his gumbo.

Several businessmen joined George Neal, the restaurant's owner at a table he reserved in a side meeting room.

"Welcome, gentlemen," he said. "Please have a seat. Tom, my waiter will take your orders. We can talk while we wait for the food."

Once all the orders were taken, one of the men was immediately in George's face.

"Neal! What's this horseshit about you hiring a nigger instead one of our veterans?"

George paused to get his temper under control.

"I don't recall any veteran applying for a soup cook's job. Just who do you think I turned down?"

Another man spoke up. "A fellow member of the GAR named Williams, I think."

George pulled out a file. "I keep all applications on file. Let me see, Williams is the name? Nope. My files go back over a year; no Williams asked for any sort of job.

"Any other members of the GAR apply here?"

"I think he got that name wrong," another man suggested. "I think it was Wilson who applied."

"Let me see," George said. "Sorry, no one named Wilson applied for a job here since I opened."

Stan Killeen and Bill Anderson joined the group.

"You all know our deputy marshals," George reminded everyone. "Since they have your valued members Williams and Wilson in their jail on assault charges, I thought you might like to hear of the sterling military record each of them earned during the late war compared to the service record of the man I did hire as a cook."

Bill went through the military service records of the two men he held in jail. After repeated convictions for stealing from fellow soldiers and finally, for cowardice in the face of the enemy, they were given jail time in a federal prison and dishonorably discharged.

Stan opened another service record. "This service record belongs to Amos, the cook George did hire. Amos had quite a different service record than Williams and Wilson. Amos served honorably with I Troop of the Sixth Michigan cavalry during their service in the Carolinas. After the war, he joined Marshal Drieborg's men in South Carolina working for the Congressional Committee on Reconstruction. When that group completed its work, he came to Grand Rapids and sought work as a cook.

"This is the service record of Amos, the cook all this fuss is about."

While Stan talked, everyone had been served his bowl of soup or gumbo and was eating heartily.

"By the way, gentlemen, the man Stan has been talking about, Amos prepared the meal you're eating. That's right, Charley, a nigger cooked the gumbo you're eating. Are you gonna throw up, now? What do the rest of you think about that?"

"Don't get all steamed up, George," the leader of the group urged. "We didn't know. I think I can assure you that neither the GAR nor any of us will give you any more trouble about this."

"I just wish you men would have had the common courtesy to come to me with your complaint instead of going off half-cocked and urging people to boycott my restaurant. After all, I'm a fellow businessman and a veteran who served honorably.

"Now that you know about the scum you supported and the hardworking man, Amos, who honorably served, I expect you to spread the good word about my restaurant and Amos just as vigorously as you damned me and him."

"Can I count on you do that?"

The men around the table looked at one another, and nodded.

# Kellogg's Washington Office

"Good afternoon, Mr. Chiniquy," George Krupp greeted. "Thank you for joining us."

"You're welcome, Marshal. I'm pleased to have this opportunity of sharing with you the evidence I have of the Catholic Church's conspiracy to kill our late and beloved president."

Charles Chiniquy was a slender man of about six feet. His black suit and clean-shaven face made him look gaunt and intense. As a Catholic priest in the early 1850s he had been an outspoken opponent of his bishop. Sued for slander, he employed Abraham Lincoln to defend him in civil court. Lincoln arranged a settlement for Chiniquy.

Subsequently, Father Chiniquy was stripped of his position as a Catholic priest. He then left that church in 1860 and became an outspoken opponent of the Roman Catholic Church.

He continued. "I must admit, however, that I'm surprised there are only three of you present. I had been led to believe that Marshal Drieborg and three other marshals would be present, too."

"Let me explain, Mr. Chiniquy," George responded. "Marshal Drieborg is on his way to Philadelphia to take his pregnant wife to her parents' home. Marshal Austry is in the hospital recuperating from surgery and our other two colleagues are on official business. But do not fear, sir. Your remarks will be recorded today by our clerk and will be included in our final report to the Judiciary Committee along with any supporting materials you present."

"Please remember, sir," George continued. "When you were sworn in just now, you promised to tell the truth and cooperate with this investigation. Any falsehoods or refusal to answer our questions will be considered contempt of congress. Do you understand that, sir?"

"Rather heavy-handed, I must say. But yes, I understand."

"Before we begin the questioning, would you like to make a statement for the record, sir?"

"Thank you, Marshal Krupp. I would."

"Gentlemen," he began. "Allow me to thank you for allowing me this opportunity to bring attention to the involvement of the Catholic Church in the killing of President Lincoln. It is something that has been ignored far too long."

"What leads you to believe the Catholic Church was involved, Mr. Chiniquy?" Bob Stephan asked.

"Your accent tells me that you are from the South, sir. Is that true?" Chiniquy asked.

"Yes it is."

"Early in the late war, it became obvious that the Pope recognized the Confederate government and supported the maintenance of slavery."

"It became obvious to whom, sir?" Frank Stanitzek asked.

"In my presence, President Lincoln showed me a letter from the Pope to Jefferson Davis. In that communication, the Pope did exactly what I have said. He supported the efforts of the Confederacy to establish a nation independent of the United States of America."

"You met with the president?"

"I met with him several times. He was well aware of the support given the rebellion by Catholics who lived in the North. He knew that Peace Democrats were mostly members of the Catholic Church. And, the opposition of Irish Catholics to the war was well known. All of this was very troubling to the president."

"He shared his concerns about Catholic citizens and the Catholic Church with you?" Bob asked.

"Yes. And, he told me that the Catholic Church posed a threat to the institutions and government of the United States as serious as that of the southern rebellion. He also told me that his life had been threatened by Catholics, on several occasions."

George Krupp interrupted. "Mr. Chiniquy, in preparation for your visit, we asked President Lincoln's Private Secretary, Mr. John Nicolay and his assistant, Mr. John Hay to verify your visits with the president. They couldn't find your name listed in any of their records. How do you explain that, sir?"

"Neither man would know because, I never had a formal appointment. The President just slipped me into his office when he had a moment."

Stephan asked, "They could not find a copy of the document about the Pope recognizing the Confederacy either. Can you help us with that, sir?"

"The president could not allow such a document to be published in the pro-Catholic press in the North. That would just encourage the anti-war movement sponsored in the North by the Catholic Church. I'm sure he destroyed it."

"Do you have any more information about Catholic Church involvement in the anti-war movement during the late war?" Stanitzek asked.

That comment was more than Chiniquy would tolerate. "My Lord, man!" he shouted, slamming his open hand on the table. "You are either a Catholic or blind. The Irish Catholics were behind the anti-draft riots in New York and Detroit. Resistance to the draft in other large cities was not of riot proportions, but there too, Catholics were prominently involved."

Krupp observed. "I was under the impression that the labor unions were involved in the Detroit riot. In fact, I think the Detroit Free Press reported that workers rioted over wages not keeping up with wartime prices and their fear of job competition from Negroes soon to be emancipated by Lincoln."

"Marshal Krupp," Chiniquy said, in obvious exasperation. "All one has to do is look at the leadership of the unions; they're all Catholics."

"Do you have anything else to add, Mr. Chiniquy?" George Krupp.

"There is a great deal more, I assure you.

"The Jesuit priests of the Catholic Church controlled Booth. It was Rome who directed his arm, after corrupting his heart and damning his soul.

"There is not the least doubt that the priests had perfectly succeeded in persuading Mary Surratt and Booth that the killing of Lincoln was a most holy and deserving work, for which God had an eternal reward in store. There is a fact to which the American people have not yet given sufficient attention. It is that, without a single exception, the conspirators were Roman Catholics."

Frank interrupted at this point, "Sir, our information is that Booth and Herold were Episcopalians, Atzerodt was a Lutheran and Powell a Baptist. Do we have that wrong?"

"Yes you do." Chiniquy insisted.

"Sir," Stephan asked. "Is it true that as a priest you had disagreements with your bishop that were so serious, you were stripped of your powers as a Catholic priest?"

"I took my bishop to court and Abraham Lincoln was my attorney. In fact, he won my case against the Church. They hated Lincoln for that. They couldn't get at him, then. But out of spite, they threw me out. They call it being defrocked. In protest, many members of my congregation left with me and I became a Presbyterian minister."

"One of the newspaper articles you sent us came from a newspaper in Minnesota," Stephan told everyone. "The reporter wrote that some Catholic priests at a monastery in the village of St. Joseph, Minnesota knew of the assassination hours before it happened."

"How could they possibly have known, sir?" Frank asked.

"Because their fellow priests from Washington were aware of the details of the plot. That's how, sir. You will note that a Protestant minister swore out an affidavit that a prominent Catholic from the village told him that priests from the local monastery told him at 6:00 PM on the 14th of April, 1865 that both Lincoln and Seward were dead.

"What more proof do you need to link the Catholic Church to the assassination of Abraham Lincoln? And remember, gentlemen, all of the conspirators were Catholics, too."

"Do you have anything more for this committee, Mr. Chiniquy?"

"Not at this moment, Marshal Krupp. But I hope you will call upon me should you need additional testimony."

"Thank you, sir," George responded. "You can be assured we will."

# THE FARM

Craig Haynes led two squads of Union troopers to the farmhouse where Bose Faute had holed up with Officer Parker.

"It's about time someone came out here," Faute told Haynes. "We're near out' a supplies and this Parker feller is drivin me nuts with his whining."

"A lot has happened since you and Henry brought Parker out here."

"Don' ya think I seen that when you didn't send out relief or food. What in hell is goin on?"

"Earlier in the week, Henry was shot while bringing supplies to you."

"What in tarnation!"

"How is he, Craig?"

"He'll be fine, I think. His uncle, General Sherman has round the clock guards and medical people taking care of him."

"He has a general for an uncle? It's not that red haired devil who burned near the whole' a Georgia a couple a years back? Don't tell me it's that Sherman."

"You got it Bose; the very same Uncle Billy."

"Well, I'll be switched. Know how the shooting happened?"

"Henry said he was leaving town last Sunday headed here; with your supplies, it turns out. Four guys with masks stopped his carriage. They started shooting and he got hit in the shoulder by a stray one."

Bose stood in the doorway. He laughed to himself and slapped his knee. "We'll I'll be a monkey's uncle."

"What do you find so humorous, Bose?" Hayes asked.

"Never thought I'd be happy to see Yankee troopers all 'round.

"Who else ya got with ya, Craig?"

"That's Dr. Mudd. He came in yesterday to testify. We weren't done when all this trouble came, so I just brought him along; one less loose end flapping around seemed to me. The other guy you must recognize. That's Parker's boss, Mr. Richards."

"Is this darned thing getting complicated, or what?" Bose exclaimed.

"What about my ol' lady? She all right?"

"She's fine. She's at the Krupp house this weekend," Craig assured Bose.

"She and Pattie Krupp seem ta' be getting along pretty well, aren't they, Craig."

"They sure seem to be. It's mighty strange, too. One lady city bred and the other country-raised."

"Sort' a like in the war when I served with men I'd a gone outa my way to avoid a' fore the fightin started. But fightin together forces men to work together. It seems that way with Ethie and Pattie, too."

"How long we gotta stay holed up here, anyways?"

"Mike and the others will return early tomorrow morning, Bose," Craig told him. "We'll pack up and meet then at 5 AM at the train station. Our escorts will take our prisoners along with Mudd to the prison. We'll go to the boardinghouse. We might even get a few hours of shut-eye."

"Ya', could be right," Bose added. "After all, tomarra is Sunday."

# TRIP TO PHILADELPHIA

Posing as Michael Drieborg and his wife Mary Jacqueline, a man and woman from the Pinkerton Agency boarded the train bound for Philadelphia. The female agent was even disguised as pregnant. Two other couples, also armed Pinkerton agents, were in the car posing as passengers, too.

"You look rather fetching all pregnant looking, Linda." Actually John Gostomski didn't think she should even be part of this assignment. He didn't think any females had a place in detective work; women belonged in the home. His boss Allen Pinkerton did not agree. But that didn't keep John from admiring the beauty of his dark- haired companion.

John had an extensive background in security work. After serving in the Union army during the war he worked as a watchman for the Pere-Marquette Railroad Company and lived in Detroit. The publicity surrounding his killing of an armed thief in the Detroit railroad yards brought him to the attention of Alan Pinkerton. John accepted a job offer from Pinkerton to join his detective agency at a big jump in pay. That was a year ago. Now, he usually was the man Pinkerton sent if the job involved the railroad.

"Why, John," she retorted, "That's the nicest thing you've said to me in weeks.

"I just wish I had had the pleasure."

John had nothing against women, especially this woman. In fact, he and Linda had often enjoyed one another's company when not working. Instead of wearing disguises, on some occasions, they didn't wear anything at all.

"You see yourself as a father, John?"

"As a matter of fact, I do."

"With me as the mother, I suppose!"

"Now that you mention it, Linda, yes."

"That is a subject for discussion in a more private setting, don't you think? Right now, I suggest we pay attention to our work, John. The train is about to get under way. Remember, Allen told us that if we're going to be attacked, it will most likely be shortly after the train leaves this station."

"You have any other reminders for me, Miss Birkholz?"

"I'll let you know."

"I'm sure you will."

The train had been underway for almost thirty minutes. With the windows closed and the shades drawn the agents could not see the passing landscape. They had opened the ceiling vents for ventilation, however.

Suddenly the thud of footsteps on the roof of the car could be heard. Alerted, the agents looked to the closed doors at each end of the car, their weapons ready. Instead, smoke bombs were dropped into the car through the roof vents.

"Raise the windows," John shouted through the smoke that filled the car. "Watch the doors!"

No sooner than the order was given, bullets were flying into the car through the broken glass of the door windows at each end of the car. Although blinded by the smoke, the agents seated against the wall at opposite ends of the car returned fire toward the door furthest from their position.

As quickly as they had started firing, the attackers stopped, and fled. But less than a minute later, two hand grenades exploded inside the car.

"Everyone report!" John shouted. "Mary's been hit. I don't know how badly, though. She's bleeding a lot," her partner reported.

"I'm ok," Bill shouted from the opposite end of the car. So is Margaret. We're just shaken up by the grenades."

"What about Linda?" Richard asked.

"She's unconscious. I see some blood on her cheek. It might be from the blast. I honestly don't know what her condition is at this point.

"Listen up, you two! Blankets are stored above the seats. Get them and put out the fires. Do it, now!" John directed.

As soon as the fires were extinguished, John gave another order. "Close the ceiling vents and reload your weapons. They might just decide to return. John, you and Bill stand by the door. Get out your sidearm. I don't want anyone sneaking up on us again. Margaret, you look after Mary."

*Shit! I should have checked those vents; was distracted by Linda. Damn it all!*

"Shouldn't we go after' em, John?" Richard asked.

"No! We were ordered to act as decoys and secure this car, nothing more. So, that's what we'll do."

The train rumbled on toward Philadelphia.

# Washington Boardinghouse

After dark, a six-passenger carriage and ten mounted troopers arrived at the boardinghouse where the Drieborg team and their wives were housed.

Bob Stephan and his wife Mary Alice and Frank Stanitzek and his wife Peggy hurriedly moved from the house to board the carriage. Aside from weapons, the only baggage they carried was a carpetbag for each couple.

"I feel badly about leaving Ethie here alone," Peggy said.

"She'll not be here, Peg," Bob reminded her. She'll be fine at the Krupp home. We have a squad of men to take her there and to stand guard until we return."

"And what of her husband Bose and Craig Haynes?" Mary Alice inquired. "They're all alone at that farmhouse of yours."

"I've told you a dozen times, dear," Bob said. "We've got six men or more guarding that place. Our Parker and Baker, our prisoners and Dr. Mudd are there under guard, too."

A few minutes later, they all arrived in front of the Kellogg home. Mike Drieborg and Mary Jacqueline quickly moved to the carriage and boarded.

"Any trouble getting here?" Mike asked.

"None at all, Mike," Frank told him. "I never thought in a million years I'd be guarded by a bunch of Yankee troopers, and be pleased to have them doing it."

"See? We're not all bad, Frank," Mike kidded him.

"Well, maybe." Frank grumbled.

"Oh, yes. Before I forget, a telegram was delivered here not an hour ago. The train arrived in Philadelphia carrying the decoy agents. The Pinkertons were attacked shortly after the train left the station this afternoon. The attackers dropped smoke bombs through the ceiling vents, fired into the car through the doors, and then threw two grenades into the car before they fled. One of the female agents is still unconscious and another agent was wounded, but is expected to recover."

"Oh, my goodness," Mary Alice said.

Mike continued. "Had the attackers known we were not on that train, they never would have attacked. So, I think it safe to assume the assailants still believe we were the passengers on that car. That means we should get to Philadelphia without a problem."

Mary Jacqueline squeezed closer to her husband. "I hope you're right, Michael."

# PHILADELPHIA

Mike was right. There was no attack and the train arrived in Philadelphia on time. It was two in the morning and still dark as the train slowly pulled into the station. Mike could see Dr. Miles Murphy waiting on the platform, with his dog Irish at his side.

Mike stepped onto the platform first. His two deputies followed him off the train. With their rifles at the ready, the three men immediately surveyed the area before they returned to the train and helped their wives down to the station's platform.

Dr. Murphy came forward and gave his daughter a reserved kiss on the cheek. He shook Mike's hand.

"I suppose all this armed caution is about your switching trains?"

"Yes sir. It is. There are some powerful people in Washington who do not want us to complete our work. We're just being careful. I think we ought to move off this open platform, sir and away from the station. This is too exposed."

"Is my family in danger, here, too?"

"I'm the one they're after, Doctor," Mike assured him. "As soon as I leave this evening, I believe I'll take any danger with me."

"We can only hope, Drieborg. Let's get Mary Jacqueline to the house. You've put her through a great deal getting here, Drieborg. For her sake and the baby's, I want her in calmer surroundings as soon as possible. It appears that means, away from you."

"For once, Doctor," Mike said, "I agree with you."

*     *     *

It wasn't long before Mary Jacqueline and Mike had arrived safely at her parents' home. The others went to a downtown hotel.

Her mother met them inside with a hug and a few tears.

251

"I'm so happy you're both here safe and sound," she told them. "I worried so."

"Is that you, Momma?" Charles called from upstairs.

He and Eleanor came running down the stairs and virtually flew into Mary Jacqueline's arms.

"I'm so glad you waited up for me," she said. "When did you two grow so big? You nearly knocked me down a minute ago. Give your father a hug too, children."

"Papa!" Eleanor shouted, hugging him.

Charles got in a boy-type hug. "Hi Mike."

Mike set his rifle aside. "That's not a real hug, Charles," Mike said. "This is a man's hug."

"Wow Mike; you practically pushed all the air out of my lungs."

Mike set Charles down and picked up Eleanor. She put her arms around his neck and rested her head on his shoulder. They held one another like this for a minute or two. "I missed you, Papa," she whispered. Mike couldn't help but tear up some.

"Hey, Mike!" Charles said. "Why do you have a rifle with you?"

"We'll talk about that in the morning, young fella. Do you realize that it's still the middle of the night? I'll bet you two kids haven't slept a wink. Come' on everyone. There are a few hours left till sunup. Let's get to bed."

"Aww! We want to stay up with you and Momma." Charles complained.

Mary Jacqueline got into the conversation at this point. "Who said your father and me were staying up? You heard him, you two. Upstairs to bed it is, for everybody."

# KELLOGG'S WASHINGTON OFFICE

Pete Oppewall walked into the congressman's private office.

"Sir, can I have a moment?"

"Yes, Pete. What is it?"

"A messenger just delivered this from Congressman Boutwell, sir."

After reading the note, Kellogg rose and left the room. "I'll be in Boutwell's office if you need me."

As Chairman of the House Judiciary Committee, George Boutwell had a much larger office than Kellogg; more elegantly furnished, too.

One of Boutwell's aids recognized Kellogg coming through the door.

"Good afternoon, sir. Go right into the committee room. Congressman Boutwell is expecting you."

"Thanks for coming, William," Boutwell greeted. "I think we're all here. So, we can begin."

It was not unusual for congressional committee meetings to be called without much notice. But he didn't see any Democrat members in the room. So, this meeting had to be a Republican caucus session called in response to some unforeseen event.

"I've called you here to discuss the Drieborg matter."

*The Drieborg matter; what the hell is talking about?* Kellogg sat bolt upright.

"Now, don't get you're dander up, William," Boutwell asked. "I may have phrased that poorly. I just want to review where we are on the investigation we asked him and his marshals to undertake."

Congressman Bingham spoke. "I don't think anyone in this room questions the purpose of the overall investigation. But it appears to some of us that the methods used by Drieborg are pretty heavy handed."

It was Kellogg who interrupted at this point. "Hells bells Bingham. I'd be embarrassed too if, like you, I had been cuffed, hooded and locked in a closet for defying a legitimate summons of a congressional committee to answer some questions."

Bingham snapped, "I told all of you we'd get nowhere with Kellogg. Drieborg's his man, after all. Just get on with it, will you? Tell him what we decided."

"Yes, George, tell me what you decided." Kellogg urged.

"Yes, of course," the chairman agreed nervously. "I've decided to call an end to investigating the various Lincoln assassination theories. After all, the committee of the whole has voted to accept the president's proclamation that Jefferson Davis and others in his government were behind the assassination. That should be enough."

"You've decided, George?" Kellogg asked.

Boutwell corrected himself. "Actually, the members of the Judiciary Committee decided, William."

"And when, pray tell, did they do that? I know were still technically out of session. So, many of our colleagues have left Washington for the summer."

Once again Bingham interrupted. "You know how it works Kellogg. Messengers or telegrams were sent around to request the vote of each member on this matter."

"Strange, that I never received such a request," Kellogg told them.

"Messages get lost. That happens occasionally. You know that," Congressman Lovejoy reminded Kellogg.

"Were the Democrat members of this committee polled as well?"

"I don't have the vote totals in front of me, William. So I can't tell you, exactly," Boutwell claimed.

Everyone silently watched Kellogg write on a notepad and then directed one of the committee's clerks to take the note to his office for his office manager Peter Oppewall.

After the clerk had left the room, Kellogg addressed his colleagues.

"Gentlemen; if you actually try to squash this investigation, let me tell you what I'm going to do. First, I've just directed my aide to notify all the Democrat members of this committee of your intended action. Second, he will make an appointment for me with the President. Those Democrats still in town will be invited to attend that meeting. It is then my intention to go public with or without their support. I intend to ask the president to authorize the continuation of the investigation by executive order, and to notify the press that he had to take that step because of your attempt to squash the investigation."

"You wouldn't dare, Kellogg," Bingham shouted.

"Watch me."

"William," George Boutwell cautioned. "You're in the minority on this. Think of what you're doing."

"I would listen to your chairman, Kellogg," Speaker of the House Colfax urged.

"Think of what I'm doing? My Lord, George! The Democrat press will savage you and our party. And, this is an election year, for God's sake. Think of what I'm doing? You can stick your head in the sand, but I'm not going down with you."

"Thinking of you first, eh Kellogg?" Bingham said sarcastically.

"I'm not the one who is afraid of this investigation, Bingham. Some people are though. One of Drieborg's marshals has been shot on duty and men with rifles and grenades attacked the railroad car on which another marshal was thought to be riding with his pregnant wife.

"The marshal who was shot is the nephew of General Sherman. As a result, troopers under his command are now guarding the wounded young man. Lafayette Baker is in custody and members of his police force are being sought for the shooting.

"Another policeman, a man named Parker is in custody, too. You might remember, gentlemen that it was Parker who left President Lincoln unguarded on April 14th. I wonder if he has something to say about his role in the assassination and about the people who put him up to leaving his post. What is clear is that there are people of influence in this town who are worried about such a revelation and want this investigation stopped. Are you among them, Bingham?"

"I resent that implication, Kellogg!"

"No implication intended, Bingham. We'll see how you'll come out in all of this, won't we.

"George," Kellogg continued. "I suspect you're being pressured by Bingham, Butler, Holt and the War Department people on this. If you give in to them and shut this investigation down, even the Republican press will blame you personally. They'll say Rep. George Boutwell is trying to cover-up evidence of some sort.

"The information gathered so far will come out anyway, you know. So, how can it hurt to give Drieborg another week or two to finish his report?"

Bingham pounded his fist on the table. "Damn it, George! Show some backbone for once. Shut this witchhunt down and protect your own people!"

"Well, George," Kellogg said very quietly. "What's it going to be? Do I go public? Do you take the heat for a cover-up? Or do you give Drieborg and his team another two weeks to get us a report?"

"But you already told the Democrats to meet with you," Boutwell reminded everyone.

Kellogg smiled. "That was a blank piece of paper your clerk took to my office, George. The next one won't be, though."

"Very well, William," committee chairman Boutwell decided. "You've got your two weeks."

# PRESIDENT JOHNSON'S OFFICE

President Andrew Johnson looked up from behind his desk. He watched as Edwin Stanton entered his office.

The president rose and moved toward his Secretary of War. As he came around his desk, he reached out his hand in greeting.

"Nice of you to come, Mr. Secretary," Johnson said as the two men shook hands. "Please, have a seat."

"How can I help you, Mr. President?" Stanton asked.

"I'm just a bit puzzled about this memo you sent me. Why in heaven's name do you intend to remove General Sherman from his current post?"

Stanton sat up straight, obviously irritated. "Are you questioning my authority to assign members of the military, sir?"

"I am aware of the authority you exercise, Mr. Secretary. Do you recognize that your actions are subject to the authority of the president?"

This time, Stanton sat quietly for a moment before answering.

"It was not my intention to question your authority, sir; only to remind you of mine."

"Of course, Mr. Secretary," Johnson responded mildly. "Why do you wish to remove General Sherman?"

"I am reassigning him because he has assigned members of the military to inappropriate duties, of late."

"Oh, you mean his use of troopers to guard his nephew who was ambushed and shot by members of Colonel Baker's National Detective Police. It appears that the young man was in the process of carrying out his duties as a federal marshal."

Stanton straightened up in his chair again. "That is preposterous, sir!"

"Or are you referring to Sherman's use of troopers to protect the other members of Drieborg's team?"

"Mr. President!" Stanton shot back. "Are you suggesting that I had something to do with any of this?"

"Was I?"

"Let me see. You convinced President Lincoln to appoint a Mr. Lafayette Baker to be the head of the National Detective Police. So, it would seem that Baker is your man."

"He is no such thing, I assure you."

"We also know that Superintendent Richards of the Washington Metropolitan Police Force, another one of your boys, was given the responsibility of protecting the late president. We all know how that turned out."

Stanton stood. "I don't have to put up with this utter nonsense!"

"No you don't, Mr. Secretary," Johnson said calmly looking up at him. "You can resign. Or, you can sit down. Choose now, sir!"

Stanton sat.

"One of the men who attacked Sherman's nephew has been identified and is being sought as we speak. I'm confident when he is questioned, he will identify his three colleagues and the man who gave them the order to find a fellow officer, a Mr. Parker.

"You might remember Parker as the man who left his post at Ford's Theater on April 14th and thus allowed Booth unimpeded access to Lincoln's box. You were in charge of all aspects of the assassination investigation and trial of the co-conspirators were you not, Mr. Stanton?"

"Yes I was, sir."

"Your investigators never did even ask anyone how Booth knew Parker would leave his post or why he left it at all. And Parker was never punished for this dereliction of duty. He was not even reassigned by his superior, your man Mr. Richards. Odd, don't you think, sir?

"Now, Officer Parker is one of the men protecting me. That fact is certainly not very comforting. Are you expecting lightning to strike again, Mr. Stanton?"

"Really, sir," Stanton stammered. "I am not in a position to respond to such questions."

"But maybe Mr. Richards will be. Possibly he will tell us why Officer Parker was never punished for an obvious dereliction of duty."

"I'm sure I don't know, Mr. President."

"Of course, Mr. Secretary," Johnson continued. "You would not have known that your man Baker would have ordered his men to find and kill Officer Parker either, I suppose."

"I certainly would not, Mr. President."

"We'll see about that, won't we though, Mr. Secretary? Baker's men will be rounded up soon. And, I believe Baker is already in custody. We'll see just what your man has to say."

"Where was I? Oh, yes. I'm sending you a written order not to remove General Sherman from his current post or impede his efforts to protect the members of Marshal Drieborg's team. In fact, I am issuing an order directing Sherman to do just that.

"Also, a provost marshal unit under his direction will take over responsibility for the Old Capitol Prison. Mr. Wood will no longer have that responsibility."

"But Mr. President," Stanton interrupted. "I'm sure we have US Marshals in the Justice Department who can be assigned to all these tasks."

"That may be, Mr. Stanton," the president said. "But I've told you of my decision and my instructions stand.

"And, Mr. Stanton," Johnson concluded. "General Sherman will report directly to me until this matter is resolved."

The president stood.

"I think that will be all, Mr. Secretary," Johnson turned his back on Stanton. "You can return to what remains of your duties."

# Willard Hotel

Secretary of State Stanton was pacing around a private sitting room at the Willard. It had only been a little more than an hour since his confrontation with the president. He had no sooner left the president than he sent messages to several men to meet him here.

Chief Judge Advocate Joseph Holt was the first to appear.

"It's about time, Holt. You've had my message for almost an hour."

"Excuse the hell outa me, Stanton. Aside from protecting your ass, I've got honest work to do."

"Don't get cute with me, mister," Stanton snapped. "One word from me and your sweet deal is over. Then you're back on the street chasing ambulances for legal fees once again."

Congressman Butler had come in the room during this exchange.

"That's all we need, you two; fighting amongst ourselves," he observed.

"What's so all fired important that you had to pull me away from a private lunch with the most beautiful young thing I've seen around here since we threw Mrs. Greenwood into jail as a spy for the South?"

Rep. John Bingham joined the three men already in the room.

"Have I missed anything?" he asked.

"Not really, John," Butler told him. "Just these two frightened birds losing their nerve."

"Why are we here, then, Stanton?"

"The president is on to something. I'm sure of it. He called me into his office not more than two hours ago. He's assigned Sherman to protect Drieborg and his men and he's given over control of the Old Capitol Prison to a military provost unit of Sherman's."

*Michael J. Deeb*

"Weren't you going to assign Sherman to some outpost west of Fort Leavenworth?"

"Yes. I had already cut the orders. Somehow Johnson got wind of it and ordered me not to, in writing."

"Do it anyway," Butler insisted. "You cut those orders before your meeting with Johnson. So you can claim to have legitimately issued them. By the time everything is sorted out, we'll have Drieborg out of our hair, one way or another, and we'll be home free."

"Easy for you to say, Butler," Stanton snapped. "You're an elected official; a congressman ta'boot. But I happen to serve at the president' pleasure. He still believes my man Holt and I tricked him into hanging Mary Surratt. And, he knows Holt lied to him about Jeff Davis and the assassination. So right now I suspect he's not too pleased with me."

"Relax for God's sake, Stanton. We've got the votes in both houses to stop him from dismissing any cabinet member the Senate has approved. He's not going to fire you unless he's willing to run the risk of impeachment."

"Butler, I've got two written orders on my desk which say otherwise. One directs Sherman to protect Drieborg's team and take over the running of the Old Capitol Prison. The other directs Sherman to report directly to the president, not me."

"Has Sherman received either your order reassigning him or the president's, taking control away from you?"

"I don't think so."

"Then send yours by special messenger as soon as you return to your office. After lunch you can mail Sherman the president's orders.

"By God, get some backbone, Stanton! You need to act, not talk. As for me, I still have a chance for a much more pleasant meeting than this."

# PHILADELPHIA

Inside Constitution Hall, the Stephans and the Stanitzeks were standing silently in the main hallway.

"Imagine, Francis," Peg Stanitzek said. "Mr. Lyman Hall from Georgia met in this very room with representatives from all thirteen colonies to discuss breaking from England."

"Don't' forget George Walton and Button Gwinnett, Peg," Frank added. "They were signers of the Declaration of Independence, too."

"I've not forgotten," Peg assured him. "Just don't you forget that those three men from Georgia worked rather well with all those Yankees."

"Thank you dear. Your point has been heard and understood."

"Mary Alice," her husband Bob Stephan asked. "Do you remember who represented South Carolina in this very room?"

"Are you kidding, Robert? Like every kid in the state I had those names drilled into my head. They were Mr. Thomas Lynch, Mr. Arthur Middleton, Mr. Edward Rutledge and Mr. Thomas Heyward Jr."

"Oh, yes," Robert added. "For heaven's sake, don't forget the Jr. after Heyword's name. In primary school I got my knuckles rapped one time for leaving it off."

"Sort of ironic, isn't it, Frank?" Robert said. "The representatives from both the Southern and Northern colonies agreed to the language of the declaration just about the time of day that Lee's Army of Northern Virginia charged up Cemetery Hill at Gettysburg. Wouldn't it have been something if Lee had won that battle and the Confederate States of America had gained its independence on the 4th of July?"

"That it would, Bob," Frank agreed. "But there's no sense pining for a lost cause. I'm learning to deal with the present situation."

"Let's go see the Liberty Bell," Mary Alice suggested. "Afterward, I want to have lunch at the City Tavern. I'm told that George Washington and Thomas Jefferson often ate there when they were in town."

"We can go to Christ's Church and see Franklin's grave after that, Mary Alice," Peg added.

"We don't have to pick up Mike at his in-laws' house until ten tonight. That'll give us plenty of time for a nap before supper," Frank told everyone. "The people at our hotel can direct us to a good restaurant."

"What's this nap business, Francis?" Peg kidded. "Since when have you needed a nap?"

"For heaven's sake Margaret; I don't need to take a nap. I want to spend some time alone with you."

"Sounds like a great idea for me, too," Bob Stephan said. "What do you think, Mary Alice?"

"Oh, my goodness," Mary Alice chuckled, blushing some. "I agree, Robert."

*     *     *

Back at Dr. Murphy's home, the Drieborgs were up and about having a late breakfast.

"As I understand this, you will be leaving for the train station shortly after dark this evening."

"That is the plan, Doctor," Mike responded.

"Aww, Mike," Charles complained. "Can't you stay?"

"I have to finish my work in Washington, son."

"When will you be back, Papa?" Eleanor asked.

"I can't say, actually. But it shouldn't be too long. I think my work will be finished before our baby is born next month.

"Tell me, children," Mike asked. "How is school going?"

Eleanor explained. "We don't go to a real school, Papa. We do our lessons at home, not at a real school like we did at St. Andrews back home."

"I thought you were going to St. Patrick's here in Philadelphia."

Charles jumped into the conversation. "We were, Mike. But they wouldn't let Helen study with us because she's a Negro. So, Grampa Murphy said we would do our lessons right here."

"A teacher comes here, every day almost. Mrs. Anderson teaches Helen, Charles and me reading, geography, history and spelling."

"And arithmetic, too," Charles added. "I like that the best."

Just then, Helen came into the dining room with some more hot coffee. She joined the conversation.

"Doctor Murphy sure toll those sisters over at St. Patrick's a thing err two. Jus the same, we doin jus fine here, Marshal. Not as good as back at St. Andrew cause there's no other kids for Eleanor and Charles to play with. But we doin jus fine with our teacher Miss Anderson; jus fine."

Ruth Murphy explained, "Miles really got upset over the school's refusal to allow Helen to attend St. Patrick's with the children. He created quite a stir about it. The pastor was so embarrassed he eventually begged Miles to allow Helen to join the children at St. Patrick's school after all. But he refused. We go to a different Catholic church, now too."

"I know Father can be stubborn, Mother," Mary Jacqueline said. "But in this case, I don't blame him. The children will be back at home and at St. Andrews school before Thanksgiving. Things will work out just fine, I'm sure."

"How about Miss Eleanor and Master Charles reads somethin fer you?" Helen suggested. "You be mighty proud' a dem how good dey read, believe me."

"Aww," Charles complained. "Do we have to?"

Mike told Charles, "You don't have to show us how smart you are, son. Eleanor and Helen will though, won't you?"

"Oh yes, Papa," Eleanor agreed. "Let me get my favorite book. I'll be right back. Come on Charles, you get a book, too."

"Oh, all right."

"How about you, Helen?" Mary Jacqueline asked. "Will you read for us, too?"

"I'd be proud to, ma'am. As long as you unerstan dat I don read as good as da children."

For the rest of the afternoon the two families sat around the table listening to the children and Helen read from their favorite book; do arithmetic homework and show off other things they had done under the stern eye of their teacher, Miss Anderson.

"I love your paintings, children. I knew you loved to draw, Eleanor. But I didn't know you could paint so well, Charles."

And so it went right up to supper.

*       *       *

Later that evening, Mary Jacqueline and Mike were alone in their bedroom. The children were in another bedroom, presumably asleep.

Lying side by side on their bed, they talked quietly between kisses.

"So much for you being home for supper each evening, eh Michael."

"I'm sorry about that sweetheart. But there's not much either of us can do about it."

"I know, Michael," she sighed. "I'm just sort of pulling your leg."

"I don't mind. And, I don't mind that other part of my anatomy you're pulling."

"Like that, do you?" Mary Jacqueline deftly slid on top of her husband and used her free hand to join them. "How do you like this, mister?"

"This is worth coming home for, believe you me."

"Don't you forget it either, Mr. big shot Marshal Drieborg." She began to move on him.

"Not a chance." He gasped.

*     *     *

Later, in the darkened room Mary Jacqueline rested in Michael's arms. The chimes on the hallway grandfather clock told them it was nine pm. It was time for Mike to get ready.

His very pregnant wife watched as he dressed. When he sat on the bed to put on his shoes, she rose and gave him a hug.

"You take care of my child's father, you hear?"

"Sweetheart; you can be sure that your child's father will return home safe and sound, soon."

Mike stood and Mary Jacqueline put on her robe to accompany him down the stairs to the front door.

Dr. Murphy was at the bottom of the stairway, waiting.

He held out his hand to Mike. "I'm proud of the work you're doing, Michael. Make sure you don't let those Black Republicans off the hook. Keep your foot on their throat until you get to the bottom of all of this dirty business."

"Sounds like the sentiments of a true Irish Democrat, sir." Mike joked.

"Well, maybe. I admit I never voted for Lincoln. But I respected his courage. If they helped kill him I want them to pay for it."

"I'll do my best, sir."

"You be sure you get back to us safely. You hear me?"

"Yes sir. I will."

Mike gave Mary Jacqueline a last hug and turned to go out the door into the night.

"Papa!"

Turning, Mike saw his daughter, Eleanor at the top of the stairs holding a doll to her chest.

He dropped his bag and bounded up the stairs to hug her in his arms.

"Don't go, Papa!" she begged."

"I have to, sweetheart. But I'll be back before you know it."

"I'm afraid that I'll never see you again."

"Please don't be frightened, sweetheart."

"I can't help it, Papa," She hugged her father tightly. "I'm afraid when you go out that door, you'll never come back."

"I'll be back, sweetheart. You'll see."

"You promise?"

"I promise."

At the bottom of the stairs, he handed little Eleanor to her grandfather. Mike noticed the tears on Dr. Murphy's cheeks, too.

"Don't you worry, son," Dr. Murphy assured him. "I'll look after all of them."

*This is tearing me up. I've got to get out of here. Look after them, Lord.*

He picked up his things and closed the door behind him.

# Washington Boardinghouse

It was ten o'clock the next morning. Mike and his companions had arrived in Washington just before dawn. The ladies were still in their rooms but the men were up and having a late breakfast. Henry Austry was the only member of their team missing. He was still recovering at the National Hotel. Mike had used Henry's boardinghouse room for a few hours of sleep earlier today.

Over coffee, Mike began the discussion.

"Just to bring you and Bose up to date, Craig," Mike began. "You and Frank were right to suspect an attack on my trip to Philadelphia. The Pinkerton decoys we sent in my place yesterday afternoon were attacked not ten miles out of town. Since we returned without incident, I suspect our enemies think their earlier attack succeeded."

'Let me bring you up to date, Mike," Craig cut in. "President Johnson stepped in and ordered General Sherman to use whatever resources he felt necessary to protect us and help us with this investigation. He also gave Sherman responsibility for the Capitol Prison. Captain Sowle and his provost marshals are there now. Parker, Baker and Dr. Mudd are in cells there. And I put Richards in a Capitol Prison cell, too."

"I'll bet he and Baker are fit to be tied."

Mike made an observation. "The Secretary of War usually has authority over all military personnel, like Sherman. For the president to step in like this means he is crossing swords with Stanton."

Haynes continued. "Word is, Mike, that Stanton was upset with Sherman for helping us. Sowle told me that he was about to demote his boss, Sherman and ship him out west to some frontier post. That's when the president stepped in and stopped Stanton. Now, Sherman is to report directly to the president, instead of to the Secretary of War."

"That is a major shift of power within the administration. I wonder if the president is aware of the Radical's fear of our investigation." Mike thought aloud.

"Sowle thinks so, Mike."

"All right, gentlemen. Let's pick up the pace. I've asked Pinkerton to assign his man, John Gostomski to work with our team here in Washington until Henry is back. He'll arrive tomorrow. As for present business, just where are we?"

"George, you start. Where are we with the warrants?"

"The warrants for the arrest of Baker's men are ready for us to go after them. The warrant allowing us to search Baker's office and take all his files dealing with the assassination is ready to be executed tomorrow. My team will hit those offices first thing in the morning."

"Who's going to be on your team, George?"

"I'm planning to use Frank and Bose."

Craig Haynes commented. "George, if Baker's people are on duty when you hit them with the warrant, you'll not have enough men for security and the search. You need at least two more men on your team."

"I think Craig is right, George," Mike said. "So, have Craig, Bose and Frank look for the red-headed police officer Henry identified. Bob will work with you on the documents. Do you think that will work?"

"Sure, Mike."

"Remember, all of you," Mike stressed. "While documents are important, nothing is more important than finding that red headed officer who was involved in Henry's shooting. When we have him in custody, I'm sure he'll turn on his three companions. Once they're in custody, they'll turn on Baker. And Baker is our best bet to get to Stanton and possibly other Radicals."

"Excuse me, Mike," Bose asked. "I thought Parker was our key witness."

"Parker worked for Baker, Bose. But we have no corroborating evidence from anyone else to support what he's told you about Baker. So we need the man who shot Henry."

"If you can't find the redhead at police headquarters tomorrow, Craig, arrest a few others and take them to the Old Capitol Prison. Scare them good. Maybe they'll give the red headed fellow up."

"George, can you and Bob put together a request for the calling of a grand jury in Washington? We need to bring charges against Parker as a co-conspirator in the assassination of Abraham Lincoln. Can you leave it open for the addition of other names should the need arise?"

"You asked two questions, Mike," George answered. "First, we can do the necessary paperwork tonight. The answer to your second question is no. But once a grand jury is impaneled it can be given additional responsibilities. So, if we see an additional need, the same grand jury can be given the additional assignment."

"Thank you for the legal education, George.

"After we're done here, I want all of you to accompany me to the prison. I need to talk with Baker and Richards. While I'm doing that Craig, meet with Sowle and ask him to have a squad of his men meet us at Baker's National Detective office quarters at seven am, tomorrow.

"Bose, you George and Frank visit with Parker. Take a rope with you, Bose. Make sure Parker sees you with it. Whatever you need to do Bose, I want him to give you more information about his meeting with Booth; things like the location and the date of the meeting. Also, get him to talk more about his absence from the president's box on April 14th. Just get him talking. Who knows what he may recall."

"George, I know you're sensitive about coercing a witness, but don't interfere with Bose. We need more information from Parker."

"I have a suggestion, Mike," Bob Stephan said.

"I hate to leave the ladies alone tonight. And George and I have a good deal of work to do on that grand jury request you want for tomorrow. So I propose that he and I stay here and work. By doing so, we can secure the house, too."

George added. "I agree with Bob. But my legal library is at my home. I don't normally do this kind of work in my practice, Mike. I really need references and such. I can find that type of thing in my library, at home.

"Since it's right on the way to the prison, I suggest the ladies be asked to go with us. Bob and I can work at my house and the ladies can stay there until you're finished at the Old Capitol Prison. Actually, I think the wives can all just plan to stay overnight at my place."

"Makes sense to me, George. Is there anything else?" Mike looked in particular at Haynes. Craig could usually smell out problems when no one else could. He didn't raise a question or make a suggestion. So Mike went on.

"I believe we're on the verge of something big, gentlemen. Given the recent attack that was made on the train, I believe the Radicals see it, too. Even the president senses we're about to uncover something.

"But we can't let up. We all need to stay alert and keep focused. So, bring your wives up to date on what we have planned, have them pack an overnight bag, get your weapons and let's get moving."

# STREETS OF WASHINGTON

It was already dark when Mike and his three men left the Capitol Prison. Walking the poorly lit streets, they headed to the Krupp residence.

"That meat they served tonight at the prison was not a good cut of beef," Frank told them.

"I thought it was some chewy," Bose agreed. "In the mountains, our beef's so tender, it melts in yer mouth."

"I wouldn't sell my customers back home the stuff we were fed tonight," Frank continued. "It not only was poor quality beef but it was badly prepared, ta boot."

"Don't want to make the meals too enjoyable for prisoners, I 'spec." Bose added.

"I was just saying," Frank began.

To the right of their sidewalk, a store's window glass shattered followed by the sound of a gunshot.

"Drop to the ground!" Craig shouted.

"Across the street," Mike pointed. "See that muzzle flash?" The globe of a street light shattered near them.

Craig was already returning fire with his Spencer rifle. The others joined him. Mike and Bose joined in with their rifles. Never having seen combat, Frank was some slower getting his rifle into action.

Mike had supplied his men with Spencer rifles when they joined him in Washington. A tube in the stock contained seven bullets. A man could chamber a shell and fire seven times without taking the weapon from his shoulder.

"Bose, follow me," Mike shouted. They rose in unison and ran across the darkened street. They set up positions to the right of the shooters, and resumed firing.

Suddenly, no fire was returned. Mike shouted to his men, "Cease firing." After a few moments of silence he told Craig Haynes. "Cover us, Craig."

The initial attack had come from behind several barrels. Behind them, two men lay dead.

Bose searched their pockets. "Neither of these guys has any identification on him."

Craig and Frank searched the street in both directions and then rejoined the others.

"The street is clear, Mike. It appears there were just two of them." Frank reported.

Craig asked, "Does either of them have red hair, Bose?"

He bent over and took off their caps. "No red hair on either of these guys, Craig."

"Good. We need a redhead who we can interrogate, not a dead one we have to bury."

"What do you mean, I can't see him?" Lucy Lambert Hale said with all the indignation she could muster. "I happen to be the daughter of Senator John Hale, and Marshal Austry's very close personal friend."

The front desk clerk looked at her with a blank stare. "I am happy for both of you, Miss Hale. But General Sherman has given very strict orders about the marshal. You are not on the list of approved visitors. So I am afraid I can't help you. You'll have to obtain a pass from the general's office."

"You've not heard the last from me, I can assure you."

"I'm truly sorry that I can't help you, miss," the clerk insisted. "Have you ever seen the general when he is angry? He has his rooms here. So I have seen him unhappy. It is not a scene I wish repeated."

Lucy knew she would get no further with this fellow. So, she went into the dining room to think about it. Maybe she would come up with a way to get past this clerk.

"Can I get you something, miss?"

"Yes, thank you," she told the waiter. "I think I'll have a glass of red wine; a light variety, please."

"Yes, miss."

She sat looking out of the dining room window. Quietly sipping her wine she had come up with nothing that would get her past the front desk to Henry's room.

"I'm told you wanted to see me."

Lucy almost choked on her wine. There was Henry, smiling like a Cheshire cat, sitting on a wheelchair a few feet behind her. He held out his arms to her.

"Henry!" she said as she hurried to his side. "Can I hug you?"

"I would like that, Lucy," he told her. "I don't think I'll break."

She slid onto his lap and gave him a fierce hug. After a long kiss, Lucy leaned back some and looked into his eyes.

"I'm not hurting you am I, Henry?"

"It would only hurt if you got off my lap, sweetheart."

"I heard about your injury and I couldn't bear not seeing you another minute," she explained. "But that awful man at the front desk wouldn't let me see you."

"Don't think too badly of him, Lucy. He was just following instructions. After all, he told me you were here."

"That's true. Besides, you're in my arms. What else could be more important?"

They kissed again. "I wish we could do more than just kiss, Henry."

"We can if you push this chair back to my room."

"Oh! My, this is exciting." She giggled. She wheeled him past the surprised guards into his sitting room.

"Push the chair into the other room beside my bed, please. I'm afraid my legs are not yet fully operational."

"I hope other parts of you are in good operating order, though."

"Let's find out, Lucy."

Henry threw off his bedclothes and watched as Lucy shed her street clothing and joined him on the bed. It was some time before they spoke again.

"What do you think, Lucy?" Henry asked. "My parts work to your satisfaction?"

"I believe everything works just fine, Henry. I just hope I didn't wear you out."

"You did, but I loved every minute of it, Lucy. Would you please get me a glass of water? There's a pitcher of on the table in the sitting room."

"I'd do anything for my wounded warrior."

Lucy jumped off the bed and walked buck naked toward the adjoining room to fetch him the water he wanted.

Propped up on pillows, Henry watched Lucy walk across the room. He especially liked the sight as she walked back toward him with his glass of water.

"I saw you smiling when I came back into the room, Henry. What was that all about?" she asked as she rejoined him on the bed.

"Just watching you walk naked across the room and back was a real treat for this wounded marshal; the smiling was for the pleasure of the sight."

"Did you trick me into parading about in my birthday suit, Henry Austry?"

"Do you mind, Lucy?"

"Not really," she admitted. "I'm just happy you like what you see. Now drink all your water like a good boy."

He did as she asked. It was almost dark before Henry was willing to let her leave his bed.

"Come back soon, Lucy?"

"I can't wait, darling," she cooed. "But my father expects me to help him open our house back in Dover, New Hampshire. So I won't see you until we return to Washington in December. Will you wait for me until then, Henry?"

"Of course I will."

On the way out, Lucy talked to the guards outside the door.

"Henry wants to sleep for a while. I guess he did something that wore him right out," she tittered.

"We'll let him sleep, miss. Good night."

Later that evening an orderly could not awaken Henry. Dr. Andrews was called immediately.

The Doctor could not awaken him, either. "Oh, my Lord," he exclaimed. "Austry hardly has a pulse. It appears he's been drugged."

# PHILADELPHIA

Dr. Murphy opened the front door of his home. His Irish setter stood at his side, growling. Standing before him was a well groomed young woman holding a carpetbag.

"Can I help you, miss?"

She was a dark-haired lady of average height. She was conservatively dressed and carried an umbrella along with her carpetbag.

"I'm Linda Berkholz," she said. "I assume you are Dr. Murphy."

"Of course, Miss Berkholz, I've been expecting you."

The dog was still blocking the door, but wagging his long tail, now.

"Please step inside," Doctor Murphy pushed the dog back. "Move, Irish. Let the lady in." Once they were all inside, he shut the door.

"Marshal Drieborg informed us by telegram to expect you."

"Yes, Doctor. I am a special agent with the Pinkerton Detective Agency. I've been assigned to protect you and your family."

"I don't believe your services are all that necessary, Miss Berkholz. But for the sake of my grandchildren I will accept the judgment of my son-in-law."

"Please follow me into the living room. Don't mind Irish. He's usually very nervous around strangers. But he seems to like you."

"Thank you for the assurance Doctor," Linda replied.

The children were working at a table with Miss Anderson. Helen was observing the instruction, too. Mary Jacqueline was sitting on the couch reading.

"Judy, will you join us in the living room, please?" Dr. Murphy called.

"I'd like to have your attention everyone," he began. "This is Miss Berkholz. She was asked to join us by your father, children. It appears that the work your father is doing has made some dangerous people angry. He fears that they may try to harm one of us. She is here to protect us from that. Miss Berkholz may wish to explain further."

"Thank you Doctor," she started. "Before I begin, I would like you all to call me Linda. Marshal Drieborg asked Mr. Pinkerton to assign me here because he wants to be sure that all of you remain safe. If I'm going to accomplish my job, I need you to follow a few rules. First, I must be the only person who answers the door. Second, I must know if any of you plan to leave the house. If at all possible, it would be best if you stayed indoors at home until Marshal Drieborg tells me that all is clear.

"Until then, I will be staying here. I will try not to upset your routine. Do you have any questions?"

Dr. Murphy spoke up. "I'm afraid you'll not be alone answering the door, Linda."

"Why is that, Doctor?"

"If he's in the house, Irish will be at your side."

"Oh, of course," she said as she patted Irish on the head. "I'm sure that will be fine."

Of course, Charles had to say something.

"Do you have a gun?"

"Yes, I do, Charles."

"Will you shoot anybody," he continued.

"To protect you, I would.

"Do you have a question, young lady?" Linda asked Eleanor.

"I thought only men carried guns," Eleanor said.

"If I were a teacher like Miss Anderson here, I would not carry a gun. But detectives carry weapons, Eleanor," Linda told her. "Remember, even though

I'm a woman, I'm a detective, too. So, I must have a weapon. I believe a revolver is best because it is easiest to carry."

*       *       *

Helen took the children upstairs for a nap. Dr. Murphy left the house as he had a class to teach at the University of Pennsylvania. The three ladies sat in the living room having a cup of tea.

Mary Jacqueline asked, "Do you know the lady who posed as me when the train was attacked?"

"I did, Mrs. Drieborg."

"Please call me Mary Jacqueline. So, were you the one who was wounded during the attack on your Pullman car?"

"Yes. I was rendered unconscious by a grenade that exploded inside the car. But as you can see, I've recovered fully."

"Please accept my thanks for the risk you took. Had I been in that car I can't imagine what would have happened to my baby." While saying this, Mary Jacqueline had her right hand over her stomach as though protecting her unborn child.

"That's part of the job, Mary Jacqueline."

"You're from Detroit, Michigan?"

"Yes. And, between assignments, I stay at my parents' home there."

Judy Murphy entered the conversation. "Are we really in danger?"

"It is hard to say, Mrs. Murphy. Given the attacks that have been made thus far, nothing seems beyond the people who oppose Marshal Drieborgs investigation. He told my employer, Allen Pinkerton, that he is about ready to present a report and believes that once the report is made public, the danger will end as well."

"That cannot come too soon. But what of us; are we to be prisoners in our own home?" Mrs. Murphy was clearly upset.

"It would be best, Mrs. Murphy, if everyone stayed put for a while. May I be blunt, ma'am?"

"Please do."

"It is understandable that you are upset with this intrusion on your life. I can also see that you are angry as well. But should you insist on going about your normal routine and an attack occurs, could you ever forgive yourself if anyone was hurt?

"I am sorry to speak to you with such bluntness, ma'am. But I urge you to follow my advice until this threat is over. I can't protect you without your cooperation.

"Please, Mother," Mary Jacqueline urged. "Will you do as Linda asks? It won't be for long in any case."

Mrs. Murphy sat quietly looking down at her hands that rested in her lap.

"You are correct, Miss Berkholz. I am not accustomed to the restrictions you suggest. And I'm must admit that I am angry about it. But for the children's sake, I will do as you ask.

"Now that we have gotten that out of the way," she continued. "I think we best discuss the practical matters like; getting fresh food into the house each day; attending Sunday Mass; daily exercise for the children; that type of thing. And what of the children's teacher Miss Anderson, coming and going safely?"

"Thank you for being so understanding Mrs. Murphy. Let's take the problems you raised, one at a time."

While the children slept, the ladies discussed each of the issues.

Judy Murphy concluded the discussion. "I think we have addressed these problems rather thoroughly and identified a satisfactory approach to each one of them. Let's stop for now and go over them with Dr. Murphy after the children are put down for the night. He must be part of this, don't you think?"

"Yes, ma'am; I agree, he should."

# George Krupp's Washington Home

It was late when Mike and his men arrived at the Krupp house.

"Where the devil have you been all this time?" George greeted. "We'd begun to worry that something had happened to you."

Mike explained the reason for the delay.

"You think Richards or Baker had anything to do with the attack?" Bob Stephan asked.

"At this point there is no way to trace it back to either of them. In fact, we had to let Richards go for lack of evidence."

"What about Baker?"

"We've still got him in a cell at the Capitol Prison. I'm hoping you find someone you pick up on your raid at his offices tomorrow who can link him to Henry's shooting. It you can't, we'll have to let him go as well."

"The ladies have already turned in, Mike. It's going to be an early day for us tomorrow, so rather than go back to the boardinghouse, why don't you all just get some sleep here."

"Sounds good, George." Mike decided. "Just point me to an empty bed or a spot on the floor."

\*       \*       \*

Peg Stanitzek, Mary Alice Stephan and Ethie Faute were already asleep together in one guest room. So George had Craig, Bose and Frank take beds on the third floor and Mike a bed in the other guest room on the second floor.

Inside his room, Mike dropped his shoes, took off all his clothing and washed his body. It was too warm for blankets so he just lay atop the bed, naked. Exhausted from the events of the last two days, he quickly fell into a sound sleep.

Later, Mike became vaguely aware of movement on the bed. More awake, he felt himself reacting to a naked body sliding on top of his. Lips covered his and a hand joined him to her.

Fully awake, he pulled his lips away. "What the hell!"

Patricia whispered in his ear, "Stay still, Michael. I can feel that you want me. Let me do the work."

Instead, Mike pushed Patricia off his body.

"Of course, I want you!" he hissed. "I'm not dead. But this is wrong, Patricia. You and I are both married; to other people."

Listening, Patricia lay on her side alongside of Mike, their bodies close, but not quite touching. While he talked, she caressed him with her free hand.

"Shush! I need you, Michael. I can see you still want me, too." She quickly moved over him again and before he could push her away or say anything else, they were joined once more.

*"Oh, shit!* Mike thought. *"She knows I want her. I shouldn't let this happen."*

# OFFICES OF THE NATIONAL POLICE FORCE

It was seven in the morning. Mike and his five armed marshals entered the offices of the Washington National Detective Police.

Mike approached the front desk as his men went directly into Colonel Baker's office and other rooms.

Standing, a police officer sitting behind a high desk at the back of the room protested.

"What the hell do ya think yer doing?" The man was stocky and not quite six feet tall. His face was bright pink with excitement, His dark blue uniform clearly showed his rank to be that of a sergeant.

"I'll have your name, Sergeant," Mike snapped.

"Sergeant Ryan, sir. And, I repeat my question. What are ya doing here?"

Mike handed him the search warrants. "These documents are warrants, Sergeant," Mike told him. "They authorize us to search the premises."

The Sergeant looked over the papers. "If ya tell me what yer looking for, Marshal Drieborg, I might be able to help ya."

"You can provide me with a list of all your personnel with ranks, assignments and current work schedules. I'll need their home addresses, too. Then, you can show me where all your records are kept."

"If you give me a moment, I'll get those files, Marshal."

"Go with him, Bose. See that he doesn't destroy anything."

"Look who we found in a back room, Mike." Craig pushed ahead of him a red headed man in police uniform. "I'll secure him to a chair for now."

Then, Sergeant Ryan returned with the files Mike had requested.

"What's that man's name, Sergeant?"

285

"Alex Williams, Marshal."

"When do you expect the other officers to report for duty, Ryan?"

"Some are due to report here within the hour. Others will report later for the evening shift. It's all in the file I gave ya."

Two more police officers reported in. They were arrested and taken to a back room.

George and Robert were going through Baker's file cabinets and boxing the contents up for later study.

George asked the sergeant, "Are any records keep at another site?"

"If there is, Marshal, I don't know about' em."

The boxes of files were carried outside and loaded on a wagon. George and Bob then took them back to Kellogg's office to begin their study of the contents.

Mike was ready to leave. So he gave his final instructions.

"Craig, you and Frank stay here with the good sergeant. You pick up the rest of Baker's crew as they report in and jail them at the Capitol Prison. Right now, I want to take the three police officers we have in custody now there. Bose will help me with the interrogation. I'll join you there this afternoon after my interview with Stanton.

"John Gostomski, the Pinkerton man, is going to meet me at the prison, too. I'll have him stay there with Bose until you arrive, Craig."

# PHILADELPHIA

The children were down for the night and Dr. Murphy had just finished listening to his wife recount the afternoon conversation with Linda Berkholz.

"What you ladies concluded makes sense," he told them. "Our loss of privacy and the restrictions you have mentioned seem necessary in the short run. You're correct, Miss Berkholz; better to be safe than sorry."

Mary Jacqueline handed her father a sheet of paper. "A telegram arrived from Michael while you were out, Father."

"I see," Dr. Murphy began. "Michael wants to have the children returned to Michigan to be with his parents. What do you think of that, Mary Jacqueline?"

"When there's trouble I'd rather have the children close to me, Father. But I believe I must trust Michael's suggestion that it's safer for them to be there, rather than here."

"This business can't be over too soon for me," Judy Murphy said.

"Amen to that, my dear," Dr. Murphy agreed.

# EDWIN STANTON'S OFFICE

That same afternoon, Mike entered the offices of the Secretary of War. George Krupp and Robert Stephan were with him.

Major Thomas greeted him. "Good afternoon, Marshal. Please have a chair. Secretary Stanton will be right with you."

The three men were kept waiting over thirty minutes.

"We should have had him come to us, Mike," Stephan observed.

"Knowing how Stanton operates, Bob," George told him, "he would have kept us waiting at our office, too. It's all about impressing us with his power. Keeping us waiting is nothing to how he openly treated President Lincoln. People in Washington often wondered why Lincoln didn't fire the bastard."

"The secretary will see you now, gentlemen," Thomas told them.

"Good afternoon Marshal," Stanton began extending his right hand to shake Mike's. He carefully turned his back on Krupp and Stephan. "Please take a seat in front of my desk."

There was only one straight-backed chair in front of a very large desk.

*That bastard wants Mike to ask if we can be seated!* George thought. *No way will I allow that.*

Without asking, George moved across the room and moved a chair alongside of Mike's. Bob Stephan and their recording secretary did the same.

"Well, now. How can I help you, Marshal?"

"Frist, Mr. Secretary, I wish to introduce my colleagues, Marshal Krupp, Marshal Stephan and Bose Faute."

"Oh, yes. I remember you, Mr. Stephan. You're the Confederate officer from Columbia, South Carolina. And, if memory serves, I believe you, Mr. Krupp, are formerly of Congressman Kellogg's staff and now a Washington lobbyist."

"Your memory does serve you well, Mr. Stanton; on both counts." George Krupp complimented him.

"Thus, it is unfortunate that your memory fails when you testified about whether or not Mr. Lincoln was in your telegraph office on April 14, 1865. Why is that, sir?"

"I'm sure I don't know what you're talking about."

"Sir, we have signed affidavits that the president was in your telegraph office that afternoon. In addition, we have your sworn statement that Mr. Lincoln was last in that office on April 13th.

"Has your memory improved yet, sir?"

"I don't think I like your tone, Mr. Krupp. I might remind you that your success in this town depends upon the good will of people like me."

George continued as though he had not heard the threat from Stanton.

"You also swore that you received the daybook kept by John Wilkes Booth with pages missing? Is that true, sir?"

"Yes, it is."

"You might find it interesting then, that we have sworn affidavits from your staff that it was given and received in this office, intact. Now that you know that, Mr. Secretary, has your sharp memory improved on that matter?"

Stanton stood, "I believe this interview has ended, Drieborg!" he shouted.

Mike remained seated. "Mr. Stanton, you received a subpoena requiring you to make yourself available for our questions. I will treat your refusal as contempt of Congress and I will take you out of this office in chains. Do you still refuse to answer our questions?" Mike asked.

Visibly irritated, Stanton squirmed and sat back in his chair.

"Let's get this over with, Drieborg. Ask your damn questions."

"On April 14th, why did you refuse the president's request that you allow Major Thomas Eckert to accompany him and Mrs. Lincoln to Ford's theatre that evening?"

"How could I have done that? I don't remember the president being in the telegraph office on that date."

"Was such a request made on a different date?"

"No such request was made on any date."

Bob Stephan questioned Stanton on the plot to kidnap President Lincoln.

"Is it true, Mr. Secretary, that you and those in your department were in complete charge of the pursuit of Booth, the investigation, arrests and trials following the killing of President Lincoln?"

"Yes. President Johnson gave me that responsibility and the authority to carry it out."

"During the trial of Booth's accomplices, both Judge Holt and the Prosecutor John Bingham argued to the military court that there had been no plot to kidnap President Lincoln in 1865. Do you believe their assertion to be true?"

"I do; absolutely."

"Then you would deny that your office knew as early as late February or early March in 1865, of a plot to kidnap the president?"

"While I have been Secretary of War, this office has received information most every day of all manner of plots and threats to the president. For that reason I was always urging President Lincoln to be more cautious about his movements."

"If you had known of a serious kidnapping plot, I assume you would have taken additional steps to protect the president?"

"Of course I would have."

"So when a member of your staff, Mr. Weichman brought you information in early March, 1865 of such a plot being led by John Wilkes Booth, it was not considered a serious threat?"

"I know Mr. Weichman, but I don't know about any serious kidnapping plot."

"It is interesting, Mr. Stanton", George concluded "that the man who planned the failed March 1865 kidnapping plot turned out to be the same man who killed the president. And, it is odd that the other men in the March kidnapping plot were the very ones you later hung for later helping Booth murder the president. Wouldn't you agree, Mr. Secretary?"

"I'm sure I don't know what you're talking about."

"How is it, sir, that during the war, your people arrested thousands on suspicion of even saying things in support of the rebellion; but when you knew of plans to kidnap the president, you did nothing?"

"I've already answered that question. Are we finished yet, Drieborg?"

Mike answered, "I have one more line of questioning, Mr. Stanton."

"I hope this will be short, Drieborg," Stanton snapped. "I have serious work ahead of me this day."

Mike sat quietly until he saw that the silence had become uncomfortable for Stanton.

"Well, sir. What is it?"

"In the aftermath of the killing, you had literally hundreds of people arrested. You even closed Ford's Theatre and had all the employees and the owners taken into custody. Is that not true, sir?"

"Colonel Baker and Superintendent Richards advised me on the proper investigative procedures. I just followed their lead following the killing of President Lincoln."

"Of course you did, sir. My advisor on such matters, Marshal Craig Haynes is the former Cleveland, Ohio Chief of Police. He said he would have given you the same advice."

"So, Marshal Drieborg," Stanton asked. "Why did you even bring the matter up?"

"Because, Mr. Stanton. Of all the hundreds you had arrested you ignored the one man who allowed the killing of the president; Officer Parker. Why was that, sir?"

"That was a matter for his superior, Superintendent Richards."

"Why did Richards not interrogate Parker?"

"I'm led to believe Richards had Parker brought before a disciplinary board of some sort."

"Have you read the transcript of that hearing, Mr. Secretary?"

"No, I have not seen it."

"Did you tell Superintendent Richards not to discipline Officer Parker?"

"No. That was and is a matter for Richards, not this office."

"Does Colonel Lafayette Baker work for you and the War Department?"

"Yes, he does."

"Did you have anything to do with an attack on one of my marshals by members of Baker's National Police?"

"Absolutely not, Marshal."

"Did you have anything to do with the attack on my Philadelphia-bound Pullman car last weekend?"

"That's preposterous. Are you so important, Drieborg, that the War Department should make war on you?"

"It would seem that you think so, Mr. Stanton," Mike snapped back.

"We are finished with you today, sir. But we're not done with you," Mike warned as he stood.

"Not by a long shot are we done with you."

Stanton also stood. Hands on his desk, he leaned forward and glared at Mike.

"You are just a little fish swimming among sharks, Drieborg. You're way out of your depth."

"You're probably correct, Mr. Secretary," Mike responded. "But you will soon discover that this little fish has very sharp teeth.

"We can prove you to be a liar, sir. And, we will show by your conduct that you could have prevented the assassination of Abraham Lincoln and chose not to do so.

"Actually, Mr. Stanton, when we're finally finished with you I believe the public will come to know you to be just another power-hungry and very dirty politician.

"If you're a shark, you're one I intend to see hung out to dry. Good day, sir."

On the way out of the building, Bose made an observation.

"So that's tha powerful Mr. Stanton, eh? I'll bet he's not used to bein called a liar. You got him so mad Mike, I swear he could a' bit hiss self."

# KELLOGG'S WASHINGTON OFFICE

Coffee cups and empty food containers from the Willard Hotel restaurant were scattered on top of the table. Mike, George, Bob, and Craig were sitting back and taking a break from their review of all the documents taken from Baker's offices.

George was the first to speak.

"Not much here, Mike. Nothing we can use anyway."

"Well then," Mike said. "Let's box it up and send it back tomorrow."

"Where are the other guys, Mike?" George asked.

"I left Frank, Bose and the Pinkerton man, John over at the prison. Frank wasn't too happy about the food, but it can't be helped. I need them there until morning, at least."

Bob Stephan had a question. "How did the interrogation of the red- headed officer go?"

Mike responded. "He caved without much persuasion. He signed an affidavit stating that Baker gave him and three other officers a direct order to find and kill Parker. Their shooting of Henry was an accident, it seems.

"The other three officers corroborated his testimony."

"What about Baker?"

"When confronted with our evidence, he caved, too. He told us that Stanton was behind the order to kill Parker. He also told us that our friends Representative Bingham, Judge Holt and Senator Ben Butler were all in on the scheme to kill Parker as well as me. But unless one of them cooperates with us, we don't have corroboration. So just having Baker's word is not enough for an indictment. Stanton is probably finished as Secretary of War, though," Mike insisted.

"By the way," Mike went on. "Henry entertained Lucy Hale in his rooms yesterday. Before she left, it appears that she managed to slip him some kind of sedative. The doctor thinks he caught it in time and has Henry on the mend.

"Lucy Hale was picked up this morning in the Philadelphia railway station. The federal marshal questioned her. She claims that she saw Henry put some powder into a glass of water he asked her to get for him. She said he told her it was a sedative to calm him."

Craig added. "So, that appears to be a dead end; her word against his, at best. Besides, I'm led to believe that she's off for Spain with her father, the new US ambassador to that country."

"That ends the chance of our getting any useful information from Lucy Hale."

"I suppose."

As the men walked toward the boardinghouse, George and Mike fell in alongside one another.

"Don't you think this investigation is coming to an end, George?"

"I think so, Mike. Good thing too. If I make any more important people angry in this town, I'll be ruined and have to move out. And, if you stay around much longer I'll have to move Patricia out."

"What have I got to do with that?" *Oh, my Lord. George knows what happened last night,* Mike thought.

"Patricia, that's what. Before I left this morning she was railing about how you were a bastard. You stole her father's love from her. Then, you dumped her twice when she thought the two of you were going to marry and then you abandoned her when she needed your support most. And, she went on about you convincing her father to put her at that sanitarium up in New York after she got hooked on laudanum."

Mike reminded George. "You knew she and I had gotten close back in '63 when Kellogg assigned me to escort Pat around town to various social events. He also ordered me to work with her at his house to plan his dinners. That was before I was sent to join my old cavalry unit at Gettysburg.

"A year later, after my wife Eleanor died and I returned to duty in Washington, Pat and I got reacquainted and even discussed marriage. But we both decided that marriage wasn't a good idea for us. Patricia couldn't see herself as a farmer's wife and I wasn't about to live in Washington as her social escort around this town for the rest of my life. Gosh, George, that was a long time ago.

"As for her addiction to laudanum, you know that situation. Kellogg had little choice. I just found a good place for him to send her."

"Ya, I know, Mike. I knew all of that. But this morning she was in high rant to be sure. I'm glad she didn't have a pistol. She was so angry, she might have shot me.

"Did you say something recently to get her all worked up, Mike?"

"Hell, George, I haven't even seen her since she and Bose gave their report to us a few weeks back in Kellogg's office. Yesterday afternoon, I saw her when we dropped off the wives at your house. When I returned late last night, she and the other ladies were asleep.

"It's sure got me puzzled too, George. Thanks for the warning, though. I'll try to stay out of her way."

# KELLOGG'S WASHINGTON OFFICE

The next day, Mike and his men were gathered around the conference table. Congressmen Kellogg and Webster were present as well.

With his usual bluster Webster spoke first.

"What the devil we doing here, Drieborg?" he began. "My Lord man, it's hardly eight in the morning!"

"Actually, Webster, we called this meeting early, just for you."

"You have to be kidding, Kellogg."

"Yes, I was. It does seem strange to me, Mike especially since you've got me agreeing with Webster. Why are we here?"

Webster wasn't done, though. "My eyes are hardly open, here. You got any a' that smooth mountain bourbon with you, Faute?"

Mike interrupted. "No he doesn't, Congressman. Our meetings here are dry; except when they're held at the Willard."

"Probably some straight-laced Yankee custom, I expect," Webster observed. "Well let's get on with it, Drieborg, so's we can adjourn there."

After the laughter subsided, Mike did just that.

"You two have been asked to join us because we are at a crossroads of sorts, and we need your advice.

"George," Mike directed. "Tell our guests what we have."

"Sit back and relax, gentlemen," George began. "This will take a while.

"I'm going to start with the charge that the late Confederate government inspired and supported Booth's assassination of Abraham Lincoln in 1865.

"On April 24th, 1865 Secretary of War Edwin Stanton declared publicly,

"*This Department has information that the murder of the president was organized in Canada and approved at Richmond.*"

"During the trial of Booth's co-conspirators, Federal prosecutors continued this theme. So that at the conclusion of the trial of Booth's companions, Chief Prosecutor Bingham said,

*'Jefferson Davis is as clearly proven guilty of this conspiracy as is John Wilkes Booth.'*

"Leading up to his summation, prosecutor John Bingham, had built to this moment with the testimony of witness after witness. Their hearsay testimony he argued supported the notion that the Booth assassination was just another part of the Confederate government's war against the United States of America; a last ditch attempt to turn the tide, perhaps.

"We already know this stuff, Krupp," Webster snapped impatiently. "Get to the meat of your presentation, will ya?"

"I'd be happy to, Congressman."

"As a result of all this testimony, Judge Advocate Holt convinced President Johnson and his entire cabinet that the case against the Confederate government was sound. Based on that, the president signed a proclamation on May 2, 1865 affirming that the assassination was "incited, concerted and procured" by Jefferson Davis and others in the Confederate government.

"However, the testimony which supported this proclamation soon began to fall apart. Rep. Rogers, a Democratic member of the House Judiciary Committee interrogated the War Department's witnesses; they admitted that their testimony had been false. In fact, it was revealed that the witnesses were coached and their perjured testimony paid for.

"Based upon this admission, the declarations issued by Secretary Stanton and by prosecutor Bingham as well as the proclamation they convinced President Johnson to sign are not supported by any evidence whatsoever.

"Since their case fell apart, Judge Holt and Secretary Stanton have not been able to produce a single piece of reliable evidence to support their earlier accusation.

"During our interview with Jefferson Davis, he reminded us of the very different positions taken by Lincoln and Vice President Johnson before the war ended. He insisted that Lincoln as president, not Johnson, promised the best chance for a smooth reentry of the former Confederate states to the United States of America.

"And, now, Holt and Stanton seem to have decided that there is insufficient evidence to convict Davis of being part of the plan to kill Lincoln. Instead, they want President Johnson to try him for treason.

"Given the facts available at this time, we have to conclude that Booth was not part of a Confederate government plot to assassinate President Lincoln."

Congressman Webster couldn't contain his glee. "I knew all along those Republican bastards were wrong," he declared. "Will Johnson rescind his declaration publicly?"

"When we interviewed him the second time, Bob Stephan asked him that question, congressman. The president said the matter was under consideration."

"Shit! Just more crap," Webster spat. "What else have you got?"

"I'll let Bob Stephan take over at this point. He'll review our findings on the charge that the Roman Catholic Church was involved."

Congressman Kellogg had been silent throughout Krupp's presentation.

"Before you begin, will you tell me once again, Michael why you're telling Webster and me all of this, not all the members of the Judiciary Committee?"

Mike gave an evasive answer to that question.

"We wanted to sort of try out our report before we turned it in to the House Judiciary Committee, Congressman."

"Michael," Kellogg said. "You know you can trust me to keep my mouth shut about whatever I hear until it is properly presented to the Judiciary Committee. But you've got to know as well that Webster will have whatever he hears all over town before he's ordered his second whiskey at lunch today."

"Oh, now that's cruel, Kellogg," Webster said with a smile. "Probably true, but cruel just the same. Besides, I believe Drieborg and his boys are counting on me to do just that."

Neither Mike nor any of his deputies said a word.

"Can we continue, sir?" Mike asked Kellogg.

"Yes you can, Michael. But do so with the knowledge that when you and your colleagues are finished, I must inform the Chairman of the House Judiciary Committee that this meeting took place."

Mike looked around the table at his marshals.

"Do what you must, sir," Mike told him. "But when one of our team lies wounded and near death at the National Hotel; when agents posing as my pregnant wife and myself were attacked; when my men and me were attacked recently on a Washington street; when War Department people ordered the killing of our chief witness; when the very Judiciary Committee that authorized this investigation tried to shut it down, we became determined that our report would not be buried. So, we too will do what we must, sir.

"We concluded that the only way the House Judiciary Committee will be forced to deal openly with our report is if it is first leaked to the public."

"Very well, Michael. Now that we understand one another, proceed if you wish."

"Thank you, sir."

"After Henry was shot, we were short of available personnel so only three members of the team were free to meet with a Mr. Chiniquy about his charges that the Roman Catholic Church encouraged and supported the killing of Abraham Lincoln."

# PHILADELPHIA

The lunch dishes had been cleared and Helen and Mary Jacqueline had taken the children upstairs for a nap. Linda and Mrs. Murphy were in the living room enjoying a cup of tea and Dr. Murphy was preparing to leave for his afternoon class at the university.

The front door chimes rang.

Irish jumped up and began barking as he moved toward the front of the house. Linda rose and with pistol in hand followed him. She slowly opened the door.

Looking at her from their position on the front porch were a man and a woman dressed in rather plain clothing. Each carried a carpetbag. The man also carried what looked like a gun case.

"Good afternoon, miss," the woman said. "Are Doctor and Mrs. Murphy at home?"

"Stay back, Irish," Linda used her leg to keep the dog inside the house, "Can I tell them who is calling?"

"This is Jacob Drieborg and I'm Rose Drieborg. Michael Drieborg is our son. May we step inside?"

"Oh, my goodness," Linda gushed. "Please come in. I'm sorry for the rather brusque greeting, but no one told me you were coming." She holstered the pistol and opened the door wider.

"And, I wasn't expecting to look down da barrel of a pistol eider, when you opened da door to Dr. Murphy's home opened." Jake said with a smile.

"Oh yes. I must have given you a fright, Mr. Drieborg. As I've said, you caught us unprepared. I'm Linda. Mary Jacqueline is upstairs lying down with the children. Dr. Murphy is in his study and Mrs. Murphy is in the sitting room. I'll let her know you're here."

Judy Murphy had heard the conversation and headed toward the front door.

"Rose and Jacob," Judy exclaimed. "Come in, please come in."

They stepped out of the open doorway into the foyer. Linda shut and locked the front door behind them. As soon as they were inside the house the dog ran circles around their feet.

"Miles," Judy shouted, "The Drieborgs are here. Stop it Irish. He gets so excited when company arrives."

"My goodness, put your bags down. Why didn't you tell us you were coming, Rose? We had no idea. Miles would have met you at the station. Come into the sitting room."

"Miles, the Drieborgs are here," she shouted again.

She had hardly finished shouting and Dr. Murphy walked into the room.

"Mr. and Mrs. Drieborg; how good to see you."

Jake stood up and extended his right hand. "Call me Jake, Doctor."

"Yes, of course.

"Are you and Mrs. Drieborg here to take the children to Michigan, Jake?"

"I have another thought I would like to share with you about dat, Doctor."

"Should we go into my study?"

"No," Jake stated rather bluntly. "What I have to say should be shared with da ladies, I believe."

"Ladies, please," Dr. Murphy asked politely. "Jake has something he wishes to tell us all." Once in the living room, Jake began.

"When Michael notified us of da trouble, we decided we'd best be with you and da children."

Rose added. "Family best faces problems when everyone is together, don't you think?"

"Of course," Judy Murphy agreed. "Can I get you something; coffee or tea? Have you had any lunch?"

"They served us some cold cuts, bread and cheese on the train," Rose told her. "It wasn't very tasty actually, but it satisfied. I would like a cup of tea, though."

"Jacob, what can I get you?"

"Coffee would be fine, Mrs. Murphy."

Mary Jacqueline rushed into the room.

"Rose! Jacob! You two are a sight for sore eyes," she said.

Rose stood and gave her daughter-in-law a hug. "You look fine, dear. How do you feel?"

"I'm just fine, Rose."

Jake was standing by the two of them. "What about me? Don't I get a hug, too?"

"Of course you do, Jacob. After all you're my favorite father-in-law in the whole world."

"I should be, young lady. I'm your only father-in-law in da whole world."

"Judy, Mary Jacqueline, I think Jake has a suggestion he would like to share with us. You can get the drinks after he speaks. Please, Jake, what do you have in mind?"

"First, Doctor," he began. "Let me start by telling you what I think we should not do. I don't think it wise to take da children out of your house and back to Michigan. If what Michael fears is true, separately in Michigan we will be more vulnerable dan together here in Philadelphia.

"So, I suggest Rose and I stay here with you until dis danger has passed."

After a quiet pause, Dr. Murphy spoke first.

"Jake," he began. "I can understand that the children and you could be just as vulnerable in Michigan as here. But how would we all be safer if you and the children stayed here in Philadelphia?"

"Because, Doctor," Jake responded quickly. "Rose and I have had experience with killers back in Lowell."

"What kind of experience, Jake? And, please call me Miles."

"A few years ago, Michael was at home on leave. On his way back to da war, he was attacked by hoodlums. They were hired by da banker in our town. I feared dey would attack us in Lowell, too. So, I taught my children how to use firearms. Even I made Rose learn to fire a revolver. She didn't like to shoot it and she really didn't like to carry it. But I insisted."

"It was awful. I hated it. But I did as Jacob asked because I knew it was necessary," Rose added.

Jake continued. "It wasn't long before hoodlums attacked our home. While Rose and I were in town one Saturday morning, two armed men entered our yard on horseback. Dey wounded our son Jacob before my daughter Ann killed one of dem and wounded da other. I got da wounded one to tell me who hired him and his dead partner. He said it was da banker."

Mary Jacqueline asked, "Why did he tell you, Jacob?"

"He told me because he wanted me to stop using my knife on him."

It was very quiet in the room.

Finally, Judy Murphy cleared her throat and said.

"Rose, that food you had on the train sounds simply awful. Cook has just put away the leftovers from our lunch. Let's you and I get some of it out. And we have some very good blueberry pie. Would you give me a hand in the kitchen?"

"I'd be happy to, Judy. I must admit, I am still hungry."

"Afterward, I'll show you to your room. You might want to rest before the children get up from their nap."

"That would be nice. I would like to freshen up, at least."

Jake and Rose enjoyed some soup and homemade bread. Judy gave them dessert, too.

"This pie is delicious, Judy," Rose commented.

"Our cook does a very good job. We're fortunate to have her."

"Oh, Mary Jacqueline," Rose gushed. "Before I forget, I have some news about a member of the Pope family."

"The Pope family lives in South Carolina, Rose. What could you possibly have heard about them in Michigan?"

"I must admit, it is a bit surprising. Tell them Jacob."

"Did you know dat Jacob and Kenny Hecht are both at West Point now?"

"Yes I do, Jacob. Michael told me Congressman Kellogg had decided to appoint them. So they arrived safely, I take it?"

"Yes," Rose broke in. "And their roommate is Richard Pope, your late husband's nephew and the son of the South Carolina landowner who called Michael the "Gentleman Major"."

"What was that all about?" Dr. Murphy asked.

"Well, Miles. If Rose will let me, I'll tell you."

"I'm sorry, Jacob. Go ahead and tell the story."

"When Michael returned to duty in January of 1865, he was sent to Savannah, Georgia where he joined General Sherman's command. His first assignment was to prepare Union soldiers who had been prisoners of war for da return trip north. After dat job was done he was given command of a cavalry troop in one of Sherman's regiments.

"As Sherman's army moved into South Carolina, Michael's cavalry troop came across many farms. Living off da land, his men took food for der use and forage for da horses. In other commands some Union troopers burned or killed everything dey did not take. Michael refused to allow dat.

"At one large cotton farm, his men took provisions but did not destroy da owner's home. And, Michael did not allow his men to kill da farm animals or burn da farm buildings. Da owner called Michael da "Gentleman Major".

"Word got back to General Burbridge, Michael's superior. Da general threatened to court-martial him for not punishing Southerners by burning homes and killing animals. But da war ended and da matter was dropped.

"As it turned out, dis landowner was a member of da Pope family Mary Jacqueline married into."

"Well, I'll be switched." Dr. Murphy exclaimed. "You must be proud of your son's fine character, Jake."

"We both are, Miles," Rose informed him.

"Did you know this about Michael when you met him, Mary Jacqueline?" her mother asked.

"No, I didn't, Mother. I didn't hear about it until the Richard Pope of Jacob's story visited us at Edisto Island a few weeks after I met Michael in Charleston. The story Richard told us about him didn't surprise me in the least. I already knew Michael was a man of good character. And, I saw that he was the very man I could fall in love with."

Her father then made a comment that greatly pleased her. "I believe you made a wise observation, Mary Jacqueline. And, I'm truly happy you chose Michael to be the father of my grandchildren."

"So am I, Father. It's nice to know that we finally agree on that."

# KELLOGG'S WASHINGTON OFFICE

Bob Stephan was about to begin.

Webster had a question, "Hold on a minute, Stephan. I want to know what you fellows have done about Congressman Julian's daily journal. My information is that it contains notes about Republican Radicals being in on the Lincoln killing.

Mike answered him. "We were going to save that for a later part of our report, sir. But we'll tell you right now. Craig, will you answer the congressman's question?"

"Certainly, Mike. I interviewed Congressman Julian and asked him about his famous journal. His immediate response was,

*"I assume you're interested in the time period just prior to and just following the assassination?"*

"He unlocked a cabinet to show me rows of journals; all clearly dated."

*"Read whatever entries you wish, Marshal Haynes,"* he told me.

"Com'on Marshal," Webster asked impatiently. "Were Julian and the others in on the assassination?" Webster asked impatiently.

"Congressman, I spent hours going through his journals for April and May. Not even you, sir could have concluded Julian either knew about a plot to kill the president or supported one in any way.

"If we are to believe the content of these private journals, I am convinced that the worst thing you could say about Congressman Julian is that he expressed relief that Lincoln and his Reconstruction ideas were out of the way."

"Congressman Webster, can we proceed?" Mike asked.

"Damn! Go ahead, Drieborg."

Bob Stephan continued.

"Charles Chiniquy was a priest in the Catholic Church. In 1851, he had a parish in the village of St. Anne, Illinois. While there, he became embroiled in a dispute with Bishop Anthony O'Regan of Chicago. Subsequently, a friend of the bishop sued Chiniquy for slander. Abraham Lincoln was hired to defend Father Chiniquy.

"He settled the case, leading his client to believe he had been exonerated. And, thus Chiniquy believed that Lincoln had won the case, and had thereby incurred the enmity of the Catholic Church.

"Later, striped of his priestly position, Father Chiniquy left the Catholic Church in 1858 and became an anti-Catholic zealot. After the assassination, Chiniquy accused the Roman Catholic Church of engineering the killing of Lincoln.

"During our interview, he insisted that the Catholic Church was the sinister force behind many schemes to destroy the United States. For example, the anti-war efforts of the Peace Democrats, the Northern Copperheads, union leaders and the Democratic Party Organization were all instigated by the Roman Catholic Church. The draft riots in New York and Detroit were likewise planned and carried out by Catholics who were dupes of the Catholic Church."

Kellogg asked, "Did he tell you how he came to know this, Marshal?"

"We asked that question too, Congressman," Stephan said. "In response he gave two answers: One, that Lincoln told him these things. And, secondly, that all the leaders of these organizations were Catholic. He claimed that all the people involved in the assassination were Catholics, too. But he presented no documentation to support any of these allegations."

"Bob, is an allegation something like an accusation?" Bose Faute asked.

"You've got the idea, Bose," he answered.

"He also claimed to have had private conversations with President Lincoln during the war. At these meetings, he claimed Lincoln told him that the greatest danger to the United States was the Catholic Church; that the Pope supported the Confederacy and that the Irish Catholics in this country were in favor of slavery and therefore supported the rebel cause.

"Before our interview with him, we had examined Lincoln's appointment records kept during the war years. We found no mention of Chiniquy. In fact, Mr. Hay, Lincoln's appointment secretary, told us the president had given explicit instructions that he was not to give Mr. Chiniquy an appointment.

"Chiniquy did give us a stack of newspaper articles which heralded his charges. It turned out that the articles were not based on research conducted by reporters. Instead they were simply interviews reporting unsupported claims made by Chiniquy. Most newspaper articles weren't news at all, but were excerpts from his speeches or the diatribes he had written."

"I was alone in this office a few days ago. This fella showed up with more of his evidence. So I got to listen to him speechify, some. He sure can get worked up. He reminded me of a good 'ol bible stump preacher; all full of hate and tales 'a gloom 'n doom. Once he started, I had a hard time gettin him to shut up. He sure hates tha Catholic Church; that's for certain.

"In my view, it's hard to trust tha word of a hater; caus' they's so determined their view is tha whole gospel an' that everything contrary is wrong," Bose concluded.

"I thought you didn't like Catholics, Bose." Frank asked.

"Now, that's not true, Francis. I might a' thought badly a' Catholics once. But during tha war, my sorry bacon was saved more 'n once by guys who were Catholic. Got to know em an' respect' em, too. An, here in Washington I got to know guys like you, Robert an' Mike. A threesome I'd go inta battle with any day, even though ya are Catholics, all a' ya."

"That's nice to hear, Bose," Frank told him. "I think."

Stephan resumed his presentation, "Much of his writing was just anti-Catholic ranting taken from the publications of the Know-Nothing party of the early 1850s.

"The story Chiniquy liked to repeat in his speeches was the one about the tunnel he claimed connected the house in which the priest lived with the convent house in which the nuns lived. Newspaper articles always said it got his audience worked up."

"That's not true?" Webster asked mischievously. "There was no funny business going on? Damn, I thought those priests had a good thing going."

"This committee has concluded that there is no evidence to support a charge that the Catholic Church engineered or even supported the assassination of Abraham Lincoln."

# PHILADELPHIA

Charles and Eleanor were playing catch in the Murphy's large back yard. Whenever one of them would miss, the dog Irish would easily beat them to the ball and grab it in its mouth. Then the dog would crouch, drop the ball on the ground and wait.

But as soon as one of the children made a move toward him, he would grab the ball in its mouth and run. Then, the children would run and shout in pursuit. The children seemed to enjoy the chase. The dog absolutely loved it.

Linda was standing at the far end of the play area and Grampa Jake sat on the back porch. As much as he enjoyed watching the children play, his eye traveled along the fences that surrounded the yard. His shotgun lay across his lap.

Suddenly, shots rang out from the front of the house.

Linda shouted, "Run into the house, children!"

The children had been drilled to respond to such a command. They ran toward the back door. Linda led them inside to a safe place. Jake crouched on the porch and waited.

Jake and Linda had talked about such a tactic with the police who were stationed in front. They expected a fake attack at the front of the house and an assault from the rear.

So, they had agreed to allow the city policemen to take care of the front; and have the ladies take the children into the windowless pantry in the center of the house. He and Linda would watch the back.

Sure enough, two men came over the backyard fence.

Jake did not hesitate. He shot one of the intruders in the chest. Before he could cock the hammer on the second barrel of his shotgun and take aim on the second man, Linda had shot him through the open kitchen window.

With both men on the ground, Jake and Linda waited and watched. After what seemed like a safe interval, Jake moved toward the intruders. Linda moved onto the porch with her revolver drawn.

"Are they still alive, Jake?" Linda shouted.

"One is still conscious, Linda," He found their weapons and picked them up.

He secured the man's arms with rope Linda brought him.

Jake drew his knife and put under the man's chin. "I think you had better tell me who sent you here, or maybe I let my partner kill you."

"You go to hell!" the man said.

"If I do, I'll find you der already, I think. Maybe you hear me better without dis ear."

Jake grabbed the man by the hair and began to use his sharp knife.

"Stop it! Stop it!" the man shouted.

"Dos are my grandchildren who were playing in dis yard. Who sent you here?" Jake asked again.

"Someone in Washington sent my boss money to attack this house."

Linda asked. "What were you supposed to do here?"

"We're just supposed ta' frighten everyone; maybe set the house on fire; not kill anybody.

"My God, ya sliced my ear. Get me a doc before I bleed ta' death."

"Sure mister, as soon as you give me the name of your boss."

"He'll kill me if'n I do."

Jake put the point of his now bloody knife up to the man's face.

"How'd you like to go through life with your nose split up da middle, eh?"

Just then Linda saw a Philadelphia policemen come into the yard.

"Let's turn this scum over to the locals, Jake. We've done all we can," Linda suggested.

Jake stood up, but not before he put a gash down the man's cheek.

"My God, ya cut me!"

"You're lucky dat's all I done, mister," Jake told the wounded man. "But I always listen to a lady."

# KELLOGG'S WASHINGTON OFFICE

"Frank, would you and Bose please present our findings on the charge against President Johnson?

Frank began. "There has been no official charge. But Senator Howard of Michigan has said that the president had a friendship with Booth going back to when he was Governor of Tennessee. I guess that could be taken as a suggestion of complicity."

Bose got into the report at this point. "Being a good ol' Tennessee boy, Craig asked me to check out the Michigan senator's claims. I talked with a bunch 'a people back in Tennessee; Nashville, Knoxville and Chattanooga. I couldn't find a whisper about such a friendship. There was plenty 'a talk about Johnson's boozing and philandering; But not a thing about Booth and him hanging out together. An' remember, I talked with folks who hated Johnson's guts for stickin with tha Union."

"What about that calling card Booth left at the National Hotel for Vice President Johnson?" Kellogg asked. "Did that mean anything?"

Frank answered that one. "We just don't know, Congressman. I talked to William Browning, Johnson's personal secretary who took the card from Booth. He told me that people left messages and calling cards for the vice president all the time. He just accepted it from Booth and put the card in with the vice president's other mail."

Kellogg then asked, "Remember Baker's contention that in 1865, he saw written communication between Johnson and Jeff Davis? He swore he could produce the documents. Did you look at that possible connection?"

"I checked that out, sir," Craig Haynes said. "But Baker could not produce any such document or proof that they ever existed. As a result, he is the one whose word can't be believed."

"What about the president's widow, Mary Lincoln? She has made a big fuss. What about her charge?" Webster asked.

"Yes sir. Her accusation has been in all the papers. She wrote:

*"My own intense misery has been augmented by the same thought – that that miserable inebriate Johnson had cognizance of my husband's death … As sure, as you and I live, Johnson had some hand in all this…"*

"I believe, Congressman," Frank answered, "that these are the words of a grieving and bitter widow looking for someone to blame. When judging her, sir, I believe we must keep in mind the guilt she must bear for requesting that Parker be assigned to the president's guard detail."

"You boys have any idea why she requested Parker?" Webster asked.

"Parker is a nephew somewhere in the family. We think she was responding to a request from a family member."

"So where are you on any involvement of President Johnson in the assassination?" Webster asked.

Frank answered that question, too.

"We have concluded that we could find no evidence connecting Booth with President Johnson; nor could we find any evidence to suggest that the president was a co-conspirator in the failed kidnapping or the successful assassination.

"We further believe that it was more likely Johnson was a target along with Lincoln and Seward on the night of April 14, 1865. Remember, we read in Booth's journal that George Atzerodt was assigned the job of killing Johnson who was sleeping at the Kirkwood House on the night of the assassination. Instead, Atzerodt had a drink at the hotel bar and then fled."

Bob Stephan joined the conversation. "The other side of that coin is rather interesting. What if Johnson wasn't attacked because the people behind the killing of Lincoln didn't want him dead?

"For some time, Andrew Johnson had been quoted widely as saying that the rebs were traitors and the leaders should be hung, one and all. That was in stark contrast with what Lincoln had been saying about his desire for a Union victory without punishment.

"Didn't Congressman Julian of Illinois say that the accession of Andrew Johnson to the presidency would prove to be a blessing for the country? Supposedly he was speaking for the Radical Republican caucus.

"At this point we have no evidence to link Julian or the others to the assassination, either."

"Do you have any questions, gentlemen? Mike asked.

Webster stood and said, "That's about all I can take in one sitting," he declared. "My mind is swirling with all this information; besides, I'm parched. So, I'm headed for the commode and then to the Willard.

Mike raised his hand. "Congressman," he asked, "you go ahead and use the necessary, but then allow us to cover one more part of our report before we go to lunch. It will only take a few minutes."

"All right, Drieborg," Webster replied, "I'll go along with that. But if you want me to hear the rest of what's in this report a' yours, you better take a break then."

"That will be fine. Everyone else stay in the room. As soon as Congressman Webster returns I want to get in the Parker report."

\*     \*     \*

Mike got right back on schedule as soon as Webster returned.

"Bose, you and Henry questioned Parker," Mike began. "Henry is still laid up, so, why don't you give the Parker report."

"A while back, Parker went missing. Me and Henry drew the short straw on him, so we went to the address we found in his file. We talked to his wife and she claimed she didn't know where he was; told us to look in tha brothels. So, we sat on his house, and waited.

"Then, we got lucky cause we were there when the slime bucket came home. We busted in and took him to the Farm for questioning. After some pursuadin, he told us some things that were real interestin.

"He said, Booth found him in a bar and bought him a drink. Parker said Booth knew it would be his turn to guard the president at Ford's Theatre on April 14th. Booth offered him fifty in gold if he would leave his post outside the door to Lincoln's box by the time a certain line was said in the play. He got a twenty-five dollar advance and was to collect the rest on April 15th."

Kellogg interrupted with a question. "How long before the assassination did this conversation take place?"

"Parker said it was at least a week; because the guard schedule hadn't even been posted for the week that included April 14ᵗʰ," Bose told everyone.

"Evidently someone knew; or at least was sure it could be arranged for Parker to have the duty that evening," Kellogg concluded.

"That seems likely, Congressman," Bose agreed. "As we know, it turned out that a' way."

Mike concluded, "Booth was so confident of that schedule that he planned to execute simultaneous attacks on Lincoln, Secretary of State Seward and the vice president; at least that's what's in his journal."

Webster showed that he was following the discussion. "Who was in charge of the presidential guard detail?"

"A.C. Richards, superintendent of the Metropolitan Police was responsible, sir."

"Was there anything that seemed unusual about the various assignments?"

"It is hard tellin, Congressman," Bose told him. "Men on that detail were tradin duty and fillin in fer one another all the time. So, there wasn't any set rotation a body could depend on.

"How Booth knew to approach Parker is still a mystery to us. We do know he did not approach any of tha other men in the White House protection detail. I'm pretty sure Parker don't know tha answer to that either. But one thing is clear. Booth was given information not available to tha public.

"Another thing," George Krupp interjected, "by admitting he was paid to leave his post, Parker has to be considered part of the conspiracy."

"How could he be? He didn't help plan it or carry it out." Webster asked.

"That's a high faulting lawyer question, Congressman," Bose replied. "I'll let George or Bob handle it."

"Go ahead, Bob," George urged.

317

"During the trial of the co-conspirators, the prosecution presented the concept of 'vicarious liability'. This states that any person involved in a conspiracy is liable for the actions of another even though that person was not directly responsible for the actions of the other conspirator.

George Krupp picked up the thread. "Prosecutor Bingham argued this so persuasively that the court accepted it. Thus, Mrs. Surratt was included as a conspirator just because she knew the others were planning something illegal which eventually became a murder. All the conspirators then, were also guilty of murder.

"So, Congressman," Bob concluded, "Parker was vicariously involved and should be tried for the murder of Abraham Lincoln, just like the others.

"But we we're having a problem with that. We haven't been able to obtain the cooperation of anyone in the Justice Department or the cooperation of Judge Advocate General Holt."

Webster chuckled, "Seems like a no brainer case, ta me. What's the problem?"

Mike dropped the other shoe. "We believe no one in either office wants Parker talking. Actually we don't think he knows much more, but the people at the War Department and at Justice probably don't know that. A grand jury investigation or a public trial could open a can of worms they don't want revealed.

"The House Judiciary Committee has the power to subpoena administration officials. If they did, we might find the answer to your question, Congressman."

Webster stood up, "Are you birds done with presenting this Officer Parker business?"

"Yes sir. We are," Mike told him.

"Well, then. I'm goin ta tha Willard. How 'bout you, Drieborg?"

# WILLARD HOTEL

The men were hardly seated when a waiter was at their table.

"What can I get you gentlemen from the bar?"

Webster spoke first, "You can get me a glass of water fer starters, waiter.

"I hope you brought that flask with you today, Bose."

"I carry it close to my heart, Congressman, cause I knew you'd need a taste today."

"Good man. What'd you call that stuff? Was it happy somethin or other?"

"It's 'Happy Sally', Congressman."

"Well, pass it down, son. I want some happy before I die a' thirst here."

Frank said to no one in particular, "I'm so full a' coffee I could burst.

"Say, Mike," he asked, "what's the name a' that fizzy stuff from Detroit you ordered for me last time we were here?"

"It's called Vernor's Ale, Frank."

"I'll have some of that, please," he told the waiter.

"Some Yankee blue belly came up with that concoction, you said. That right?" Bose asked Mike.

"That's right. He's a pharmacist in Detroit, Michigan now. Two men from my old unit stopped at his place on their way to join me here a couple of years ago. They brought a keg of it with them. Willard's has carried it ever since."

"What tha hell; give me a shot 'a that stuff too, waiter," Bose ordered. "It didn't hurt my buddy Frank, here, none."

"Say, Bose," Webster shouted across the circular table. You want a swig a' this Happy Sally? If yer not careful, son. I'm liable to finish it off."

"Thank you kindly, sir," Bose answered. "I'll just pass fer now. Mike's liable to ask me to present somethin this afternoon; gotta keep my wits about me, don't ya know."

Congressman Kellogg had been silent thus far.

"I'm sorry you're uncomfortable with what we're doing, sir," Mike began. "I hope you understand."

"Yes I do, Michael. But let's play it out this afternoon."

"Thank you, sir."

"I'm sure loose-lips Webster will play his part. But I hope you intend to give the first hard copy of the report to Chairman Boutwell of the Judiciary Committee."

"Yes sir. He'll have his copy later today."

Just then, Peter Oppewall came into the restaurant.

"Mike! This telegram was just delivered at the office for you."

As soon as Mike opened the folded paper, Pete announced.

"Congratulations Mike! It's a girl."

The men around the table started to clap.

"How is Mary Jacqueline, Michael?" Kellogg asked.

"Apparently, she's fine, sir. Dam-it! I should have been there."

Kellogg reminded Mike. "The baby's a few weeks early, Michael or you would have been, just as you promised."

"I know that. But it meant a lot to both of us; and the children. Damn!"

Mike wrote a response on the back of the paper Pete had just handed him.

"Would you please get this message off when you go back, Pete?"

"What ya gonna name tha little tyke, Mike?" Bose asked.

Mike turned to Kellogg and asked, "What did you say your wife's name was, sir?"

"Her name was Maxine."

"You heard the man, gentlemen; Maxine Drieborg it will be."

The men raised their glasses of Vernor's Ale.

"Hear! Hear! We wish long life and happiness for Maxine Drieborg."

# KELLOGG'S WASHINGTON OFFICE

On the walk back to his office, Kellogg told Mike.

"I can't begin to tell you how grateful I am to you and Mary Jacqueline. I expect that I will want to be little Maxine's patron, too."

"Actually, we'd like you to be her godfather. But only Catholics are allowed to take that role and stand in the shoes of the biological parents. Even so, could you be present, and be her honorary godfather?"

"I'd be honored, Michael."

"By the way," Kellogg continued. "I think you got us out of the Willard just in time. I'm afraid Webster is definitely in his cup, as they say."

Mike agreed. "I noticed. He finished off the flask Bose gave him and started throwing back shots of whiskey from the bar. I don't think he touched the soup he ordered. It appeared that he drank his lunch, instead.

"I hope he doesn't fall asleep this afternoon. I need him awake to hear our entire presentation dealing with Stanton.

"He may be awake, Michael," Kellogg chuckled. "But with all that liquor he's just consumed, I doubt he'll be very alert."

"I'm guessing, but I believe he doesn't want to miss any of this," Mike surmised. "We'll see, Congressman."

\*       \*       \*

"All right everyone," Mike announced. "Get settled. We've got a good two hours to go. We need to get started. Craig, would you begin by summarizing this morning's presentation?"

It took Craig less than an hour to summarize the findings that had been revealed before lunch.

"We have some recommendations that may apply to this morning's report, too. All of those will be included later in the report. I'm finished, Mike."

"Thank you, Craig."

$*$      $*$      $*$

"President Lincoln made Edwin Stanton Secretary of War in 1862. Stanton wasted no time exercising the wartime power of his office.

"He began with a witch hunt for Army officers who might be 'soft' on secession and purged them without mercy. His Judge Advocate General, Joseph Holt was given the power to determine if the action of any citizen fit the category called 'disloyal practices' covered in Lincoln's earlier proclamation.

"Holt was relentless in his search for the guilty, arresting almost ten thousand people during the remainder of the war, suspending individual rights and the freedom of the press while using military courts to enforce his decisions.

"Stanton too, was known to be ruthless. Until the very end of the war, he insisted that harsh punishments be carried out on farm boys whose crime amounted to no more than falling asleep on guard duty. Only Lincoln stood between these kids and a firing squad.

"Most say that Edwin Stanton had become a very powerful man in Washington. Many would say he was the second most powerful man in Washington; exceeded only by Abraham Lincoln.

"In the wake of Lincoln's killing, Stanton moved quickly and snatched control of all matters associated with the assassination from the Justice Department. He convinced the new president to sign an order giving the Secretary of War full authority to do what he felt necessary in the pursuit, arrest and trial of any suspect he believed might have been involved in the assassination.

"With this order, Johnson made Edwin Stanton arguably the most powerful man in Washington. What did the Secretary of War do with his new power?

"With the assistance of Colonel Baker's National Detective Police and Major A. C. Richards' Washington Metropolitan Police Force, hundreds of people in the Washington area were arrested. Even Fords' Theater was closed and the owners arrested along with the entire theatre staff and cast.

"Among those arrested within days of the assassination, were several people who had been involved in the unsuccessful kidnapping plot. We find it interesting, that while denying that there had ever been a plot to kidnap President Lincoln, Stanton's office knew the names of the kidnappers thanks to the information supplied by Wiechmann through Gleason.

"It is also interesting that Officer Parker, the man who could have blocked Booth's access to the president' box at Ford's Theatre was not among the hundreds arrested. In fact, he wasn't even questioned. We asked Stanton to explain this strange omission. He said he was too busy at that time; he still had a war to wrap up. Besides, he said, Parker wasn't his responsibility.

"As to the kidnapping plot, the prosecutors of the assassination conspirators went to great lengths to deny there had been a March plot to kidnap the president.

"We asked Stanton what he knew about the March 16th attempt to kidnap the president. Lincoln was to attend a stage play at the Soldier's Home three miles outside of Washington. Stanton claimed to know nothing of such a plot or of its March failure.

"We have testimony that Stanton was apprised of this plot well early in March. In fact, a worker in his department a Mr. Wiechmann knew of it and the names of the conspirators. Another worker a man named Captain Gleason, passed the information to Stanton.

"Admitting that there was a credible plot to kidnap the president would embarrass Stanton especially because he didn't do anything to stop it. The public would soon realize that if he had arrested the known kidnapping plotters, the assassination would probably never have happened. By the way, the kidnapping plot failed only because the carriage the kidnappers stopped on that date wasn't carrying Lincoln.

"Stanton's people also had possession of Booth's daybook at the time of the trial. In it, Booth wrote of the failed March plot to kidnap Lincoln. So Holt and Bingham had to keep the existence of that book a secret or reveal that the War Department had dropped the ball on that, too. Such a revelation might move the public to wonder if Stanton ignored that threat on purpose."

"Dr. Mudd was involved in the kidnapping plot. Keeping that plot a secret was another reason for keeping him a prisoner and insisting he was part of the assassination plot instead.

"To keep Mudd and the others quiet, Stanton ordered them to wear leather hoods he had specially made for everyone except Mary Surratt. None of the prisoners were allowed to remove the hood for any reason. The physicians' reports we read about the effect their use had on the prisoners made my stomach turn. He also kept the prisoners in isolation to prevent them speaking to anyone, or to each other.

"So, as far as we could determine, there are no recorded conversations with the prisoners.

"As it turned out, after the kidnapping plot failed, the plotters turned to plan two; the killing of Lincoln."

"Frank, would you present our findings about the next lie Stanton told?"

Kellogg bridled at that judgment. "Isn't saying the Secretary of War lied a bit harsh?"

Bose chuckled loudly. "What da you Yanks call it; stretching tha truth?"

"It was well known that the president went to the telegraph office adjacent to Stanton's office every day. He went there to check reports from the war front. April 14th was no exception. We have sworn affidavits to that effect.

"But following the assassination, Stanton testified under oath that the president was not in that office on that date. We gave him the chance to

correct his earlier testimony and he clearly refused.

"Could this be just a small mix-up in the Secretary's mind? Possibly it was; but maybe not. You see, we have sworn statements from eyewitnesses, one from David Bates a clerk in the telegraph office, and another from William Crook, Lincoln's guard, that the president was there on the afternoon of April 14th.

"So what does it matter if the president was in the telegraph office that particular day?

"It matters because on that occasion, in front of witnesses, President Lincoln asked Stanton:

*"Give me your best man."*

"The president was referring to Major Thomas Eckert, who was in charge of Military Telegraph Operations. And he wanted Eckert to be his guest at the theatre that evening. The major told the president that it was up to his boss, Secretary Stanton. That's when his boss, Stanton, told Lincoln, no, you can't have Eckert tonight because I need him for some duty that evening. Actually, Eckert had no assignment and was at home that night.

"We also discovered that it was Stanton who urged, some say ordered, General Grant not to go with the president that evening as had been advertised in the newspapers. It appears that the general welcomed an excuse to back out since his wife had become very uncomfortable with Mrs. Lincoln's recent outbursts of temper.

"Can we draw any sinister conclusion from all of this? Was Stanton just trying to impress his staff by saying 'no' to the President of the United States? Or, did Stanton want to leave the president unprotected at Ford's Theatre that evening? There is no way we can determine either possibility with any certainty."

"But without doubt, Stanton's actions on that afternoon left Abraham Lincoln more vulnerable that evening at Ford's Theatre."

"So what's the bottom line about Stanton?" Webster asked.

George Krupp answered first. "We have concluded, congressman that if the Secretary of War and his staff had simply followed the operational pattern he set for his department dealing with regard to those suspected of plotting against the United States, two things would have happened: first, John Wilkes Booth would have been in jail on April 14th, 1865; and second, Lincoln would have slept in his own bed that night."

# KELLOGG'S WASHINGTON OFFICE

Peter Oppewall walked into Congressman Kellogg's office with a copy of last night's Daily Evening Star newspaper.

"I thought you would want to see this as soon as you got in, sir."

At the top of the first page, the headlines were three inches high:

## Assassination Could Have Been Prevented

*The House Judiciary Committee's investigation into the various assassination conspiracy theories appears to be concluded. After weeks of painstaking investigation, the report documents grave oversights by Edwin Stanton and his War Department staff. This paper's informants revealed that:*

*First: Stanton knew of a plot to kidnap Lincoln in 1865. He also knew that John Wilkes Booth was organizing such an attempt. Despite having this verified information in his possession, no arrests were made; not even for questioning. **Why not?***

*So, the kidnapping plot went forward. On March 16th, the carriage which was supposed to carry President Lincoln to a function at the Soldier's Home outside of Washington was stopped by the kidnappers.*

*They were well organized and set to spirit the president south into Confederate held territory. The only reason their kidnapping failed was that Lincoln was not in the carriage. At the last minute he had to cancel his appearance. Still, there were no arrests made of the men known to have attempted the kidnapping. **Why not?***

*To cover up this grave oversight, Stanton himself has denied there was ever a plot to kidnap President Lincoln. Our readers might remember that at the trial of the assassination conspirators, Prosecutor Bingham and Judge Advocate General Holt argued that same thing; and they insisted that Booth's intention was always to kill the president; never to kidnap him.*

*They even hid Booth's daybook which confirmed a March kidnapping plot. We know this now because Colonel Baker of the National Detective Police recently swore under oath that he turned such a journal in to Stanton before the start of the co-conspirators' trial. Why would Stanton's people deny its existence?*

*Would it be because then the public would know there had been a kidnapping plot led by Booth? We think so. Then too, the public would know that had Stanton's people arrested the plotters of the kidnapping attempt, Booth and his co-conspirators would have been in jail on April 14th!*

*This is either bumbling of the worst sort; or a conspiracy by highly placed government officials to allow the killing of the president. If it was simply an inept response of overworked bureaucrats in the War Department, they should be dismissed immediately.*

*If however, it was part of a conspiracy to expose President Lincoln to the worst sort of danger, they should be arrested as co-conspirators in his murder, tried and punished.*

"Good Lord! This is a catastrophe for the Republicans; and with us facing an election next fall."

"There's more on page three, sir."

Sure enough, other articles laid out the conclusions made by Drieborg's investigators exonerating the Confederate government, President Johnson and the Catholic Church of any association with the killing of President Lincoln.

On the opinion page, the editor made the following statement.

*This report forces even the most partisan of us to consider the possibility that the powerful and trusted Edwin Stanton allowed the killing of President Lincoln.*

*May God have mercy on the United States if President Johnson does not investigate this matter with all the powers at his command.*

**Do it now, Mr. President!**

"What will Johnson do, sir?' Pete wondered.

"He'll crucify Edwin Stanton. I'm sure of it."

# Philadelphia

Mike was standing in the terminal of the railroad station. He had some time before his train to Philadelphia would be ready for boarding. Who should he see walk into the station walked but his team of marshals. Peg Stanitzek, Ethie Faute and Mary Alice Stephan were with their husbands, too.

"What in heaven's name!" Mike exclaimed. "I thought we said our goodbyes at the boardinghouse. What are all of you doing here?"

Bose spoke first. "Well, ya see Yank; me an' tha wife here ain't ever been north or much east of Tennessee. An, we heard tha Stephans and tha Stanitzeks talkin about the grand sights they saw in Philadelphia. So, we thought we'd go and see em fer ourselves. Sides, I got all this Yankee money ya' know an' no place ta' spend it."

"You don't mind, do you Michael?" Ethie asked.

"I don't mind at all, Ethie." Mike responded. "I'm pleased to have your company. Just puzzled, that's all.

"But you, Frank; and you, Bob; you and your wives have already been there."

"Somebody gotta show Bose and Ethie around, Mike," Frank answered with a grin.

"Besides, Michael; you're not the only one who wants to meet your new baby," Mary Alice Stephan added.

"So what's your excuse, Craig?" Mike asked.

"Ya know, Mike," he replied, "in all my years of running around, I missed Philadelphia. So, I thought I'd just tag along. Besides, I have to thank my friends at the Philadelphia Police Department for agreeing to look after Mary Jacqueline and her family; don't you think?"

"John Gostomski is here, too?" Now I know something is amiss when a Pinkerton man is following me. All right John, why are you joining this motley crew? Ladies excluded, of course."

329

"Evidently you have forgotten, Mike," John replied. "My colleague Linda Berkholz is still at your in-law's home in Philadelphia. I want to surprise her with a marriage proposal. What better way to bolster my case than to have all of you around vouching for me."

"We might be talked inta that, sonny," Bose kidded him.

"And, you're all carrying your Spencer rifles, because?" Mike asked.

Just then, Henry Austry came walking into the station carrying his carpet bag and rifle.

"Because, Marshal Drieborg, you just never can tell when you might need it."

# PRESIDENT JOHNSON'S OFFICE

The president was sitting behind his desk apparently reading a newspaper. There was a knock on the door and it was tentatively opened.

As soon as he saw who it was, President Johnson stood and came around his desk to greet his visitor.

"Thank you for coming, Mr. Secretary. I know my request gave you short notice, but I didn't think we should put off discussing a matter of grave importance."

Edwin Stanton closed the door behind him and moved toward the president.

"Please take a seat, would you?" the president asked.

"You know Mr. Browning my personal secretary. I've asked him to take notes of our little conversation."

"I find that highly irregular, sir; insulting even," Stanton sputtered.

"Even so, he will be taking notes," Johnson insisted.

"Have you seen last evening's Daily Evening Star newspaper, Mr. Secretary?"

"I don't read that trashy paper," Stanton snapped irritably. "What little time I have for the newspapers, I'll give to the New York Times."

"Well, I'll bet you're the only one in Washington who hasn't read this edition, sir. The front page article isn't long. Please take my copy and read it before we continue our conversation."

"Must I, sir?" he complained. "I've got a desk piled high with work back in my office."

"Yes, I'm afraid you must, Mr. Secretary."

Reluctantly Stanton took the offered copy and read the front page article. "Rubbish! That's all it is. I can't believe you've called me away from my work to read such nonsense."

"Even your favorite paper, the New York Times is carrying the story today in their afternoon's edition. It will be printed in all the nation's dailies in another day or two. And, it will be in all the weekly papers by next week."

"What is your reaction to the suggestion made by the Star's people? Should I ask for an investigation?"

Stanton struggled to regain is composure. "You'll investigate because of allegations made in a trash newspaper? You wouldn't dare, sir!"

"It appears that I have no choice, sir." Johnson informed Stanton. "The leaders of the Democratic minority in the House and the Senate have already visited me. They think such an inquiry essential to preserve the public's trust. That's political speak which means that they think such an investigation might favor them at the polls in next year's elections.

"I'm not surprised those traitors would leap at an opportunity to embarrass me." Stanton claimed.

"I suppose you're right, Mr. Secretary."

"But even a few of your staunch Republicans fear that very thing, too. So, they have agreed to support a full and public inquiry. Except for the few Radicals who joined with you to stop Drieborg's investigation, you are quite isolated on this, Mr. Secretary."

"This is preposterous, sir!"

"The leaders of your own party don't want to be seen as shielding a person who might have allowed the killing of the late President Lincoln. I'm sure you can see that, Mr. Secretary."

"So have your damn investigation," Stanton spat. "You'll find nothing to the allegations made in that trash newspaper."

"I'm sure you're right, Mr. Secretary. But this office cannot be seen to be favoring you during the inquiry. So, regrettably, I'm suspending you from the duties of Secretary of War pending the results of the investigation."

"You forget, sir. There is the Tenure of Office Act."

"To be sure, Mr. Stanton; there is that. But read my Executive Order and you'll have to agree I'm not firing you; only suspending you, with pay of course.

"As we speak, General Sherman's Provost Marshal has occupied your office. They have sealed all of your files and taken over the telegraph center as well. Major Eckert and his staff are in custody and wait questioning. Judge Advocate Holt is also in custody and all of his files have been taken, too. General Grant will carry out your former duties as Secretary of War until this entire mess is clarified. Do you have any questions, sir?"

Visibly shaken, Stanton stood behind his straight backed chair. He seemed to grip it for balance.

"You will never get away with this, Johnson. It's very clear that you're subverting the intent of the Tenure of Office Act, which was passed over your veto."

The president continued to sit calmly and just look at Stanton. "My, my, Mr. Stanton," Johnson replied with a smile. "Calm down, sir. It's not good for your blood pressure, I'm sure.

"I'm told you helped write that law. You can only blame yourself if you did a sloppy job. By the way, you will notice that my order is dated August 12, 1865; yesterday. So, today you will not be allowed back into your office. I suggest you make a list of personal items and submit it to the provost marshal, a Captain Sowle. I'm told he will be very accommodating.

"I believe we're done here today, sir. You may leave."

# THANKSGIVING IN MICHIGAN

It was the day before Thanksgiving. Jacob was still in the house after finishing his noon meal. Rose was cleaning the top of her stove when she heard a commotion in the yard.

"Jacob," Rose asked. "Who could that be out in the yard?"

She turned and went to the kitchen window.

"Oh! My heavens, Jacob," she exclaimed. "You'll never guess who is getting out of a carriage in our yard."

"I don't guess too well, Momma," he said irritably. "Just tell me."

"It's the Murphy's."

"You mean da ones from Philadelphia?"

"Yes. Don't just sit there, Jacob. Go let them in; help them with their bags."

Jake didn't even bother putting on his winter clothing. He just rushed into the yard. Rose was right behind him.

"Miles," She scolded. "Why didn't you tell us you were coming? We would have met your train in Grand Rapids."

"Quite frankly, Rose," Miles Murphy responded. "I didn't know myself. Judy didn't give me much notice. I returned home from my last class two days ago to find our trunk and overnight bags packed and loaded in a carriage. She didn't tell me much more until we were on a train headed west. And, here we are."

"What a nice surprise," Rose said. "But it is freezing out here. Judy, you get inside. Jacob, you and Miles bring in the bags."

"Women are always telling da men what to do, eh Miles?"

"Don't I know it, Jake?"

"I thought you were da master of your home, Miles."

"I am, in my classroom; just as you are, in your barn, Jake. But let's not kid ourselves about the home."

*   *   *

Thanksgiving Day brought the Drieborg children home with their families. Susan Deeb and her husband Joseph lived just down the road; so they were early with their two children. Susan Neal and her husband George closed their Grand Rapids restaurant for the day and brought their two boys, along with several pies and a pot of Amos's famous soup. The youngest, Jacob, called Little Jake, was a student at West Point in New York.

Michael's carriage pulled into the yard last. He had gotten to his Grand Rapids home late from some work he insisted had to be done in his office. Mary Jacqueline was irritated with that choice and gave him the silent treatment on the ride to Lowell. The children took their cue from her and were cool toward him as well.

Once inside the house, Eleanor and Charles were anxious to join their cousins. So, it was a struggle for their parents to hold them back and get off their boots and winter coats.

Mike and his wife were so preoccupied with this that they didn't notice Mary Jacqueline's parents in all the confusion of the room. Then, Miles and Judy Murphy stood and stepped forward.

"Mother; Father; oh my goodness, look Michael. Look who's here."

All of them embraced in the doorway. She was full of questions for her parents.

"When did you arrive? Why didn't you tell us? How long can you stay?"

But she didn't wait for them to reply.

"I don't care about any of that; I'm so happy to see you. What a wonderful Thanksgiving surprise. Children; come here and give Grampa Miles and Gramma Judy a hug."

Through the noise of all the greetings, Rose heard something.

"Jacob, I think there's someone pounding on the door."

When Jake opened the door, he found himself looking into the eyes of a tall man dressed in a soldier's great coat.

"Oh! My God, Momma! It's Jacob!" Jake grabbed his son in a tight embrace pounding him on the back at the same time. The adults in the room behind them became quiet, wondering what it was all about. Rose seemed to know and rushed through the crowd of children around her to join in the embrace.

Ann broke the silence, "For Lord's sake! Come in to the house, you three. You're letting in the cold."

She quickly joined her parents, Susan and Michael in a family hug. Everyone was crying with joy, even Jake.

# Historical Figures

Colonel Lafayette Baker (1826 – 1868)

Appointed by Edwin Stanton as head of the National Detective Police in 1862 he arrested large numbers of subversives during the war; most of whom were quickly released after suspected bribes were paid. In charge of the Booth manhunt, he swore that the assassin's daybook was intact when he turned it in to Stanton's office. He soon died after his 1868 retirement from meningitis, later determined to be arsenic poisoning.

John A. Bingham (1815 – 1900)

After losing his congressional seat in 1862, he was appointed Judge Advocate of the Union Army. After the assassination of Lincoln, he was the chief prosecutor of Booth's co-conspirators. He denied the existence of the earlier failed plot to kidnap President Lincoln. Toward that end, he hid the existence of Booth's daybook which showed the assassination plot dated from the failed kidnapping plot of March 16. He insisted that "Jefferson Davis is as clearly proven guilty of this conspiracy as is John Wilkes Booth". Bingham is considered largely responsible for the death sentences of the co-conspirators. As a member of the Thirty-ninth Congress, Bingham wrote the final version of the 14$^{th}$ Amendment to the U.S. Constitution. After another election defeat, President Grant appointed him U.S. Minister to Japan.

George S. Boutwell (1818 – 1905)

A self-educated man, he served various electoral and appointed posts, such as Secretary of the Treasury, Governor, Senator and Representative from Massachusetts. A member of Congress during the impeachment trial of President Johnson, he was one of the special prosecutors.

Benjamin F. Butler (1818 – 1893)

A Massachusetts lawyer and politician, he was made a general during the Civil War. An incompetent military leader, he earned the notorious nickname the "Beast of New Orleans". After the war, he entered the House of Representatives.

A Radical Reconstructionist, he fiercely opposed President Johnson's policies and was one of those members of congress who sought his impeachment.

Mr. Charles Chiniquy (1809 – 1889)

Defrocked Catholic Priest who left his church in 1860, he conducted an anti-Catholic crusade for the rest of his life. In1865 he claimed the Catholic Church hated Lincoln and had engineered his assassination. He published his charges in 1886, *Fifty Years in the Church of Rome.* His popery theory gained prominence after Lincoln's assassination. It is reported that his book was the biggest seller in Canada at that time. His grand Catholic Conspiracy theme was revived at the time of the Kennedy assassination in 1963 as well.

Lucy Lambert Hale (1841 – 1915)

Youngest of two daughters of New Hampshire U.S. John Hale, she was the mistress of John W. Booth and claimed to be his fiancée. She provided him with a pass to sit behind Lincoln at the President's March 4th second inaugural speech. After the assassination, her father shielded her from public embarrassment and took her with him to Spain. After he died in 1873 she married a New Hampshire politician, William E. Chandler and returned to Washington D.C. She predeceased her husband in 1915.

Joseph Holt (1807 – 1894)

During the secession crisis, he worked to hold Kentucky in the Union. As the result of his efforts, Lincoln appointed him Judge Advocate General. He was especially vigorous in defense of the Union arresting almost 15,000 citizens for what he viewed as subversive activities. Few were ever convicted. After the assassination of Lincoln, Holt convinced President Johnson to declare the Confederate Government complicit in the killing of Abraham Lincoln.

Even though the evidence which supported this declaration was proven false, he still believed that Jefferson Davis was behind the assassination. His reputation was also hurt by the controversy over whether or not he had shown the president the military tribunal's recommendation of clemency for Mary Surratt.

Andrew Johnson (1808 – 1875)

A tailor's apprentice, Andrew Johnson had no formal education. Despite this handicap, he gained the support of laboring people and was selected by them for local and state positions culminating in election to the U.S. Congress and as governor of Tennessee. At the time of the secession crisis, he was a U.S. Senator; the only senator from a secessionist state to retain his seat. A Jacksonian Democrat, he was a staunch Unionist. He was deemed a traitor in the South; his property was confiscated and his family driven from the state. Lincoln appointed him as the military governor of Tennessee and later chose him as his 1864 vice presidential running mate.

Sworn in as president after the assassination, President Johnson clashed with the Radicals over Reconstruction policy. Impeached by the House of Representatives the effort failed in the Senate by one vote. Tennessee returned him to the U.S. Senate in 1875, but he died the same year.

Francis William Kellogg (1810 – 1879)

A Grand Rapids, Michigan businessman was elected to the U.S. House of Representatives in 1858. During the Civil War, he organized the Michigan Second, Third and Sixth Regiments and served as the Colonel of the Third Michigan. During Reconstruction, he served as the collector of taxes in Alabama. Upon readmission to the Union he won a seat from Alabama in the 40th Congress as a Republican.

Mary Todd Lincoln (1818 – 1882)

Called "Mother" by her husband, Mary was raised in a slave owning family in Lexington, Kentucky. Never-the-less, she became a fervent abolitionist. As the president's wife, she found herself caught between Northern suspicion for her Southern background (three of her brothers died while in the service of the Confederacy) and Southern anger for her Northern sympathies. During her husband's presidency, she was the center of controversy caused by her extravagance, her temper and her sharp tongue.

She publicly accused President Johnson of being part of the conspiracy to kill her husband. She went to Europe in 1868, not returning until 1871. In 1875 her son Robert had her committed to an insane asylum.

John Parker (1830 – 1890)

He was a member of the District of Columbia's Metropolitan Police force. At the request of Mrs. Mary Lincoln, he was assigned to the White House as one of President Lincoln's body guards. He was accused of dereliction of duty for leaving his post and thus allowing Booth access to President Lincoln. That charge was mysteriously dropped. Even more mysteriously, he was returned to duty as a presidential guard. Within a week after Edwin Stanton left his position as Secretary of War, Parker was fired. He returned to his carpenter trade.

A.C. Richards (1827 – 1907)

A teacher in Washington D.C. he was appointed Superintendent of the Washington Metropolitan Police force in 1864. His team of White House guards was responsible for protecting the president. He brought charges against John Parker for dereliction of duty and then dropped them. He then returned Officer Parker to his former position as a presidential guard. Richards was forced to leave this position in 1878.

General William T. Sherman (1820 – 1891)

A Union general who was most famous for the scorched-earth tactics he used during the Civil War in Georgia and South Carolina. After the war he was outspoken in his belief that Indian policy should be set by the army and that its aim should be the subjection of all Indian tribes and their placement on reservations. After he became commander of the Army under President Grant, he carried out this policy.

Edwin Stanton (1814 – 1869)

Stanton began his political career as anti-slavery Ohio Democrat. He had a large legal practice in Washington D.C. when he was appointed Attorney General by President Buchanan. Under Lincoln, he replaced the wartime Secretary of War, Simon Cameron in 1862. Thousands of Northern citizens were arrested after he issued this order in August 1862:

"...to arrest and imprison any person or persons who may be engaged by act, speech or writing, in discouraging volunteer enlistments, or in any way giving aid and comfort to the enemy, or in any other disloyal practice against the United States."

After the assassination, President Johnson put him in charge of the pursuit and prosecution of any and all conspirators. After the identification and capture of those believed to be co-conspirators, Stanton ordered a military trial and isolation of the accused. He also ordered that the prisoners wear hoods and manacles which were not to be removed. Within days of Lincoln's death, he pronounced the Confederate government guilty of ordering the assassination as another war measure.

Stanton joined the Radicals and opposed President Johnson's Reconstruction program. Their clash eventually led to his firing in February of 1868. A year later, President Grant appointed him to a position on the U.S. Supreme Court, but he died before taking the oath of office. Some historians suspect him of complicity in the assassination of Abraham Lincoln.

# CHARACTERS

## Michael Drieborg's Family

| | |
|---|---|
| Michael Drieborg | US Marshal: MI |
| Mary Jacqueline (Pope) Drieborg | Wife |
| Eleanor Drieborg | Daughter |
| Charles (Pope) Drieborg | Adopted Son |
| Maxine Drieborg | Daughter |
| Helen | Children's Nanny & cook. |

## Jake Drieborg's Family

| | |
|---|---|
| Jake Drieborg | Farmer Lowell MI |
| Rose Drieborg | Wife |
| Jacob Drieborg | Son |

## Ruben Hecht's Family

| | |
|---|---|
| Ruben Hecht | Farmer Lowell MI |
| Emma Hecht | Wife |
| Kenny Hecht | Son |
| Ruth Hecht | Adopted Daughter |
| Emily Hecht | Adopted Daughter |

## Kellogg Staff

| | |
|---|---|
| William Kellogg ® | US Congressman: MI |
| Mable | Household Cook |
| Adam | Butler (Mable's husband) |
| Peter Oppewall | Washington Office Manager |
| David Lyman Gould | Grand Rapids Office Manager |

## Michael Drieborg's Washington Team

| | |
|---|---|
| Craig Haynes | Chief Deputy Ohio |
| Henry Austry | Deputy Marshal: Illinois |
| Bose Faute | Deputy Marshal: TN |
| Frank Stanitzek | Deputy Marshal: GA |
| George Krupp | Attorney: Wash D.C. |
| Robert Stephan | Attorney: SC |
| John Gostomski | Pinkerton Agent: MI |

## Michael Drieborg's Grand Rapids Team

Craig Haynes — Chief Deputy: OH
Stanley Killeen — Deputy Marshal: MI
Bill Anderson — Deputy Marshal: MI

## Joseph Deeb Family

Joseph Deeb — Old Kent Bank: MI
Ann Deeb — Wife
Michelle Deeb — Daughter
Stephen Deeb — Son

## George Neal Family

George Neal — Restaurant Owner: MI
Susan Neal — Wife
Robert Neal — Son
George Jr. — Son

## Jacob Drieborg's Squad

Hans Krause
Joe Gillet
William O'Brien
Alfred Ryder
Fred Schmalzried

## Kenny Hecht's Squad

Tom Shaw
Ed Cornelius
Luther Trowbridge
Benjamin Clark
Gilbert Chapman

## Grand Rapids Personalities

Paula Bacon — Wife of Harvey Bacon (dec)
Amos — Cook

## Washington Personalities

Andrew Johnson — President of the United States
Edwin M. Stanton — Secretary of War
Harry Webster — Congressman (D) TN
Owen Lovejoy — Congressman ® IL
Salmon P. Chase — Supreme Court Chief Justice
John F. Parker — Presidential Guard Detail
Colonel Lafayette Baker — Chief of D.C. Nat'l Police
Joseph Holt — Judge Advocate General

| | |
|---|---|
| John A. Bingham | Congressman ® Ohio |
| Andrew J. Rogers | Congressman (D) NJ |
| George F. Boutwell | Congressman ® Mass |
| Benjamin F. Butler | Congressman ® MA |
| A.C. Richards | Superintendent: D.C. |
| | Metro Police |

## Military Personalities

| | |
|---|---|
| Captain Tom Quinn | Troop CO Dakota Territory |
| Sgt. Major Riley | Sgt. US Dakota Territory |
| Gen. William T. Sherman | General of the Army |

## Wives

| | |
|---|---|
| Mary Alice Stephan | Wife of Robert Stephan: SC |
| Margaret (Peg) Stanitzek | Wife of Frank Stanitzek: GA |
| Ethie Faute | Wife of Bose Faute: TE |
| Patricia (Kellogg) Krupp | Wife of George Krupp: D.C. |
| Ellen Stanton | Wife of Edwin Stanton: D.C. |

## Other Ladies

| | |
|---|---|
| Lucy Lambert Hale | Booth's Fiancée: NH |
| Linda Berkholz | Pinkerton Agent: MI |
| Miss Anderson | Teacher in Philadelphia |

# BIBLIOGRAPHY

Bak, Richard. *The Day Lincoln was Shot.* Dallas, Texas: Taylor Publishing Company. 1998

Eisenschiml, Otto. *Why Was Lincoln Murdered?* Boston: Little, Brown and Company, 1937.

Hanchett, William. *The Lincoln Murder Conspiracies.* Urbana and Chicago: University of Illinois Press. 1986

*The Lincoln Assassination: Crime & Punishment, Myth & Memory.*
Ed. Hoilzer, Symonds & Williams. New York: Fordham University Press. 2010.

Mills, Robert Lockwood. *It Didn't Happen the Way You Think: The Lincoln Assassination: What the Experts Missed:* New England, Conn. Write-Ideas. 1993

Roscoe, Theodore. *The Web of Conspiracy: The Complete Story of the Men Who murdered Abraham Lincoln.* Englewood Cliffs, NJ. Prentice-Hall Inc. 1959

Steers, Edward Jr. *Blood on the Moon: The assassination of Abraham Lincoln:* The University Press of Kentucky. 2001

Steers, Edward Jr. *The Lincoln Assassination Enclopedia.* New York: Harper Perennial. 2010.

# DUTY AND HONOR

Book One

The Drieborg Chronicles


In the summer of 1862, the United States is torn by Civil War. What what was supposed to be a short conflict has turned into a bloody struggle with no end in sight. Teenage farm boy Michael Drieborg lives with his family and longs to join the cause, but he can't justify abandoning his parents and their farm.

But fate intercedes on Saturday morning on the family's weekly visit to town. Michael saves a young boy from being bullied. Unfortunately, he strikes the bully – the son of the town banker – and is arrested and charged with assault. He is given a choice: go to jail or join a cavalry unit being formed in the area. Against the wishes of his parents, Michael leaves home and marches to war.

Thus begins the story of a naïve farm boy's journey to becoming a seasoned cavalryman. From the harshness of training camp we see Michael drawn into the intrigues of Washington D.C. and the arms of the congressman's daughter. Wounded at Gettysburg he only survives to be later captured and sent to Andersonville Prison.

# DUTY ACCOMPLISHED

Book Two

The Drieborg Chronicles

The reader is returned to the turbulent years of the American Civil War in this second installment of the acclaimed Civil War trilogy, "The Drieborg Chronicles".

It is December 1864. Major Michael Drieborg had escaped the dreaded Confederate prison at Andersonville, Georgia. The war is won but not over so recuperation at his parents' home in Michigan, is cut short. He was ordered to return to Washington for reassignment.

Once in Washington, President Lincoln sends Michael south to assist Union war prisoners recently liberated at Savannah, Georgia by Sherman's army. But things grow complicated when Michael arrives and discovers the enormous task in from of him. Worse, while his is gone, old enemies threaten his family back in Michigan, and there is little he can do to help.

With the war drawing to a close, Michael must adjust to new challenges, ones that will take him from the burning ruins of South Carolina to the Indian country of the Dakota Territory. Finally home, he is forced to confront his enemies in a final showdown.

# Honor Restored

Book Three

The Drieborg Chronicles

After four years of civil war, Lincoln's determination to keep the union together had prevailed.

Then a new conflict began, this time over the nature of that Union. Would the Northern victors allow the old Southern ruling class to regain control, or would a new political and socio/economic structure prevail in the states of the former Confederacy.

President Johnson and the Congress were at odds over that issue.

Michael Drieborg had returned to the life of a farmer. He was no sooner settled than enemies of the Drieborg family killed his wife and adopted son. Michael settled the score, but could not face the memories at home.

He returned to Washington to work for Congressman Kellogg. There he found himself in the midst of the early struggles of Reconstruction. Reunited with troopers from his old unit and allied with Congressional Republicans, he had to deal with Washington intrigue, wartime enemies, a fleeting romance and South Carolina's struggles to recover.

CPSIA information can be obtained at www.ICGtesting.com
Printed in the USA
BVOW051955181011

273964BV00005B/1/P